SHOW STEALER

Scholastic Children's Books
An imprint of Scholastic Ltd
Euston House, 24 Eversholt Street, London, NW1 1DB, UK
Registered office: Westfield Road, Southam, Warwickshire, CV47 0RA
SCHOLASTIC and associated logos are trademarks and/or
registered trademarks of Scholastic Inc.

First published in the UK by Scholastic Ltd, 2018

ISBN 978 1407 17968 1

A CIP catalogue record for this book
is available from the British Library.

Printed by CPI Group (UK) Ltd, Croydon, CR0 4YY
Papers used by Scholastic Children's Books are made
from wood grown in sustainable forests.

1 3 5 7 9 10 8 6 4 2

www.scholastic.co.uk

SHOW STEALER

HAYLEY BARKER

■SCHOLASTIC

For Mum and Dad

HOSHIKO

I'm not sure if it's the sound of the traffic building up outside as the rush hour approaches or the gleam of the sun breaking its way through the cracks in the blinds that wakes me, but I'm the first one of us to stir this morning. Around me, the sleeping forms of the others remain still and tranquil, oblivious to the brightening light and the concert of horns and engines going on outside.

I stretch out my limbs, luxuriating in the unfamiliar feeling of peace. I don't think I've felt this calm since … well, since ever. Life was certainly never calm in the Cirque – not when Death was always hiding in the shadows, stealing people away every night with a smile on his face. And since I threw that grenade, blowing the arena to pieces and obliterating the evil ringmaster, Silvio Sabatini, life hasn't exactly been serene.

It's been nearly a year now and we still haven't made it out of London. We were so hopeful at first. We were going to spend a little time recuperating, and then we were heading straight to one of the Essex or Kent ports, on to a boat and away to freedom; away to a better place. It never turned out that way, though. Everywhere we go, suspicious eyes stare at us, and we're always just one step ahead of the sound of whistles and sirens and pounding footsteps. Roadblocks bar our way every time we try to escape the city as the net closing in around us gets tighter and tighter and tighter.

Being the most wanted criminals in the country means always running, running, running. Always looking over your shoulder, never being able to rest, never being able to stop, hunted every step of the way.

So many times, it's nearly been over. So many times, we've nearly been caught. Our photos are beamed up on to practically every building and there's a huge reward for anyone who can provide information on us. It's hard to hide anywhere when you're so notorious, especially when there's a circus monkey coming along for the ride.

This is the fourth night in a row we've been camped out in this abandoned office on the top floor of an apartment block. According to Jack, all the staff turned up for work one morning and were told the company was bankrupt, and they'd lost their jobs and should all go home.

I don't know how he knows these things, but Jack always seems able to find us the next safe place to hide out. He was a Pure police officer for over twenty years before he blew his cover whisking us from the Cirque right under Ben's mother's nose. He saved Greta and me from certain death that night and he's the one reason we've managed to survive this long. He's got contacts everywhere and he's been with us every step of the way – not that we've managed to get very far. Not that we've managed to get anywhere.

I look around the vast office space. It felt kind of creepy when we arrived here, looking around in the dim light of Jack's torch at all the disused and empty desks, at the cups that had just been left there on them, and the photographs of smiling Pure children grinning back at us from their frames. If it wasn't for the musty smell and the dead plants drooping forlornly, you'd think they'd only left yesterday. It's as if it's frozen in time, holding its breath, waiting to be useful again.

It doesn't feel creepy now. It feels like a friend. It's given us shelter, protected us without asking for anything in return.

Every morning, Jack's been saying we ought to pack up and move on to another place, that it's a mistake to stay in the same place for too long, that it's too risky. He's getting twitchier and twitchier. Across the room, I see him shift and my heart sinks; as soon as he wakes up, he's going to make us get up and move on again.

I don't understand why we can't just stay here. Nobody else is using the place, and surely it's safer staying put than going out there again where we'll just be more exposed? Jack's resistance friends can keep bringing us food and drink, and if we can't get away properly, we can just hide out here – for ever, if that's what it takes.

I'm going to suggest it to the others when I wake up. I'm sure Ben and Greta will back me up.

My back aches, and my cheeks feel rough from lying on that scratchy carpet. I wriggle my toes. I've got pins and needles from lying in the same position all night. They don't hurt though – not like they used to. It's taken a while, but I'm finally fixed back together, on the outside at least. Ben's the same – his leg has nearly healed completely; the skin has grown back over the once gaping wound, and you wouldn't even notice his limp unless you were looking for it. Even the wounds inside, the gaping holes that will never heal – the Amina and Priya shaped ones – have got a bit easier to bear. The pain will never go away, of course, and I wouldn't want it to anyway; they were both killed because of us, after all – but we can talk about them now without losing it completely.

My mouth is so dry, I really need a drink. As quietly as I can, I ease myself up out of the threadbare blankets I've been huddled in and sit up. Next to me, Ben's head turns and his hand reaches out to settle on my legs but his eyes stay shut and his breathing stays heavy and regular.

When I look at him, lying there like that, my breath catches in my throat. His cheeks are dark with stubble now and, when he's up and about, he looks just like the man he's become. When he sleeps though, his sweet face looks exactly like it did on that first morning, when I watched him sleeping under my bed back at the Cirque and tried so hard to hate him.

I'll get a drink in a minute. I ease myself back down and spoon myself into him. His arms wrap around me and I nestle there, matching my breathing to his.

For a few moments, I am joyous. Not a dancing, jumping, ecstatic joy, but a calm one. A deep, quiet joy. We're on the run, we don't know what's coming next, but we're alive and we're together and that's all that matters. This is where I belong, right here.

Suddenly, gunshot. The sound of wood splitting, of footsteps, hundreds of them, running up the stairs.

Immediately, we all sit bolt upright. My eyes meet Ben's, wide and panicked.

"What's happening?" Greta has hold of Bojo, who she insists sleeps right next to her, snuggled up on the same pillow, even though we've all told her it's not hygienic, sharing a bed with a monkey. His little arms are wrapped tightly around hers and he's looking around at all of us in concern and confusion at the sudden disturbance.

Jack's already jumped up.

"What's happening?" He repeats Greta's question, his face grim. "They're here, that's what. They've found us."

BEN

It takes me a moment or two to collect myself enough to work out what's going on. Even when Jack says "They're here," my brain can't make sense of his words. I don't know why it comes as such a shock to me – we've been waiting for this day for almost a year now.

The day when they finally catch up with us.

Dozens of times now, we've tried to escape from the city. Dozens of times we've had to turn back when we've hit a roadblock, or a police barrier blocking our way. Dozens of times we've had to run, had to hide. Dozens of times, we've been seconds away from being caught.

I don't know if Mother's personally funding the efforts to catch us or, more likely, is using public money to do it but, either way, no expense has been spared. Every lamp post, every shop window, every vast skyscraper seems to have our faces on.

We were all hoping that the fervour to find us would die down, but all it seems to have done is escalate.

A few weeks ago, we woke up to find our faces beamed up on the PowerHouse, the huge government building in the centre of London. The colossal statue of a grinning gold man – supposedly symbolizing the Purer, superior group of society standing tall on the heap of poor oppressed Dregs he crushes beneath him – is doubling up now as the world's biggest Wanted poster, plastered with images of England's most sought-after villains. Day and night our scowling faces stare down over the city. Hoshi, Greta, Jack, me – even Bojo's got his own personalized mugshot.

The reward money they're offering keeps increasing too, higher and higher with every passing week. That's why Jack says we're never safe.

"Most people have a price," he always says, "even the good guys. The police won't stop looking for us, not after what happened to the Cirque, and not when the son of one of the most important people in the country is with us. They'll catch up with us eventually: they're bound to."

And now they have, and they're here, in this building, coming up the main stairwell. You can hear them, heading directly towards us. Footsteps, lots of them.

The others spring into action faster than me, turning tail as one and heading for the fire exit. When they reach the door, Hoshi turns.

"Quick!" she hisses, urgently. "Hurry, Ben, we've got to get out now!"

Only then do I jolt into reality. I dash after them, turn back, grab my gun and follow.

The footsteps are closer now and there's a booming voice shouting out commands. There's no stealth tactics here, they aren't even bothering to be quiet. Why?

Because they've already got you surrounded, a voice in my head says.

As I push through the fire door my eyes meet Jack's, his mouth resigned, and I know I'm right.

We run down the stairs, Jack, Hoshi and me all holding up our guns. In front, Greta stops abruptly and looks back at us, wild-eyed.

They're streaming up from below us, scores of them.

We turn back, but even more of them are above us, swarming through the doorway, riot shields up, guns pointed at us from every direction.

This is it, then. This is the end.

Time's up.

HOSHIKO

"Freeze!" a voice calls out, and a policeman steps forward on the stairs. "Drop your guns. You can't go anywhere; we have you completely surrounded."

Armed, uniformed figures block the way above us, block the way below us. Through the window, I can see dozens of police cars and flashing lights.

What do we do now? I look to Jack, searching his face for answers. He always finds a way out, always manages the impossible, ever since he drove us out of that circus as brazen as anything.

I try to catch his eye, but he doesn't look up. His face looks downcast. It's never looked like that before, never, not even in the darkest of times.

We've had days over the last year when Greta has put her head in her hands and sobbed, days when Ben has sunk down to the floor in exhaustion and despair, days when I've been so moody and sullen I haven't spoken to anyone for hours. We've all had our moments of bleakness, the three of us. Not Jack though. No matter what happens, Jack's eyes keep shining with that twinkle of optimism and hope. He never gets down. He never gives up.

Not until now.

My heart plummets as he lowers his gun down, placing it carefully on the floor and holding his hands up. He's surrendering.

What else can he do? We're finished.

They'll probably kill us all. They'll definitely kill me, Greta and Jack. Jack's a traitor and Greta and I are even worse than that. Dreg arsonists, Dreg abductors – Dreg devils, if you believe the posters and the news reports.

Bojo scrambles up and down the banister, chattering in panic as he looks at the police surrounding us and Greta clings on to me, her arms squeezing me so tightly that it's hard to breathe.

I stroke her hair.

I turn to Ben. I guess this will be the last time I ever see him. I need to remember every detail of his face. I need to etch it in my mind, so that, for as long as I am alive, I never forget it, in the way I've forgotten the others – forgotten my parents, forgotten my baby brother. Even Amina's image hasn't stayed fixed. Sometimes, when I search my memory for her face, it won't come straight away, not sharp and crystal clear. I won't let that happen, not with Ben. I need to take a photo in my head, or better still, a video, keep it with me, playing on repeat.

He's not looking at me though, and he hasn't put his gun down. He's holding it high still, staring at the man who's stepped forward; the man who's obviously in charge.

"Drop the gun," the man repeats. "You're wasting your time, Benedict Baines."

Ben lowers his arm down. He looks at Greta; looks at Jack; looks at me. For the longest moment, he looks at me. Our eyes drink each other in. We don't speak, but our eyes say a million words.

Then he raises himself up, holds his head high, steely-eyed. He lifts the gun back up, but he doesn't point it towards the police; he points it at his own head.

"No," he says. "No. I will not drop the gun. Let the others go, or I'll shoot myself."

BEN

It's not as if I'm suddenly making a spontaneous heroic gesture. I've always known this is what I'll do if I get the chance. It's not a selfless act: it's a calculated gamble that might pay off.

Hoshi, Greta, Jack – what have they got to bargain with? Their lives mean nothing to the police; nothing to the government; nothing to my mother, who is no doubt controlling all of this behind the scenes. She must be desperate to see them all die.

Not me though, at least I don't think so. That's not her style. If I know anything about how my mother works, she'll want the chance to see me repent. She'll want to exert her will on me, mould me back into being her good little boy again. She'll want to win.

These officers will have been told not to harm me if they can possibly avoid it. That's what I'm gambling on. And if I'm right, they certainly aren't going to want me to put a bullet through my own head, not after all these months of searching for me.

Next to me, Hoshi's mouth is open, her expression shocked and fearful.

"Ben, you're scaring me."

"It's OK," I tell her. And then I say loudly, in a confident voice, "They don't want me dead. They've been told to bring me in alive, no matter what the cost. Isn't that right?"

The policeman at the top of the stairs doesn't answer my question.

"Lower your weapon, Benedict," he says. "It's over now."

"Yes," I answer, my voice shaking, just a little bit. "Yes, it is over, or it will be for you once I've shot myself. I'll do it. I promise I will. Let the others go, or I'll do it right now."

There's panic in his eyes. I'm right. I know I am.

"I swear to you, if you let them go, I'll put the gun down. I'll come with you as soon as they're free."

I can almost see his thought process: what's more important, one live Benedict Baines and three escaped outlaws, or one dead Benedict Baines and three captured outlaws? He looks around at the other officers for answers, but they look just as bewildered as he does.

"Why should I believe you?" he says. "How do I know that as soon as they're out of sight, you won't shoot at us, or you won't just shoot yourself anyway?"

"You don't," I tell him. "But think about it." My hand reaches out and grabs hold of Hoshi's, clutching on to it for the last time. "What's left for me if you take them?"

"We'll keep you together," he says. "We just want to talk to you. No one's going to get hurt."

"You really expect us to believe that? Believe that you'll let Hoshi go, that you'll let Greta and Jack go? What are you going to do, send them away with a smack on the wrist after what they've done? We all know exactly what you'll do to them!"

I lower the gun. Hold it to my own heart.

"Please," I say. "Please let them go. I'll do whatever you want then, I give you my word."

I can't believe this is happening. He's about to turn the gun on himself, right in front of us.

"Ben, you have to stop this," I say, carefully. "It's too late now. It's over – we have to do what they say."

He turns to me, and his eyes are on fire. He whispers to me, urgently. "It's the only way we all stand a chance of surviving! Please. Please, if you get the chance, just go. Run, as fast and as far as you can." He's gripping the gun hard, still holding it to his own chest. "I'll find you," he says. "Wherever you go, I'll find you, one day."

Jack reaches for Ben's arm.

"Mate, you can't do this." He speaks to the police officer, waiting silently at the top of the stairs. "Let the girls go, keep us." He gives a dry laugh. "There, I've upped his offer. Two for one."

"No!" Ben's tone is resolute. "Let them all go, or I end it, right here."

The policeman at the top of the stairs finally seems to have regained his composure.

"None of you are going anywhere, except with us," he says. "If you want to kill yourself, Baines, please go ahead: saves us a job later."

Ben shakes his head. "It's too late for that now," he says. "You've hesitated too long – you've given the game away. You aren't going to shoot me; you'd have done it by now."

There's a silence. It feels like it goes on for ever.

My mind is whirring. He's right about one thing – they'll

definitely kill Greta and me; we're just Dreg scum to them. And they'll kill Jack too – a turncoat police officer – he's committed treason as far as they're concerned. But Benedict Baines, son of Vivian, Dreg Control Minister and wannabe Prime Minister – what will they do to him when they've got him? That one's harder to call. He's a traitor to his country too, or so they say, but his blood's a damn sight Purer than the rest of ours.

Still, it's way too risky. We've been through too much. We come as a unit now, the four of us.

"We said we'd stick together," I tell him. "I'm not leaving you. I *can't* leave you. Not after everything."

His eyes are brimming over, desperately pleading with me.

"Please," he says to me. "Please let me do this. You have to." He looks pointedly at Greta, still holding tightly on to me, uncharacteristically silent for once.

I look down at Greta, so frightened that I can feel her trembling, and I know he's right. She's so young still. I can't let them take her and kill her, not if there's a chance she can get away, and she won't go anywhere without me – she's made that pretty clear by now.

We'll have to run, if we get the chance. I'll have to leave him; there's no other way. Damn him for playing the Greta card! He knows my weaknesses too well.

"Keep the guns on them," the guy at the top of the stairs says. "I need to make a phone call."

He pushes roughly through the officers crowding the stairwell behind him and walks off, through the doors and back into the office.

He's gone about a minute. Nobody speaks.

When he returns, he looks even more panicked than he did before.

"OK," he says to Ben. "OK, you've got yourself a deal. Just do not fire that gun."

BEN

"I want to see they're not followed," I tell the officer in charge. "I want to watch them go."

I look once more at Hoshi. "I'll be OK," I say. "I promise." I nod to Jack, smile at Greta, and stare at Hoshi again. "Be careful," I say. "Stay safe. Whatever it takes."

I turn away and the officers part as I walk through them back up the stairs to the office, gripping the gun to my head.

I walk over to the big panoramic window, raising the blinds up with my free hand.

It's a glorious day out there, not a cloud in the sky.

The PowerHouse building dominates the skyline from here, just as it does across London. All the other monuments – Big Ben, the old clock tower, the crumbling remains of the old parliament buildings, the big white palace – pale into significance beneath the triumphant smile of the gleaming statue. That was exactly the intention when they built it all those years ago: to signify the new world order.

Beamed up on to it, five faces stare down into the city below, draping the whole building in their translucent colours.

It's pointless thinking they'll escape. How can they when the whole city, the whole country, the whole world knows what they look like?

At least they can try, though. I haven't saved them, but I've given them a reprieve, and, for now at least, it's the best I can do.

"I won't lower this gun until I've seen them disappear from sight," I say to the mass of people standing behind me. "I can see your reflections: if you come any closer, or I see anyone following them, I'll pull the trigger."

The boss guy heaves a large, exasperated sigh. "You heard what he said!" he barks angrily at the rest of the police officers. "Let them go!"

At the bottom of the stairs, someone opens the door up and daylight floods in. The officers below us lower their guns and stand back against the walls, forming a narrow passageway between them. I feel their eyes boring into me as I pass down the stairs and into the warmth of the morning, right past all the police cars and their blue lights.

I turn and look up.

Ben's at the window, high above, still holding the gun to his own head.

What are the chances of us ever seeing each other again if I leave him now?

I take a step backwards.

"Hoshi." Jack's hand clamps down on my arm. "We have to do this."

"I can't. It can't end like this!" I wrench away from him and start running back towards the building.

"Hoshi!" Greta screams out. "Don't leave me!"

The sheer fear in her voice stops me in my tracks.

Jack catches up with me.

"I made a mistake," I tell him. "I have to go back. If I hand myself in, maybe they'll leave Ben alone! I'm the one they want to punish. Take Greta with you, look after her. You'll be safer without me. Less visible."

"You heard what Ben said! He's thought about this. He's doing it for you, for Greta, for all of us."

My head is whirling.

"You know I'm right, Hoshi. We keep going. For him.

For Ben. And for Greta. It's not the end. Things are going to change for the better. As soon as they do, you'll be together again."

Jack believes that with all his heart, I know he does. He left his fiancée, Alice, behind the day he saved us. She was resistance too and, as soon as his cover was blown, she had to flee to Europe. He called her as soon as we got away from the Cirque and told her to run before she was hauled in for questioning. She had fake passports and money all lined up and by the time the police came calling for her, she'd gone.

A woman we've never even met is in danger because of us. Jack says she won't blame us, that they both always knew what the deal was, being in the resistance.

He thinks she'll be able to come home soon. He says that pro-Dreg sentiment is so strong now that we're on the brink of a new world, where we can all live as equals. There's an election next week and, for the first time ever, a pro-Dreg candidate is running for office. Jack says there's a really good chance she'll win and, if she does, Alice can come out of hiding and we might be granted pardons.

I wish I could share his conviction, but I don't. This world is too cruel for things to be any different.

When Jack speaks again, his voice is uncharacteristically stern. "Don't you dare let Ben down now, Hoshi! You know how we make what he's doing worthwhile?"

I shake my head.

"We fight, that's how! We fight to stay alive, just like we always have."

I stare at him, and then back at the tiny blonde girl behind us, clutching her monkey. Then I look back up at Ben. He lifts his other hand and waves.

I wave back. I mouth the same words I mouthed all those months ago – the last time the police had us surrounded. *I love you*. He mouths the words back.

"Come on," Jack says. "Let's get out of here."

And we walk off slowly, Jack, Greta and me, the eyes of a hundred police officers on us.

At the corner, I turn once more. There he is, a tiny figure now, at the window. I raise my hand again and he waves back and I feel like my heart is breaking into a thousand pieces.

I stay there at the window, holding the gun to my head and watching as they get smaller and smaller and then disappear from sight.

The first time I ever saw Hoshi tumbling and turning on that wire the day the circus came to town, I knew even then, somewhere deep inside me, that she'd change my life.

We've been on the run for so long that a part of me started to think it would always be that way. The four of us, outlaws for ever.

I had such an easy life before: always had food on demand, a warm house, clean clothes. To be without things you've always had in abundance, always taken for granted, is a shock to the system. My back aches all the time now from sleeping on dirty floors and crawling into cramped spaces. My head itches permanently, desperate for the rich, creamy lather of shampoo. My lips have cracked, and my stomach's concave now, and shrinking more every day.

I don't miss my old life at all though, not like you might think. I was deluded then. I lived in a bubble. Everything I had was paid for by evil and coldness and cruelty.

Hoshi and me, and Greta and Jack, we've become a team: so tight, so strong. I've never had that before. Never had that feeling of belonging, of being with people who I knew I could rely on to be by my side through everything, through anything.

Sometimes, I used to look at the three of them and wonder if they knew what on earth they were doing, sacrificing so much for a boy like me, a boy whose mother had done such terrible things. And yet they never blamed me for it, not once, not any of them. For some unfathomable reason, these people – people who were so much braver, so much wiser, so much better than me, somehow saw something in *me*, loved something in *me*.

They might make it now, without me. I'm one less person to worry about. They might finally get to the continent and Jack can be reunited with his fiancée. Things are better there. People are more tolerant, borders are open, society is inclusive. I could put up with anything if I knew Hoshi and Greta were free, really free, for the first time in their lives, even if it meant them being in another country; even if it meant not seeing them again.

A lump constricts my throat as I contemplate a life without Hoshi in it. What does it matter what happens to me now, really?

I turn around.

They're all still there, at least a dozen police officers, their shields up, their guns trained on me. I've imagined this scenario loads of times, planned it exactly this way: me bargaining myself so Hoshi and the others can go free. It's worked, gone exactly as I wanted. The trouble is, I just psyched myself up for this bit. I never really let myself imagine what would happen afterwards. What *are* they going to do with me: Benedict Baines – the rebel? Benedict Baines, the outlaw?

Like a light going on in my head, I realize I know the answer. I know exactly where they're going to take me, exactly who they're going to take me to.

"You're going to take me to my mother, aren't you? As soon as I put this gun down."

Their eyes flick nervously at each other but nobody says anything. If they're not denying it, it must be true.

21

My mother is the Dreg Control Minister, and now she's running for office. My mother hates anyone who isn't "Pure" English more than anything in all the world. She calls them vermin. She thinks the world would be a better place without them. She wants to "do away" with them.

She must be absolutely livid about all the things I've done. My mother is used to controlling people, used to getting her own way, and yet I, her own son, ran away from home, assaulted a security guard, posed as a police officer, helped to blow up a circus and spent nearly a year on the run. A year embarrassing her, casting shame on her, and why? Because of a Dreg tightrope walker, that's why.

What's she going to say? What's she going to do?

Whatever it is, I don't care. Her power over me has gone. She'll never turn me back into her meek little boy again. She'll never win.

I know myself now. I know what's right. I know what's true.

I want to see her, all of a sudden, to tell her that. I want to look into her eyes: defiant, unrepentant. I want her to see who I am now, see that I'm nothing like her, see that she means nothing to me.

I look at the police officers, all still petrified that I'm going to turn the gun on myself. Maybe I should. Maybe I should just shoot myself, right now. I won't though; I don't want to. I don't want to die, not while Hoshi, Greta and Jack are still out there. I want to keep fighting, for them. I want to live.

I throw the gun down, step forward with my hands up.

"Come on then, let's get on with it," I say. "Take me to Vivian Baines."

Once we're out of sight, we break into a run.

"Where will we go?" I ask Jack. "They're bound to find us, anyway. They can track us now, surely; there are cameras everywhere."

"No," he says. "Not everywhere."

He's leading us further and further away from the city centre, into the outskirts. He runs down a dark alley, then another one, then another.

"Where are we going?" asks Greta. Bojo's little monkey arms are wrapped around her neck, and she's panting already, as she tries to match Jack's long-legged pace.

"The only place the cameras can't find us." Jack says. "The only place they haven't bothered installing them."

There's only one place he can mean.

We're heading for the slums.

Pulling on my hand as we run, Greta's voice is urgent.

"Where does Jack mean, Hoshi? Where are we going?"

I look down at her. As soon as I mention the "s" word, she'll get hysterical, I know she will.

"Just keep running."

"Jack," she calls after him. "Where are we going?"

"The slums," he answers abruptly over his shoulder.

Greta stops in her tracks, wrenching my hand back.

"No! I don't want to. You said we'd never have to!"

"We don't have a choice any more, Greta! They'll be following us. Come on!"

I pull her arm, but she won't come.

In front, Jack turns and heads back towards us, his eyes panicked.

"What are you doing? Come on! As soon as Ben drops that gun, they're going to try and grab us!"

"But you said we'd never go to the slums! You said we'd be safer out here!"

"I know I said that, Greta, but they'll be tracking us! The slums are the only place we stand half a chance of losing them!"

She still won't move. There's the sound of a siren in the distance, getting louder. Jack gives a sigh of frustration. I can tell how desperate he is, but he tries to talk gently and calmly.

"Greta. We have to go into the slums. We don't have a choice. It might not be that bad."

"No," she says, stubbornly. "I don't want to."

He throws his hands up in exasperation. "Come on! We don't have time for this!"

There are more sirens now: louder, closer.

What can I do? We've always tried to protect Greta when we can, always tried our hardest to make being on the run seem like an adventure. It's too late for that now. It's time to let her know how high the stakes are.

"You hear that sound?" I say. "That's for us, Greta! They're coming after us and if they catch us again, this time they *will* kill us. Do you understand? They'll kill us all!"

I pull her arm, hard, and drag her along with me as I start to run.

She stops resisting and her feet pound along with mine as she gasps stifled cries of shock and fear.

The buildings we wend our way past become ever shabbier,

ever more run-down. More and more of them are boarded up, covered in graffiti, and we have to dance our way through the dogs' mess and broken glass decorating the pavement as we run past burnt-out cars and battered shopping trolleys.

I've heard of streets like this: the streets they call No Man's Land. Not slum territory, not yet, but close enough to the slums that no respectable, clean Pure wants to spend any time here. We see someone eventually: a man, slumped in a doorway, clutching a bottle.

"Spare us some change," he calls out as we pass.

There are more people after that. Curled up in doorways, like him, the stench of urine announcing their presence, or walking towards us, grabbing at us as we pass.

They all have the same empty, crazed look in their eyes.

"Who are they?" I ask Jack as we run. "Pures or Dregs?"

"Neither," he answers. "They're in limbo, poor devils." He slows his pace a little and talks as he runs along next to me. "They're Pures, probably, or they were once. Pures who, for whatever reason, lost their way. Maybe they've committed a crime and they're on the run, like us. More likely though is that they're just broken in some way ... mentally ill maybe, or the victims of some kind of tragedy or loss they can't recover from."

"Why can't they get help?"

I thought all Pures lived in a land of milk and honey. I thought they lived in paradise.

"If they come forward, and ask for medical or financial help, or somewhere to sleep for the night, they'll be written off," he replies. "The Pures don't want people like these guys messing up their world, making it look less than shiny and perfect.

They'll have their status taken away, be immediately classed as Dregs and, once you're a Dreg, there's no going back. That's why they're out here; they're hiding from anyone who might discover them. They think it's a better option than life in the slums."

"And is it?"

He looks at me with a shrug. "There's not a lot in it as far as I've seen."

He was a Pure, once. He had a job. He had a home.

It dawns on me all over again what they've sacrificed for us, Jack and Ben: the police detective and the minister's son. They've turned their backs on the life they knew: a life of easy comfort, a life of privilege, to stand up for us, to stand beside us.

Where does Jack belong now? And Ben, where does he belong? They too are in limbo. Are they Dregs now, like us, or are they the same as these desperate creatures, clutching at us as we pass?

No. They are neither of those things. They have defied the labels branded on them at birth. They are heroes, both of them, my heroes, and they belong with us.

The ache for Ben fills me up. I hope he's OK. What will they do to him? What if I never see him again? I can't lose him. Not now.

I push the thought away. I can't think like that; I'll crumple to the ground in a heap if I do. I have to focus on running, on staying safe. For Greta.

We reach the battered wooden fence which segregates the slums from the rest of the city.

"We can't go through the main checkpoint; we'll have to

duck in along here somewhere. If we keep walking along, we should find a gap sooner or later," Jack says. I can see what he means. It's a ramshackle fence, rotting wood, slumping inward on itself.

"I thought it'd be more secure," I say. "The Cirque fences were all electrified. Surely any Dreg who wants to could jump these, or kick them in."

Jack nods. "You'd think so, wouldn't you, and they do, from time to time, but why would any Dreg want to leave the slums, unless it was for work?"

"To escape!"

"To escape to what? Where would they go? What would they do?"

I think about it. He's right: there's nowhere for a Dreg to run to, nowhere safe to go. None of us have money, none of us have passports. At least in there, behind that fence, they're away from the Pures.

We run along the perimeter, looking for an easy opening. Within seconds, sirens sound, louder and closer by the second.

Jack starts kicking at the fence in front of him. I join him, and then Greta does too, her little leg booting it as hard as she can. It's so old and rotten that it gives way easily; a whole panel splinters in half and you can see through the gap into the slum beyond.

"Climb through," Jack says. "Quickly!"

I scramble through. A splinter of wood catches my arm and scratches it. Greta slips through next, passing Bojo gently through the gap to me first, followed by Jack, who carefully slots the wood back into place.

We press against the fence, panting, eyes wide, as the sirens get closer and then pass by.

I look around, curious and apprehensive.

Huge mounds slope up on either side of us, dotted all around the outskirts, like mountains. The stench alone – a rotten, cloyingly sweet smell – is enough to confirm that they're rubbish dumps. It's a smell that makes Greta's nose wrinkle and bile rise in my throat. There are dark shadows hovering over each one: fuzzy, moving clouds. Flies, I realize as one lands on my cheek and I brush it away in disgust. Crows and magpies, pecking away busily amongst the rotting litter, pause to look down briefly at us before resuming their scavenging ways, and fat, gleaming rats slink brazenly along. Around the corner, a bigger figure emerges, hunched over, rooting through the rubbish. It's a human being, a tiny, dirty boy rummaging for scraps. He looks at us with dark, hollow, disinterested eyes. Further away, on the other huge heaps, I can see more children doing the same thing.

In front of us, stretching as far as the eye can see are thousands and thousands of tiny, ramshackle dwellings. At least I think they're dwellings, it's hard to tell. They're all falling apart, all leaning on each other exhaustedly. Corrugated iron, wood, cardboard, a slumping metropolis of poverty and decay.

We stand there, taking it in. The great London slums.

When the Pure Protection laws were first passed – the ones that categorize people and their rights according to race and background – the Pures didn't want Dregs living alongside them any more, polluting their lovely city, so they kicked them all out of their homes. The trouble was, they still needed them close enough to keep everything running in the manner to which they were accustomed: to keep the sewers functioning, the trash collected, the roads built – all the jobs the Pures deemed too lowly for themselves, so they commandeered miles of green belt land and piled everyone in.

They did the same thing in all towns, but the London slums are the most notorious, for lots of reasons. They're over twenty-five years old now and there obviously hasn't been any cash spent on them since they first vomited them out.

I can't really remember much about my own slum; I was only five when they took me away. I wonder if it looked like this place. It's probably miles away from here, but I don't know. I don't think my mum ever told me the name of where we lived and, if she ever did, I've forgotten it. I've always told myself I'll find my way back one day but, even if I had the chance to start looking, I wouldn't know where to begin.

Once my eyes have adjusted, I think I can make out movement from inside some of the shacks, and then we hear shrieking voices and a group of shabby children run past, kicking a can and laughing.

"What do we do now?" Greta asks, her lip trembling.

Jack shakes his head. "Not much we can do," he says. "We're going to have to go and ask someone for help."

BEN

The officers in front of the car are silent as we move slowly through the heavy city traffic. We don't make our way south, towards my old house, and we drive straight past the grinning, gleaming PowerHouse monument, so they aren't taking me to my mother's office either.

I stare up at the huge image of Hoshi as she glares down at me. The image has been manipulated, of course – all of the beauty and grace that make up Hoshi erased with the touch of a button. Her eyes are narrow splinters of cold hard flint. Her mouth is set with aggression. It isn't her at all. It's a million miles away from the girl I know.

I look away. Where on earth are we going? At first, I think we're heading towards the prison, that they're going to lock me up straight away, but we drive past that too.

The traffic eventually eases as we make our way out of the city and on to the open road.

We drive up a steep hill and then dip down again, and that's when I realize where we're heading.

A huge arching dome soars up from the trees, shooting lines of red and white cascading down from the top hypnotically. I stare at it, stare at the other buildings which rise up around it as we get closer. More domed roofs, orange and green and pink and purple, like delicious swirled sweets.

My blood runs cold.

We knew it was happening, of course we did. We've been on the run, but we haven't been on the moon. As soon as the arena burnt down, the government made plans to rebuild it, plans to construct a bigger, better, permanent Cirque, here in the capital city. I think it was their way of claiming victory, their way of snubbing all the protesters and campaigners who came out against the Cirque. They secured land on the outskirts of London, acres and acres of land, and they started rebuilding it. Permanent structures this time: *A bigger, better, bolder Cirque*, the posters said, *with a few magic tricks up its sleeve.*

As we approach, a helter-skelter looms in front of me, rising up over the fences and, in the distance, an enormous big wheel towers over everything. It's not enough any more to just have the shows and the side stalls – there's a fairground now too. No, not a fairground, a theme park: vast, expansive.

I think of everything we've been through, Hoshi and Greta and me.

We blew up the arena. We escaped. So what?

They killed Amina, the person Hoshi loved most in all the world – strung her up in the arena and auctioned off her parts on the internet to the highest bidder. They killed Priya – the first person in the world to ever tell me the truth about anything – and turned her into a zombie, there to be used as target practice by excited thugs with their shotguns.

What did they die for, Amina and Priya?

Nothing. We achieved nothing.

The Cirque has picked itself up, dusted itself off and risen up, bigger, better, stronger than ever.

People will go on dying in the name of entertainment, just like they always did; there'll just be someone new at the helm.

Still, whoever it is can't be as bad as Silvio Sabatini. I shudder just thinking of him. At least we destroyed him. They'll never be able to take that away from us.

"Why have you brought me here?" I call out, as the car rolls ever onwards.

The officers ignore me.

We pass a road sign. *The Cirque*, it says. *Two hundred metres*.

"Stop the car!" I shout.

We turn left, past a huge plastic clown face grinning inanely at us as we pass, its wide eyes moving from side to side, and proceed up a long driveway, past the huge empty car parks until we reach a wall, covered in bright three-dimensional images of lions and elephants and acrobats and more clowns.

The officer driving the car winds down his window, tapping a code into a panel outside. The wall moves then, and I realize it's not a solid wall at all; it's a pair of huge double gates. They swing slowly open, the action apparently signalling the start of music.

It's the same music as before, gaudy hurdy-gurdy circus music which once, a lifetime ago, filled me with excitement but now fills me with dread and fear and loathing. Waves of panic rise up inside me.

"Stop the car!" I cry again. They just ignore me. I try the door. It's locked. "Stop the car! Stop the car!"

There's nothing I can do.

I don't want to be here. I should never have let them take me. Once I'd seen Hoshi and Greta and Jack were gone, I should have just shot myself.

We're in a huge open-air entrance hall lined all across with ticket booths, gleaming and new and unused. In the middle of them, a huge sign flashes its greeting in bold neon lights.

Welcome to the Cirque! it declares. *The Show Must Go On!*

HOSHIKO

We make our way hesitantly towards the shacks, Greta and me behind Jack, Bojo bounding along at Greta's heels. It's eerily quiet everywhere; I suppose most people are out in the city working, doing all the jobs the Pures think are beneath them – the dull ones, the dangerous ones, the dirty ones. There are people here though, I can feel them. A million eyes, hidden away, watching us.

I keep my gaze on the ground. I don't remember ever feeling so shy and uncomfortable. The mud beneath our feet is squelchy, even though there's been no rain for a couple of weeks.

When we reach the outskirts of the shacks, Jack stops.

"I think it might be better if you two go first," he says, "and I hang back a bit."

The dismay on Greta's face must match my own. The media might say we're fearless renegades, but it's not true. I really don't want to do this: find the nearest stranger in this place and ask them for help.

How can they help us when they've got nothing themselves? And why should they?

"Why?" I ask him.

He grimaces. "I don't look enough like one of them, that's why. I'm nearly forty-two years old and I've still got all my teeth. My hair hasn't fallen out, and I'm still fairly strong, even after a year on the run. As soon as they look at me, they'll see a Pure."

My heart sinks further.

Jack's told me all about the slums. He told me and Ben that they were the one place we could never run to, the one place we should never hide, not with Ben and Jack being Pures. Even the police, armed with their guns, avoid the slums if they can help it, Jack says. The Dregs are left to their own devices here, and there are far too many hungry, angry, desperate people for it to be a place where anything good happens.

Greta squeezes my hand.

"We'll do it together," she says.

I look down at her and my heart swells. She's recovered from her panic already: she's ready to do whatever she has to. She always was the bravest of us.

"What are you going to do?" I ask Jack.

"I'll be behind you. I'll keep my head down and try and stay in the shadows, if I can. I'll keep within hearing distance though. If you need me, shout."

As we start walking, I glance behind me at Jack, skulking along behind us. He's wearing a beanie hat and he's adopted that slumped, defeated look most of the Dregs have, but he was right; he does look different to the Dregs. Of course he does – he was born in another world.

Jack never talks much about his life before. One night though, back in the early days on the run, he told me and Ben about what happened to him to make him the way he is – so brave and loyal and good.

We were camped out in the woods. It was a really cold night and we made a fire and sat there, talking through the night while Greta and Bojo curled up in the warmth of the flames and slept.

Jack said being out in the woods reminded him of his home, when he was a kid. His parents owned a big farm and a lot of land, but his mum died when he was young and his dad was always busy overseeing the management of his estate. Nobody had much time for Jack, so he was shipped off to boarding school.

"I was pretty much left to my own devices in the school holidays," he said. "I could roam around as I pleased, as long as I kept out of the way and didn't cause any bother.

"There was always a lot of manual work to be done, which meant a lot of Dregs – working in the fields, clearing out the livestock, that kind of thing. Mostly people would come and go – we were always especially busy at harvest time – but there were some families who lived on site, in cottages my father gave them in exchange for labour.

"There was a Greek family living in one of the homes and the oldest boy, Andreas, was the same age as me. Ever since we were little kids we used to play together, down in the fields and woods. I spent every waking minute with him if I could. It wasn't allowed, of course, but nobody paid much attention to things like that on a rural farm in the middle of nowhere.

"When you're young, you think days like that will last for ever. It didn't matter that he was a Dreg and I was a Pure, or that his dad was a serf, working long, hard hours under the heavy hand of my father."

His eyes filled with tears when he said that. He stopped for a while, and stoked up the fire. Then, when he sat back down, he started speaking again.

"Andreas was my best friend. I lived for those days when it

was just me and him, free and wild. We would fish together, and build camps out in the woods, and then, when our stomachs told us it was time, we'd go back to his cottage and scrounge some food. His family were as different to mine as it was possible to be. There were seven of them living in that tiny place: Maria and Alesandro, the parents, and five kids. It was always noisy and it felt like everyone was happy, all the time. They didn't have money, obviously, but Alesandro was an expert hunter and forager and there always seemed to be something cooking away. Maria always found a bit extra for me, and I always ate it, even though I could have had anything I wanted at home. The food our cook made was never as nice as the stews she'd dish up.

"One summer, I came home and I went straight down to the cottage to find Andreas like I always did, but he wasn't there. His mum told me he had to help out with the labour on the farm now he'd turned fourteen, so that was the pretty much the end of our friendship. I'd see him all the time, working away, but we never got to spend much time together any more. I know it was wrong of me, but I resented him for it. It felt like he'd grown up and I was still a boy, like he didn't have time for our childish adventures now he was a man."

Jack stood up then and walked off into the woods. I wanted to go after him, but Ben said we should wait.

"He'll come back," he said. "He'll tell us, in his own time."

So we waited there by the fire. He was gone ages. It was really late, and as I stared into the flames, my eyes felt heavy, but I didn't want to go to sleep. In the end, Ben was right: he came back and carried on like he'd never stopped talking.

"I've never told anyone this before," he said. "It's the worst thing I ever did. You two think I'm a good person, but I'm not." And then he sat down with his back to us and told us the rest of the story.

"That was the summer that everything changed. My father was selling a lot of our land off to build new houses. The livestock was taken away and the builders were all moving in.

"The day before I left to go back to school, I was wandering around on my own, bored as usual, and I ran into Andreas, clearing the crops in a field. He looked at me all sympathetically when he saw me, like he felt sorry for me, even though I was a Pure and he was a Dreg. He put his arm on my shoulder and asked if I was OK.

"For some reason, it got my back up. I felt like he was patronizing me, like he just saw me as a little kid. I pushed him away, really hard, with two hands, and told him to get his hands off me. I called him a filthy Dreg. His face dropped, but it just made me angrier. I don't know to this day why I did it, but I punched him, right in the face. I remember looking at him, lying there in the mud, his nose spurting with blood, and then just walking off and leaving him. The next day, I went back to boarding school.

"It didn't take long for the guilt to set in, of course. I couldn't believe how awful I'd been. I still can't. All I wanted was to get home and apologize for what I'd done. I knew it would be hard but I'd make up for it, somehow. I'd find a way to help him with his work. I'd try to explain why I did it, although I didn't really understand myself.

"When I arrived back that Christmas though, Andreas and his family were gone. Their cottage had been torn down to make way for the new houses and my father had dismissed them.

"He seemed totally bemused by my dismay at first and then, when I kept asking him to find out where they were, he got angry.

"'You want to be careful, Jack,' he said. 'People will start wondering if you're a Dreg sympathizer.' I remember him sneering at me. 'Maybe you should join the underground resistance.'

"He meant it as an insult, but the phrase stuck with me. I didn't even know there was a resistance movement until then. It got me thinking: it must mean there were people out there who didn't like the way things were, people who thought we should all be treated equally.

"I needed to find my best friend. I needed to tell him I was sorry, that I hadn't meant what I'd said, what I'd done. I only joined the police so I could try and track down Andreas's family. I never did though – nobody bothers keeping records of the whereabouts of Dreg farm workers.

"It doesn't take long when you work for an institution like the police for people to work out that your views maybe aren't as fixed as they should be – for you to be regarded as something of a liberal. The resistance are always looking for new blood and eventually, and very carefully, over many months, they recruited me.

"Helping others was the only way I had of apologizing, I guess, to Andreas. If I ever meet him again, I want to show him that I'm not the spoilt, spiteful Pure kid I was back then. That's why, when the Cirque came to town, I made sure I was on the security task force. I didn't know what I could do, but I knew I had to do something. As soon as they said that Vivian Baines's son had been fraternizing with a Dreg girl and they were trying to escape together, I knew I had to try and help you."

He looked at Ben then and his face was all shameful. "You were braver than me. You'd put your neck on the line straight away. Not like me. You'd never have behaved like I did."

"Andreas would have known you didn't mean it," I said. "He wouldn't have hated you. He'd have realized that you were just hurt and confused. You were just a kid then, Jack. Look at what you've done since. You saved us. Greta and I would be dead without you."

He just smiled then, a sad kind of smile, and I wondered if he was missing Alice, his fiancée. Now, I realize, he must have been, not just then, but all the time. He must miss her every second of every day, just like I'm missing Ben now, but I think he never says much about it because he doesn't want to make us feel guilty.

He gave everything up for us and he still thinks he's a bad person.

I'm not excusing what Jack did, but the shame he feels, deep inside, and the guilt which is still eating away at him — they've made him what he is today. He's determined never to let anyone down again — hell-bent on doing the right thing, whatever consequences it might have for him personally. He seems so confident most of the time, so bright and cheerful, but when you really know him, you see that there's an emptiness there, deep down inside him. I wish I could take it away. I wish he would judge himself on the man he has become, and not the foolish boy he once was.

I think about what he sacrificed for us, and for the millionth time I'm flooded with gratitude. This must be the first time he's been this far from Greta and me since we went on the run and I have no doubt that if I called now, he'd come running.

What would we have done without him these last few months? We'd have died out there on the streets, that's what, or been captured, which amounts to the same thing.

He's spent nearly a year now without even speaking to the woman he loves, the woman he wants to marry. He doesn't even know if, or when, he'll see her again. Every day, he must have had that ache inside him that I do. That cold, empty feeling.

Where is Ben, right now, I wonder? I hope he's safe. What if he's not? What will they do to him? What if they've locked him up somewhere? What if they're hurting him?

A piece of cardboard draped over the front of one of the shacks moves suddenly and a woman emerges. Her skin is grey, her hair is sparse and thin; she's really skinny. She's wearing an orange uniform so I guess she's heading into the city to earn her food tokens.

I hold my breath, flash her a look which must be more grimace than smile, and walk past her, gripping hold of Greta's hand tightly. She doesn't step aside to let us past, so we have to squeeze around her, awkwardly.

Once we're past her, we take a few more steps and then I stop and turn around. She's still there, standing in the middle of the path, the cold stare of her hollow eyes replaced by a glimmer of recognition.

Her eyes keep darting from us to something else, something beyond us, high and in the distance. I don't have to turn back around to know what she's looking at. The PowerHouse, adorned with our pictures, casting its shadow down over the slums.

I turn back around and keep walking, clutching Greta's hand the whole time.

After a few seconds, I hear her footsteps, running off into the distance.

I stop and wait for Jack to catch up with us.

"She recognized us," I say.

He nods, grimly. "She ran out of here just then as if she was on fire. Three guesses where she's going?"

He doesn't need an answer. We all know what he means.

She's running to find a police officer, as quickly as she can. She wants to get her hands on all that lovely reward money before anyone else does. Damn it, we've hardly been here five minutes.

"What do we do?"

"Stick to the plan. They were hot on our heels anyway."

We walk on, more quickly this time. Greta keeps looking behind us, her face full of fear and panic. I wish I could say something that would make her feel better.

Use your instinct, Jack said, but after a while everywhere looks the same. Decay and despair drape over everything, as rancid and rotten as the smell of the rubbish tip hanging in the air. Then, as we turn another corner, I see somewhere different.

A hut, as tiny as all the others, but a little more upright, a little crisper, a little neater, a little prouder-looking than the rest. It's got real windows, for a start, clean enough to see through and beyond them, in the dim interior, there's a vase of wild flowers.

Flowers, here, in the slums.

I squeeze Greta's hand and point towards it.

"Let's try that one," I say.

Her eyebrows rise in surprise when she sees the windows and the flowers, and she nods.

"Agreed."

And so we do. Hand in hand, we walk slowly up to the tiny shack and knock on its thin wooden door.

BEN

Neither of the police officers has said a word to me since we got into the car.

"What are we doing here?" I demand, time and time again, but they just stare straight ahead.

They stop the car and get out, the female officer opening my door and taking a firm hold of my arm, all without any response.

I shake her hand away, roughly.

"I'm not going anywhere until you tell me what's going on!" I yell.

The other officer comes round to our side of the car and pushes me on to the bonnet.

"Do you want us to cuff you?"

I stop struggling and let them lead me through the open ticket barriers and into the main courtyard.

I look around, overwhelmed by it all.

Pristine multicoloured pathways lead everywhere, neat flower beds fully in bloom alongside them. The buildings are all different colours too, all gleaming with fresh paint, all solid, all built to last.

It's like a larger than life version of the old Cirque: the travelling circus that came into town, put on its dazzling display of death and destruction for a week or two and then moved to another town to do the same thing there.

There are no scaffold frames up, no sign of any construction going on. Everywhere is empty, but it's ready. Ready to open, waiting impatiently to put on a show.

The officers lead me forward towards a huge hill right in the middle. Its grassy slopes are dotted with flowers and trees and various life-size figures are meandering about. Traditional shepherds holding crooks, tend their sheep. Ethereal maidens, dressed in white robes, wander and pick flowers. Girls with rosy cheeks carry milk churns on their shoulders, whilst nymph-like creatures frolic amongst the trees, tumbling together in ponds and streams.

Mythological creatures like these don't really exist, not in real life. They must be projected images, so lifelike that you can't tell the difference. If you touched one, would your hand go right through it, I wonder, or would you grasp something physical, something real?

A large hive is perched right on the top, hundreds of bees flit busily in and out of it, and behind it, letters, twisted from flowers: *Arcadia: the Land of Milk and Honey.* Arcadia: I've heard that word before. It's Greek, I think. What does it mean? I wish I'd paid more attention at school.

I look at it. It's obviously the centrepiece of the whole Cirque. Why? What happens inside?

Dread and fear twist in my stomach. I don't want to go in there.

I brace myself for a second and then wrench my arms away from the police officers holding me, spin around and run towards the gates.

They run after me.

They're quick, but I'm quicker.

I reach the ticket booths and vault right over one of the turnstiles, sprinting off down the sweeping entry road.

Behind me, I hear whistles blowing frantically and then sirens, lights flashing, the sound of footsteps sprinting in pursuit.

Something huge swoops past me, so fast I feel the air rush, and there's a screech of tyres as it skids to a halt in front of me.

It's a motorbike. A police officer leaps off it and stands there, barring my path, gun raised.

I stop. What else can I do?

I look around; I'm surrounded by armed forces. Twice in one day. There are the two officers who brought me here, flanked by six other officers. Behind them, security guards, wearing the government uniform.

One of them looks familiar. It's Stanley, my old bodyguard. My heart gives a little jolt at seeing him again. It's silly, I know, but I was fond of him in a funny kind of way. For years, he was always there next to me: a silent companion, my own personal shadow. I try to catch his eye, but he gazes passively into the distance. Some things never change.

What's he doing here?

Something catches my eye as it glints in the sunlight, beaming down on the arena roof. I look up. There's a sniper up there, his gun trained on me.

What's going on?

Stanley, the sniper, the government uniforms. They can't all be here for me, can they? No. There must be something else that's brought them here. Some*one* else. There's only one possible explanation. *She* must be here.

My mother.

Why?

I guess I'll find out. I step forward with my arms held out in front of me.

"Go on then," I say. "Since you lot are so obviously rubbish at keeping hold of me, you'd better put those cuffs on."

The officers who brought me here break out of the line and walk towards me.

"No," a deep voice says; it's an older man in a black suit. "The boy's right, you lot *are* useless. You nearly lost him all over again then. How can one boy escape two armed officers? Why wasn't he cuffed in the first place? Get out of here! Consider yourselves suspended until further notice!"

The two officers look at each other and then slope away slowly.

"Cuffs?" says the man, and the other police officers scramble around for some.

He steps forward, grabs my arm, slaps the handcuffs around us both and pulls me forward, dragging me past the other officers, along the path, all the way into Arcadia.

There's no sound from inside the shack, and no movement either. It's a minuscule little place, like all the others are, so when the door's not opened within ten seconds, it's clear there's no one there.

Next to me, Greta looks dismayed. I know how she feels: now we've got to psych ourselves up again to bang on another door, and there's something about this place that looks friendlier than the others. Maybe it's just the flowers, or the fact that it's cleaner than everywhere else, but there's a different feel to it, a more welcoming feel.

"It's the middle of the day," I say to Greta. "I suppose it's not surprising that there's no one about. They've probably gone into the city to work, like that woman from before."

There's no sign of any more people, just the sound of the kids in the distance, still kicking their can around the rubbish heaps. I can still feel the eyes on us though. These huts are so squashed together, there must be people in some of them, listening to us, watching us.

"What shall we do?"

"Keep trying, I suppose, until someone does answer."

"Hoshi?" She's looking up at me with big, worried eyes. "What are we going to say when we do speak to someone?"

"Tell them the truth, I guess. Tell them about the Cirque. Tell them we ran away. Hope they're on our side – they should be."

We turn away from the little door and that's when he appears. Hands in pockets, scowl on his face, sloping right up to us: a boy, about Ben's age, I'd say. Thin, freckled face, floppy, dirty hair hanging over his eyes, hands in the pockets of his ill-fitting orange work suit.

"What do you want?" he asks, abruptly. "What are you doing outside my home?" He steps closer to us, suspiciously. "Do I know you?" His jaw drops in surprise when he sees Bojo staring out at him from Greta's arms and when he looks at me, his eyes widen even more. "Bloody hell, you're the circus runaways, aren't you? The ones the police have been hunting for all these months. What are you doing here?"

I give a quick glance behind him to check Jack's still there. He is, stooped in the shadows a few yards away. It makes me feel a bit better.

"We don't want trouble," I say. "We've got nowhere to go."

"And what's that got to do with me?" There's a challenging tone to his voice. "Why are you telling me that? There's a cash prize for you," he says. "Big money. They've said they'll even reward it to a Dreg if they're the ones who shop you."

My eyes flick towards Jack again. He's crept a little closer now and his pose is different. He's poised, he's ready. Could we get away if we ran? Get out of here before this boy shouts out and other people come running, all desperate to be the ones to catch us, to grab the golden tickets?

No. We couldn't.

Greta steps forward from where she's been hiding behind my back.

"You should help us," she says, bravely, "because we'd help you. Because we're Dregs too and because Dregs stick together."

He looks down at her, and an expression of amusement flickers across his face. "Is that right?" he says.

"Yes," I say. "Yes it is, actually. We're not going to beg you but, just so you know, if you turn us in, they'll kill us."

He sighs wearily.

"I'm not going to turn you in, but someone will. There are plenty of people around here who are hungry enough. You should leave."

"And go where?" I ask, desperately. "Where is there for us to go?"

"Don't know, don't care. Not my problem." And he pushes us both roughly aside, opens the little rickety door up and slams it in our faces so hard that the whole shack shudders.

BEN

Once we're at the door, the black suit guy releases me from the cuffs and pushes me inside, slamming and locking the door.

I'm all alone, for the first time in almost a year.

Alone in Arcadia.

What is this place?

The last time I was inside a circus building, it was the arena: a traditional big top, with circular rows of plastic chairs surrounding the central ring and the smell of sawdust and sweat and stale beer.

This place is completely different. I've never seen anything like it before; I've never heard of anywhere like it before.

I'm inside a forest.

Great gnarled trees curve around the edges, ancient and majestic. Way up high, the branches strain together so that they arch overhead in a leafy canopy. The air feels lush and alive; they must be real. Sunlight twinkles through, or what feels like sunlight, warming my back and casting dappled spots on to the springy grass beneath my feet. It's dotted with tiny daisies, yellow buttercups and delicate blue forget-me-nots. I reach down and feel it with my fingers.

Dozens of tiny yellow birds – canaries, I think – are flitting about the branches. They sing and chirp continuously, their creamy voices soaring high into the air. It's just an illusion, it has to be, but they're buying into the myth. There are other birds too, their wings beating vigorously while they sup the delicious nectar – hummingbirds. On the ground, real peacocks strut around, ignoring me completely, their tails fanned proudly.

There aren't chairs; the places where the audience will sit

are mossy indents, formed somehow in the grassy slopes which meander towards the stage where the woodland theme continues.

The trees up there are tiny and adorned with thick blossoms. I breathe the heady smell in; it fills my lungs with perfume. The law of the seasons doesn't apply in this wonderland; it's spring, summer, winter and autumn all at once, for the trees bear fruit too – their boughs laden with golden pears, yellow lemons, shiny red apples. Vines, rich with clusters of purple grapes, curl around the trunks, entwining themselves among the branches.

There's a high waterfall, right at the back, gushing down serenely. The water cascading down is rainbow-coloured, changing mid-flow from red to orange, from blue to green, twinkling and dancing as it rushes down to a bubbling brook below.

I tread my way over to the stage and reach up and pick a cherry from the nearest tree. I put it tentatively to my lips, but it's real. It explodes in my mouth, the rich, sweet juice trickling down my throat. I take another one, and another one, and another one, cramming them into my mouth. I stand on the spot and rotate around and around, captivated by the smell of the blossom, the song of the birds, and of the babbling stream, the waterfall, the sights so rich and lavish.

Who created this place? They've surpassed themselves. How much did it cost? And what on earth happens in here? It might look like the Garden of Eden, but it can't be anything good.

The door opens, and there she is, framed in the sunlight, the serpent herself: my mother, Vivian Baines.

"Well, well, well," she says. "After all this time, the return of the prodigal son."

"Well, he was friendly!" I say. "Come on, let's get out of here, quickly."

We turn away. I look over the road at Jack, answering his quizzical look with a shake of my head.

Suddenly, the sound of sirens fills the air again. Louder. Closer.

The police are in the slums. That woman must have told them we were here.

"Where can we go?" Greta gasps. "Where can we hide?"

"I don't know." I look around for an answer. "Deeper into the slums, I suppose."

We both look towards Jack. He points to the left and starts running, fast. We start running too, until there's a shout, from behind us.

"Wait!"

I look back. It's the boy from the hut, standing in the middle of the path. "They're coming this way," he says. He gestures towards his tiny home. This time the door's open. "You'd better come in."

BEN

We stand there, my mother and I, facing each other, either end of the forest.

She steps forward, slowly coming closer and closer. I fight the urge to step away from her. I don't look down. I will not let her intimidate me, will not let her bully me. I raise my chin, thrust back my shoulders, and keep my eyes fixed on hers.

Her hair is longer than before and she's ditched the power suits she always used to wear for softer, more casual clothes.

"Benedict," she says, tentatively stepping even closer. "I've been so worried about you. I haven't slept for months." Her voice wavers. "I was so scared I'd never see you again." Her tone is less abrasive than it used to be; it's mild, reasonable.

"A lot's gone on," she says, gently. "Too much for one conversation. Right now, I'm just relieved to see you in one piece. Why don't we leave the talking for tomorrow? You can come back home, where you belong. We'll have pizza, if you like, watch a film. You don't have to talk at all if you don't want to."

I just keep glaring at her. It's the only power I have: the power of defiance.

"We've missed you," she says. "All of us. Let's just go home and be together as a family again."

She's almost pleading with me. My mother, pleading: I don't know what I expected, but it wasn't this.

I try and picture it for a second, what it would be like, walking away with her now, going back to my old life. Living in that house again, going to school, settling back into the way things used to be.

It's a ridiculous suggestion. I'm not that person at all any more.

"Benedict," she says, softly. "I love you, we all do."

Blimey, she's really pulling out all the stops. I don't think she's ever said she loves me before. I'm surprised the word's even in her vocabulary.

"You're my baby," she croons. "We're a family."

I can't be bothered to have this conversation, to play these games. They're pointless, can't she see that? They're not my family any more, her and Father and Francis. Hoshi is. Hoshi and Greta and Jack: they're the only family I need.

The last eleven months, being on the run, they've been hard, really hard, but they've been so precious too – to me anyway. When you know that every day could be – probably will be – your last day together, everything is intensified, every moment becomes sacred. There's no time to play games, to waste precious seconds.

I turn away from this grasping, evil woman.

She doesn't even know what it is to love someone. She never will – the only person she's ever really cared about is herself.

Love that wants to own people and curb them to its will isn't love at all: it's the opposite of love.

Thinking of Hoshi, out there somewhere, without me, makes the fluttering panic I'm trying to suppress rise up in my chest. How am I going to cope, not knowing where she is, not being beside her every day? Not even knowing if she's—

I steel myself. It won't do to think like that. I have to stay strong. For her, and for Greta and Jack. I have to somehow find a way to help them. Nothing else matters but that. Certainly not my mother, with her big house and her big cars and her endless food and her endless money and her piles and piles of luxury goods, mounting up all around her, while the Dregs she crushes have nothing.

"Benedict." There's tension in her tone for the first time now. "I'm trying here."

I still don't speak. What is there to say that would make any difference?

My thigh's aching, as usual. I massage it with my hands, easing the stiffness a little. Ever since Silvio Sabatini shot me, it starts throbbing if I stand on it for too long. I was lucky, really lucky, not to lose my leg.

The first thing Jack did when we escaped was get us to a safe house and arrange for a doctor to come and look after us; Beth, her name was. She was a proper doctor, six years training and everything, but she wanted to help. She was like Jack, like a lot of the Pures apparently, part of the resistance network which stretches across the country. She visited every day until Hoshi and I were healed, or as healed as we'll ever be now.

Hoshi's hands and feet are much better than they were when the infection took hold, but she'll probably never be able to get up on a wire again. As for my bullet wound, it's doing well, considering. I hardly even limp now but the scarring will never go away. There's an indent in my leg where I used to have muscle; it's concave now. I don't mind really – you can't even tell when I've got my jeans on, and Hoshi says it's a battle wound, which, in a way, I guess it is.

A shadow looms over me. I look up; it's my mother. She's moved to the stage and is standing there, looking down on me.

Two little dots of colour burn on her cheeks and, when she next speaks, all the softness has gone. Her voice shakes with rage.

"You don't even have the decency to meet me halfway, do you? You arrogant, foolish child. Do you even know what you've done? Do you even care? You have brought shame on me, brought shame on your family, shame on our name! You've caused me personal and public embarrassment. There's an election next week, did you know? The moment I've spent my whole career working towards, and I don't even know if I'm going to win it! Your bleeding heart performance all those months ago stirred all those sentimental do-gooders into action, made them think they had a duty to stand up for the poor little innocent Dregs. You have betrayed me in the worst possible way and yet you look up at me with that insolent look on your face and you say nothing! The very least you could do is apologize!"

I look up and smirk at her; I know how much it will irritate her.

"My son!" she cries. "My own son, a violent criminal, wanted by the police! His head turned by a Dreg trapeze artist! I still can't believe it! You should be begging at my feet, begging for my forgiveness! Do you know what? I'll tell you something incredible, shall I? I was nervous about seeing you today, worried about what I'd say to you! All those months of not knowing if you were alive or dead, I promised myself that if they found you, I'd forgive you anything. Now I look at you and I realize I don't think I can. It's too much, Benedict, it's too much!"

It's hard for me to look directly at her. All I see is what

she's done, what she is. I close my eyes and remember Priya how she was when I last saw her, and I think of Hoshi: this woman ordered her death. I think of the piano – her favourite possession – with its gleaming white keys, and all the Dregs she's destroyed – how many? Too many, far, far too many.

I can't keep quiet any more. Why should I?

"What do you want me to say?" I adopt a whingeing, whiny tone. "*What a silly, naughty boy I've been! I'm so sorry that I dared to question you. I'll never break the rules again, Mummy dearest! I'll do whatever you say in the future if you'll just forgive me. You were right all along: I could never really love a revolting Dreg girl!* Do you know what? I *am* sorry. I'm sorry it took me so long to work out who you were, sorry I went along with it all for all those years. I don't want your forgiveness! I don't want anything from you! Everything that happened, everything I did, I'd do it again in a heartbeat!"

She lets out a cry of rage.

"I don't know where you came from!" she says. "I don't know whose genes you've inherited, but they sure as hell aren't mine! I would never have spoken to my mother like you've just spoken to me! Never have behaved in such a reckless, selfish way! I respected my parents. I respected authority! How can *my* son be a rebel? *My* son be a filthy Dreg lover?"

"Let me go then," I say. "If I'm such a disappointment, give up on me. I gave up on you a long time ago. Do us both a favour, disown me."

She laughs. "Disown you? All of a sudden, it's a tempting idea. If only it were that simple. No. You've humiliated me, Benedict; you've made me look a fool. There's an election around the corner and your ridiculous behaviour has cost me votes. The world needs to hear you say how sorry you are! You owe me that at least!"

Ah, now it makes sense. I should have known; it seemed very unlike her to be so desperate to regain my affections. She needs me, that's why she's so persistent. My infamous betrayal has dented her reputation. She needs me to repent, publicly.

She turns away from me, pacing up and down the strange woodland wonderland. Then she whirls around, walks back towards me, crouches down on the stage, grabs hold of my face and thrusts hers towards it, baring her teeth at me in a snarl.

"You will apologize, my boy, I promise you! It's just a matter of how difficult you make it for yourself."

"You want me to say sorry, tell the voting public I've made a mistake?" I say. "You want that? Put me in front of a camera then, I'd be delighted to tell the world how I feel!"

She throws her hands up in exasperation. She doesn't know what to do. For once, my mother is at a loss.

"Why am I here anyway?" I say. "And why are you? Why on earth are we meeting at the circus?"

She's silent for a second and then she climbs down from the stage and sinks into one of the grassy indents. When she looks at me again, there's something in her eyes I've never seen before. It looks a bit like guilt, a bit like sorrow.

"It was only ever meant to be an insurance policy," she says. "I promised your father it was just something to threaten you with, should you make things difficult. I didn't think I'd have to do it. I thought it would be too much, that it would be too hard on you. Now, looking at you, standing there so brazen and so defiant, I realize we *do* have to take drastic measures. Not for me, but for you. For your own good. We *do* need to show you the error of your ways, show you what it would really be like on the other side."

She stops for a second, and her voice, when she speaks again, sounds bewildered. "Who'd have thought it? He was right all along."

"Who was right all along? Do you mean Father? Is that who you mean?"

She slumps down further and puts her head into her hands.

"Sometimes you have to take the hardest path," she says, quietly. "Make the difficult decisions, even if they seem cruel at the time. No, Benedict, I'm not talking about your father; he doesn't see it quite that way."

She looks across at me and that unfamiliar, regretful expression is still there.

"I'm talking about the ringmaster."

HOSHIKO

We dash back down the path and through the door. The boy pushes it shut just in time: blue lights flash on the walls, intermittently lighting up his and Greta's faces as we all stare at each other fearfully.

Through the window, we see three police cars plough down the narrow path that the huts and shacks cluster either side of. It's a tight squeeze for them – this track wasn't made for vehicles – and they leave a wake of destruction behind them. A bit further along, the road tapers even more and a tiny cabin precariously overhangs the dusty trail. The cars don't stop, they just plough through it. Debris flies up as they bulldoze through, leaving behind nothing but crushed and flattened wood and cardboard.

"There goes Molly and Joe's pad," the boy says, wryly. "At least they weren't in there. I guess that's something."

"That was someone's home? What will they do now?" Greta says.

He shrugs. "What can they do? Scrabble around in the rubbish tips to try and find enough stuff to build a new one, I suppose."

Jack's still outside, lurking suspiciously in the shade. He's lucky the police cars didn't stop.

I glance at the boy again. There seems to be a permanent scowl on his face.

"Thank you for taking us in," I say.

He rolls his eyes. "Didn't feel like I had much choice. Don't imagine you're staying long though."

"But we've got nowhere else to go," Greta says, dejectedly.

He shakes his head. "Look around you. What exactly do you think I can do for you?"

I take in our surroundings.

The tiny shack is neat and clean, inside as well as outside. There's a little broom in the corner, made of bound-together rags, and the floor beneath our feet is dust and mud free. A large wooden crate, with a couple of smaller crates around it, functions as a table and chairs. The flowers we saw from outside are in a glass bottle. They look like they've been freshly picked. Two thin sheets, hung over some string, make up a curtain, dividing the room up. I crane my head a little to peer through the gap. Beyond are two buckets and three neat rolls of blankets: beds, I guess, at night.

"Do you live here on your own?" I ask him.

"No. With my mum. It's ... just the two of us." His words jolt, as if they're hard to get out. I wonder if there used to be more of them: a dad maybe, or a brother or sister. I wonder what happened.

"You think you can't help us," I say. "But you can, if you want to. You must know how it works around here: *we* don't. We don't know who we can trust – we don't even know if we can trust you. We don't know where to avoid. We don't know anything. There must be something useful you can tell us."

"Why did you have to bang on my door? I don't need this hassle, especially not at the moment." He sinks down on one of the little crates, kicking his legs out in front of him so that they almost fill the tiny room.

"Avoid everyone," he says, curtly. "Avoid everywhere. You can't trust anyone." His eyes narrow dangerously. "Including me."

"Well, why did you let us in, then?" I say. "Why did you call us back?"

He laughs dryly. "That's a good question."

There's a silence. Greta and I exchange uncertain glances. The sirens start up again; they're heading back towards us. I need to get Jack in here, quickly.

"Our friend," I say. "He's outside. Can he come in? Just for five minutes, until the police have gone."

"Who is it?" he asks. "That Pure boy from the posters? Benedict Baines? The one who made that speech they all talk about?"

"No, it isn't him. It's—"

"Where's he, then?" he interrupts me, inquisitively. "Did he change his mind? Go back to his mother?" His expression is gleeful.

"No!" This boy is making me angry. "He didn't change his mind. The police caught him. He turned himself in!"

In my mind's eye I see Ben again, standing at the window with the gun to his head. Please, God, please let him be OK. What will they do to him? How will they punish him? I don't think I'll be able to keep going if anything happens to him, not even for Greta.

"He gave himself up," I say, "for us."

The sirens are close now.

"Our friend, his name's Jack. He's outside. Can he come in? Please!"

The boy runs his fingers through his lank, sandy hair and sighs heavily.

"It's the copper, isn't it? I hate Pures and I hate the police. Why would I let him in here?"

"He's not a Pure, not any more. And he never was a policeman, not really. He only joined so he could help the Dregs! Please," I beg. "Please. They'll find him otherwise, and they'll kill him. They'll kill us all!"

He scowls even more. "What have I got myself into? Fine, bring him in, but only until the coppers have gone."

Opening the door a crack, I beckon Jack over. He looks quickly around from side to side and then darts across the path and into the hut. We shut the door just in time.

The police cars appear, driving back over the little house they destroyed, crushing it even flatter. They're cruising slowly this time. Looking for any signs of us.

"Duck down," the boy says. "They'll see you through the window."

Greta and I crouch down, keeping our heads low. Jack can't though: he's too big for this tiny hut. He has to lie flat out on the floor. The boy doesn't lie down, but he pushes himself against the wall so that they won't be able to see him unless they really peer in.

Once the cars have rolled their slow way past, we scramble to our feet.

"Thanks, mate," Jack says to the boy, and holds out a hand. "You don't know how much we appreciate what you've just done."

The boy looks down at Jack's hand but doesn't take it.

"You can't stay here. There's no space."

He's right; the four of us fill this room up.

"Fair enough. You've done more than enough to help," Jack says. "If we could just stay here five minutes more, until we know they've gone, we'll leave you alone after that."

"Good," the boy says, curtly.

There's an awkward silence. I can feel him staring at me.

"You were in the Cirque for a long time, weren't you?" he says, eventually. "What was it like in there?"

How am I supposed to answer that?

I could use a million words and I'd never be able to describe it. I'd never even be able to come close.

It was hell. It was a prison.

It was home, the only one I remember.

We all jump at once as the door is pushed open, and my heart bangs in my chest. It's not a police officer though: it's a woman, wearing one of the green catering uniforms. She looks just like the boy: same sandy-coloured hair, same freckles, same nose, same eyes, but her face is all softness where his is angular and sharp. She stops in her tracks when she sees us and her mouth opens in surprise.

"I don't believe it!" she says. "The runaway circus stars!"

I stare at my mother.

"The ringmaster? What do you mean, the ringmaster?"

The sadness that crossed her face before has been replaced by a glint of amusement.

"You don't know, do you? You don't know he survived?"

There's only one ringmaster I know.

Only one ringmaster I *knew*.

"He can't have survived," I say. "I was there. The arena blew up. I saw the grenade land at his feet. I felt the explosion."

"I'm afraid not. Your little tightrope walker didn't quite manage to finish the job. They thought he was dead when they pulled him out of the rubble, but there was a fragment of life left and he clung on to it like a leech. I suppose he would have died in the end though, if it hadn't been for an anonymous donor coming forward and paying for his treatment – one of those obsessive circus fans, I imagine. Anyway, once it became apparent that he was going to actually survive, they decided it would make a bigger impact if they could keep it all a secret and reel him out to the public on opening night. It's all been kept incredibly hush-hush – there's some ridiculously extravagant unveiling planned."

"You're lying."

She raises an eyebrow. "Benedict. Have you ever known me to lie?"

My mother doesn't lie; she doesn't need to. She always gets what she wants anyway.

She spins around and strides up and down the soft grass. A

tiny rabbit up ahead bolts suddenly, its little tail bobbing up and down as it darts away from her. Sensible rabbit.

She stops and reaches up into a tree, pulling down a shiny red apple. She sinks her teeth into it and chews, staring at it musingly. "Hmm, not bad, not bad at all." She looks around. "They've done a good job in here, better than I hoped for. I'll say one thing about Sabatini: the man's got vision. This place is all his idea." She takes another delicate bite of the apple, crunching it slowly. "As I said, he survived. He's different, very different now, to how he was before, but he survived and he's running this whole show. He petitioned me last week, when he heard, somehow, that we were closing in on you. He begged me to let him have the two Dreg girls back in the circus, said he sought his sweet and justifiable revenge. When I refused, when I told him they would be immediately executed – which they will be as soon as we find them, Benedict – he asked for you instead. He suggested that it might be a valuable lesson for you, if you were unrepentant, to give you some work experience here, in the lovely shiny new circus. He said it might make you more humble, might make you realize what life is really like on the other side."

"Why would you listen to him? You hate the circus! You hate him! Why would you even talk to him? I don't believe you. I saw him die!"

"You didn't see him die: you saw him blasted to pieces and that's a different thing altogether. He was *almost* obliterated. Almost, but not quite. He's a very determined Dreg: resilient, like a germ. What with one thing and another, I've had no choice but to liaise with him directly over the last few months. You see, as much as I hate to admit it, the reopening of this circus is playing a large part in the finale of my election campaign. Those who know how these things work have insisted on pouring pounds and pounds of our funding into building this place. It will send a message, so they say: a loud, clear message that we will not respond to violence. Terrorists like those two Dreg girls, like you – my own son – will not prevail."

She tosses the apple core over her shoulder.

"I met with Sabatini because we have a mutual concern. We both need to see this place flourish. He needs my political support and I, well, I have reluctantly been forced to concede that I need him: need the impact he will make, need his oily charisma, his creepy little stage presence." She laughs. "His drastically different but nevertheless compelling stage presence."

"What's happened to him?"

"What do you think's happened to him? A grenade blew up at his feet. His face was blown off. His body was shattered."

I picture Silvio, his face a mangled mess.

"He rose up from the ashes," she says. "Someone paid for his hospital treatment, whatever the cost. They paid for rehabilitation, they paid for reconstruction. He was on the brink of death, you understand, for a long time, but in the end, he used the situation to his advantage."

"What do you mean?"

She laughs, coldly. "What do I mean? He got what he'd always wanted, or as close as he's ever going to come to it, anyway. He's managed to get rid of his obvious Dregness, outwardly at least. He's Pure now, Benedict, according to him, pure as the driven snow."

Why is she talking in riddles?

"I don't know what you're talking about. I don't understand you, and I don't believe you."

I do believe her though.

Silvio Sabatini made Hoshi and Greta's life hell. He tortured them. He killed their friends. He killed Amina. The memory of him haunts them. They both wake up in the night, crying out, screaming. What are they going to say when they hear he's alive?

My mother turns the watch on her wrist towards her and raises it up to her face. "Very well, if your own mother's word isn't enough for you, I'll bring in the little freak himself, let you see exactly what he's become."

She taps a button on the watch and speaks.

"It's me. Send him in, will you? Who do you think I'm talking about? Sabatini, of course! Send in Silvio Sabatini!"

The woman who's just walked into the hut steps towards me, cupping my face with her weathered hands.

"Look at you!" she says. "Beautiful! The posters don't do you justice. And you—" She bends down so her eyes are level with Greta's. "You're my hero, do you know that? Taking on those bad guys!" She winks. "You showed them a thing or two!" Greta grins back at her, her little face lighting up with pride.

The woman gives a friendly smile to Jack and then holds her hand out tentatively to Bojo, who scrambles immediately behind Greta, peeping out from between her legs and chattering to himself indignantly.

She chuckles. "I'm Rosie," she says, and then looks at her son, sprawled on the little crate. "Felix! Where are your manners?" she scolds. "Have you offered our guests a chair?" She tuts crossly. "Just because we don't have a lot doesn't mean we shouldn't make the effort, I always say, and don't forget, politeness costs—"

"Yeah, yeah, I know; politeness costs nothing," says the boy, rising reluctantly to his feet. "I let them in. I stopped the police catching them, what more do you want?" He glares at me and Greta and then gestures towards the crates. "Go on then, sit down!"

Greta sits down obediently, scooping Bojo on to her lap, where he presses himself up against her, looking accusingly at Rosie and the boy, Felix.

Felix frowns at me.

"Sit then!"

"I'm OK, thanks," I say.

He gives an exaggerated sigh.

"Fine. You can't say I didn't try," he says to his mother, and sits back down on the empty crate.

"Yes, I can! That's exactly what I can say! You've embarrassed the poor girl! Have you even offered our guests a drink? Get up, you silly boy, get up!"

She bats him over the head with her hand until he stands up again.

"Go and get some water to make tea!"

He rolls his eyes again, pushes back one of the sheets and grabs one of the buckets.

As he's about to leave, Rosie grabs his arm. "Felix, you won't mention our guests to anyone, will you?"

"I'll keep my mouth shut, I suppose. But it's only a matter of time until someone reports them, and then we'll all be dead."

He looks directly at me, puts two fingers up to his temple and mimes the action of a gun, blowing his head off, before sloping off through the door. I watch him through the window, sauntering nonchalantly off down the path.

"Honestly, I don't know where he gets it from sometimes." Rosie laughs nervously. She coughs and her eyes flick towards Greta. "He's got a point though, I'm afraid. The police have said they'll give a huge reward to anyone who can lead them to you, even if that person's a Dreg. Did anyone see you arrive?"

Jack winces. "Yes, at least one person, probably more. There was a woman who looked straight at us and then ran off as fast as she could. We should go now. We don't want to make trouble for anyone."

My heart sinks. I know he's right, but I don't want to go back out there. Next to me, Greta starts to cry.

Rosie steps forward and sweeps Greta into a hug. "Shh, shh, it's OK, sweetheart. You don't have to go anywhere! We'll work something out." She grabs two of the rolled-up blankets from behind the curtain. "Sorry I don't have anywhere for you to sit," she says to Jack. "You can use these though, if it will make it a bit more comfortable."

"Thank you," Jack says. "But we can't put you in this position. It's not fair."

"I've never turned a person in need away and I'm not about to now," Rosie insists firmly. "Anyway, I'm not being totally selfless. There are lots of things I'd like to ask the girls about, if it's not too painful for them. Please, sit down."

What can she possibly want to ask me and Greta? Jack looks at me questioningly, and I incline my head towards Greta. Her lip is still trembling as her big eyes plead with him. Jack's eyes flick from her to Rosie and then he nods.

"Thank you. We'll just stay here for a bit longer then, if that's OK. Just long enough to rest awhile and then we'll go."

He sinks down on to a blanket and Rosie does the same, both hunching their long, adult legs up awkwardly. I stand there uncertainly for a few seconds and then lower myself on to the empty crate.

"That's better," Rosie says. "You poor things, you must be exhausted. As soon as Felix comes back with the water, we'll all have a nice cup of tea. There's nothing like a nice cup of tea, that's what I always say."

BEN

All at once, darkness descends upon the whole forest. The second it does, all the birds instantly hush. It's only in the silence that I realize how loud their soaring song was before.

There's nothing for a moment or two – and then a sound, coming from above, quietly at first and then louder and louder, until it echoes through the whole place.

Tap. Tap. Tap.

Finally, a single light flickers above, a thousand speckles of dust dancing in its beam. Way up high, a thin wooden walkway stretches right across the stage, all the way over the waterfall.

A silhouette emerges from the wings and slowly works its way across the dimly lit boards. The tap is the sound of a cane knocking on the wooden floor.

Slowly, slowly, the figure moves towards the centre of the stage.

I hold my breath.

It steps into the pool of light, slowly turning to face us.

The blood rushes from my body.

It's not him.

It's not even a human being. It's a ghost. I stare at it, aghast. Maybe it's not a ghost, maybe it *is* a man: a man from a horror film. His skin is the same brilliant white as the suit he wears. Not a normal flesh colour, not a colour at all, a white devoid of colour. A white *like the driven snow*. A bleached white, a brilliant white, a *Pure* white. His hair is white too and his eyes – the eyes staring down at me – are a piercing blue.

He stands there, in the spotlight, straining forward, peering towards me. He steps a little closer, peers a little harder, and a triumphant smile settles on his face.

"My oh my, it's Benedict Baines. How wonderful to see you again!"

It's a cold voice. A determined voice. An unforgettable voice. It's only when I hear it that I finally understand.

This ghost: it's Silvio Sabatini.

The boy, Felix, has sloped off around the corner, out of sight.

"He's gone to warm up the water," says Rosie. "There's a communal fire over the back. It might take a while, I'm afraid."

There's an awkward silence for a second, broken by Jack.

"Thank you," he says. "For taking us in like this. I know what a risk it is."

She smiles. "You're very welcome. I hope Felix wasn't rude?" She looks at each of us sternly, searching for any indication that he might have been.

I don't say anything. I mean, he was kind of rude, to be honest, but I'm hardly going to say that to his mum, and he did let us in.

In the end. Right at the last minute.

"No," Jack says. "He was amazing. He hid the girls from the police." He winces at her, apologetically. "They've already driven through looking for us, I'm afraid. And then he opened the door for me too. We would have been caught by now if it wasn't for your son. We'd probably be dead. He's a credit to you."

You can tell she's proud; her whole face lights up.

"He's a good boy, really," she says. "He might come across as a bit moody at first, but that's just his way. You know what teenage boys are like!" She lowers her voice. "He's been a bit of an angry young man since we lost his father a few years back, to be honest … and then, late last year – round about Christmastime it was – his brother was taken off the streets."

"Taken? Taken where?"

She looks around at us all fearfully; her smile has gone now and her face is pale and drawn.

"Taken into the Cirque."

Greta and I both cry out at the same time.

"I'm so sorry to hear that," Jack says, softly.

She turns to me. "That's what I wanted to ask you about, if you can bear it. What's it like, being in there?" Her eyes are filled with fear.

"Well, I don't really know what it's like any more," I say. "It's a different place now to the one we left – it might be much better. There's a fairground there now, isn't there? That doesn't sound so bad."

"The explosion killed the ringmaster, Silvio Sabatini," Jack says. "He was the mastermind behind the whole place. Most of the cruelty and violence came directly from him."

Silvio Sabatini. I hate the way his name still has such an effect on me, even after what I did to him. I look at Greta. She's staring at the floor, biting her lip.

"When was your son taken?" Jack asks, softly.

"It was just after they announced they were revamping it. They must have needed extra people, I suppose. They came in big lorries and pulled a load of kids off the street. It wasn't just him, a lot of families around here lost someone." Her voice breaks and she's silent for a moment, and then she looks right at me, her eyes searching my face. "Do you think we'll ever see him again? Do you think he's still alive?"

How am I supposed to answer that?

"He's bound to be," Jack says, confidently. "They'll be training them all up for various acts, I should think. Won't do them any good to harm them now, not before the place even opens."

If his words are meant to make her feel better, I don't think they're working very well. "And what about when it does open?" The pitch of her voice rises higher. "What then?"

"I'm really sorry," I say. "We don't know what it's like any more. We don't know what they've got him doing in there. We can't tell you anything."

It's true, what I'm saying. I'm as ignorant as anyone about what's happening in the place. The last time I saw the Cirque, it was a glowing ball of flames, lighting up the night sky as we drove away from it.

We tried to find out what happened, of course we did. Every time we spoke to anybody from the resistance, we'd ask, but nobody ever knew anything. And every time we could get hold of a newspaper, or near a TV screen or tablet, Greta and I would search frantically for information but there was never anything.

There was obviously a news freeze on it. We'd escaped from right under the police's noses – it must have hurt. They wanted to catch us, yes, but they didn't want anyone to focus on the carcass we'd left behind.

There was nothing, for months: it was like the Cirque had never existed at all. And then the big announcement came – it was returning, bigger and better than ever before.

I don't know whether all the people I knew will be a part of it. I don't even know if they're still alive.

It's thinking of Ezekiel that hurts most of all. It's he who haunts my dreams. I only knew him for a few days but he was already dependent on me, I know he was. He wasn't much more than a baby and I just abandoned him there without a second glance. Emmanuel, Ezekiel, I left them all behind. My friends. My people. Left them to burn or, what's worse, left them to stay there, and face whatever came next after the trouble we'd wreaked.

"Was it as bad in there as everyone says?" Rosie asks. "It can't have been. The rumours are exaggerated, aren't they?"

Memories creep and crawl from the pit of my stomach, clawing their way up to the surface, clutching and twisting at my insides, beating and pounding against my chest.

I can't do this. I know she wants answers, but I can't. I can't talk about that place, not to her, this woman whose son's been taken. I can't talk about it to anyone.

I wish Ben was here.

I stand up, sending the crate across the floor with a clatter.

"I'm sorry."

I push the door open and gulp in the air.

"Hoshi! Come back inside! Anyone could see you!" Jack hisses urgently.

"I'm sorry. I just need to breathe."

I feel a gentle arm around my waist.

"You don't need to be sorry, I do." Rosie's voice is mournful. "I was beyond insensitive. I won't ask you about it again. I should have realized. Please forgive me. It's hard to think of anything else when someone you love is in danger, when they might already be dead."

The poor thing's in agony. I know how she feels. I know because my Ben is gone too, and I don't know where he is either, and I don't know how he is and it's my fault. I left him all alone. I ran away as fast as I could and left him up there, with a gun pointing at his own head.

Just another person I've left behind to deal with the mess I've made.

I turn to face Rosie. Her cheeks are pink with shame and her head is hanging down low.

"It's OK," I say. "Really it is. I know what it's like when someone you love is suffering and you can't help them." I do too, God knows I do.

I must stop this. I take another deep breath. "Like Jack says, they're bound to keep everyone alive until the new place opens."

Her face turns even paler and she gives a little whimper.

She raises her head and her eyes, alight with panic and fear, meet mine.

"Haven't you seen the posters?"

Greta's beside me now, tugging at Rosie's sleeve. "What do the posters say?"

There's silence for a moment.

"They say it'll be unforgettable," Rosie says, finally. "They say it'll be dark. They say it'll be deadly."

"When?" I ask, dread cold and hard in my stomach. "When's it opening?"

"This week." Her voice is trembling. "Saturday night, two days from now."

BEN

I stare up, open-mouthed, transfixed by this ghost addressing me in Silvio Sabatini's voice.

Finally, I turn to my mother. She's smiling at me, smugly.

"Surprised?" she says.

"I don't understand," I gape.

The spectre above laughs, a jubilant cackle.

"I look the same as you now, Benedict, don't I? I don't look like a Dreg any more. I look like a Pure. I *am* pure now, aren't I? You can't deny it." There's a pleading tone to his voice, like he wants my confirmation.

"Shut up!" barks my mother angrily. "Shut up, you silly idiot! You're lucky I don't have you hauled away for treason! Whatever you do to yourself, you'll never remove the Dreg that's within you, you vain little fool." Her tone is disgusted as she stares at him in the same aghast way she always did. "The dirty, horrid, Dregness within you will always be there, right at the core of who you are!"

The grin has frozen on Sabatini's face. He struggles to compose himself for a moment, and then speaks.

"Anyway, Benedict, has your mother told you about our little agreement?"

She smirks. "I thought I would give you that pleasure, Ringmaster. Don't say I never help those less fortunate than myself."

He claps his hands together and the cane he's holding crashes to the wooden floor. "You have made a very wise decision. He'll be begging you to take him back once he's spent a day or two seeing what life is really like in the real world!"

"What do you mean? What's going on? Where am I going?"

"I was hoping that having a chat with you would be enough to make you see the error of your ways," my mother says, ruefully. "I thought your months on the run would have made you see reason." She gives a funny little snort. "I even had visions of you apologizing! Ridiculous of me really – I should have known that little witch had cast too toxic a spell on you."

"Hoshi is not a witch!"

"No. No, she's not a witch. She's a vile, verminous creature who's sunk her claws into my son."

My whole body shakes with rage and anger. I stand up. "I'm not listening to this. I'm leaving!"

I walk up the aisle and open the door, blinking in the sudden light. Stanley's on the other side, his gaze fixed blankly over my head.

"Excuse me," I say. I try to push him aside, but he stands there, unmoving, a wall.

I turn back. My mother is facing me now and Silvio Sabatini is directly above her, framed in the spotlight.

"Benedict," she says. "You aren't going anywhere. You will remain in this circus until you have seen the error of your ways. It won't be long before you'll be begging to return to the bosom of our little home."

I stand in the doorway, staring at her.

"What do you mean?"

"What I mean is this: until further notice, this is your place of work." She turns and calls up to Sabatini. "Remember what I said: backstage only. No performance work; it's more than my marriage is worth. You may punish him if required, but no lasting injuries."

"Yes," he simpers, "yes, of course, madam." He's actually rubbing his hands together in glee.

"You can't make me work here!" I tell them both. "You can't make me do anything!"

She laughs, loudly this time, long and hard and cold. "I think you'll find they have their ways of persuading you," she says. "Remember, as soon as you want to come home, just say the word and I'll send a car. You can save yourself a lot of trauma and come now, if you like. One apology, that's all it will take."

"Never," I say. "I'll never apologize to you."

Her eyes narrow. "We'll see, Benedict, we'll see. Oh, I almost forgot, before you begin your work experience I have something to show you." She moves closer to me and takes her phone from her pocket. "Look at this a second, will you?"

She holds the screen up and waves it around. I can't see what it is she's showing me, and whatever it is, I don't want to know. I roll my eyes and turn away.

She moves so close that I can smell her sickly perfume.

"It's the latest news," she says. "About your girlfriend."

I grab her hand, pulling it towards me.

There's writing on the screen, a news report:

The Cat and two of her accomplices evaded arrest yet again this morning, it reads. *The three outlaws remain at large, and are believed to be armed and dangerous.*

They escaped! My heart soars.

I turn to my mother and I laugh in her face.

"We've made you look like fools! Again!"

I feel her arm suddenly snaking around my waist and there's a click. I move away, but it's too late. She's taken a photo.

She looks at the screen. "Perfect," she says. "A joyful family reunion, captured on camera. It's amazing what you can do with these phones. Sounds and images can be manipulated in so many ways. Thanks, Benedict, you've given me exactly the material I needed. OK, now let's get on with business. Ringmaster," she calls up to Sabatini. "You may take your latest recruit!"

He pulls a whistle out from his jacket, blowing hard on it.

Three security guards come running in, looking from Sabatini to my mother expectantly.

"Gentlemen, we have a new addition to our little circus family!" he says, gesturing to me grandly with both arms.

"Take him to the sleeping quarters; show him his new home."

They grab hold of me. I kick and shout but it's useless. As the door shuts behind us, the lights go out and the last thing I see are two darkened figures: my mother and the ghost of Silvio Sabatini, both watching me go.

I stare out into the dwindling light, looking towards the Cirque.

In two days' time, its lights will shine bright again. Hundreds of people queuing up eagerly, jostling for the best spot to watch the action, keeping their fingers crossed, praying for a death.

Who will they be watching? Will it be my friends? Have they made it this far? Will it be poor Rosie's son? What will they be doing in there?

Is there a tightrope?

My toes tingle. My back arches. My heart beats fast.

My soul and my head hate the Cirque. Hate everything it was; hate everything it will be again, but my body, my fickle selfish body, craves it. Craves the sound of the crowd, cheering and yelling; craves the smells: the smoke and the sweat and the sawdust; craves the twang of the wire, vibrating beneath my feet.

I've never told anyone this, not even Greta, not even Ben, but when I dream of the Cirque at night, it's not always a nightmare. It's not always about the death and the horror and the cold, cruel ringmaster.

Sometimes I dream of the performances. Sometimes I dream that I'm dancing up there, way above the crowd. Soaring and flying, arcing above them all. Sometimes I don't want the dreams to end.

I shiver. This won't do. It's not right to feel like that when people are imprisoned there right now, frightened and vulnerable and desperate. It's not right to feel like that when so many people – Anatol, Astrid and Luna, my lovely Amina – are dead.

I step inside, shutting my betrayal out, on the other side of the flimsy door.

The awful, desolate sound of Rosie's sobs fill the room. I know I should say or do something but I don't know what. Greta knows though; she lowers Bojo gently down to the floor and wraps her little arms right around Rosie.

"I'm sorry," Rosie says after a few minutes.

"You do *not* need to apologize," Jack says firmly. "You must be living in hell."

She nods. "Every day, every minute, every second," she answers. "I'm petrified about Sean, that's my oldest son, and worried sick about Felix too. He's become so angry, so bitter." She looks at Jack. "I'm surprised he let *you* in at all," she says quietly. "What with you being an ex-Pure police officer. If there are two thing he hates more than anything, it's the Pures and the police." She strokes Greta's hair. "Thanks for the hug. I can't tell you how much I needed that. You're a tonic, that's what you are."

She's stopped crying now, but you can tell it's taking every part of her not to start crying again.

"Listen to me, all I've done is go on about my own problems! I can't even imagine what the three of you must have been through. Tell me," she says, her voice a little calmer now. "How can we help? What can I get you or do for you that will help you? I've got to be honest, I think you've done well lasting this long. The authorities have been here already, you know – three times there've been door-to-door checks, looking for you."

My heart sinks. I knew they were looking for us, of course I did. But they've been to this one, random home three times already. This one tiny shack in this huge big city – talk about leaving no stone unturned. How long are we going to be able to stay hidden for this time?

"They did find us," Jack tells her. "This morning. It's a long story. The other person we were with gave himself up for us. It was a huge sacrifice; he's a very brave lad."

"Ahh," she says. "Benedict Baines. He's become something of a folk hero – you all have. I wondered where he was but I didn't like to ask, in case ... well, you know, in case all wasn't well."

Benedict Baines: *a brave lad*, Jack said; *a hero*, she said. They were right; he's both of those things.

"Any information you can give us," Jack says. "Insider information, about how things work around here, would be really helpful. I'm guessing not everyone's as sympathetic as you. Who should we avoid? Where should we avoid? That kind of stuff, and who do we need onside if we want to survive?"

She walks over to the little window and peers out. "Well," she says. "I'd like to think that most people around here would help you out. It's the Dreg way, isn't it? We stick together through thick and thin."

I feel so relieved hearing her say that. That's how it always was in the Cirque, but I thought it might be different out here on the streets.

A frown creases her face. "A lot of people out there are hungry though. Hungry and desperate enough that there's not much they wouldn't do for bit of cash." She winces apologetically. "And there's a big price on your heads. We need to act quickly. If you're going to last more than a few hours in here, we're going to need to try and get you protection."

The door opens and the boy, Felix, comes in, carrying the bucket of water, steaming hot now. Rosie busies herself making tea. "Excuse me a second, sweetheart," she says to Greta. "I just need to get something out from underneath you." When Greta stands up, she lifts the lid of the little crate and takes out a pot of teabags, four chipped mugs and a little container of milk. She pours water into each of the mugs.

"Felix," she says as she stirs the cups. "Did you see anyone? Did anyone mention our guests?"

He shrugs. "Didn't speak to no one. Kept my head down."

She nods. "That's good."

Felix tuts. He catches my eyes for a second and I narrow them at him and scowl. I know he's been through a lot and Jack's right: he did save us, but still, he is *very* rude. He glares back at me, and then at Greta, who's noticed our silent exchange. She eyes him defiantly, and the tip of her tongue pokes out, just a couple of millimetres. I grin and turn my head away.

Rosie hands us steaming hot cups of tea and we drink gratefully. I can't even remember when we last had a hot drink.

There's silence for a few moments and then Rosie coughs. "Felix," she says tentatively. "Listen, we're going to have to let Kadir know they're here, don't you think? Better he finds out from us than from someone else."

Felix stares at her incredulously.

"Are you kidding me? Why would you even think of getting involved with him? What the hell makes you think Kadir would help them anyway? What makes them so special? He's just as likely to kill them himself as give them any shelter, and you and me too if the mood takes him!"

"Felix! I'm sure that's not true!" She looks at Jack and gives a nervous laugh. "Kadir's sort of the unofficial leader around here," she says. "You'll need him onside if you're to have any chance of staying concealed."

Jack nods, grimly.

"The police might not know much about the slums, but we've all heard of Kadir," he says. "And he's either Robin Hood or Genghis Khan, depending on who you speak to."

Rosie laughs, nervously. "He can be a little unpredictable. I think it might be best if I speak to him first, see how the land lies, and maybe arrange for you to meet with him, if I can."

"You'd do that for us?" Jack says. "That's more than we can ask."

"Yes!" Felix's voice is angry. "Yes, it is more than you can ask! Kadir's dangerous!"

Rosie's voice shakes as she answers.

"Kadir is fair, Felix, whatever you think. What's the alternative, anyway? You wouldn't turn these lovely people away any more than I would, not really."

"Oh, do what you want! You will anyway! Don't say I didn't warn you, though." He shakes his head and turns away. "I'm going out."

Rosie's voice is suddenly panicked. "Where are you going?" She positions herself between Felix and the door. "Please, Felix, please don't go off again. How can you talk to me about danger when you're running around out there doing God knows what? Jack, you used to be in the police, maybe you can make him see sense. What would you say about the Brotherhood? What would you say if you met someone foolish enough to want to join them?"

"My God!" Felix gives a cry of rage. "You idiot, Mum! Do you want to get me killed, is that it?"

The Brotherhood. Curiosity prickles inside me, and a hint of recognition. There's something about the phrase that's familiar.

"No! I want to stop you from doing anything stupid! I want to stop you getting yourself killed! I've already lost one son. I can't lose another!"

"Sean isn't dead!" he shouts. "Not yet anyway. Not as far as we know."

"Hey," Jack says. "Can we rewind a minute? Why are we talking about the Brotherhood?" He steps towards Felix. "Please tell me you aren't getting involved with all that, son? It's not the answer. It's never the answer."

"What do you know? What's it got to do with you?"

"I know plenty!"

I look at Greta. She hates shouting. It makes her feel frightened, it always has. Her hands are over her ears and her eyes are screwed tight shut.

"Please!" I interrupt. "Stop it, all of you! You're upsetting Greta. What are you all talking about?"

Felix throws his hands up.

"Now look what you've done!" He goes over to the window and looks out then speaks in a low voice. "Keep your bloody voice down, all right!"

Rosie shoots Felix a withering look.

"The Brotherhood are a group of foolish people, mostly male as you'd guess from the name, who think that the only way to fight the Pures is through violent means. They are not heroes, as my son seems to believe. They are dangerous and deadly criminals. They—"

"They *are* heroes," Felix interrupts her. "They don't just sit back and wait for change. They fight. Like you did in the Cirque."

The Brotherhood. I knew I'd heard the word before; they were the ones who grabbed Ben and his brother once, at a football match. Ben said the whole group had been hunted down and executed. Obviously not.

A year ago, I'd have been all for groups like that. I hated all Pures back then – I'd probably have cheered if you told me a load of them had been blown up and killed.

Now, though, I realize that things are far more complicated than that. I've met Jack now, and I've met Ben. The two bravest and kindest men I know also both happen to have been born as Pures.

You can't hate people just because of the group they were born into. There are good Pures; there are good Dregs. There are bad Pures; there are bad Dregs. Silvio was a Dreg, although he was desperate to prove otherwise, and he was the cruellest man I ever met.

The truth is, nobody is born better than others, and nobody's born worse either; scratch the surface and we're all the same. It's the labels put on all of us that are the problem. The labels used to categorize us, to define us, to say who we are, what we can do.

Felix's fists are balled up and his face is red with anger and frustration. "The Brotherhood are the only people who can really change things around here," he says, angrily. "That's why I'm joining them."

Rosie's face drops and she sinks down on her blanket roll. She clutches her stomach like she's just been punched.

"No!" she wails. "No, Felix, you agreed!"

"I never agreed. I said I'd think about what you were saying. Well, I have thought about it and I still feel exactly the same! What's the alternative? Sit back while they parade my brother up and down in the circus like a performing animal? Sit back while they kill him? Stay here in this shithole and wait for change to come to us?"

"Felix! Mind your language! There are ladies present! And yes, change will come to us. Things *are* changing!" she says. "They'll change anyway without you putting yourself and others at risk like that!"

"Your mother's right," Jack says. "Change is coming, son. It's coming soon. Not through blowing people up, not through cranking the hate up even more, raising even more animosity and resistance, it's coming right from the top. Proper, permanent change. You know about the election, right?"

Felix nods, sullenly, his eyes downcast and hooded.

"You know about the candidates, then? You know about Laura Minton? That she's pro-Dreg? That she's running against Vivian Baines? She stands a pretty good chance of winning, from what I understand. A couple of years ago no one would have dreamed that would be possible. If she wins, they'll bulldoze over these slums, shut down the Cirque, start all over again. Equality for all, opportunity for all, that's what she's fighting for. That's how things change: by rebuilding the structure of society, not from blowing up innocent people."

"The Pures aren't innocent!" Felix snarls. "I hate them! They all deserve to die!"

He's so angry, so full of hate. I know those feelings; I've felt them myself, every second of every day for the whole of my life. I don't know him and I don't think I like him, but I understand where he's coming from. I get it now, why he was so moody with us. He's damaged inside; broken and embittered.

Jack speaks again, softly, reasonably. "Listen, son, the Brotherhood are bad news. The answer to hate is never just to hate harder. We need *peace*. Proper, lasting peace, and more Pures want it than you know! Give Laura Minton a chance before you think about doing anything radical."

Felix mutters something under his breath and then looks from Jack to Greta and me and then at his mother, her eyes pleading with him.

"There's no time to sit and wait for some do-gooder Pure politician to try and win an election that the Dregs can't even vote in! People are being suppressed and killed right now! My brother is in that circus right now, and the only people willing to stand up and fight back, right now, are the Brotherhood! That's what I've always said, that's what I still say!" He glares at his mother. "Anyone who doesn't like it will just have to deal with it!"

He stands up and walks out of the hut, slamming the insubstantial door so hard that the cardboard walls wobble dangerously, and one of them leans in at the top, exposing the sky above.

Rosie bursts into tears and Greta throws her arms around her again.

"Please don't cry," she says. "He didn't mean it."

"He did mean it!" wails Rosie. "He meant every word he said. He's going to join the Brotherhood and there's nothing I can do about it!"

Jack's on his feet, attempting to manoeuvre the wall back in line with the ceiling. She looks up at him. "I'm sorry," she says. "I'm sorry to behave like this when you've only just arrived. What on earth must you think of us? It's just ... I can't stand the thought of him getting into trouble, or doing something he'll regret. He will, though. He won't change his mind!"

"He might do," Jack says. "We'll try and talk to him again, give him some more information. I know a lot about the Brotherhood – I used to be a copper, after all. You need to be seventeen before they let you join, right?"

She nods. "You can sign up on your seventeenth birthday."

"And when is Felix seventeen?"

She looks at me, and then back up at him, her eyes welling.

"Last week," she whispers quietly, before bursting into tears all over again.

The Cirque guards are dragging me across the vast courtyard when there's a loud whistle from behind and a big white golf buggy comes trundling towards us, its mechanical whirring sound loud in the empty courtyard.

Silvio is behind the steering wheel.

He glides to a halt as he approaches us and switches the engine off, stepping down with a flourish.

"Ah, Benedict, you must forgive me my transportation method; my leg just hasn't been the same since your girlfriend blew it up! Then again, your thigh probably still aches a bit where I shot you at point-blank range!" He laughs, his white teeth flashing. "Can't believe I was such a poor shot. You'd think I'd have managed to kill you there and then! Bit embarrassing, really. Oh well, all in good time, I guess! Anyway, I've just had a wonderful idea! Before we acquaint you with your new bedroom suite, why don't I take you on a little tour? Give you the chance to really get a feel for all the things we've done here?"

"I don't want a guided tour," I answer quickly. "I don't want to see it."

"I say what goes on around here!" His voice, vengeful and bitter, cracks like a whip before he reverts to the same ingratiating tone as before. "Anyway, you loved the last circus, I know you did! You couldn't stay away from the place! We've excelled ourselves, if I do say so myself! It's a much more interactive affair now and there's far more action, far more blood and guts. You see, I know exactly the kind of things you teenage boys like!"

He laughs again, and nudges me. "Oh, silly me, you're not like the others; you're a little more ... romantic than most, aren't you? Well, fear not; you'll find plenty of other pretty Dreg girls to replace Hoshiko in here, Baines. You may as well see if there's anything you like – your last girlfriend's as good as dead, after all!"

Rage floods through me. I grab hold of him by his suit lapels, lift him up high, and throw him to the ground. Within a split second, the guards have grabbed hold of me, but not before I see him crumpled in the dust, see the shock on his face, the fear in his eyes.

He looks up at me, his crystal-blue eyes wincing in the sunlight. "OK, you want it like that, do you? Fair enough, don't say I didn't try to be hospitable. Guards, cuff him and put him in the trolley. You'd best stay close by though; we've got a wild one on our hands here."

He pulls himself to his feet and brushes the smudges of dirt from his white suit. "Well, Benedict, let's begin our guided tour!"

Once Rosie's sobs have finally subsided, she stands up and starts busily sloshing the cups in the bucket of water and drying them with a cloth she pulls from inside one of the crates.

"I'm so sorry. You barely know us and suddenly you're caught up in the middle of our family conflict. You've got enough on your plates." She laughs. Well, it's sort of a laugh; it has the sound of a laugh, but her face is still sad and exhausted-looking. "I bet you're regretting knocking on our door now!" she says.

"Not at all," Jack says. "I just wish there was something we could do to help you in return."

She tidies the cups away and lowers herself back down.

"Felix has been angry for a long time, even before they took our Sean away. Their dad ... well, he was in a bad place. He was angry too. He took it out on us, sometimes. He wasn't always very kind. And then, one day, he just snapped. He was working in the quarry, mining for stone, and he just lost it. He hurled a huge chunk of rock at one of the guards. Caved his head right in, they said. He was shot on sight. Felix was only a little lad then, but that's when all his hatred for the Pures started."

"I'm sorry," Jack says.

"It's OK. The truth is, we're better off without their dad. I wouldn't let Felix hear me say that – he'd never forgive me – but it's true. He wasn't a nice man, not in the end. He's damaged him: Felix, I mean, my lovely boy. He used to be so kind, so gentle. He always looked up to his big brother, especially once his dad was gone, and when they took Sean away, the last little bit of softness went with him. It's torturous for him, not knowing if his brother's alive or dead, not knowing what they're doing to him. I'm trying to calm him down, trying to stop the hurt, but it's hard. He feels it all so deeply. He works on the roads, digging them up, laying tarmac, that sort of thing. He goes to work, keeps his head down, gets his tokens, eats his rations, sleeps, goes to work again. The only thing that keeps him going, the only thing that fuels him, is his determination to get Sean out of the Cirque. That and his hatred, his need for revenge." She shakes her head. "It's eating away at him from the inside."

Listening to her, I can't help thinking of my own family. It must have been the same for them when I was taken, must still be the same for them, if they're even alive any more. I wonder if they know about me. I wonder if they've heard the stories. They're bound to have – everyone seems to know who we are.

"Rosie," I ask her. "How *do* you cope when something like that happens? How *do* you keep going?"

She sighs. "It's very hard, almost impossible some days. I just hold on to the belief that the world is changing, that he'll be freed one day, and he'll come home to me. That's why I keep the place as neat and tidy as I can, that's what the flowers are for. I find fresh ones every day, put them in the window so that when my Sean comes home he'll see them and he'll know we're still right here, waiting for him."

She stands up briskly. "Anyway, why am I still waffling on? I don't know why I'm putting all this on you. As soon as Felix comes back, I'll send him out to go and make an appointment with Kadir's guys. He won't have gone far. He'll be back soon."

Felix doesn't come back though. Rosie keeps glancing at the door so much that, in the end, we all are. His absence becomes more and more palpable in the room as the minutes go by.

Who is this infamous Kadir? *Request an appointment*, she said. It sounds funny to me, like something the Pures would do, not us. They make appointments all the time. Appointments with doctors, or dentists, or lawyers, and then they sit in a waiting room in their smart clothes, waiting to be called by a receptionist. There's a water cooler, Ben said, if they get thirsty, and teas and coffees are available too, if desired.

Does Kadir have a receptionist? A secretary?

I don't like the thought of a Dreg having that much power; it reminds me of Silvio. Dregs don't make appointments, and they don't sit in smart clothes in waiting rooms. I don't want to meet this guy who Jack has to suck up to – cower to – if you read between the lines.

I look at Jack. He's thinking the same thing as me, I'm certain of it.

"I'm not sure about this," I say. "I don't like the sound of Kadir."

Jack frowns. "You heard what Rosie said. He runs the slums. Even the police leave him alone to get on with it. If he's got that much power and influence, the sensible thing is to try and make friends with him as quickly as we can."

"That's right." Rosie nods. "You won't get very far without him."

"What if he won't help us? What if he just turns us in straight away?"

"He'll find out about us anyway," Jack answers. "Loads of

people must have seen us earlier. If he's that well informed, he'll soon hear about our arrival."

Rosie laughs, nervously. "You'll have to a bit careful how you talk to him, especially you," she says to Jack.

"Why especially me?"

"You used to be a Pure. Not just any old Pure either: you were a copper. Kadir might be wary of that. He'll want to make sure you understand who's in charge."

Jack raises his eyebrows. "I'm sure you'll be safe," she says hastily. "As long as you're respectful to him, as long as you understand who's boss. We'll go soon. I'll take you myself."

"If there's any chance you're going to be put in danger by your association with us, then we can't let you get involved," Jack says, and Greta and I nod.

"There's no danger," Rosie says. "I promise you. Not from Kadir, anyway. I'll take you to him myself." She peers out of the window. "We should probably just wait until it gets a bit darker before we go out there, though. *Everyone* knows who you guys are. You're famous." She smiles at Greta. "Famous heroes."

"Famous criminals, more like," I say. "As soon as they see us, people are going to inform on us. Why wouldn't they? What do they owe us?"

Rosie frowns. "That's why we need to see Kadir, for protection." Her eyes flick towards Jack. "Better you go to him than he comes looking for you."

BEN

It's only when I'm on the back of Silvio's golf buggy, trundling across the acres and acres of land, that I begin to comprehend just how huge this place is.

Hundreds of fairground rides, all still for the moment, stretch on into the distance, their bright colours gleaming and fresh.

At first, I feel quite reassured. Maybe they've taken a conscious step away from all the horrible stuff that used to go on in the old Cirque. Maybe it'll all be OK. There's nothing wrong with fairground rides, after all.

I start to read the signs though, and a cold shiver of doubt whispers its way up my spine. *Fatal Blow*, one reads, *Buried Alive*, another. It's when we whirl past a bumper car ride – *Dodge the Dreg* – that I know I'm right. This isn't a normal fairground.

The huge Ferris wheel dominates the skyline to the right, its carriages lightly swinging back and forth in the breeze.

"Ah, I see you're impressed by our big wheel," Silvio calls to me, glancing over his shoulder. "You're right to be. It's a historical artefact, you know. It used to be the pride of the city, that wheel: the London Eye, they called it, because of the panoramic views it offered. They dismantled it when the slums started spreading everywhere. The Pures didn't like seeing the way the Dregs took up so much space, the way they were polluting everything. They stopped using the wheel and it was eventually dismantled and shoved in an old warehouse. It was your mother's idea to resurrect it; she thought it would make an impressive set piece. She's clever, your dear old mum; you must be proud of her. It's going to be one of the stars of the show when we open."

He looks up at it fondly. "Do you know, it still worked? After all these years. It only took a few minor adaptations to turn it into a suitably dramatic ride for this place. We've called it *The Wheel of Misfortune!* Maybe you can have a ride one day, if I can persuade your mother to relax her restrictions a bit!"

His eyes light up with excitement. "I can't tell you how much I'd love to get you into one of those carriages, Benedict!"

I don't say anything; I won't give him that pleasure. I stop looking about me and stare down instead, keeping my eyes fixed on the shiny metal floor of the buggy as we move on and on and on.

Eventually, the whirring stops and we come to a halt.

Silvio eases himself out of the buggy and comes round to the back, his cane tap-tapping on the ground.

"Well." He grins, holding out a gloved hand. "Shall we?"

I ignore the offer of assistance and push myself up, trying not to let him see how difficult it is with my hands cuffed. My thigh always stiffens up if it stays still for too long, and being hunched up in the back of this buggy, even just for this short journey, has made it feel numb and inflexible.

Sabatini watches as I prise myself out and then reaches forward, prodding my leg with his cane.

"You could do with one of these, couldn't you, Baines? Too proud, are we? Or maybe you didn't like looking weak in front of your little tightrope walker. Didn't want her to know you weren't the big tough guy after all, is that it? I shouldn't worry, my cane doesn't bother me at all. In fact, I've grown rather fond of it. It lends me a certain … gravitas, wouldn't you agree? And it has several custom-made adaptations. I'm sure you'll become familiar with them at some point." He squares his shoulders and thrusts his head forward. "I feel stronger than ever now. Stronger and purer and better, despite your girlfriend's efforts."

For the first time, I look at him properly, taking in all the details. He makes my eyes hurt. Everything bleached, blank, white. From the crisp, starched suit to the gloves, the tie, the handkerchief in his jacket, all the way down to his shoes: white. And it's not just his clothes, either. His skin doesn't contrast to them at all, not in the way it should. It matches them perfectly; it's the same colour, or to clarify, it's no colour at all. I remember learning about colour and light at primary school; about how white is a negative. That's what Silvio Sabatini has become now. He's turned himself into a negative. Even his eyelashes are white, even his grinning teeth. Only his piercing blue eyes and red lips, stretched into their usual leer, break up the blank canvas.

I smirk back at him. "You don't look stronger, and you don't look purer, either. You look like a joke. I bet everyone round here's laughing at you behind your back."

I look round at the guards, lingering discreetly a few feet away, pretending not to hear. "I bet they are, I bet everyone is."

One of the guards' mouth twitches. I'm sure he's holding back a grin.

The leer has frozen on Sabatini's face and two tiny spots of colour have appeared on his alabaster cheeks.

"We will see who's the joke, Benedict," he hisses. "You will soon realize who has the power around here: I will make you see. Before I'm done with you, you will bow down at my feet, I promise you that. You and Hoshiko have lost. You tried to defeat me, but I have risen! I have risen and my circus has risen and we are bigger and we are stronger than ever before! What do you have, Baines? You have nothing. You don't even have your girlfriend to hold your hand any more. She's probably already dead!" He throws his head back and laughs. "You don't really think they let her go, do you?"

His words renew the fear inside me all over again. It courses through me, filling me up. He's right; why would the police stick to the agreement? They'll have followed Jack, Greta and Hoshi, of course they will. They'll have captured them and locked them up by now … if they were lucky.

I take a deep breath. He's taking a low blow, trying to hit me where it hurts the most. I must brace myself against the force.

It's not true, what he just said: I saw it on the news report my mother showed me. They escaped, and they're free, and somehow, they'll all make it. I have to believe that. I will believe that. And I'll be free too. I'll see Hoshi again soon, I know I will. And until then, I'll be strong in here, just like she was. I'll make her proud of me.

"I hope Bojo's OK," I say, studying Sabatini's face for a reaction. Immediately, his jaw slackens, his eyes widen.

"Bojo? Bojo is dead, isn't he? I was never sure, but I told myself he must be!" He clutches my arm. "Are you telling me he survived? He's OK? Oh my goodness!" He fans at his face with his hands. "This is such a shock to me. Is he well? How is he coping?"

"Oh, don't worry." I smile. "He's absolutely fine! He hasn't missed you at all, you know – but then, he always did love Greta the most, so I understand. After all, he chose her over you that night we blew up your arena, didn't he? Wise choice: that's what saved his life – his preference for her. He made it out unscathed and you turned into –" I look him up and down and scratch my head "– this."

His eyes narrow, dangerously. "I don't believe you. Benedict Baines, you are playing with me. It does not do well to toy with my emotions."

He pushes me in front of him and jabs at me with his cane, propelling me towards a strange spherical building. It's painted to look like a planet. Saturn, I think, going by the spinning rings of pink and black light arcing around it.

"This is one of my favourite attractions," he purrs in my ear. "We call it the *Globe of Death!*"

I feel cold suddenly, cold and shivery. He keeps on prodding me, all the way up the little brick pathway and through the door, towards whatever awaits within.

As soon as the shadows begin to lengthen on the walls, Rosie tells us, "It's time." She roots around in one of the crates and pulls out a couple of thin woollen hats which she passes to Greta and me to wear, surveying us critically when we put them on.

"It's no good. Your faces are too recognizable. Everyone will know who you are, even in the dark."

She picks up one of the blanket rolls and starts wrapping it around Greta's neck like a scarf. Greta's mouth, nose and most of her face soon disappear. I do the same thing and Jack zips his collar up high and pulls his hat down low.

Rosie steps back and looks again.

"Scoop your hair up inside the hats, girls," she says. She picks up the rest of the blankets. "Will the monkey stay still if you hide him under your jumper?" Greta nods.

Rosie turns to me. "You're the most famous one of all. Maybe you should roll one of the blankets under your top." She starts cramming one up my jumper.

I pull away. "That won't work," I say. "I'll just look like one of the Cirque clowns. We survived on the run for nearly a year without wearing fake stomachs!"

"Hmm. They found you this morning though, didn't they?" says Rosie, gently but pointedly.

"There's not a lot I can say to that, is there?" I sigh and stuff the blanket under my jumper.

We creep out into the night. The slums seem different now. It's that eerie twilight time of the evening when the sun has gone but the light still lingers. Although the day has been a warm one, it's cold now, but there's a lot more people about than when we arrived. A lot of it is foot traffic; people traipsing past, returning from shifts, or leaving to work through the night. The orange and green work suits are everywhere. As well as the comings and goings though, there are people clustered together in groups around the little fires dotted here and there.

"Keep your heads down," Rosie whispers. "Don't make eye contact."

She hurries us along, bypassing people whenever she can, so quick that we're almost jogging.

Every group we come near seems to stop talking as we pass. Every time I lift my eyes up, I glimpse suspicious eyes. I feel them behind us, watching, staring.

"Hey!" someone calls. "What's the hurry?"

"Quick." Rosie moves even faster as we wind our way into the heart of the slums. The tiny shacks become even smaller and closer together, the little paths between them narrower and narrower.

Eventually we reach a different sort of dwelling. It's bigger than the others – about ten times the size of the ones which cluster around it – and it's taller too, towering above them. The structure seems more permanent; it's made of thick wooden planks nailed together, and there's a roof of corrugated iron.

There's a story Amina used to tell me when I was younger, one that I still tell Greta sometimes, about the three little pigs hiding from the big bad wolf. This place reminds me of the third little piggy's house. It's not made of brick, but it's stronger-looking, more resilient. A shelter from the storms outside, maybe, offering protection from the evil which scratches relentlessly at the door but can't find its way in.

It always reminds me of the three of us, that story, and whenever I tell it to Greta, the big bad wolf in my head has Silvio's face. In our grim reality, the wolf caught one of the piggies, and there are only the two smallest left now. Still, at least we destroyed him in the end. No more big bad wolf for us – at least not that one, anyway.

Rosie leads us up to the door, a real door with an arched window of frosted glass at the top and a rusty metal knocker. She looks around at us and gives a nervous little grin before tapping gently on it. There's nothing for a moment or two, and then the sound of footsteps inside and a man opens the door.

He's big – muscular and tough-looking. His face is scarred, his nose has obviously been broken more than once and there's a scowl on his face. He peers down suspiciously to get a closer look at Greta and me. Instinctively, I lean backwards and I feel Greta dart behind me.

"I'd like to see Kadir, please," Rosie says.

"What's your business?"

"I've got some visitors here," she says. "He'll want to meet them."

"Wait there."

He walks off, leaving the door open. I poke my head in, pulling it back quickly when I see what's inside.

In front of us is a room; there are actual armchairs in it with a load of people, all male, sprawled on them, looking towards the door suspiciously. I only get a quick glimpse, but some of them are older, I think, like the guy who let us in, and some of them must only be about Ben's age. They all have this look on their faces though, and that's why I shoot my head back so quickly. They all look like lions do when they're ready to pounce.

The guy comes back.

"You've got five minutes."

My eyes meet Rosie's. Why does she look so worried?

It smells funny inside, a sweet, musky smell, and there's a thick cloud of smoke hanging in the air. I avoid making eye contact with the men, who all stare at us silently as we cross the room towards the thick, hanging curtains which the guy in front pushes aside as he gestures us into the inner sanctum.

It's larger in the curtained-off section than the part we've just left – that was the entrance hall, I suppose. The walls are lined with thick, dark material and the ground is covered with boards, so it's like an actual floor. There's nothing else in the room except for a platform about a metre high at the back of the room, covered in the same material as the walls. On top of it sits a large chair: shabby when you look closely at it, with ripped upholstery and chipped wooden arms, but very grandiose nevertheless. It reminds me of the thrones they used to put in the royal box in the arena sometimes when VIPs came to the Circus. The ones Ben and his family sat in; the ones he says made him feel like an idiot.

There's a man sitting on the chair, looking down on us from his elevated position.

He's about thirty years old, olive-skinned, with a little round hat perched on his bald head. He has a goatee beard and he's wearing what can only be described as robes. His hands, the hands which clutch the arms of the throne-like chair, are dripping with jewellery – huge gold rings, flashing under the light from the candles surrounding his little podium – and there are heavy gold chains around his neck. He smiles and his teeth flash too; there's a jewel in his mouth, right where his front tooth would normally be. It's a diamond, I think, or a crystal, white and twinkling.

I wonder if they're real or not, the diamond and the gold. It doesn't really matter; the overall effect is the same. Anyway, even if they *are* fake, they still feel inappropriate. Here, in the slums, where children scavenge on rubbish tips for food and people root around for enough sodden cardboard to build their houses with, sits a bejewelled figure on a throne.

I look down at Greta. She's holding Bojo inside her jumper with one hand, but her other one's over her mouth and she's looking at the ground. She's trying not to laugh. I know what she means; it's ridiculous. Ridiculous and bizarre and contemptuous. I already know this Kadir guy is going to irritate me.

He lifts his hand and beckons us forward.

"Come closer," he commands. "Speak. Tell me who you are and what it is you desire."

BEN

Inside, the Globe of Death is like nowhere I've ever seen before. Lasers run up and down and all around, flashing lights of red and then orange and then green. In between the flashes, darkness, so that it takes me a while to figure out exactly what I'm looking at.

Black seats line the whole orb, stretching all the way around, to the left, to the right and above my head. Each one has what looks like a steering wheel in front of it, and some kind of control panel, like it's a car.

In the middle, raised up on a platform is another sphere, a transparent one.

Silvio looks remarkably pleased with himself.

"What do you think happens in here, Benedict?"

I sigh and turn my head away from him while he fiddles around unlocking my handcuffs.

He jabs me in the ribs with the cane again so that I give a little involuntary jolt.

"I don't know!" I answer quickly. "I told you, I'm not interested!"

He pushes the sleeve of his suit up a little to reveal what looks like a large old-fashioned gold watch, standing out in stark contrast to his white flesh.

"We only have a minute or two to be seated! The full dress rehearsal is about to begin."

He gestures grandly around the room. "Pick a seat. Any seat, it doesn't really matter, they are all equally good. I hope you don't get motion sickness?"

I cross my arms together and stay where I am.

His eyebrows arch. They aren't real – they look like they've been tattooed on. His plastic face stretches. It reminds me of the stress putty everyone used to have a few years ago. You could stretch it out until it was stringy and elastic. A horrid image appears in my mind of Silvio's face, stretched out like dough, expanding lengthwise, getting thinner and thinner, the blue eyes still gleaming, the manic laugh getting louder.

"Shall I tell you a secret about this cane? I don't even really need it any more! I can get on perfectly well without it! The truth is, I've grown quite fond of it. It's become such a useful little prop." He waves the end in my face; it's sharpened to a tiny point and it whirrs round like an electric pencil sharpener.

"See this bit? I like to call it my corkscrew! It's a good name for it, don't you think? Do you know, I did actually use it once to open a bottle of wine! Such a good party trick." He leans forward and winks at me. "Of course, that's not its primary purpose." He prods it into me again; the corkscrew whirrs around, pushing into my skin.

"Stop that!"

Silvio caresses the top of the cane with his finger and the corkscrew retracts.

"That was just a tickle! Such a shame your mother said no lasting wounds – she's ruining all my fun!"

His thumb taps the top of the cane again and he grins at me as an electric jolt buzzes through my body, making my fingers and toes tingle, and giving my teeth a funny fuzzy feeling.

"Get off!" I shout.

I look around. Armed guards are stationed at the door and the apparition next to me has an electric shock stick. What can I do? I lower myself down into one of the chairs.

"Fasten your belt, Baines! You're going to need it!" Sabatini grins and secures his own with a click. I reach behind me for the seat belt. It's a full harness, coming down over my chest in diagonal strips which pin me down on either side. It's uncomfortable and I don't like the restriction of it, but something about this round room and the glee on his face makes me glad I've got it on.

He glances at his watch again.

"They should be here any minute. Now, what should we chat about while we're waiting? Perhaps you'd like a little background info, a recap of what you've missed while you've been playing hide-and-seek?"

His icy blue eyes gleam unnaturally. "Well, despite your intentions, the little grenade-throwing act you and Hoshiko carried out last year has only made the Cirque stronger. Such was your mother's disgust at your betrayal that she resolved to strengthen what you attempted to destroy. She wanted the world to see that Pure blood will never be threatened. It will fight back. It will crush. It will vanquish. She had a complete change of heart! She began to understand the delight people feel when those who foul and taint our society with their stinking presence get their just desserts at last. She was never our biggest fan before but now she can't get enough of this place! She loves it, she really does, and you could say we owe it all to you and Hoshiko! Your failed act of rebellion ended up being the best thing of all that could happen, for the circus and for me!

"Anyway, I digress. Your mother has helped to fund the rebuilding of this circus, Benedict. She's been so generous, so kind. She has raised its legitimacy with her political approval and she has given me almost entirely free rein. She appreciates my genius, Benedict! The only insistence she made was that there was to be more action, more bloodshed than ever before!" He laughs excitedly. "Of course, that was music to my ears!"

He leans in closely.

"She's very keen for the experience to be a more interactive one too. She suggested that the audience would like to feel a part of it all more, would like to make an impact, would like to be more than just spectators.

"I knew straight away that she was right. That's why we've brought in all the fairground rides – so that the paying public can really get involved in the action. And there are many truly wonderful new acts, too, where the audience play a vital part." His eyes glitter with delight. "I think this one might be my very favourite of all!"

He sighs. "Time is ticking by, where are they?" Then he looks over his shoulder and barks at one of the guards. "Hurry the Dregs along, will you! They're keeping us wait—"

Before he can finish his sentence, the throaty, throbbing rev of engines reverberates through the room.

I feel myself being tipped backwards and then the seats begin to spin. I'm turned upside down, again and again, my empty stomach lurching as we rotate around the sphere.

Suddenly, from the ceiling – at least I think it's the ceiling;

I'm so disoriented it's hard to tell – a huge motorbike drops down into the central sphere. On its back is a rider, anonymous in helmet and suit. Another person drops down after it – a girl. She scrambles to her feet and stands there, bracing herself, waiting for whatever it is that's about to happen in the Globe of Death.

We step into the pool of light from the candles surrounding Kadir and he leans forward.

I slowly unravel the scarf from my neck and pull the blanket roll from under my top. Beside me, Greta's taking off her scarf too and Jack's removed his hat.

When I lift my eyes up to meet Kadir's, recognition dawns immediately on his face.

"Well, well, well, I do declare, it's the runaway tightrope walker! The outlaw and her band of merry men, or at least part of them."

"I wondered if you might be willing to help them." Rosie's tone is deferential. "They're good people." She looks at Jack and smiles. "Very good people."

"Hmm." He sounds suspicious. "Where's the Pure boy?"

I feel my eyes welling up. I wish I could answer him. I wish I knew where Ben was. I wish he was here now with me, or I was there with him, wherever there is. I'd rather be in chains, living together, dying together if we have to, than here, without him, in this weird slumlord's headquarters playing these stupid games.

Jack takes a step forward.

"He got captured," he says. "And we got away. We're hoping we can hide out in the slums for a while until the police stop looking for us."

"Stop looking? Yeah right! They ain't never going to stop looking for you, not while they still run the show, anyway."

"There's nothing special about us now," Jack says. "They've

caught Benedict Baines. He was the golden prize. He's the one they wanted — we were just collateral. They aren't going to waste time and money looking for us for much longer."

"You're wrong, I'm afraid," Kadir says. "You've made them look stupid. While you're still on the run, they look weak. They won't stop looking until they find you and string you up." He nods his head towards me. "*She's* the devil in human form if you believe what all the posters are saying, what the police have been saying when they've come looking. And they *have* come looking. And they will come looking again. Anyone concealing information about you puts themselves at risk. Why should people around here bother gambling with their lives to protect you?"

None of us says anything. I knew I wouldn't like this stupid man, with his big ego and his big throne.

"Give me one reason why I shouldn't just hand you over right now? There's reward money in it, I believe, substantial reward money."

"Like I said," Jack answers coolly. "I doubt they'll offer anything for us, not now they've caught Benedict Baines."

I've had enough of this game. I'm not playing. If he wants to turn us in, so be it. Suddenly, I don't feel shy any more.

"Look," I say. "If you want to help us, that's great, thank you very much, much appreciated. If you don't, that's fine too. We haven't begged anyone yet, and we aren't going to beg anyone now."

He leans back and laughs, the diamond in his tooth twinkling.

"I heard you were fiery," he says. "Fiery is good. We'll need fire in the times ahead." He crosses his hands together under his chin and regards us thoughtfully for a moment or two.

Bojo pushes his way up out of Greta's jumper, his little wizened monkey head surfacing at her neck and peering around curiously.

"Oh my!" A smile forms at the edges of Kadir's mouth and his eyes dance with amusement.

"Little girl, your monkey is adorable! Do you think he'd let me stroke him?"

"Maybe," Greta answers, doubtfully. "He's a bit nervous around new people usually."

She gently lifts Bojo from her jumper and steps a little closer. Kadir steps off his throne and lowers himself down on to the edge of the platform, leaning forward and petting the little monkey softly with his jewelled hand.

Bojo reaches his paws up, playing with the rings on Kadir's fingers, turning them around and chattering away excitedly; he's always had a thing about sparkly objects. He looks up at Kadir, cocks his little head to one side enquiringly, and then springs right up from Greta's arms into his lap, his delicate little paws reaching up to his face. His tiny monkey fingers gently probe Kadir's lips; I think he's trying to get to the diamond in his mouth.

Greta gasps. "He must really like you!" she says. "He never goes to anyone like that!"

I scoff, quietly. "Maybe he reminds him of Silvio," I mutter to myself. "All that glitters isn't gold, Bojo."

"I must say, the feeling is mutual!" Kadir says, stroking Bojo, reverently. "I always wanted a pet of my own." He catches

Greta's stricken look. "Oh, don't worry; I wouldn't take him away from you! But I do like him. I like him very much."

He looks down at the four of us.

"I'll help you," he says. "I'll give you somewhere to live. I'll make sure you don't starve and I'll make sure no one talks ... but I will want something in return."

I knew it. This guy isn't going to do anything for nothing.

"What is it?" Jack asks warily. "We're in enough trouble as it is."

"I'm not sure yet," Kadir muses. "There are things happening, big things, happening soon. Change is coming. The balance of power is shifting." He caresses his beard. "How can you help me?" he says thoughtfully, and it's as if he's asking the question to himself, not us. "I'll tell you what, I'll help you now, but you owe me. Agreed? I scratch your back, you scratch mine, if and when the time comes. What do you say?"

I look at Jack and Greta. Greta is staring up at Kadir, fascinated. She's just as smitten with this creep as Bojo is; she thinks he's a king from a fairy tale. I can't blame her, I suppose – I know how romantic she is and it's exactly the look he's going for; he only needs that hat on his head to be a crown to complete the image.

Jack looks back at me.

"What do we say?" I murmur under my breath, my lips not moving.

"Beggars can't be choosers," he answers, in the same way. He steps forward.

"Thank you," he says. "For your offer. We would be grateful

for your support, and we will do our best to repay you, if we can, should the opportunity ever arise."

I don't like this conversation. I don't know what we're agreeing to. I don't know what he wants. Jack's right though; we don't have any other option.

Kadir stands up and hands Bojo carefully back to Greta. "Thank you," he says. "I'd like to see him again, if I may. Perhaps I could get him a treat. What does he like to eat?"

Greta smiles happily. "He likes bananas best. He hasn't had any for a long time, though."

"Bananas? So what they say about monkeys is true. OK, how about I get him some bananas? Do you think he'd like that?"

"Oh, he'd love it!"

"And you? What would you like? What food can I get for you? You name it, I'll get it."

She gasps and looks at me excitedly, and then back at him, gazing up at him in wonder.

"Anything?" she says.

He nods his assent.

I know exactly what she's going to say.

"Can you get chocolate cake?" she asks. "I've never had chocolate cake!"

"Chocolate cake? Why, of course! Chocolate cake it is. And you, policeman?" he asks Jack. "What can I get for you?"

"Thank you, but you're doing more than enough for us already," Jack answers.

"It would be a pleasure," Kadir says. "Call it a goodwill gesture."

"Thanks," Jack answers again, "but we're fine for now."

Kadir's benevolent smile drops a little and his eyes harden.

"If that's how you feel. And you?" he says to me. "There must be something you'd like. More chocolate cake, perhaps? Anything else? Anything else at all."

I've only had cake once; a Pure passed me some in the Cirque and I stuffed it into my mouth before anyone saw. I've never forgotten it. My mouth waters and the gnawing pain that's always there in my stomach intensifies at the thought of sweet sponge cake filling my mouth.

If what he's saying is true though – if he can get hold of anything – how's he doing it? He's not some genie in a lamp, or the fairy king Greta seems to think he is. What's he got that gives him so much power?

I don't want to owe him anything else. I don't want him to think he can buy us.

"No, thanks," I say. "I'm fine."

His eyes are like pinpricks. He doesn't like us refusing him. He wants to play God.

Suddenly, I think of something. It's not food, but it's the thing I want more than anything else. The thing that's gnawing away at me even more than hunger.

"There is one thing," I say. "Can you get hold of information as well as food?"

He raises his eyebrows curiously. "Yes, of course. What is it?"

"Can you find out where Ben is?" I ask. "Can you find out what's happened to Benedict Baines?"

"Benedict Baines?" Kadir's tone is curious. "The rich boy? He really gave himself up for you guys?"

I nod. "And now we don't know where he is. Please, if you could just find out if he's OK."

He leans down and looks carefully at me.

"You've really fallen for a Pure kid, then? It's not just a romantic myth? You really ..." He raises his both hands up, making inverted commas. "... *love* him?" His tone is sneering.

"Can you find out where he is or not?" I say.

He leans forward further, like he's scrutinizing me.

"You don't like asking for help, do you, Black Cat? You hate coming here cap in hand to me. I've got you figured out already. You're proud and stubborn and you like to stay in control. Hmm." He sits back and strokes his little goatee. "That boy must really mean a lot to you. That's interesting. I'll remember that. Yes, I'll do some digging. I'll find out where your boyfriend is. Please bear in mind though, we are friends now, you and I, and friends expect loyalty."

It feels like he's threatening me. I don't like it, but I need to find out where Ben is.

"Anything to say?" he asks me.

"Thank you," I murmur, looking at the ground.

Kadir throws his head back and roars with laughter.

"Ooh, that scowl! That hurt you, didn't it! You know what? I like you, Hoshiko." He smiles at Greta. "And I especially like you and your monkey. We will be good friends, I can already tell."

There's a movement at the door and one of Kadir's heavies moves in and stands deferentially at the edge of the room. It's the same guy who answered the door.

"Sven!" Kadir smiles warmly. "Have you met our famous guests?"

The man gives a sullen nod, looking distinctly unimpressed.

"It's time," he says. "You asked me to tell you."

"Thank you, good man." Kadir springs down from the stage like a ninja, the chains around his neck clanging as he leaps. "Well, it's been lovely meeting you all, but I'm afraid I have somewhere I need to be. Don't worry, leave everything with me."

Then he claps his hand to his forehead.

"Silly me, where are my manners! You should join me! Let me introduce you to my people!"

"Where are you suggesting we go?" Jack has positioned himself in front of Greta and me and his hand is lingering at his side, right where his gun used to be. Habit, I guess.

Kadir frowns at him. "I have done nothing to deserve such a hostile reaction. I have already told you, I will keep you safe, even you –" his lip curls into a sneer "– although that's a big ask, ex-copper." He grins again. "I give you my word, no harm will come to you. This will be the perfect opportunity to tell the masses that I have assured you of our protection. Plus, just as a little extra bonus –" he winks at me "– you, my dear, might even get to see your mother-in-law."

BEN

The throb of the engines subsides and we stop spinning, our seats suspended halfway up the globe.

A familiar voice fills the room: Silvio's. It comes from all around me, reverberating like the engines did. The whole globe must be one big speaker.

Ladies and gentlemen! Welcome to the ride of your life! Buckle up, sit back and enjoy your spin in the Globe of Death! I look at Silvio; the sadistic light in his eyes is as gleeful as it ever was. "It's prerecorded," he informs me, rather unnecessarily.

Before you is an orb of the very strongest reinforced glass! Fireproof, shatterproof, waterproof! Do not fear, what happens inside will stay inside! Our rider must circumnavigate the sphere, attempting to avoid the obstacles in his way and maintaining a speed of fifty miles an hour or above at all times! Dropping below that will cause his bike to immediately blow up, turning the whole globe into a deadly inferno! Above the orb, you will see a speedometer, enabling you to track the rider's speed.

The control panel in front of each of your seats contains a single button. At a random point in the ride, you will each find your control panel light up. This gives you the opportunity to control what happens in the wheel. Press the green button to increase the speed at which it turns. Feeling dizzy and want to slow things down a bit? Simply press the red button for a calmer ride, momentarily at least. And finally, depressing the large blue button will add a mystery object to the globe, making things trickier for our rider. Ladies and gentlemen: you control the ride!

The flashing of the strobe lights ceases, plunging us into

darkness while the globe in the middle lights up, illuminating the people inside. The girl, all dressed up in a spangled circus leotard, must be the obstacle the rider has to avoid.

The revving sounds begin again.

Five, four, three, two, one! Let the fun commence! Silvio's voice counts down.

The motorcyclist revs his engine.

The illuminated sphere in the middle of the room begins to spin and turn, while the larger circle surrounding it, the one I'm strapped into, revolves around it.

The rider begins to drive around the spinning sphere. I don't know how he isn't falling. I think it's something to do with the speed he's going at; he's already up to sixty miles per hour. The girl is scrambling desperately out of his way, like a hamster around a wheel.

The smell of petrol and burning rubber fills the room.

We spin and they spin. How long can this go on for before he hits her? Any second now, one or both of them are going to get crushed. I close my eyes.

My arm is shaken roughly and, when I open my eyes, Silvio is leaning forward in his seat, shouting frantically above the engine.

"Your panel. It's lit up! It's your turn!"

I look down. The buttons are glowing. I frown at him. Does he really think I'm going to join in?

"Quickly, Baines, you'll miss your chance!" His face contorts angrily and he reaches over me and pushes the blue button.

Trickles of water start to run down the middle globe. The

bike slips and the girl grabs desperately at the smooth walls around them, now wet and slippery.

I close my eyes again.

I feel Silvio shaking me. Feel him slapping me, but I don't open my eyes. I keep them screwed shut tight until the engine stops, until the wheel stops turning, until the world stops spinning. Only then do I slowly open one, then the other, and take in the sight in front of me.

I might see my mother-in-law: what does Kadir mean by that? He can't mean Vivian Baines, can he? She can't be here, in the slums.

Kadir sweeps from the room and his men form a ring around us, their cold, hard faces blocking out the light above me as they usher us out of the building and through the streets.

My heart pounds. All that talk of friendship was just a lie. He's going to hand us over to her.

I stop moving. "Where are you taking us?" I shout. "Where are we going?"

One of the men clamps his hand over my mouth and propels me forward, roughly.

"You don't get to ask questions," he snarls.

"Get your hands off her!" Jack demands. The men stop in their tracks, every single one of them turning and regarding Jack, their eyes burning with malice.

"She won't make a fuss again," he says, quickly. "None of us will."

The man lets go of me. I wipe my mouth but I don't make another sound and we move forward again, Jack's arms clamped protectively around me and Greta.

There's a sound, distant at first, and then progressively louder as we move closer to its source. I know exactly what it is; I used to hear it every night, not so long ago. It's the sound of people, lots of people. It's the sound of a crowd.

We round a corner and there they are: hundreds of people, clustered in the narrow paths of the slums, surrounding a stage, like one of the temporary ones we used to have at the Cirque.

What are they all waiting for?

Kadir has dropped back now, entrenched with us in the middle of the ring of his men. The track we move along is dense with people but they step aside for us as we go, carving a pathway for us right up to the stage.

There's a ladder at the bottom. Kadir rests his hands on it, turning to address us over his shoulder.

"Follow me," he instructs. "And don't look so worried! This will be fun!"

I don't move, and neither do Jack or Greta. We stand there, trapped and surrounded by a wall of muscle as the king of the slums takes to the stage and addresses his people.

BEN

Even after the room has stopped spinning, it takes a while for my head to catch up. I look up, towards the globe, my heart racing.

The rider is still on his bike; the girl is scrunched up on the floor. They're both alive! The rider pulls off his helmet and bends down to the girl, helping her unsteadily to her feet. He's a bit older than me, I reckon, tall, with sandy hair that's tousled and damp with sweat where it's been under the helmet. She looks a few years younger – just a child – with dark hair and eyebrows and wide, brown eyes.

I glance at Sabatini. He's frowning irritably. He pushes some buttons on his watch. The glass walls of the sphere drop down. Water gushes out, the smell of burning tyres grows even stronger and heady smoke catches in my throat.

"This is no good! I knew it was wrong to give you too much rehearsal time! She was scrambling out of the way far too easily, even when the water came down! Where's the fun in this act if you don't even come close to crushing her under your wheels? It's going to be a complete anticlimax! Where's the risk? Where's the thrill factor? Baines – got any bright ideas? Don't be so shy! Dregs, we have our first guest! We can't let him leave disappointed! Don't you recognize him? Don't you know who he is? We have Pure royalty here for a little holiday!"

I feel their eyes boring holes into me. They think I'm with Sabatini. They think I'm on his side.

"Your eyes do not deceive you!" he cries. "It really is him! It's Benedict Baines! I kid you not, *the* Benedict Baines is here, with us, in our humble little circus! The same guy who tried to destroy us last year. Such a funny turn of events! He's always loved getting in on a bit of circus action. He's ever so keen to join us!"

"That's not true!" I cry. "They forced me to come here! They're keeping me prisoner!"

"Benedict, spare us the theatrics! You aren't fooling anyone!" Silvio's voice is sharp. "Right, back to business. Any bright ideas? How can we make this act more thrilling?"

He sighs heavily. "Do I have to think of everything around here? You, boy! What's your name?"

The boy mumbles something incoherent.

"Speak up!" shouts Silvio. "What. Is. Your. Name?"

"Sean," the boy says more clearly.

"Right. Well, Sean, take off your shirt!" The boy stares at him. "Come on! Take it off!"

The boy lowers his helmet and takes off the ragged shirt he's wearing. His emaciated chest is covered in cuts and bruises.

Silvio releases his seat belt and pulls himself from his chair, tap-tapping across the room towards the boy. He snatches the shirt from him, holding it at arm's length with a look of disgust on his face, and lifts it up between his fingertips, turning his head to the side delicately. He reaches up to the boy's head and ties it around, rolling it up to make a blindfold.

"That should make it a bit more fun!" he says. "Right, let's go again."

"I can't do it," the boy says, his voice high and panicked. "I won't be able to control it!"

"Erm, that's kind of the idea." Silvio's voice drips with sarcasm. "Well, it will be interesting to find out anyway. Now, how else can we improve this act? Hmm. I've drawn a blank."

He scratches his head theatrically, and then looks up at me.

"Oh yes, you made a suggestion earlier, didn't you, dear Benedict? Said I should make it harder for them to concentrate."

"No!" I cry out. "I didn't! I never said that!"

"There's no need for false modesty!" he chides, turning back to the girl and boy. "Benedict begged to be appointed as my creative assistant! He's taking it extremely seriously. He wants a fully immersive introduction, he said. He wants to live amongst you in order to fully understand what motivates the lesser, animalistic races. Those were the words you used, weren't they, Baines?"

"He's lying!" I shout.

"Oh, Benedict! You shouldn't be afraid to show creatures like this your true leanings! It hardly matters what they think! They'll probably both be dead by the end of the season, dead by the end of the day for that matter! Right, back to the act. Benedict's right: we need to put you under more pressure. Light a fire maybe, or have some kind of animal prowling around, wasn't that what you said, Baines? Yes, that could be perfect! I'll make arrangements for opening night. For now, the blindfold will have to do."

He throws the controller towards me. "Switch on the wheel, won't you, Benedict?" He reaches forward with the cane, pushing it into the boy Sean's chest and holding it there. The boy looks forward steadily, but he's biting down on his lip, and his chest is still where he's holding his breath. When Silvio pulls his stick away, a little round red wound has joined all the others on Sean's bruised and abused frame.

I look at the girl, her big eyes round with fear, her face pained and pale. I look at the blindfolded boy. I look at the guards, armed and silent.

I look at Silvio.

He raises the cane again, holds it towards the boy's chest. "Come on, Baines!" he says. And pushes it into Sean again. This time, he doesn't take it away. Little wisps of smoke curl out of it and there's the horrible smell of burnt meat.

He raises his non-existent eyebrows at me. "Are you going to get on with it, or are you going to keep standing there, watching him fry?"

I reach down for the panel. There's a big red ON button.

I click my seat belt off and lunge towards Sabatini, knocking the cane flying.

The guards spring forward and pull me backwards, wrenching my arms behind my back. One of them retrieves the cane and handles it to Silvio.

"Baines! You can't keep playing the double agent like this! It's not fooling anyone, not even these brain-dead Dregs! We all know you're a Pure! We all know who your mummy is! We all know you get off on acts like this!"

I feel the girl's eyes on me, accusing me, dissecting me.

"Do it again, with the blindfold on this time," Sabatini orders. "I'd love to stay and watch but I've promised Benedict a tour of the whole place. He's desperate to see it all!" He turns to the guards. "You!" he instructs one of them. "Go and tell them to bring in a firepit for the bottom, will you? And then

131

let me know how it goes. You'd better come with us," he tells the other guards. "Benedict is a VIP, after all. He may require protection from all these savage Dregs!"

He turns and hobbles out of the room, moving with surprising speed. The guards grab hold of me again, pushing me roughly after him.

At the doorway I turn. Sean has taken off the blindfold. His fists are clenched, his gaze is fixed on me, and his eyes burn with hatred.

Amidst a roar of applause, Kadir stands in the centre of the stage, facing the cheering people gathered below him.

"Thank you! Thank you all!" he calls as the noise subsides. "Why are we gathered here? Why? Because we are on the brink of a new era! An era of renewal, an era of opportunity, an era of hope! Before the show begins, however, I would like to introduce you to some friends of mine, some good friends. People, we are among star-studded company tonight!"

He looks across and down to where we're standing. "Come, don't be shy! You, of all people, should be used to the limelight!"

"It's the Black Cat!" someone calls out. "It's Hoshiko!"

They all start shouting then, roaring and cheering and calling my name. Word of our arrival in the slums has obviously spread.

"Come on!" Kadir calls down. "Don't keep your public waiting!"

I feel myself pushed towards the ladder. The noise of the gathered masses is getting louder and louder, pounding, just like it used to. As I grip on to the cold iron bars, memories wash over me like a wave. For a few seconds, I'm transported, back to the time before.

The crowd are calling for me to perform for them.

I stand above them, way up high, curling my toes around the wire. The very worst thing in my life; the very best thing in my life. Time to let the conflict go.

Time to leap, time to soar, time to fly.

A sharp dig in my back jolts me to reality.

"Get up there!" Sven orders.

I look around at Jack and Greta, take a deep breath and begin to climb.

At the top, I stand on the stage before the crowd, my eyes lowered, listening to the wave of hysteria grow.

Before long, Greta appears next to me and then Jack, standing awkwardly behind us.

Kadir holds up his hands, and eventually, the noise hushes.

"Yes! They need no introductions! Please, give a warm welcome to the runaway circus stars!"

He waits, grinning, for the din of the wolf whistles and shouting and applause to subside again.

"These people have sought sanctuary in the slums and I have assured them we will protect them: every single one of us."

"What about him?" someone shouts. "He's police!"

"Who said that?" Kadir's head whips to the left, and he steps forward, peering down into the crowd. "Who was it? Remove him." Below us the sea of people parts again as two of Kadir's men move through the crowd and drag someone away.

"As I was saying, these people are my guests. Now, you may well be aware that there's a reward on their heads, a big reward. You may well be thinking that you'd like to get your hands on all that lovely money. You may even be tempted to turn snitch, but—" He pauses and his eyes glint. "Money ain't no good when your throat's been slit."

He doesn't have a microphone up here. He doesn't need to; the people below us are silent now, deathly silent.

"These people are heroes, living legends, and we are honoured to have them here with us." He grabs my arm and raises it high. "This girl here blew up the circus! The circus which has stolen so many of our sons and daughters from us! The circus which is back and which must be brought down again!" There's a roar of approval from the crowd.

"We are gathered here to watch the first televised political debate in over twenty-five years! To watch the first ever pro-Dreg candidate take on the system. In just a few short days we could be given the vote! The circus could be shut down for good!" There's more roaring applause. "After years in chains, we will be free again! Would we be here without the brave actions of these people you see before you? I. Think. Not! I have promised them we will protect them. I know you will all honour that promise."

There's silence again.

"OK, people, let's get on with things. Let's start the show!" He raises his hands above his head and begins to clap, slowly, rhythmically. Below us, the crowd of people begin to join in until every single person's hands are raised in unison.

This man next to me can play a crowd like a musician plays a fiddle. Applause, silence, clapping – he's working them at his will. I've only ever seen one man before who had such presence onstage: Silvio Sabatini, the ringmaster himself. The man I killed. The man who turned me into a murderer. An unrepentant murderer.

Behind us, a giant screen descends. Dramatic music begins to play.

Whatever it is that's going on here, it's about to begin.

BEN

It's dusky by the time we get back outside, and there are pink smudges in the sky; it's going to be another warm day tomorrow. It's cold now though, cold and crisp. You can smell the shift of season in the air, feel it in your fingertips.

Nearly a year has passed since I sat there in that big house on the hill and watched the circus come to town.

I was so excited, so desperate to see all the action. It was all I could think about. How could I ever have been so deluded, so naïve?

I remember how Priya's shoulders hunched when I said I wanted to go to the Cirque, how her gentle eyes were suddenly hard and angry.

Decide for yourself, she said. *Judge with your head and with your heart.*

She risked everything to tell me that. She knew it was treason; she knew what would happen if they found out. And they did find out. My own brother, my own twin, told them. Francis killed her, or he may as well have done.

I miss her so much. I hope I've done her justice, wherever she is. I hope she's proud of me. I renew again the promise that I've made to her every day since I discovered what they'd done to her.

One day, if we ever get out of this mess, if the world ever changes enough, I'm going to find her children, Nila and Nihal. I'm going to tell them how brave she was, how brave and wise and true. I'm going to look after them.

We're going to find Hoshi's family too, as soon as we can,

and Greta's. It makes Hoshi sad that Greta hardly talks about her parents any more. She used to all the time, she says, but they've stopped seeming real to her now and I don't think she even misses them any more. She just loves Hoshi so much, and she loves me and Jack and Bojo. It's not as if she wants for affection, far from it, but that doesn't make it right. There's a mum and dad somewhere who must be desperate to see her. And Hoshi: she's got a mum and a dad and at least one brother, or she did have. Miko would be twelve now.

The girls were both so young when they were taken away that neither of them even know what part of the country they're from.

One day we'll find a way to track them all down though.

We'll all be together. We'll all be free.

I look up. The first star has appeared, twinkling determinedly, waiting for its friends to join it.

The name Hoshiko means *child of the stars*. Everything about Hoshi, even her name, is beautiful. I remember how enchanted I was by her when I first saw her, how enchanted by her I still am. Now that I really know her, know the broken and brave girl under the greasepaint and glitz, I'm more bewitched by her than I ever was.

I wonder where she is. I wonder if she's somewhere out there, looking up at that star too. I hope she'll be warm enough tonight, wherever she is. I hope she'll be safe.

"Darkness is descending." Silvio's ominous statement breaks my thoughts. "This is my favourite vantage point, you know, of the whole Cirque. You can see the entire place from here."

He presses a button on his watch and talks into it.

137

"Turn everything on, will you? Yes, all of it. Yes, now! When do you think I mean, next week? Get on with it!"

There's nothing for a second, and then, one by one, a million lights begin to twinkle.

Every ride, every attraction, bright against the darkness. All the pathways between them stretching off like the arcs of fireworks. The great wheel rotates slowly, the waltzers spin and whirl. Up, down, left, right, the lights of the circus dance.

For a moment my heart betrays me. For a second, for less than a second, my breath catches in my throat.

No. I will not let myself feel anything but disgust for this place. It's just electricity, that's all it is.

I turn to Silvio, adopting the same disdainful manner for him my mother's always had.

"Is that it? After all this time, that's the best you can do. It's hardly impressive, Sabatini." His face drops, just for an instant, and then the deathly white mask is back.

"Tell you what, before I show you to your sleeping quarters, why don't you accompany me to our cinema room? There's a live television event starting in just a few moments." He gestures towards the golf buggy. "Shall we? Leap aboard, Master Benedict; it will do you good to see how the land lies."

The music fades away and there's a few seconds' pause as the audience below us wait in hushed silence beneath the blank screen.

I look over their heads, across the slums and towards the sprawling city. The temperature has dropped further now and, away to the west, the sun is dipping below the horizon, streaking the sky pink.

One tiny star twinkles bright. Seeing it sparkling defiantly up there makes me feel hopeful for the first time today.

I'll see Ben again, I know I will.

In the distance, a dark mass beyond the lights of London, the new Cirque squats, waiting to rise up once more.

Suddenly, as if it knows I'm watching, it transforms. From darkness to light, from stillness to movement, from dead to alive.

My heart leaps. Goosebumps tingle across my arms and back. Greta clutches hold of my hand and we both stare, transfixed.

No. We must not let it charm us.

Under that bright canopy, people are suffering, just like we did. Caged up, frightened, desperate, fighting for their lives. I shake my head. I break the spell.

"Don't look at it," I say to Greta. I put my arm around her and turn us both gently around to face the screen.

After a second, an image projects on to the stage.

It's a holograph one, so solid-looking, so real, that it feels like the person is actually there, right beside us, the static haughty smile on her face directed straight at me.

My mouth goes dry.

Vivian Baines.

She looks different to before. The sleek bob and power suit are gone. She's wearing a baby-pink sweater and her hair curls on her shoulders in loose waves. Looks like she's trying to soften the ice queen aura she gives off – attempting to come across as warm and gentle. It doesn't work.

Bojo springs out of Greta's arms and bounds over to the edge of the image. He cocks his head curiously and reaches out a paw cautiously, jerking it back when he feels nothing but air.

She's speaking, I think; it's hard to tell. The crowd below us are deafening: jeering, booing, shouting obscenities. Eventually, they quieten a little and if I strain my ears and stare closely at her horrid sour little mouth, I can make out the words.

"—romantic story of my son running away with a circus tightrope walker captured the nation's hearts. Love conquers all. Love can build a bridge. Love is stronger than hate – these are some of the sentiments I have heard expressed over the last few months."

She smiles. It's almost convincing.

"It's a nice idea. It's an idea we all like. The idea that we are all, somehow, the same. That, deep down, we're no different – we *can* share, we *can* live in harmony. This is the story that Laura Minton and her followers are selling you. The notion that everyone, Pure and Dreg, can coexist peacefully. The notion that if we allow Dregs more rights, they will appreciate it, somehow. They will behave themselves. They will live happily amongst us."

She leans forward. Stares intently.

"It is a *lie*. It is a *fairy story*. Do *not* be seduced by the myth. We must be smarter than that. We must consider the facts.

"Turn back the clock thirty years and you will see what it is really like to live in a country with open borders. Dregs swarming here in their millions: benefit tourists, grasping any handout they can get; health tourists, bleeding the NHS dry. Children, Pure, English children, forced to learn in schools where their own language is not even considered the primary tongue any more.

"And worse, far worse than that. Rapes. Muggings. Theft. Anarchy. This is the truth. This is the reality.

"What is a Dreg? What does the term mean? When we examine its etymology, we find that it is entirely the appropriate word for a group of people who are, all of them, even the sparkly circus performers, scum: unclean, murky sediment which must not be allowed to rise up and taint our purity.

"Do *not* destroy our country. Do *not* turn back down the path to ruin.

"Look around you: look at your home; look at your children's school; look at our hospitals. Are you really prepared to lose everything you hold dear to support the false and dangerous notion that we are all equals?

"We are not equals. Biology and history do not lie."

She pauses, and her voice softens again.

"I was heartbroken over my son's actions. Heartbroken and shamed, but he was *groomed*. He was singled out because of my position and he was brainwashed. My son was poisoned. He was sick.

"I am delighted to tell you that he that is sick no more. I

141

have my boy back! He has seen the error of his ways. Benedict, my son, is back with me. He's back and he's sorry. Don't believe me? Let's hear what he has to say."

Behind her, another image appears, a static one. It's a photo. It's Ben.

Her arm is wrapped around him and he's looking up at her face and he's smiling. At her. They're both smiling.

Ben, my Ben, is there with her, and he's smiling.

BEN

There's no point refusing any of Sabatini's demands. I'm a prisoner here and there's nothing I can do about it.

He pushes me into the back of his golf buggy and drives me across to another building. Black and circular, it's painted to look like one of those really old-fashioned film reels from the twentieth century.

Inside, the nostalgic theme continues. It's set up like one of those cinemas they used to have, with rows of uncomfortable-looking chairs that flip up when they aren't being used and a big flat screen dominating the front wall, red velvet curtains draped either side of it.

"This is where we will broadcast all televised national events," Silvio informs me. "Such as the one we're about to see." He looks at his watch. "Damn. We've missed the start!"

He presses a button. The screen flickers into life.

My mother's there, on the screen.

She's dressed in different clothes now, a soft, pastel jumper. It really, really doesn't suit her. It's like putting a baby's bonnet on a shark.

A photo appears behind her.

It's me. It's the one she took before, after she told me Hoshi was still on the run.

I was laughing in her face. It doesn't look like it though. It looks like I'm smiling up at her, adoringly. It looks like we're reunited.

A voice starts to speak. It's my voice. Silvio turns the sound right up so that, even with my hands over my ears, I can still hear exactly what she's done. I can still hear my words, still hear my voice:

I'm so sorry that I dared to question you. You were right all along. I'll never break the rules again … forgive me.

I feel sick. How dare she do this to me? How dare she take my angry words and turn them into a betrayal?

What if Hoshi and Greta and Jack see this? What will they think?

This can't be happening. After everything we've been through together. He wouldn't go back to her. Not now. Not Ben.

It's not an old photo though. It's a new one. It's Ben as he was when I left him. He's still got his scruffy old clothes on, and his face is stubbly and gaunt.

And it's his voice, saying those things.

Next to me, Greta's hand is over her mouth and her eyes are unblinking, as if she's frozen to the spot.

She's in shock. She thought she knew him, but she was wrong. Turns out she didn't know him at all. Turns out none of us did.

There's something heavy inside me. Heavy and cold.

I should have realized all along that this would happen. Out of sight, out of mind, isn't that what they say?

We've been on such an adventure together: a heart-pounding, breathtaking, unforgettable adventure. A whirlwind, a roller coaster, the adrenaline-fuelled ride of Ben's life. But the thing about a roller coaster is, if you spend too long on one, you start to feel sick. You start to miss the feeling of solid ground beneath your feet. You start to miss real life.

When Ben first met me, I was glamorous, I guess, to him at least. I was a sparkly circus star, but the sheen has worn off. Now that the lights and the sparkle and the glitz have faded, he's finally realized that I'm nothing special at all. I'm embittered and angry and broken and tired, and life on the run with an ex-tightrope walker is anything but romantic.

Hey, Ben, come into hiding with me! You'll never sleep in a warm, comfortable bed again in your life! You won't be able to wash for months on end and your clothes will all fall apart! You'll be hungry and thirsty and cold and the police will be one step behind you, wherever you go. It'll be a riot!

I'm surprised it took him this long.

His mother's obviously slapped him on the wrist for his little lapse of judgement, then smiled indulgently at his foolishness and invited him back into the fold.

I bet she's told him that if he forgets the last year has ever happened, he can have anything he wants. And she can give it to him too; whatever he likes, she can get for him. Why wouldn't he go back to her? Who wouldn't? What can I offer him I return?

He's bound to be relieved it's all over.

That must be why he put his gun down like that and walked away with them so meekly.

He wasn't sacrificing himself for us at all. He was making a choice. The choice of comfort and safety, of warmth and family.

The choice to leave me.

BEN

I feel a nudge in my ribs. Sabatini is staring at me, a smile of glee and triumph fixed on his face.

"She's good, isn't she, your mother? Now the whole world will put your little love story down to a moment of madness. Teenage hormones which got a little bit carried away. Hoshiko will hear about it: she's bound to. They'll catch up with her soon. They'll catch up with her and shoot her. She'll die thinking that her lovely-wuvvly Benny-Boy has betrayed her. She'll never know the truth!"

I stare back at the screen. Stare back at the photo, looking for all the world like a family reunion. Listen to my voice, still playing.

I am sorry. I'm sorry it took me so long. Sorry I went along with it all.

"You're wrong!" I tell Sabatini. "Hoshi will see right through this! She knows me better than that! She'll see exactly what my mother's done."

He throws his head back and laughs. His little white teeth are like fangs.

Greta's pulling at my arm.

"Hoshi?" I have to bend my head to hear her subdued little voice.

"Why is Ben saying those things? He told me his mum was a baddie. He told me he hated her."

"It's not true!" I tell her. "That's not Ben. Not really. Ben would never turn his back on us. Never!"

She looks from me to the smiling holographic image metres away from us.

I could never really love a revolting Dreg girl, says the voice. Ben's voice.

"It looks like him," she says, doubtfully. "It sounds like him."

I look back at the screen. She's right. It does. It's not though. It can't be.

Ben loves me. He would never say those things about me, and he would never, never, never go back to her. His cold, hard, evil mother.

As suddenly as it came, the feeling of horror inside me goes. This means he's alive. This means he is of use to his mother. That's good. It means he's safe.

The crowd below us are still booing and shouting. Jack kneels down to face Greta and me so that we can both hear him.

"Hoshi's right, Greta. This isn't real. They've generated it somehow, manipulated the imagery. It's just clever editing, that's all. You know Ben. You know he'd never say those things. Don't let that woman fool you, Greta. Don't let her win!"

His words confirm what I should have known all along.

Below me, hundreds of angry Dregs are shouting terrible things about Ben.

I step forward to the centre of the stage, screaming down at them.

"It's not true. It's fake!"

They shout even louder.

"Don't listen to her! It's fake, can't you see that!"

They're jeering at me, though. They won't believe me.

I stare at Vivian Baines. I hate her so much. I hate her more than I hated Silvio. At least he only had the power to hurt us, the circus people. *She* has the power to hurt all of us, and she wants even more. Nothing will stop this woman. She'll hunt down and kill every one of us. She won't stop until there are no Dregs left.

She's still talking. This time about the Cirque.

"In just a few days, the Cirque will reopen. You will see a show like no other. It will demonstrate exactly who is in charge of our country and who must remain in charge. If you are with me, if you are prepared to face what we need to do to ensure a strong, Pure future for our country, come along. Be my guest. The first thousand people who like and share this broadcast will receive a complimentary ticket for opening night."

She smiles warmly. "Let's celebrate. Let's celebrate Purity. Let's celebrate superiority. Let's celebrate strength."

I feel a hand on my back. Kadir firmly moves me to the side of the stage and points at the screen. "Look. The best bit's about to start."

The photo has gone now and I can't hear Ben's voice any

more. Vivian Baines is standing to one side, an unconvincing smile fixed on her face, as a man in a suit appears on the screen.

"Ladies and gentlemen. In the name of fairness and democracy, both of your main candidates are here to make their pledges and to take part in the first televised debate for over twenty-five years. We've heard from Vivian Baines, now let's hear from her nemesis! Please, give a warm welcome to Laura Minton!"

You can hear the studio audience applauding. Some of the people below us are too, but not like they were cheering Kadir when he took to the stage.

A woman appears. It's Laura Minton. She's very tall and she's wearing a flowing purple dress. Her wild red hair cascades down her back and her green eyes are warm and familiar. She's had such a high-profile campaign that she's become nearly as infamous as us over the last few months.

"Good evening." She smiles right into the camera. "Let me ask you a question. Who, exactly, do you think you are?"

BEN

Laura Minton is smiling into the camera.

"History is a rich tapestry woven by many people. People of all colours, people of all creeds, people who were not Pure English at all. Victoria and Albert, Christopher Columbus, Plutarch, Leonardo, Galileo – the list could go on for ever."

She leans forward and whispers into the camera.

"*Dregs*, all of them. Dregs: the scourge of mankind, apparently. A blight on the world, every single one of them. Think. How can that be? How can people with dirty inferior blood have had such an impact on the world?

"Think.

"I am like you. I am special. I am Pure. My grandparents were Pure, my parents were Pure." Her voice drops to a stage whisper. "But let me tell you a secret…"

The film is showing both women now. My mother is looking on, a sneer on her face and her eyebrow raised cynically.

"I've had my DNA tested. DNA: the fibre of my very being. The fabric of life. My genealogy: the very root of who I am. And what did I discover? Something interesting: something very interesting indeed. I am not pure English at all. I am part Gaelic." She flicks her auburn hair. "That explains the hair colour. I am also part Slavic, part Scandinavian, part Israeli and part Ghanaian."

She turns to my mother. "What do you think about that, Vivian Baines?"

My mother's face is victorious.

"Well, that explains a great deal. I'm not sure why you have chosen to make such a revelation, but surely you must realize the implications of your confession. You are a Dreg! A Dreg cannot stand for office; it is clearly stated in our country's statutes. You must stand down. You must have your rights and privileges stripped. You must be taken immediately to the slums!"

Laura Minton smiles. She doesn't look fazed. Not at all.

"It looks like you may be right. With such blood coursing through my veins, how can I possibly argue that I am Pure English? Let me tell you something else. My entire team had their DNA tested too, every single one of them. Oh yes, and another two hundred people: volunteers from across the country. Doctors, university professors, lawyers, bank workers. How many of them, do you think, were Pure, Vivian Baines? What would your estimate be? Surely none of those people could be tainted like me, could they?"

My mother's smile is fixed on her face.

"Genetic testing is illegal. You have committed a criminal offence."

"Hmm. Why is it illegal, I wonder?" Laura Minton cocks her head to one side. "It's almost as if there's something the current government don't want us to realize. Well, perhaps you could humour me before they drag me off to the slums, Minister Baines. How many of our volunteers turned out to be –" she makes little inverted commas of her fingers and quotes the national anthem "– *Pure of soul and Pure of body*?

"How many? I'm waiting for your answer..."

"Oh, for goodness' sake!" my mother snaps. "You are

employing sensationalist tactics. You are showboating. Why would I, or anyone else, be interested in your little tests and trickeries? We are here to debate the dangerous notion of allowing Dregs more freedom. I am here to warn people again of what a catastrophic mistake it would be. Let me give you some statistics about Dregs, and about crime—"

"Why have you not answered my question?" Laura Minton's voice cuts through my mother's. "How many of the two hundred people we tested at random were, it turned out, not actually *Pure* English at all?"

"I fail to see how this has any bearing on the matter at hand! You are avoiding the subject and you have committed a criminal offence."

Laura Minton steps forward.

"The answer is all of them. Every single person we tested. Not one person turned out 'untainted.' Would you believe it? We found one hundred and twelve ethnicity strains in our random group of Pures. One hundred and twelve. What does it tell us? It tells us that we are wrong! That we have always been wrong! We are all Dregs together, all part of the same melting pot! We are one and we are the same. None of us are Pure. Not one of us!"

She's so compelling. My mother, standing behind her, looks like she's been punched in the face.

"We are a tiny island nation. Romans, Saxons, Vikings, Normans: they've all invaded us, all left indelible marks on our country's heritage. And before we became cold and hostile and insular, we welcomed immigrants to these shores with open arms. We celebrated diversity! Africans, Indians, Chinese,

Pakistanis, Spaniards, Italians, I could go on for days. People from all of these nations and so many more have settled here over the centuries. They made us who we are. They made Britain great. They are a part of me." She stares unblinkingly into the camera. "And you, watching this, I'll bet they're a part of you, too."

Her green eyes twinkle mischievously. It feels like she's talking directly to me. "Are you really sure you are as Pure as you think? Can you be sure your blood is not tainted? Can you? Can any of us? Why not take the test? Why not find out? You won't really punish anyone for seeking the truth, will you, Minister Baines? Why would you if you've got nothing to be afraid of?"

"This is irrelevant!" My mother finally finds the words to interrupt her. "We cannot allow the Dreg plague to spread further. We must be more radical, not less radical. We must make tough choices. We must protect our country. We must protect our children."

"Minister Baines, why don't you humour me? Will you have your blood tested? Here. Live on TV? Why not quell my outrageous suggestions once and for all? I have scientists standing by. Will you take the test? Will you show us how Pure *you* really are? Will you?"

There's a pause. The camera zooms in on my mother. Two pink dots have appeared on her cheeks, and her face looks like it's about to crack. She doesn't know what to say. She doesn't know what to do. For the first time ever, my mother's lost for words.

HOSHIKO

I didn't know much about Laura Minton before tonight but now I think I actually love her.

"Take the test! Take the test! Take the test!" A pounding chant resounds across the slums.

It's so loud that you can't hear what Vivian Baines is saying. You can see though. See her leave the stage. See her walk out of her own debate.

I look at Greta and Jack and Kadir. The same look of awestruck delight is on all of their faces.

Below us, the crowd have gone totally mad. They're screaming, shouting, laughing.

There's something powerful in the air: something palpable, like we're all connected.

It feels like the end of something.

It feels like the beginning.

BEN

Silvio, me, the whole world watches as my mother refuses the test and walks out of the debate.

I turn to Sabatini.

"She knows," I say, triumphantly. "She knows that the whole thing, all that Pure and Dreg stuff, is all just one big lie. She has to, otherwise she'd have taken the test."

Silvio looks confused. More than confused: he looks ill. I thought it was impossible for his face to get any paler, but I swear it's turned so white it's ultraviolet.

"But I'm Pure now. I mean, I always was, really. People like Hoshiko, like Greta, like all the Dregs in my circus, they aren't Pure. Not like me. Not like you, Benedict. We're superior. We are."

He clutches at my arm. His hand is shaking. He's desperate to believe it.

I smirk at him.

"I think you might be wrong about that one."

He stands up. Pulls himself up to his full height.

"I've had quite enough of you for one day, Baines!" He lifts his arm and speaks into his watch. "Guards!"

Within seconds, they appear. Large, unsmiling, armed guards.

"Take Baines away, will you?" he hisses. "Show him to his sleeping quarters. I'm sure he'll be very comfortable there."

Once the crowd below us has finally dispersed, Kadir pulls his hood over his head.

"I've got places to be," he tells us. "Sven will show you to your new home."

He vaults down from the platform and melts away into the night.

Sven steps forward with a torch – the first time I've seen one in the slums – and we follow him through the winding alleys.

We don't bother with the disguises this time, and I feel more vulnerable than ever, flinching every time someone looks at me.

Rosie's waited for us and she puts a maternal arm around me as we walk.

"It'll be OK." She smiles at me. "Kadir doesn't go back on his word."

"What's his story?" I ask her. "How did he get so much power?"

She drops back a little further, lowering her voice. "There was a lot of trouble before Kadir. Gangs, drugs, guns. There were riots. Not out there, but in here, in the slums. Kadir came out of nowhere, really. He was just another kid on the streets at first. And then, one day, the riots stopped. Suddenly, all the old gang leaders were dead and he was in charge. It's been like that ever since."

"But if he was in the gangs, he must have been involved in all the trouble. He didn't just ask nicely to take over. He must have killed people. How else does someone like that gain power in a place like this? He must have been worse than they were!"

"Shh!" she whispers, looking about anxiously. "You can't go around speaking like that! Trust me, it's better now Kadir's here." She shivers and hugs her arms around herself. "Much better than it was."

"But it doesn't make sense. How does he keep his power? What happens if people refuse to do what he says?"

She frowns. "No one does. Well, no one has for a long time. Us older Dregs remember only too well what it was like before Kadir took control. It was a horrible time, a dark, lawless time. There was so much violence back then, so much trouble. All the young men fighting like dogs against each other, stabbings and murders – lots of crime; awful, violent crime. The worst kinds of crime. Crimes against women." Her eyes flick to Greta. "Crimes against young girls. No one wants to go back to those days. Kadir did what he needed to restore order. Yes, there are lots of stories of things he did back then, but there hasn't been anything like that for a long time; there hasn't needed to be. He keeps things safe around here."

I don't like it, the way she speaks about him so reverently. Letting someone have that much power doesn't seem that different to making one group Pure, one group Dreg to me. It's dangerous. Surely the people living in the slums should want to tear down hierarchies, not build up new ones?

I know I'm being ungrateful; Kadir's giving us a home and he's promised to protect us. I don't like owing someone that much, though, I don't like it at all. He's the one person keeping us from being informed on. What happens if he changes his mind?

Greta drops back and trots along next to me. "So, what happens to us now?" she asks.

"Well, it's obviously dangerous for you to leave, but you should be OK if you stay here in the slums. If the police come, we'll hide you. We'll keep you safe, all of us."

"We've got no way of providing for ourselves," I say. "We can't exactly go out and find work."

"Kadir will provide for you."

She's nice, Rosie – more than nice. She's warm and kind and she's taken us under her wing. It seems a bit bizarre to me, though, that she's so keen to give her trust and respect to this guy who clearly uses violence to get what he wants.

Well, I guess that's her choice. It's not mine though. I don't want to get any closer to him than we have to.

"Why?" I ask. "Why would he do that?"

"Because he's a good man. I told you," she says simply.

I roll my eyes. I don't buy it. Kadir will cash in his debts somehow. He's already made it crystal clear that we owe him. What use can a couple of runaway circus acrobats and an ex-Pure possibly be to a guy like him? No use that I can think of. If we can just stay on his good side until we find out what's happened to Ben, hopefully, after that, he'll forget all about us and we can slip under his radar. If he's found us somewhere to stay for a bit and keep our heads down, that's all we need.

We come to a stop outside a tiny, battered little hovel strung together from odd pieces of cardboard.

We duck down and enter.

Sven shines the torch around and I look where the beam shines. The room, if you can call it a room, is empty. There's no furniture in here, no bedding, just soggy cardboard and the smell of mildew. When Sven shines the torch upward, the light reveals gaps and holes in the roof.

"Home sweet home," he says. "I'll leave you the torch so you can get used to it. It ain't much, but it's all we've got to offer." His face seems a bit softer now, nicer than it did before. "Got to be better than the circus, I guess, if what they say is true." He smiles at me sympathetically in the darkness.

I stare around me. His words give me a funny feeling, deep inside in the pit of my stomach.

Anything should be better than the circus. The circus was cold and cruel and deadly. It took my Amina away from me. It hurt me. It hurt Greta. Silvio was there.

The circus was hell on earth.

It was bright though. It was exciting, sometimes. It was magical, now and then, being up on that wire, feeling it beneath my feet – tense, humming, like it was alive with energy. When I stepped out on to it, when I danced across it, we were a team, the wire and me, performing our beautiful, deadly art.

It was a bewitching, fickle friend and I had to read it, had to understand it, had to let my toes, let my heart, feel it; feel the give, feel the resistance. It changed all the time – depending on the weather: the humidity and temperature in the room, and I changed too, depending on whether I'd had anything to eat that day or not, depending on my rhythms and cycles.

I miss it so much sometimes that my body aches.

That's because they institutionalized you, the rational part of me says. *That's because they tried to break you. Fight it. Resist it.*

It's hard, though. It's in my head. It's in my heart. It's a part of me, a part of who I am.

I hated the Cirque.

I hated it, but I miss it.

How can that be?

I look around me. This place, this dingy, smelly, dark little hovel will never be home, not when the circus – the bright, shiny, evil, intoxicating circus – still calls me back.

BEN

I don't bother struggling; I just walk with the guards to wherever they're taking me. When I turn round, Silvio Sabatini's silhouetted up on the hill, still surveying his dominion.

We stop in front of a long fence, bright with moving acrobats and clowns, like the entrance gate was. One of the guards has taken out a key fob. He pushes up to a control panel and one of the panels swings open.

On the other side, things are not quite as neat and tidy and colourful. There's a field stretching out in front of us. Horses cluster together, standing still in the moonlight, and I can make out the shapes of other animals too: camels and llamas I think. In the distance, two dark elephants raise their heads at our appearance, swishing their trunks slowly from side to side.

There's nothing else except a gaping hole opening up in the ground in front of us, revealing a narrow flight of concrete stairs leading downward. The guards push me towards the steps and we climb down. There's so little room that we have to go in single file and it gets darker as we descend further and further underground.

At the bottom is an iron door. The guard in front lifts up his key fob and it swings open. He pushes me inside, so hard that I fall to the floor.

"Welcome to your luxury accommodation," he sneers. "I hope it lives up to your high standards!" The guards turn and pound back up the stairs again, slamming the door shut behind them.

Suddenly, I'm in real darkness. Pitch black. I can't see my

own hand in front of me. This place is so far underground that it's never seen any natural light. I feel my heart speeding up, just like it did that time when I was pushed into the prop box, back in the old Cirque.

There's an unfamiliar, earthy smell in here, making my stomach heave.

"Hello?" Although I'm whispering, my voice sounds loud in the silent darkness. "Is anyone there?"

There's no response. There's nothing. There's no one. I shiver. It's really cold down here, even though it's a fairly mild evening outside. Maybe this is my tomb. Maybe they're just going to leave me here until I die, until I rot away. I wonder if this is what Hell feels like.

I stand up, slowly. My head bumps something above me and I raise my hand, feeling a rough, rocky ceiling above my head. It's lucky I stood up carefully; I'd have knocked myself out otherwise.

Hunched over, I walk forward, blindly clutching my way with my hands. My feet bump into something. There's a sloshing sound and I spring back in fear.

"Please," I protest weakly, to no one in particular. "Please don't leave me in here."

As if someone's answered my prayers, there's a flicker above my head and the place lights up. Thank goodness.

I go back and try the door, although I know it's pointless.

Looking forward again, I see that I'm in a long, narrow corridor, empty apart from two great big containers of water. It was one of those that I bumped into. I look around, and then walk slowly down the passageway.

On either side of me, barred gates section off tiny little cupboard-like rooms. They stretch down away from me, all exactly the same. Behind each gate is a tiny bunk, topped with a thin grey mattress and a blanket. There's a hole in the corner of each one, and that's it.

Prison cells.

At the very end is a stone door. I push at it; it's cold and solid.

I walk back along. There's nothing else in here, just these tiny cells. I count them; there's forty of them.

Suddenly, the celling shakes and tiny fragments of rock fall to the floor. Footsteps, lots of them, are pounding above me, coming closer, descending the stairs. The door swings open again and a large group of people file their way through it before it shuts resoundingly behind them. They stand there, clustered together, looking back down the corridor at me.

We stare at each other. Then a girl's voice from somewhere in the middle of the group cries out, "It's Benedict Baines!"

It's strange, settling down in that cold little shack. Not strange because of the environment so much; this is a palace compared to some of the places we've spent the night over the last few months, but strange because Ben's not there. There hasn't been one night over the last year where I haven't slept in his arms; not one night where I haven't woken up and seen his face. It feels so wrong, him not being here.

Rosie disappears off and then, after a while, there's a tap at the door. Jack opens it cautiously. Felix is outside, wearing his trademark scowl.

"Mum told me to give you this food," he says, thrusting a wrapped-up package into Jack's hands.

"Where did she get it from?" Jack asks.

"Kadir. He's waved his magic wand and you'll never go hungry again."

He turns around and walks off down the path.

"Wait!" I call. I look towards Greta. Her eyes are fixed on the food package; she's practically eating it with her eyes.

"Open it up," I say. "I just want to speak to Felix quickly. You can start without me."

Jack's eyes search my face, concern and curiosity etched on his brow. When he nods, I step out of the hut, pulling the fragile door shut behind me.

Felix glares at me blankly, as hostile and resentful as ever.

"I want to ask you something," I say to him. "About Kadir. What's he really like?"

"How should I know what he's like?"

"Well, your mum talks about him like he's some kind of saviour … is he?"

He gives a thin smile. "Better the devil you know, ain't that what they say?"

"Is it though? How does he do it?" I ask. "Keep everyone in line like that? It doesn't sound right to me. What happens if people refuse to follow his commands?"

He looks around and then leans towards me, lowering his voice.

"The Pures, Laura Minton, Kadir, they're all the same when you scratch the surface. They all want power. They all want to rule. Why would Kadir want his little kingdom toppled? He's quite happy in here on his throne. Kadir only supports change if he thinks he's going to benefit from it. The only ones really prepared to tear everything up and start again are the Brotherhood. What my mum says about us, she's wrong. We're only dangerous when we need to be."

We. He's joined them. Rosie was right: it is too late.

He lowers his voice even further and looks at me with intense, fervent eyes.

"We're the only ones radical enough to get out there and do what needs to be done. Even Laura Minton just wants her turn in charge. My brother's in that circus right now. Things need to happen right now. Not next week, not next year. Now. We're gonna—"

He stops.

"What? What are you going to do? What needs to be done?"

He shakes his head. "I don't even know why I'm talking to you about it." He turns away and starts walking off again.

"Stop!" I call. "What are you going to do right now? I've got friends in that circus, I deserve to know."

He looks over his shoulder at me.

"Enjoy your meal," he says, and runs off into the darkness.

By the time I get back inside the shack, Greta and Jack are both sitting on the floor, the torch placed between them, its thin beam illuminating a pile of sandwiches spread out in front of them. Bojo's already holding one in his paws, nibbling at it delicately.

"He couldn't wait," Greta says, apologetically. "We did though." She pouts. "Jack said we had to."

"You should have started," I say. "Come on then, let's eat."

The sandwiches are fresh: fresher than I've ever had before. The bread is thick, soft and doughy, not dry or stale at all, and there's a thick slab of pink meat in each one. Ham, I think.

Fresh meat sandwiches. Just another of the many wonders Kadir is capable of delivering.

We eat ravenously and then spread the blankets out on the damp floor and lie down. Greta snuggles right up next to me, like she used to do in the Cirque, and Bojo buries his way in beside her, a soft warm ball under my blankets.

What I should do right now is turf them both out. I've nagged Greta every day for months about sharing a bed with an animal.

I don't say anything though. I'm grateful to have them here; it makes me feel a bit less lonely.

"Hoshi?" Greta whispers.

"Yes."

"Are you thinking about Ben?"

I sigh.

"Yeah, I'm thinking about Ben. I wish we knew he was OK."

Her head shoots with up urgency and she gives a little gasp. "He is though, isn't he? He said they wouldn't hurt him."

I should know better than to worry her unnecessarily.

"Yes. He's fine, I'm sure he is. I just miss him, that's all."

"I miss him too."

I hold her close, breathe in the smell of her hair. How can she still smell so sweet after all this time? I don't even know when she last had a proper wash, but all the dirt and muck never seems to stick to Greta.

I stay as still and quiet as I can, for her sake, and try to feign sleep until she drifts off, but I know peace will never find me, not until I know where Ben is.

BEN

It's as if they all jolt into recognition at the same time. "It *is* him!" I hear someone saying, and the whisper echoes among them. "It's Benedict Baines!"

These are Circus people: they must know Hoshi and Greta. They must know that between us we blew up the last arena and have been wanted ever since. How does that make them feel about me, then? Looking at the cluster of blank faces, all staring at me, it's hard to tell.

I search the faces for the boy and girl from the Globe of Death. At first, I don't see them, but then I make them out, right at the back of the group. Thank God.

The boy, Sean, glares at me unblinkingly. The girl's next to him; her eyes flick anxiously across from him to me and she rests a cautionary hand on his arm.

I need to speak to them. I need to tell them Silvio was lying.

A figure steps forward, a man. He has to stoop his head and lean forward to avoid hitting the low ceiling. He's huge, muscular, dark, and he has a scar stretching right across his face.

It's Emmanuel.

He stares at me silently for a long second and then steps forward and walks towards me with long, powerful striding steps, clapping me on the back with his big hand.

Hoshi's spoken about Emmanuel so often that I feel like he's an old friend. He's different to how I remembered him though. He's even taller up close than I thought he'd be, but he doesn't look fierce and warrior-like, as he does on the posters and holograms we've seen dotted around the city these last few weeks. He just looks really, really tired and really, really sad. He must be freezing, because he doesn't have a shirt on. Criss-crossed welts cover his body, and there are claw marks clear as anything on his chest and back. There's a cavernous hollow under his ribs, where a part of him has been ripped out, I suppose. The promotional images all show close-ups of his scars, particularly the one stretching across his face. I think it's supposed to make him seem like some kind of monster. It doesn't though: it shows what monsters they are. The people I used to be part of, the people I took far too long to see for what they were.

Hoshi told me about Emmanuel losing his partner, how he watched her die in front of him. I feel like it's all my fault; I feel like I did it. And I did, in a way. He knows who my mother is. He knows where I came from. I'm a Pure – or I used to be. Last time I saw him, I watched him narrowly avoid being eaten by lions. Does he know I was there, in the audience?

I force myself to meet his eyes. There's no hatred there, though, no animosity, just a calmness, a wisdom.

There's a commotion as another figure pushes his way through the masses, a little boy. He steps forward and grins up at me, a beautiful, wide smile. "You know Hoshi, don't you? I know her too. I'm—"

"Ezekiel," I say. "Hoshi and Greta have told me all about you. They miss you."

His face lights up even more. "Do they? I miss them. Hoshi was my first friend in here."

"She misses you a lot. She misses all of you a lot. She hated leaving you behind."

Emmanuel gives a sad smile. "Hoshi and Greta made it out of the circus. They give all of us hope." He frowns. "*Gave* all of us hope. Where are they?" His face is creased with apprehension. "They're all right?"

"Yes. At least, I hope so. I don't know where they are. They're still on the run, I hope." He looks at me, waiting expectantly for me to elaborate, but my leg's aching again and I don't even know how to begin explaining everything that's happened.

"It's a long story. Is there somewhere we can go and sit down?" I don't know why I'm asking. I've already seen what's in this place. Prison cells and a corridor, that's it.

He shakes his head. "Nowhere. They didn't give us any communal space this time round. Your mother has been very specific, from what I understand. She said it was having too much freedom to associate with each other that spread ideas of rebellion to Hoshi and Greta. They don't even want us to talk to each other any more." His expression is mournful. "They've taken away the one thing we had: our sense of community. We thought things were bad before, but they're worse now, far worse."

"How do they stop it? They can't just stop people communicating, not unless they fill the place full of guards all night." I look around. There are no guards in here at all.

"They have their ways, believe me." He clutches my arm urgently. "We must prepare you for what comes next. If there's anything you want to tell us, you'd better do it quickly, and you'd better do it here, in this corridor. There's nowhere else. Are the girls OK?"

So, as quickly as I can, I tell them about Hoshi and Greta and Jack escaping. I don't mention the way I bargained myself, it's too embarrassing, and it'll sound like I'm trying to paint myself as some kind of hero, which I'm not. I just tell them that the others got away, but I didn't. Somehow, though, I think Emmanuel knows anyway because he gives me a knowing smile.

"You love her, then, Hoshiko?"

It's a funny word, love. We use it for so many things: *I love chocolate. I love dancing. I love this song. Would you like to come over? Thanks, I'd love to.* How can one word mean all those different things? And how can the same word sum up what I feel about Hoshi, when that's so much more than I could ever capture in a million words, let alone one?

Hoshi turned me into a different person. She made me better, made me stronger, made me fight for what's right, for what's true. She made me look at the world in another way altogether. She inspires me. She fascinates me. She fills me up.

Hoshi is everything.

I don't say that though. Instead, I just nod and smile back. "Yes, I love her." And I look down at the floor, feeling embarrassed and shy.

When I look up, I catch the eye of Sean. His fists are clenched together. His jaw is tight.

"I still don't get it," says Ezekiel. "Why are you in here? You're not a Dreg."

"I am now, or I may as well be. You know who my mother is, right?"

He nods, wide-eyed.

"Well, she's not very happy about the things I've done, as you can probably imagine. She wanted me to say I was sorry, and she wanted me to go back, to become a part of her family again. When I refused, she put me in here. She said it was to teach me a lesson."

There's the sound of a slow hand clap and Sean steps forward, his expression twisted and angry.

"Oh, how heartbreaking," he says. "Poor you. Poor little rich boy." He turns to the rest of the group. "Didn't any of you see Sabatini giving him the guided tour? Don't let him fool you. He *asked* to be here. He's just watched us out there, me and Leah, both of us nearly dying, and he *loved* it."

"That's not true," I protest. "They caught me. They've put me in here as a punishment."

"You girls had better be careful," he says to the others. "He's probably after another poor Dreg to *rescue*. He likes playing the hero. Don't believe a word he says. Sabatini said he's working with him!"

"He was lying!" I say. "He wants to turn you against me! He hates me!"

"Not what it looked like. We saw you strapped into the ride next to him all cosy, didn't we, Leah?"

She shrugs. "He was there," she says. "He didn't look happy though. If Silvio's playing some sick kind of game with him, what choice does he have?"

"He had a choice when he paid to come and watch the shows. He's missed the action, that's why he's back. He's come back for more."

"Enough!" Emmanuel commands. "Since when do you

173

trust anything Sabatini says? Think about it, just for a moment. If he had any kind of choice, he wouldn't have asked to be in here tonight, would he? Not if he knew what was about to happen?"

I look at Ezekiel, staring up at me gravely. I look at the rest of the group. "What is about to happen?" I ask.

Sean snorts. "Like he said before, welcome to hell. Poor little Pure boy, never had to suffer before in your life and now you've been thrown to the wolves." He smirks. "Literally. Welcome to reality, *mate*. Welcome to the circus."

HOSHIKO

As the night deepens, the slums get quieter and quieter until I feel like I must be the only person for miles who's awake. Jack, Greta and Bojo are all fast asleep; I can make out their steady breathing.

What a day it's been. I woke up this morning with Ben. I'll wake up tomorrow without him.

I creep over to the door and open it a crack. The slums are quieter now. It's soothing somehow, breathing in the crisp air, but after a moment or two, I push the door shut. I know how cold this insubstantial cardboard shack will become in the dead of night; I need to keep it as warm and snug as I can.

I seek out the sleeping forms of Jack and Greta; I can just make out their shapes in the darkness. What's in store for us, I wonder, and what's in store for Ben?

I hope they're looking after him. I hope he's safe. What will they do to him? He's made such a mockery of them for so long. Will they want to make an example of him? What if he's already dead? What if they've killed him? What if he's killed himself? I keep seeing his gun pointed to his temple, and then I keep seeing it going off...

Standing there, listening to the unfamiliar night-time sounds of the slums — the shouting, faraway, odd bangs, the occasional muffled laugh — the panic and fear I've squashed down into the pit of my stomach all day creeps out of the darkness and envelops me like a shroud.

Ben told me once that he spoke to me, in his head, back at the Cirque: when they took me away and he was scared they were going to kill me. He made a promise that he would get me out. "It was a bit like a prayer," he said. "I felt like you could hear me somehow." I remember his eyes flicking up at me and then back down when he said that; all shy in that cute little way he has. He was embarrassed but he still told me.

I didn't think much of it at the time. I thought it was just Ben being Ben: romantic and hopeful and idealistic – the opposite of me. I never told him that though; I didn't want to disappoint him so I just smiled.

Now, though, after all we've been through, I think maybe he was right. Maybe we are bound together, so tightly that we can feel each other, even when we're not there. Maybe I could feel him, even back then, but I blocked him out. Maybe I just needed to let him inside.

He's inside now. Inside my head. Inside my heart. He's a part of me. I'd know if anything had happened to him.

I close my eyes. Picture his face. Not the graphic scary pictures like before, but his face when he looks at me. It wobbles a bit in my mind, but I wait for it to settle and still, until it's clear, until I see him, see his beauty and honesty and bravery. See it right there, shining in his eyes; his love, his need for me: vulnerable, open, strong.

In my mind, I reach forward and touch his soft hair.

I look back into his eyes. I don't look away, like I still do even now when I can't cope with the intensity of the moment and I have to break it, even though I don't want to, even though it's the best feeling on earth.

You'll be OK, I tell him, talking in my head just like he said. *And I'll be OK too. And we'll find each other again. We've defied the odds before; we can do it again. I'll keep believing. For you. I'll keep strong.*

I squeeze my hands together, pretend I'm holding his, and I shut my eyes tight. I feel him next to me. If I think hard enough, if I don't lose sight of him, even for a second, I'll keep him safe through the night.

I'll see you again, he says. *I'll see you soon.*

A different sound out there makes me jump. A shuffling noise, loud in the silence.

I creep over and peer out of the window.

There's no one there.

Clutching hold of the torch Sven left us, I open the door a crack and peer out. I turn the torch on and search with its narrow light, making sure I don't shine it into any of the huts opposite.

There's a figure crouching down behind the shack next to us. I hold my breath.

I sweep the torch in front of me and make out another shape edging its way towards the building. I jolt my head backwards.

When I peep out again, the shape's gone. Maybe it was never there in the first place. Maybe I was imagining it.

Behind me, Jack and Greta are still sleeping soundly. The monkey's not though. He's sitting up, looking at me, his little brow furrowed in annoyance.

"Sorry, Bojo, did I wake you?" I whisper. I try to coax him over to me, but he presses himself into Greta and eyes me accusingly. Looks like you have to be a seven-year-old child to win Bojo's trust. Or a psychopathic ringmaster. Or a bejewelled slumlord.

I open the door and peep outside. All is quiet. All is still. There's nothing there. There's no one.

Suddenly, a hand over my mouth. My body grabbed, roughly. I try to shout, try to kick, but it's no use. They've got me.

They've got me and they're dragging me away.

BEN

Emmanuel glowers at Sean.

"You've only been here a short while; you don't know our ways. This not how we behave in here. We don't fight amongst ourselves. We never have. We look after each other, as best we can. If we do not have that, we have nothing. We have such a short opportunity to be together and you are cutting it short further."

Sean shakes his head, disgustedly. "His girlfriend didn't look after you, did she, when she set fire to the place and ran away? She ditched you all as soon as she damn well could. Anyway, he's not one of us. He's a Pure. Once a Pure bastard, always a Pure bastard."

He turns on his heel and storms into one of the little cells, slamming the door behind him and, rather dramatically, locking himself in.

There's a heavy silence, and then one of the boys who'd been standing with Sean at the back turns around and walks into one of the other cells. Four others do the same. The girl, Leah, sighs and begins to turn away.

"He was watching us perform," she says almost apologetically to Emmanuel before disappearing into one of the cells.

For the first time since this morning, I feel tears filling up my eyes. Being here, with the circus folk, makes me miss Hoshi even more. She lived with these people. She was a part of them and they were a part of her. They still are a part of her, that's what Hoshi says. She says that being in the circus together, going through all the torture and pain, all the grief and fear, bound them together, so that when one of them suffered, they all did.

I tried to understand, but I knew I never would, not really. Not when I'd always had such a safe and protected life, and not when I'd never really felt close to anyone until her, except Priya.

I can't bear what Sean said about her just now. Hoshi could never have forgotten about the people she left behind. She's agonized about them, and so has Greta; tormented themselves every day with worry about what was happening to their circus family.

Suddenly, I hear her voice in my head.

You'll be OK, she says. *And I'll be OK too. And we'll find each other again.*

I feel her next to me, feel her hand in mine.

I'll see you again, I tell her. *I'll see you soon.* And for the first time, I believe it.

Emmanuel's hand on my shoulder jolts me back to reality. "Come, Benedict, let's sit down; we have only a few minutes at best to talk."

He gestures to the dirty mud floor.

I sit down and he lowers himself next to me. Ezekiel comes around to my other side and does the same. The rest of the people, the ones who haven't walked away, sit down too.

There's another difficult silence. "It's not right," I say, quietly. "What he said about Hoshi. She hated leaving you all behind. She thought about you all the time."

"Hoshi had no choice," Emmanuel says, loud and firm, so that his voice must carry into every cell. "She was brave.

She came so close to destroying Sabatini. She could never have known what would happen to him, what he would turn into."

The hairs on the back of my neck stand on end. "What has happened to him? I still don't really understand."

"Someone paid for his reconstruction and rehabilitation," Emmanuel says. "It was his family, it must have been. You've heard the rumours about them?" I nod. "They gave him a blank cheque, apparently, and he used it to recreate himself. He says he's a Pure now. The guy's deranged. He thinks it's his God-given duty to make as many Dregs suffer as he can. Hoshi could never have predicted what he'd do."

"What did he do?" I whisper, even though I don't think I want to know. There's a lump in my throat and it's hard to swallow.

"After what happened with you and Hoshi, they locked us up. I guess they were trying to decide what to do with us. They chucked bread and water in once a day and left us to rot for months. We didn't know how long we'd be in there for, or if we'd ever get out. Some people couldn't cope; they lost their minds, it was a terrible thing to witness.

"Then one day a few weeks ago, they brought us here, told us the Cirque was reopening, made us start rehearsals straight away. They took anyone who was sick, either in the body or mind, away and brought in a whole load of new people from the streets.

"None of us could believe it when we first saw Sabatini. Even in our wildest nightmares, we could never have imagined the monster he would become. He's worse than he ever was

181

before. You'll need to be on your guard; he seems to have it in for the teenage boys the most – people like you and Sean. It's like he's envious of their strength and their age. He's only been here a month and he's already killed three people. He never used to like getting his hands dirty before but he shot them himself, right in front of us at point-blank range, for no reason at all. And every time – before, during, after – do you know what he did?" His voice shakes with rage and indignation. "He laughed. He was taking a life away and he loved it. I've never seen him so happy. He's power-hungry – addicted to inflicting pain, addicted to killing."

My stomach heaves. If it wasn't empty, I think I'd be sick.

"He's working closely with your mother now; she's made the Cirque her pet project, a way of getting revenge on you and Hoshi, I guess. He says she's told him he can take as many people as he likes from the slums. We think he's been encouraged to keep the turnaround high: the authorities want as many of us dead as possible. We're completely replaceable to them, especially those of us who aren't yet trained in a circus skill."

I feel like a huge cold weight has settled in the pit of my stomach. People have been thrown in prison, people have lost their minds, people have been murdered, because of what we did, because of what my mother is doing.

"I'm so sorry," I say, my words coming out in a whisper. "We never knew this would happen."

"It's not your fault. No matter what anyone says." His words ring out. "It's *their* fault. Silvio's, Vivian Baines's, all the people out there who fund them, who pay to come to places like this. All the people who support the regime."

That was me once. I don't say that, nobody else does either, but I bet they're all thinking it.

Emmanuel carries on talking.

"All of the acts are dark, all of them are violent. They want the circus to pull in even bigger crowds than it did before and they think more bloodshed and death is the way to do it. The new circus is only going to open once a month, so they can replace any performers who die, bring new ones in and start all over again.

"There have been no deaths for two weeks now, not since they announced when opening night would be. Sabatini keeps going on about getting maximum entertainment out of us. They work us like dogs all day and we've had lots of injuries, but he wants to keep the rest of us alive for opening night and then he's going for a high death count, he says. There's going to be a lavish ceremony on opening night. It's all top secret. Not even the performers know what's happening. Your mother's the guest of honour – she's made it part of her election campaign."

"When is that?" I say, the heaviness in my stomach growing by the second.

Before he can answer, a klaxon sounds, so loud that it makes everyone jolt.

Immediately, they all scramble up to their feet.

"Get up," Emmanuel says. "Go. You've got one minute. There's an empty cell at the bottom, I'll show you." Everyone is suddenly dashing past us, pushing past each other urgently. They all run into the little caged rooms and there's the sound of metal doors clanging shut and bolts being pulled across.

Why are they so keen to lock themselves up?

"Take that one," Emmanuel says urgently, pushing me towards a cell. "Get in there. Make sure your door's locked. Quick, before they let them in!" He turns away, sprinting down the suddenly empty corridor to a cell nearby. He dashes into it and slams it shut.

I stand in the doorway, looking into the tiny bare room in front of me.

I don't like enclosed spaces. I don't want to shut myself in. Why can't I just leave it open?

"Quick," the woman opposite me hisses. "Shut your door, before it's too late!"

I swing the door shut, but I don't lock it.

There's a loud clanging sound and an iron gate descends from the ceiling, about two metres from the entrance door, and then another one drops the other end of the corridor, so that we're sandwiched into the middle.

There's a furious scrabbling noise from overhead and then, with a click, the heavy stone back door of the cell swings open and they appear, pushing against the metal gate. Snapping, snarling, frenzied.

The gate rises and they stream down the corridor. I shoot my head back quickly and pull the bolt across.

The corridors are full of animals. An angry, snarling pack of them. That's why everyone stays in their cell so obediently. They rush past along the corridor, snapping at each other's feet and sniffing the ground desperately.

One of them stops right outside my cell. My hands fly back off the bars. It stares at me with cold yellow eyes and bares its sharp teeth. I flinch back.

This is what Emmanuel meant, then. This is how they keep us in check. This is what's cheaper than paying security guards.

Wolves. Dark, lean, mean.

We're being guarded by wolves.

I try to kick, try to fight, but the grip round me is too tight. I'm dragged through the dark alleys and narrow paths. Eventually, we come to a halt, right on the edges of the slums, in the shadows of one of the huge rubbish tips.

The hand over my mouth is sweaty and smelly and foul.

I look up at the bloodshot eyes and cracked skin of the man holding me. His breath on my face is rancid.

There's another man here too: thin and pale and wiry.

"We're early," he says. "Didn't think it'd be that easy, did you?" When he laughs, he has hardly any teeth, just gaping holes in his gums.

"Might as well have a bit of fun while we're waiting," the man holding me says. He pulls me tight against him and wraps his arm across my waist. "She's even better-looking in real life."

I try to wriggle from his grasp. He laughs and holds me even tighter. "I like them feisty."

For a second, the dirty hand over my mouth loosens a little. I bite down hard.

"Damn it!" He snatches it away. "Little bitch bit me!"

The gummy one laughs again and grabs my arm and twists it hard behind my back.

"Help!" I scream as loud as I can. "Help!"

He clamps his hand down over my mouth.

"Shut it! You're going nowhere. You're going to make us our fortune. You're our ticket out of here. Cops are going to give us a nice big pile of cash in return for you!"

He talks to the other one over my head. "Why didn't you get the little girl too? She'd have been easy."

"Opportunity was too good. This one was right at the door. They might have guns for all I know. I don't know what Kadir gave them, do I? Anyway, she's the one they want. She's the only one they were going on about – they didn't even mention the kid."

He's still nursing his hand, looking up and down furtively. "How long do you reckon until they get here?"

"Stop being so twitchy. We've done the hard bit already."

"Can't I have a closer look at the merchandise, then?" He steps closer to me. "The police won't care what state she's in."

"If anyone sees us … if anyone saw us. You heard what Kadir said. He's guaranteed them protection."

"By the time Kadir finds out she's gone, we'll be gone too: long gone. And we'll be rich. Just calm down. The police will be here any minute."

I wait for an opportunity to shout out again, or to get away, but it never comes.

The thin guy's grip on me doesn't loosen for a second.

The other one keeps leering at me, licking his dry lips.

I see the blue lights before them, gliding silently along the street outside and stopping just the other side of the fence.

A car door opens and shuts lightly, and then another one and a searching torchlight spans across us as two police officers duck through the broken fence panel and walk slowly towards us.

They come closer, a male and a female.

"Well done, lads," says the man, his voice low. "Did anyone see you?"

"No. All good," answers the shorter guy. "Vicious little cow bit me though. Hand over the money and you're welcome to her!"

"It's not quite that straightforward," says the woman. "We aren't the ones who give out the reward. You'll have to come to the station for that."

"Come to the station? You never said that." The thin one sounds panicked. "We've risked our lives getting her to you! We need to get out of London before it's too late! Get the girl and we'll get you the money, that's what you said."

"And we will. At the station. Let's just all get in the car and we'll sort it out there."

"I'm not getting in no cop car!" The short one's voice is getting louder.

"Keep it down! You don't have a choice if you want the cash."

"You ain't getting the girl, then," the tall one says.

The male officer laughs and shines his torch over to the woman's gun and then his own.

"I think you'll find we are," he says.

There's a tense silence for a few seconds as they all eyeball each other, and then another, different laugh, loud and hard, from behind, and a figure steps out from behind the rotting heap of rubbish.

The officers swing their beams round, illuminating Kadir.

"Well, well, well. What's going on here then?" He grins, his teeth flashing in the torchlight.

BEN

A lone wolf howls. Others join it, raising their grizzled heads until the air is full with the cries of the pack: an eerie, collective moan that fills your head and makes the hairs on your neck stand on end. After a few minutes, it stops and then they start prowling about again – looking for food, I suppose.

I count fifteen of them. Fifteen huge wolves, pacing up and down. Every now and then there's snarling and snapping as a fight breaks out between them. One of the skirmishes happens just outside my cell and the bars jolt as wolves fling themselves against them.

I bolt backwards and scrunch up in the corner of the room with my hands over my ears. It doesn't stop the sounds though: the cries and the howls and the panting breaths.

From time to time, the wolves stop whatever they're doing and break out into their mournful howls and there's another sound too, a human sound; the sound of someone crying, a loud, hysterical sob.

"Shut up, Maggie!" a voice shouts out. "For God's sake, you're worse than the wolves!"

But Maggie, whoever she is, doesn't stop. The shout only makes her cries louder.

I try to think of nice things, of Hoshiko and the feel of her hand in mine, the softness of her hair, the sound of her voice, but I can't: it's impossible.

In the end, I give up. I crouch there, listening to the wolves, jumping every time one stops outside my door. I don't sleep. No one could sleep through this. I just sit there, huddled in that corner all night. It's the longest night of my life.

HOSHIKO

My eyes flick to each of their faces in turn: the police officers, the kidnappers, they all look equally petrified. All except Kadir, who stands there – smiling, self-assured, in control.

"Who wants to explain?" he asks, softly.

"It's not what it looks like!" blurts the tallest guy, releasing his hold on me.

"I see." Kadir's voice is low and pleasant. "That's good. Because it *looks like* you were about to hand over my guest to these officers. I guaranteed this girl protection; I assured her of her safety in the slums. I informed everyone of this a few short hours ago. It *looks like* you were about to disobey my orders." He takes a step forward and his eyes glint. "It *looks like* you have forgotten whose side you are on."

He takes another step forward.

"Hoshiko, come here, please."

I run over to stand next to him. I still don't like the guy but he's got to be better than these horrid men.

"Not so fast!" The policeman raises his gun, points it at Kadir. After a second, the woman does the same.

Kadir looks at them, his eyes widening in mock horror, and then laughs, a booming, hearty laugh. "What rank are you two? Been in the force long? Didn't think so: you're still a bit green around the edges, still not clear on how the land lies around here."

He raises his hand and clicks his fingers. Out of the darkness, figures appear, encircling us. Thirty, forty, too many to count.

High up on the rubbish tip, more dark figures, looming over us.

190

"These are my slums. Mine. I've put up with a lot from your end lately. Cars driving through, destroying people's houses. Officers banging on doors, upsetting my people. I'm getting a bit fed up with it."

He takes another step towards the officers. Their guns are still raised but they don't look very confident.

"Tell you what, I'm feeling generous. Here's what's going to happen. You turn your backsides round, right now, and slink off back to where you came from. You don't mention your little discovery. You tell your bosses, the boy's mother, anyone who asks, that the girl's not here. You tell them that the next time a police officer sees fit to step into my slums, I will let my people do whatever they like to them."

"You're forgetting something," the policewoman says. She's trying to sound tough, but her voice cracks with nerves. "We're the ones with the guns."

Kadir's head snaps round and the smile is gone as he stares at her through lowered lids.

"You are beginning to irritate me," he says. "Like I said, I guaranteed this girl my protection. One way or another, she will have it, and one way or another, you will be going back to your station. Whether it is intact or in pieces is up to you."

He raises his hand again, clicks his fingers twice more. The ring of figures steps closer, tightening around us.

"I have long had an unspoken arrangement with your seniors: you leave me to get on with things in here, and I will leave you to carry on out there. My people won't riot. My people won't attack, not unless I tell them to. I will keep control, I will maintain order here, just as I have done for many

191

years now. We have been at peace, your side and mine, but it is a fragile peace, a tentative one: and you would be wise not to test it. If my dominion in the slums is challenged, I will have no choice but to react; no choice but to let my people off their leash."

The policeman lowers his gun. The woman glances at him and then does the same.

Kadir smiles. "That's better. Now—" He raises his voice suddenly to a roar. "Get out!"

The police officers both turn tail and run. There's the screech of tyres as the car speeds away.

In the middle of the circle of men, my kidnappers cower.

Kadir stares at them, coldly.

"Kadir—" the thin one begins.

"Don't speak!" he roars again. The big one starts snivelling. I find myself grinning. I can't help it.

"Take these men to my office. I will deal with them shortly," he orders, and holds out an arm to me. "Hoshiko. Let me escort you; your companions are waiting."

After a second, I take his arm and we glide off through the silent streets of the slums.

When we approach his headquarters, he turns to me. "It's been rather an eventful day."

He's waiting for me to say something. I know what he wants, but it's hard to get the words out. He's just saved me, but I still don't like him, still don't trust him, and I don't like being in his debt.

"Thank you," I say after a moment.

He waves a dismissive hand in the air. "Don't mention

it. As I said, you have my protection. All I ask is that you remember, when the time comes, who your friends are," and he doffs his little hat to me. Then he leans closer, anger darkening his face

"Those turncoat fools won't get the chance to challenge my command again, I can promise you that."

BEN

Everything passes, even the longest and darkest of nights. Eventually, even this one reaches an end. The lights come on, glaring and harsh, but I stay huddled up in my corner, wincing at the brightness.

The metal grid near the back rises and there's a rush like a sudden wind as the wolves all turn and run to the back door. I creep to the edge of my cell and peer out cautiously.

A hatch at the top has opened and something is dropping out of it, down to the frenzied pack below, like post falling through a letter box. This isn't paper cascading down on them though. It's meat, bloodied and raw. The sound as they eat is horrible: growling and whimpering and snapping and gnashing and tearing.

In the middle of the pack, the largest wolf of all, a black, shaggy beast, raises its head. A hunk of meat hangs out of its mouth, blood dripping from it on to the scrabbling beasts below. Its cold yellow eyes meet mine for a second and then it tosses back its head and gulps the meat down.

I've always been fascinated by wolves, about the way the packs operate. This one must be the alpha, the dominant male. There'll be an alpha female too and then a hierarchy stretching all the way down.

One of the wolves, a mangy, lean one, pushes its way forward from the back. The others turn on it, snarling, and it scampers back out of the way. Its leg is bleeding and it licks at it forlornly, whimpering to itself. The omega; the weakest member of the group.

It doesn't take long for the meat to disappear, but the animals remain there, sniffing the ground frantically for scraps and licking up the blood that stains the floor.

After a few minutes, the door clicks and swings open. The wolves all turn tail and head out as one. I can hear them running above our heads. Where are they going? I wonder. Presumably they don't just roam around the circus as they wish.

After a minute or two, there's the sound of bolts being pulled back and people start creeping slowly out into the corridors.

It feels unsafe, coming out from the tiny room I've been huddled in. I can see now why everyone entered the cells so willingly.

I thought the stench last night when I arrived was bad, but now it's unbearable. It's an animal odour; the smell of meat and the earthy reek of the wolf droppings spattered everywhere. At one end of the corridor, a girl has an old broom and she's sweeping up, a disgusted look on her face.

Emmanuel steps towards me.

"OK?" he asks simply.

I nod.

"Does that happen every night?"

It's his turn to nod now.

"Every night. They're trying to break us, take away what we are." He scowls. He looks intimidating when he scowls. "We can't let them. We won't let them."

"So what happens now?" I ask.

"Breakfast, if we're lucky, and rehearsals for most of us."

"But I'm not performing. That's what Sabatini said. What will I have to do?"

"Build stuff, clean stuff, set stuff up, I suppose. They'll certainly find a use for you. It's all hands on deck for tomorrow."

"What's happening tomorrow?" I ask.

He looks at me. "What's happening tomorrow? You don't know? Tomorrow's opening night. Tomorrow, the show begins again."

HOSHIKO

In Kadir's waiting area, Greta, Jack and Rosie all sit, anxiously perched on the edges of their chairs.

"Hoshi! Thanks goodness!" Greta nearly knocks me off my feet with the speed and strength with which she throws herself at me. "What happened?"

"Some guys grabbed me when you were all asleep. They were going to hand me over to the police." I glance towards Kadir, silently watching. "Kadir saved me."

He smiles graciously. "Like I said, it was nothing. In fact, I believe Bojo here is the real hero of the day."

He holds a hand out to Bojo, who looks at Greta, seemingly for approval, and then bounds over to him.

"Bojo told us you were missing!" Greta declares proudly. "He woke us up! He was very upset. He kept pointing at the door and covering his mouth with his paws, like he was shocked. That's how we knew something had happened! We ran to Rosie's and she said to come here."

Jack has risen to his feet. He holds his hand out to Kadir. "Thank you," he says, all his previous prickliness gone. "Thank you so much."

"I gave my word," Kadir says. He looks down at Jack's proffered hand. "Please excuse me. I have business to attend to. Ah," he says as the door opens again and some men drag the two kidnappers in. "Right on cue."

He ushers us out and we walk Rosie home and continue onward to our little hut. Nobody says much; I think we're all a bit shell-shocked. All the way back, Greta is yawning, Bojo copying her theatrically every time and, within minutes of our return, the pair of them are asleep, scooched up in my arms. They fall asleep deeply so they don't hear any more sounds that night.

They don't, but we do. My eyes meet Jack's as the dim light of morning begins to break. They stare back at me, grave and anxious, as the dreadful sounds of human pain – sounds of torture, sounds of agony – continue from the direction of Kadir's, echoing across his slums.

After a few minutes, the doors open and guards appear, guns in the air, marching us up the steep concrete stairs and outside to a big barn, old and rickety, at the back of the field. It must have been here for years, long before they decided to build the shiny new Cirque here.

I don't think I've ever been in an actual barn before, but its inside still seems familiar; it's just like every barn I've ever read about or seen on TV. Dimly lit, full of the pungent odour of hay and animals. It's sectioned off into different areas with drinking troughs and mangers, and there's a huge hay loft at the back.

The horses we saw last night are there. One of them, the tallest by far, is the gleaming golden palomino Silvio rides: it whinnies as we come in and tosses its silken mane. Apart from that, everything's pretty much as you'd expect in a barn, if you ignore the camels and the quite literal elephants in the corner of the room. There are two of them: the same ones I saw yesterday, I suppose, squashed up side by side next to each other, big heavy chains wound round their legs. The animals all look up as we enter and then resume their patient munching. There are no lions, I'm more than relieved to see, and no wolves. This must be where the grazing animals are kept overnight. It's like some kind of exotic nativity scene.

The guards herd us together like another group of cattle into the largest pen.

"What's going on?" I ask Ezekiel, who's found his way next to me.

"This is where we eat." He grins up at me delightedly, as

if he's giving good news. "They'll bring the food and water in a minute."

There are hay bales scattered around and people perch on them, staring at the door expectantly.

Eventually, four guards enter, each pair carrying a huge container between them. One is a vat full of water, the other a feeding trough full of an indistinct grey slop. As soon as I see the food, I realize how hungry I am. Everyone else has jumped up and they're already standing in line. The intensity in the air is immense: they're all straining forward desperately.

Still, no one pushes, no one shoves, there's no frenzied clamour, like the wolves. Strength is not what prevails here; fairness is, fairness and goodness. The children are ushered to the front so that the smallest girl is the very first in the queue, and then they arrange themselves in height order, all the way to Emmanuel at the back.

One by one, people come forward, slurp out of the huge container and move away to make room for the next person, moving on to the trough, where they kneel down, scooping handfuls of the gloopy mush into their mouths.

Watching them eat animal food from this dirty manger fills me with shame. Not of them, never of them, but of the appalling, reprehensible place the world has become. How did we ever let things get this bad?

Emmanuel notices me, hovering at the back.

"Ben? Are you not thirsty? Not hungry?"

I'm starving, but it doesn't feel right: me taking food meant for them; me draining their meagre resources.

"Not really, not as much as you guys."

"Nonsense. You are one of us now. Take your place in the line, please." Emmanuel ushers me forward and people part to make way for me. My height places me in the middle of a group of older boys, and I can feel their resistance. It's palpable, prickly and intense, but nobody says anything. Emmanuel's hot glare is stern as he fires them warning looks. Maybe there is a hierarchy at work here after all – he's definitely the alpha wolf in this pack, but he's got where he is by being fair, by earning everyone's respect and because he's the oldest in here, I reckon, although being the strongest probably doesn't do him any harm either.

I glance behind me. Sean is a couple of people back. His hands, bandaged up with thick, dirty-looking wadding, are curled into fists. His eyes drill holes into my back. I'm so close now that I can hear exactly what the whispered insults are that he's aiming at me.

"Pure bastard," he hisses under his breath. "Pure scum."

I stand there with my head bowed. I don't blame him for hating me. Look at how he lives, look at how he's been treated by the Pures, treated by my mother. I'd hate me if I were him – even Hoshi hated me for a while.

There's a commotion at the front, the barn doors swing open and four more guards enter, carrying a table and chairs, which they lower carefully down in the middle of the barn.

The table is wrought iron, ornate and old-fashioned, and it's laid with a starched, white cloth. Another guard comes in, carefully laying down napkins, silverware and glasses.

Judging by the muttering around me, the rest of the Dregs are as confused as I am about what's going on.

A minute passes and then, like a spectre, Silvio Sabatini appears in the doorway, ghastly and ghostly and deadly.

"Ahh," he says, his eyes scanning over us. "The animals are all feeding." His gaze lingers on me and he claps his hands in the air, dramatically. "Baines!" he commands. "Come here, if you please."

I freeze to the spot. What should I do? What does he want?

"Come on, then. Quickly, boy."

The eyes of the whole barn are upon me. I step forward reluctantly.

"How was your night? Eventful, I imagine!" The gleam in his blue eyes sends shivers down my spine. "Do not fear; you, my friend, will not be scoffing away with the other performing animals."

He gestures towards the little table. "Shall we dine? Please, be seated."

I glance over at the others. I can feel the waves of hatred and resentment coming from half of them, and a few looks of sympathy too.

The barn doors swing open again and four people I haven't seen before come in. They've got green overalls on – catering colours – and they're bringing in food. Not animal food this time, but real food, delicious food. The saliva fills my mouth quickly and my stomach aches in response to the aroma of sausages, eggs, bacon, warm bread, fresh fruit, coffee that they place down on the table.

I haven't had food like that since I ran away from home.

I look again towards the performers, all watching silently.

"No, thanks," I say. "I don't want it."

I turn around and make my way back to the queue.

Behind me, I hear Silvio laugh.

"Oh, how wonderful, I've just won a little bet with myself! I predicted your reaction perfectly. *Silvio, my friend*, I said. *Benedict Baines likes to play the people's hero, likes to get down and dirty with the Dregs*. Now, Benedict, as I said yesterday, your little show of loyalty isn't fooling anyone. Let's just step outside and have a chat, shall we?"

He nods at the guards. "Go on," he says. "As instructed."

A guard grabs someone from the line – it's Sean – and drags him out of the barn. At the same time, two more guards step forward and roughly manoeuvre me between them, outside into the field.

After a second or two, Silvio appears in the doorway and taps his way out towards us.

He stands between us, fondling his cane, then furrows his brow, scratching off an imaginary dirt mark. Then he takes out a cloth from his pocket and polishes the cane with it.

Quick as a flash, he steps forward and pushes it into Sean's ribs.

"Stop!" I cry. I launch myself forward, desperate to reach him, but the guards pull me back.

He turns to me, smiling, all the while pushing the cane into Sean.

"Stop! Please, stop! I'll do whatever you want!"

He lowers the cane down. Sean crumples to the floor, clutching his side.

"Ah, now that's what I wanted to hear! I must say, you've hurt my feelings a little, Baines. It was intended as an honour, you know, the invitation to dine with me."

"If I eat with you, you'll stop, right? You'll leave him alone, leave them all alone?" I ask, frantically. Panic and fear jumble up inside me alongside the hunger. I feel nauseous. I think I'd throw up if my stomach had anything in it.

"But of course." He smirks. "For now, at least."

"Fine," I say. "As soon as he gets some help." I try to reach Sean, but the guards pull me back.

"Oh, don't be so sensitive! I want him alive for tomorrow too, you know! Take him to be seen to," he commands, and then ushers me back into the barn.

"Where's he gone?" Emmanuel calls out. "Where's Sean?"

Silvio whirls around and stares at him. "How dare you speak before you're spoken to? The boy's whereabouts are nothing to do with you. I suggest you eat: this is the last opportunity you will get for some time. Benedict, shall we?"

I move quickly forward and sit down on one of the chairs, all the while feeling the group's eyes on me. Sabatini perches on the chair opposite and pours me a glass of freshly squeezed juice.

The glug of the liquid, the clink of the ice cubes and the gentle snorts of the horses are the only sounds in the barn.

"Well, cheers!" He raises his glass. "Now." His smile slips. "*Eat.*"

I stare at the plate of food in front of me.

I can feel everyone watching me.

"You heard me," he says, quietly, and then hisses again. "*Eat.*"

I pick up the heavy knife and fork and cut into the egg. The top of it is still phlegmy, and despite my hunger, my stomach heaves again.

I scrape it from my fork, cutting into the toast instead. I put a piece into my mouth. Chew. Swallow. Cut into the bacon. Chew. Swallow.

Opposite me, Silvio is eating too, smacking his lips joyfully and dabbing his mouth with the napkin after each bite. "Oh my, such fine fare! So delicious, wouldn't you agree?" He smiles gloatingly over at the performers, who have silently resumed their line and, one by one, are kneeling down and scooping handfuls of slop from the trough.

You're one of us, Emmanuel said just now. Well, I'm certainly not that any more, Silvio's made sure of that. This isn't meant to please me: it's meant to set me apart, make sure they never accept me, make them hate me. He's thrusting my status in their faces: forcing them to eat like animals while I sit and dine alongside them. He knows exactly what he's doing.

I can't risk him hurting anyone else. I have to do exactly what he says.

And so we dine. The Dregs from their trough, Silvio and me from our table, laden with food. I keep my head down but I can still the feel eyes in my back, sharp as daggers, as I eat.

Cut. Chew. Swallow.

Cut. Chew. Swallow.

What else can I do?

I jolt upright early in the morning, at the sound of whispered voices just outside.

Jack and Greta sit up too, and we all look at each other apprehensively.

Slowly, slowly, the cardboard is pulled back a millimetre and two little dark eyes stare into mine for an instant before they vanish. A second later, they appear again, and then another pair below them, both staring through the crack.

"It *is* her," a voice whispers. "You speak!"

"No, you speak!" another replies.

We're all grinning bemusedly now. It's only a couple of kids. Thank goodness.

Greta leans forward and puts her face up to the crack and the eyes vanish again.

"They've seen us now anyway!" one of the voices whispers. "You might as well speak."

After a second, the cardboard parts open again, a bit further this time, and a boy and a girl look in at us, their faces curious and cautious all at once. They look the same age as each other, both about eight or nine, I guess. They're obviously brother and sister; they both have the same dark, shiny eyes, the same neat little grins and the same slight, wiry frames.

"You speak!" The girl nudges the boy. He nudges her back.

"No, you!"

This is getting annoying.

"OK, we've all seen you now so you might as well both speak. Who are you?" I ask. "And what do you want?"

They look at each other. Finally, the girl says something. "You're Hoshiko, aren't you? The tightrope walker?"

I nod. "And you know Benedict Baines?" I nod again.

They look at each other.

There's silence for a few seconds and then the girl takes a deep breath and speaks again.

"I'm Nila and this is Nihal. Benedict Baines knows our mum. Her name's Priya, Priya Patel, and we want to know where she is."

For a little man, Silvio certainly has a big appetite. The table is overflowing with delicacies and he works his way methodically through all of them, pausing only every now and then to urge me to: "Eat, boy, eat!"

When every last morsel has gone, he takes a slurp from his little china coffee cup before leaning back and rubbing his protruding belly contentedly.

"What a wonderful feast! Don't you agree? Did you all enjoy your breakfast too?" He calls over to the performers in a sing-song tone. They're clustered together protectively in a circle now, Emmanuel and the other adults on the outside, the children in the middle. Silvio tuts loudly.

"Honestly, it's a nightmare getting conversation out of these people! You'd think they'd be keen to express their gratitude, wouldn't you?" He sighs. "Some people are so hard to please! Right, I'd love to stay here all day, chewing the fat like this, but we really ought to get on with things!" He stands up, indicating to me to do the same. "Showtime tomorrow!" he says loudly. "Lots to do!"

He clicks his fingers, and the green-overalled man and woman come forward, clearing the table while he watches them critically. They seem nervous. I don't blame them. He always did rule in the circus, until my mother came along that is, but now he seems to have even more power than before.

He catches me staring at him and it's as if he can read my mind. He leans forward and speaks to me, so quietly that no one else can hear. "Must be a shock for you, Baines. You thought your girlfriend had killed me, but I have risen up – stronger, more powerful, more determined than ever before to protect my circus from destructive influences. I know what you think. You think you hate me, but you don't even know what hate is, not yet." He lowers his voice even more. "I'll make you hate me. Hate me and fear me. You're going to regret what you did. I'll make sure of it. I have wonderful plans for you." He grins wickedly and whispers in my ear, his hot breath tickling my face.

"Your mother's orders clearly state that you are not to be asked to perform *onstage*. At no point has she forbidden *backstage* assistance."

I move my head away and we eyeball each other for a moment before he pushes back his chair.

"Right. Everyone out. Get on with your allocated tasks. Everyone except the clowns. You stay here."

The performers stand up and begin to silently shuffle out. In the end, only one small cluster of people remains. Leah, and the group of boys, Sean's friends – the ones who clearly hated me even before their mate was dragged away and I sat and ate breakfast with Silvio in front of them. They stand there, staring sullenly at the floor.

"As you all know, there has long been a niggling problem with your little clown act, as entertaining as it promises to be. For some time, I have needed someone to assist with props and –" he pauses "– administer the required effects. Someone backstage, to make sure everything runs smoothly. I have had to rely on an assortment of people who would all be better used elsewhere. Until now, that is. Like an answer to my prayers,

Benedict here has been delivered to me. I'm sure you'll agree that there's something particularly fitting that these specific duties should be performed by someone who was once such an eminent Pure! During this final dress rehearsal I shall be personally on hand throughout, to ensure that Benedict knows exactly what is required of him. Oh my!" He gives a peculiar little leap, clicking his heels together into the air. "This is going to be so much fun!"

My heart plummets at the expectant little faces of Priya's children. What on earth am I supposed to say to them? I'm rubbish at stuff like this. It took me weeks to tell Greta about Amina.

I close my eyes and see Amina's body, swinging up there on the wire, just like I see it every night and every day, sometimes at the strangest of times. Then I see Greta's stricken face when I finally broke it to her. I tried not to go into the details but she wouldn't let it go: she asked question after question until she knew the whole horrific story.

Ben grieved Priya just as much as I grieved for Amina. It took us a long time to even talk about them but when we eventually shared the loss we felt, and the guilt which tore at us both, it brought us closer together than ever. If it wasn't for him, Ben said, Priya wouldn't have been killed and she wouldn't have been punished in such a shocking way. And if it wasn't for me, my Amina would be alive. She died protecting me, protecting Ben.

I hated myself for it, really hated myself, but time and time again, Ben repeated the same words to me:

"Silvio killed Amina. Silvio and the circus, not you." And he said it so often that I started to see that he was right: it wasn't my fault Amina had been killed, it was Silvio's, and Silvio was dead. Whatever happened now, I'd destroyed him and Amina could rest in peace. And time and time again, I told Ben:

"You didn't kill Priya either. It wasn't your fault. It was your mother, your mother and the circus. All you did wrong was care. You saw the truth behind the lies."

It was even harder for him than me, I think. The way he saw Priya at the end, what they did to her, it was unthinkable, unimaginable.

And now her children are here, and they're looking at me and they want to know why their mum hasn't come home.

Ben's spoken about them a lot, although he's never met them. He made a promise to himself, when Priya died, that he'd find them. He told me what Priya used to say about them, how her face used to light up when she spoke about them. He said he wanted to tell them that. He feels responsible for them. He feels he owes them.

And now he's not here, because he's given himself up for me, but they are and they're asking me to tell them where she is and I know that I have to tell them the truth.

Greta and Jack's faces both look grave and pensive, like mine must be. It's not their place to do this though. It's mine: mine alone. I have to do it for Ben.

I take a deep breath. "I've heard so much about you," I say, my voice shaking, just a little. "And there are some things I need to tell you. Let's go for walk, shall we, just the three of us?"

And so we do.

I step out of the shack and we walk down the narrow path and sit on a grassy little mound on the outskirts of the slums and I tell them about their mother. Not the whole truth, not the awful, ghastly way they treated her afterwards but the truth they need to hear. The truth that makes their faces crumple, that makes them cling to each other, cling to me. The truth that makes us all weep. The truth that their mother's never coming back. The truth that she's dead.

BEN

Silvio remains seated at the table while the guards chaperone me, along with Leah and the others, out of the barn, driving us like cattle across the field, through the gate, past dozens of rides and strange buildings towards a huge clown's face, perched on the top of one of the little hills.

As we get closer, I realize it's a building. The red–and–white flashing domed roof I saw in the distance when I first arrived is the clown's pointed hat. His huge face is the front facade, painted and moulded into a grinning painted face. There's a shiny red nose jutting out, and masses of curly red hair, ruffled by the wind, billowing out of the sides. The doorway is cut into the huge white teeth.

As soon as we step on to the little red path that leads up to it, the hurdy-gurdy Cirque music starts up.

I look at the wide, smiling face.

I wish Hoshi was here.

I mean, I don't. Of course, I don't wish she was here. I hope she's a million miles away by now. I hope she's free.

But I wish she was here just for one second, that's all. I think if I could see her right now, I could be brave again. She always made me braver. Being with her made me want to be a good person. She made me better. If I could just see her, hold her, just for a moment, I could draw some strength from her. It's harder to be brave when I don't know where she is, when I don't know what she's doing, don't know if she's safe.

What would she say if she knew I'd just eaten with Silvio Sabatini while her friends slurped food from a cattle trough?

Would she understand why I did it? Would she understand that I couldn't fight? That I had nothing to fight with? That he had hurt someone, that he was going to keep on hurting him unless I did what he wanted? Would she have done the same, in my shoes? Or would she have been stronger than me? Would she have resisted? If she could see me now, would she look at me like Sean did, with that same accusing glare?

After a moment or two, there's a mechanical whirring sound that's already becoming familiar, and Silvio appears on his golf buggy.

He switches it off before stepping down delicately. "Wait outside," he orders the guards, pushing a button on his watch. The clown's mouth opens wider, and he pushes us towards it, prodding at us with his cane.

We step into the grinning jaws, swallowed one by one. I wonder if we'll all make it out, or if some of us will be eaten alive.

After a long time, we stop crying, the three of us, and just sit there silently for a while.

"I knew she was dead anyway," Nihal says. "She'd never have left us. Whatever they did to her, she'd have found a way back to us."

"I don't know if this makes any difference to you," I say. "But Ben loved her too."

"She wasn't his mum though, was she?" Nila answers, fiercely. "She was *our* mum and now she's gone."

"That's not fair," Nihal admonishes his sister. "Mum loved Ben too," he tells me. "She told us all about him, about how he was always kind and respectful to her. She said he had a good soul. She said he gave her hope that one day things will change."

"We wanted to meet him," says Nila. "Mum always said that maybe one day we'd be able to."

"You will. He wants to meet you, too." I smile, but inside I feel cold and frightened. Where is Ben? What's he doing now?

"Do you think Mummy's in heaven?" Nila asks me.

What am I meant to say to that? Should I tell her what I really think: that heaven is just a story we use to try and convince ourselves that there's some meaning in this crappy existence we call life? That even if God does exist, he's doing a pretty damn awful job of things? Isn't it about time he got off his sorry backside and did something to sort out this malfunctioning world he's responsible for creating, instead of sitting up there living the high life on some cloud or whatever it is he's doing?

"Yes," I answer, emphatically. "I think she is. And I think she's very proud of you both."

Nila gives me a sad little smile.

"I hope I get to see her again one day."

"Of course you will," I say with a certainty I don't feel. And then I add something true, something I do believe. "She's not really gone away, you know. She's there all the time: she's a part of you. Close your eyes. Feel your heartbeat."

I show them how. I can feel Amina there, deep inside me where she always is. I can feel her love, feel her goodness. I can't feel Ben. That's good. That means he's alive.

"When we were in the Cirque we used to light candles to remember people," I tell them, my voice wobbling. "We used to celebrate all the goodness they brought into the world. Maybe we could do that for your mum."

"Where will we find a candle?"

"I don't know. I'll try and get one, if you like."

"We'll have to have a funeral," Nihal says, gravely. "Uncle said we should have had one before. He and Auntie have been arguing about it. We could hear them at night, when they thought we were asleep. Uncle said we needed to say a proper goodbye. Auntie said it wasn't right, because Mummy might still be alive somewhere, and having a funeral was like giving up hope." She begins to sob again. "We have to tell her. Our auntie. What will we say?"

"I'll come with you," I say. "We'll tell your aunt together."

"Will you come to the funeral too? And light a candle, like you said?"

My first instinct is panic. I didn't even know Priya. I don't belong at her funeral. How can I grieve for her when I never even met her? It would be false.

Looking down at their little upturned faces though, I know I don't have a choice. Of course I can grieve for her. The tears I've just shed weren't for me, for my life: they were for her, for Priya and her beautiful children. I didn't know her, but they loved her, and Ben loved her. She helped to make Ben good, sweet and kind and brave. She showed him the truth. I need to honour her, to remember who she was; for him, for them, for her.

"Yes. If the rest of your family are OK with it," I say. "Come on, I'll walk you home."

The clown auditorium is big. Not as vast as the Arcadian one, but still larger than the main arena from the old Cirque. Just like everything in this new version: more dramatic, more extravagant, more lavish. They must be expecting big crowds.

It's not lit, but the colours stand out solid and bright, even in such poor light. It's decorated in bold blocks of red, green, blue and yellow, like we've stepped inside a nursery school classroom.

"Go and get changed into your costumes, and tell Minnie I want full make-up!" Sabatini barks at the others, and they all head off up on to the stage and through the wings.

"I shall now explain your new role to you, Benedict. You ought to thank me, you know – there are so many other uses I could have made of you. I could have had you mucking out the animals, dealing with piles of stinking manure all day, or I could have got you involved in manual labour: chopping, building, sweeping. But I am a kind man and I wanted you to feel valued, to feel you that you were making a really important contribution. Even if you cannot be onstage, I have ensured that you will still play a key part in this, one of our biggest and newest acts!"

He leads me to the back of the room, into a little square booth with glass walls overlooking the whole theatre. It's lined with plastic panels, full of levers and buttons and, in the middle, there's a large black object. It looks a bit like a piano; it's a similar size to one, and there's a stool there for someone to sit at. It doesn't have keys though; instead, the top of it is plastic, inlaid with large blue buttons, labelled alphabetically: A, B, C, all the way up to N. I reach a tentative hand forward to the nearest one.

Silvio pushes himself between me and the machine. "Now, now, Benedict, all in good time! Once your co-workers return, all will become clear. All you have to do is sit back, enjoy the show and press one of the buttons every now and again." He hands me a booklet. "There is even a script here for you to use until you get the hang of things. Just follow the prompts: press button A at the appropriate time in the script, follow along again, press button B when instructed to, and so on and so forth."

I look down at the script in my hand, then look at the machine.

A knot of fear twists inside my stomach.

"What do the buttons do?" I ask, nervously.

"You will see, Benedict, you will see."

One by one, the others appear: dark figures on the stage. Silvio presses a button on one of the side panels and they are instantly illuminated. Staring up at us nervously is a group of colourful clowns.

I look down at them, taking in the changes.

There's a court jester, complete with his funny hat and juggling balls.

There's Pierrot, looking a little like Silvio himself with his white costume and painted white face, except for the black skullcap on his head, the little black tears painted on his cheeks and a sad mouth sloping downward.

There's Harlequin in his bright patterned suit.

In the middle is the circus clown from all the posters, the one whose face is painted on the gates, the one we all see when we think of clowns. His face is white, with thick eyebrows painted on and a big artificial red nose and a crazy curled red wig. His shiny shoes are huge, like boats, and he's dressed in bright yellow pantaloons of puffed-out silk, with a red jacket and blue waistcoat and a tie full of different brightly coloured spots. Despite the costume, I can see that it's Sean. His scowl gives it away, evident even beneath that huge red painted-on smile.

He's up and about. Relief floods through me and, for the first time today, my jaw unclenches a little.

Leah is wearing a floral dress, pulled in tightly at the waist, its skirt stretched wide over a hoop beneath so that she looks like a character from the top of a cake. She's got a wig on: blonde plaits, looping up and then straight out at the sides of her head. The make-up she wears, the huge extravagant painted-on eyelashes and round pink spots on her cheeks, makes her look permanently shocked.

The artificial smiles don't do their jobs very well. The last thing this group of people look is jolly. Even from way up here, I can see the fear on their faces.

Silvio's face, on the other hand, is full of malicious excitement. His eyes keep flicking between me, them and the machine with its large blue buttons.

A dozen memories flash into my mind.

Hoshiko, balancing way up high with no safety net. The lions. The twins in the shark tank. Poor Anatol, blasted from a cannon and left to die. Priya.

Panic wells up in my chest.

"I'd like to clean the animals out instead," I blurt out. "Or I could help with the labour, like you said. I'll work really hard. I'll dig, I'll build. I'll do whatever you want. I'm strong; you won't be disappointed."

Sabatini laughs. "Dear Benedict, you really are *too* kind! No, this will be the perfect role for someone with your background." When he turns to face me, the smile drops from his face and the cold hatred in his eyes makes me shiver. "Until I get the chance to finish you off properly, I'll make the most of having you here," he whispers. "You are my pawn, Benedict. I will use you to inflict as much suffering on these Dreg buffoons as I can."

He claps his hands together. "Music!" A boy I hadn't noticed before is sitting down at an organ in the corner of the theatre and he begins to play the trademark Cirque tune, its notes filling the air.

"Right." Silvio's sadistic smile is fixed back on his face. "Let the rehearsal begin!"

HOSHIKO

Nila and Nihal lead me through the winding pathways of the slums to their little shack. A woman outside breaks into a run when she sees us.

"Where have you been?" she cries, grabbing hold of them both tightly. "I've been worried sick!"

"Mum's dead," says Nila bluntly. "She told us."

The woman slumps down to the ground.

"My sister!" she cries. "My baby sister!"

I don't know what to do.

A man comes out of the shack and leans over her.

"Come on," he says gently. "Let's get you inside."

She looks up at me. "How?" she asks. "How?"

"They punished her," I say. "For consorting with a Pure."

She nods, as if I'm confirming what she already thought. "Is it definite? Did he see it?"

I can't say what Ben really saw.

"He saw her afterwards," I say. "He said she looked peaceful."

The woman wails, a terrible, heart-wrenching sound. She grabs hold of Nila and Nihal and they clutch on to her and begin to cry again. The man puts his arms around all of them. He looks at me over their heads and smiles. It's a sad smile, but there's no blame there.

"Thank you," he says. "It's been torture not knowing."

I nod my head and then I turn and walk slowly away.

"Hoshiko, where are you going?" Nila calls, panic in her voice.

"I'll come back," I say. "I promise."

And I give them a tiny wave, leaving them there in their huddle of pain. I need to leave this shattered family to mourn.

BEN

"Assume your positions!" Silvio barks, and the clowns all disperse to the sides of the stage. He pushes me on to the little stool, holding me down, his hands pinching into my shoulders. I shrug his hands off, but I can still feel his touch – like I'll never get rid of it, even if I get the chance to have a proper wash again one day.

"Go on then!" he says to me, impatiently. "I told you: it's easy, just follow the script."

I look down at the leaves of white paper in my hand.

It is a beautiful sunny day, the first page reads, and then, in brackets, there's the letter *A*.

Silvio nudges me hard in the back with his cane.

I look around at him. His thumb is hovering over the torturous little button on top. I take a deep breath, lean forward and tentatively push button A.

A backdrop of patchwork fields descends, seemingly stretching off into the distance. On the floor of the stage, yellow ears of corn spring up from nowhere, swaying softly in a gentle breeze. The hum of electricity has been replaced by the sound of birds singing in the distant trees and, if you concentrate really hard, you can hear the distant engines of farm machinery at work. The air itself seems to have changed: when I breathe in, the gentle air of spring fills my lungs and I inhale the sweet smell of flowers and freshly mown grass. Above, little fluffy clouds slowly drift across a cornflower-blue sky and the golden hue of sunlight gently drapes over everything.

My senses are beguiled. The effect is so real that, for a

moment or two, I forget why we're here. It's like a spell has been cast on me.

It's broken by a sudden movement from the side of the field. Sean, the jolly clown boy, the one who hates me, appears, pedalling on to the stage and trundling down a little winding path in an open-top yellow-and-red bumper car – like an old-fashioned toy car a child might have, but bigger. It's still way too small for him, though, and he's hunched up inside it, his legs looking ridiculous and his oversized shoes hanging over the edge as he pedals furiously.

Leah appears next, skipping merrily across the field, gathering the flowers which have suddenly sprouted out of nowhere. When the clown sees her, he squeezes his nose and there's a loud noise: a *honk-honk* sound. He's so busy staring at her that he pedals his car straight into a tree which has sprung up in his path.

Bang! Crash! The sound of drums signifies the car crashing and it recoils inwardly, springing into a zig-zag shape.

I feel Silvio's cane jabbing me on my shoulder again. "Look at your script!" he hisses.

I glance down. *Augustine sees Columbina*, it reads, *and is so overcome by her beauty that he crashes into a tree: (B.)*

"Oh, for goodness' sake!" Sabatini snarls and reaches over me to press the button. Billowing smoke immediately wafts up from the car, which starts flashing and making loud alarm sounds.

OK, so I'm the special effects guy. Maybe this won't be so bad.

I look up at Silvio; his eyes are bright with anticipation.

This isn't a normal circus, a voice in my head says.

Below me, Sean, or the hapless clown Sean is pretending to be, gets out of his car, awkwardly, and opens the front bonnet, scratching his head in puzzlement. Leah sees what's going on and starts to walk over to him when another figure appears on the stage, precariously riding a unicycle and juggling at the same time: the jester. He sees Leah, gives a loud wolf whistle and drops all his juggling balls in excitement. He jumps down from the unicycle and, out of nowhere, produces a large bunch of flowers. Meanwhile, Leah has walked over to the car and seems to be offering her help. Sean puffs his chest up and puts his hand inside the car's bonnet. For a telling second, he slips out of the role as he glances across the auditorium to Silvio and me. Video screens on either side of the stage close in on his face. His eyes look frantic and there are beads of sweat on his forehead.

I look at my script. *Augustine lifts bonnet: (C)*, it reads.

I stare down at the button labelled C, then turn to Silvio. "What does it do?" I say.

"Oh, for God's sake, man, just push it!" he answers.

My hand wavers above the button.

I walk slowly down the path, heading back the way we came.

The clouds gathering above are darkening by the second and the shadows of the city rise up all around me.

I look up at the PowerHouse, still lit up with our images, and think about all that it is and all that it stands for. That's where Ben's family will live, if Vivian Baines is victorious. Those great glass eyes will be her office windows. I stare into them, imagining her standing there, proudly surveying her domain.

Way over on the other side of the city, I can see the new Cirque.

It's nothing like the old one. The trailers are gone, and so are the warren of aerial tunnels they used to keep us out of the way: the tunnels we escaped through. The old arena's gone too – it must have been irreparable after I blasted a bloody great hole in it.

There must be another arena replacing it now – several, by the looks of it – there are loads of buildings down there, all the colours and shapes you can imagine and a huge Ferris wheel with scores of other fairground rides below it.

For a while, I was stupid enough to think we'd destroyed our enemy, but it's just risen up, even stronger than it was before.

We didn't accomplish anything, not really, Ben and Greta and me. All we did was focus the world's attention on what happened in the Cirque. We turned it into a battleground. If the government allowed a Dreg tightrope walker to blow the place up and destroy it, then we'd won, and that would never do.

It looks like it's ready for its grand unveiling. There's no more scaffolding, no more cranes, no signs at all of any building works going on.

I wonder if Emmanuel's there somewhere, getting ready to perform. I wonder if Ezekiel is. I wonder if they all are.

Poor Rosie. Poor Felix. It must be agonizing for them, knowing their boy, Sean, is in there and being unable to do anything about it. I don't know how they bear it; I don't think I could.

That must be how my family felt when I was taken. How they still feel, maybe – if they're still alive. Miko, my brother, won't remember me at all. He'll be twelve now, nearly a teenager. What do they tell him about me? Maybe they don't tell him anything. Maybe it's too hard to say the words: *You had a big sister but the circus took her away.* Maybe he doesn't know I ever existed. Maybe that's what they do: pretend I was never there at all.

I'll find them, one day, if I live long enough to get out of this city.

I don't know how, though. I don't even know where I'm from; I was too young when they took me away. I know it's somewhere in England, but I don't know if it's north or south, east or west. I don't know anything.

How must they have felt when I was taken? They must have thought that I'd die in that place, like so many others, but they wouldn't have known when, or how. They must have wondered, every night, if it was my last one alive on earth.

Maybe not. Maybe they kept track of me. I was the golden

pin-up girl for a good few years before I blew the place up. Maybe they saw me on the posters. The Cirque could have pitched up in my hometown and I wouldn't even know it.

And if they didn't know then, they must have heard about what happened by now.

It was big news: the biggest, not just locally but nationally – internationally, by all accounts. How do they feel, knowing the little girl who was snatched from them turned out to be a violent criminal, on the run from the police? Maybe they don't tell anyone I'm their daughter. Maybe they're too ashamed.

It's dreadful, not knowing the truth. Always wondering, always searching, for answers which never come.

At least Priya's poor children have some kind of closure now.

No, that's not right. It's worse, much worse for them than it is for me. Before, they had hope, something to cling to. Now, they just have grief and emptiness. Now they have to somehow find the strength to face the cold, hard reality of growing up without her.

Death is the end of all hope.

Tears blur my eyes, threatening to spill over again. I shake them away. I have to be strong. I have to try to focus on the positive.

At least Silvio's not in the Cirque any more. Whoever's running the show now, however depraved they are, they can't be as bad as him.

I won't think about that place.

It's hard not to, though; it's caught up with every memory I have. I feel so angry with myself every time I feel that betraying tug.

My mind is wandering so much that I don't pay much attention to where I'm going. I turn down one of the little bends, the one I thought led to our little cardboard shack, but it's not there.

I try to find my way back to it, but I just get more and more confused, twisting and turning so much that, in the end, I don't even know which direction I'm heading or even which way I came from. This whole slum is a massive labyrinth of tiny clustered dwellings and, after a while, they all look exactly the same.

The clouds above thicken even more and it gets dark really quickly. Groups of people start to appear, gathering together again around the fires. No one speaks to me; they all just stop talking and stare as I walk past them.

They must have heard those cries of pain last night, coming from Kadir's. Those terrible, torturous cries, for hours. And then nothing. A silence that went on and on.

Do they know it was because of me?

A group of children dash past nearly knocking me off my feet and a big rat with gleaming eyes runs across my path.

It starts to rain, a thin drizzle at first, but then falling heavier and heavier. The cold penetrates my thin clothes, penetrates my bones. The groups gathered around the fires quickly disperse back into their tiny homes and I tread the abandoned paths looking for my own people.

Is Ben somewhere in this big sprawling city? Is he dry and warm? Is he safe?

I'm totally disoriented now.

I find myself at the edge of the slums again, near where we

came in yesterday, and where the men took me last night. I walk towards the huge rubbish mound and turn and face inward. I should be able to find my bearings from here.

A noise breaks the silence and a group of dark figures appears, slinking along the fence.

I step back, pressing myself into the shadows of the stinking mound behind me, trying not to think about the rats and the rotting food. I don't really know why, but it becomes suddenly vital that they don't see me. Maybe it's because they look so sinister, so secretive.

They're talking in muffled whispers, but I'm so close I can hear what they're saying.

"So, everyone knows what they've got to do, right? And not a word to anyone else. If this gets out, we'll all be dead."

"I still don't like it," says another one. "We're not ready. There's no point rushing into a place like that unprepared. There'll be way too much security, especially after what happened before. Things will go wrong, they're bound to."

"We have to do it now," the first guy says. "His brother's in there, remember. We promised him. And anyway, we are prepared. Felix has been staking out the place for weeks and Billy's gone tonight to have one final look."

"What if they catch him?"

"They won't. You know how good he is at stuff like this."

There's a pause. "Tomorrow night," says the first guy. "Agreed?"

"Agreed," the others say, and they all give each other a strange little handshake. "The Brotherhood!" they say in unison and then walk off, one by one, in separate directions.

There's something familiar about one of them, even in the darkness. The way his hands are thrust in his pockets, the way his shoulders are slumped. I wait a moment or two and then follow behind him. I walk closer and closer until I'm sure.

"Felix, stop!"

The rain is even heavier now; it flicks from his hood when he spins around. "I heard you," I say. "Back by the rubbish heap. What are you planning?"

He looks blankly at me.

"I don't know what you're talking about. I'm not planning anything."

"Yes, you are." I step towards him. "You're planning a terrorist attack on the Cirque."

BEN

A horrible feeling of foreboding squats deep in the pit of my stomach. I don't know what will happen if I press this button, but I do know it won't be anything good.

Suddenly, Silvio's arm shoots out and he slams my hand down, holding it there from above.

There's a flash and Sean jerks forward. His body jolts and his eyes bulge as he shakes, spasmodically.

I look at Leah's face on the screen. Her eyes flick upwards and she whispers something to herself: a prayer, maybe? And then she puts her arms on Sean's waist. As soon as her hands touch him, the shock travels through her body too and the two of them convulse helplessly on the stage: jerking, jolting, juddering.

They don't look human any more.

I wrench my hand from under Silvio's but it's too late; they just keep shuddering.

My stomach heaves.

Their hands were both bandaged already. They've been through this before, and they'll go through it every night from tomorrow. Every night, until when? Until they die, I suppose. How much electricity can a body take before it just gives up?

Eventually, the jolts stop and they both crash heavily to the floor. I'm not even sure if they're alive.

"Come on, you should be used to it by now!" calls out Silvio. He rolls his eyes at me. "Honestly, it's only a minor shock. These people are so feeble!"

The jester is staring down at their crumpled bodies. His

face on the screens shows pity, grief, horror: a mix of churning emotions.

"Get your act together!" shouts Silvio. "Or you know what the consequences will be! This performance is just not good enough! You should all be seamless by now!"

Leah slowly pulls herself up to a sitting position. The jester steps forward hurriedly and presents her with the bunch of flowers.

She stares up at him in confusion for a moment, but then she seems to pull herself together because she takes the flowers and scrambles to her feet. She's a bit wobbly, but she stays upright and plants a kiss on the supposedly delighted jester.

Sean is still lying on the floor. He hasn't moved.

Is this part of the scene? Is he acting? I hope he's acting.

Seeing him lying there, I remember Anatol, the poor boy they shot from a cannonball and left to die. For the first time, I wonder if it was better for him that he didn't survive that day. He'd still be here otherwise. Here to be tortured at Silvio's whim.

From the wings, a third clown – the Pierrot one dressed all in white – appears. When he sees Leah and the jester together, he rubs his eyes with fisted hands in a crying gesture and the cheery music is replaced by the sad cadences of a single violin. Pierrot goes to the wings, dragging out an object, a giant mousetrap by the looks of it, which he positions carefully on the stage, glancing upwards and placing it directly below a trapdoor in the ceiling.

The jester takes Leah's arm and they walk across the stage while Pierrot looks on, apparently seething with jealousy.

Sean is still lying there.

The happy couple act as if they don't see the huge trap that has been placed in their path, both stepping on to it at the same time. It springs shut hungrily, clamping down around their ankles. Neither one of them is a good enough actor to disguise the fear they feel. Their faces contort, their bodies shrink and their shoulders hunch as they brace themselves for whatever it is I'm about to release from the door directly above their heads.

"Push the button!" Silvio hisses at me. "Push the damn button!" His arm reaches over me again.

The anger burns inside me. Hot, red hot. I push the stool back, push him away, hard, stand up, turn around to face him.

"No," I answer. "There's no way I'm pushing that button, and I'll tell you something else … you're not pushing it either."

"Shut up, you stupid girl!" Felix hisses and turns from me, walking quickly away up the path.

"Stop!" I call. "Tell me what's going on!"

He hurries from me faster. I run after him, tramping through the puddles. "If you don't talk to me, I'll give myself up to the police and tell them everything I just heard!" I raise my voice. "Don't think I won't do it!"

He spins around and glares at me, before taking my arm and pulling me down into one of the little side alleys, glancing around furtively as he does so.

"Keep your bloody voice down! The Brotherhood have been planning this for months, you're not going to come along at the last minute and spoil everything!"

"I've got friends in that place!" I answer angrily. "People I care about! Do you expect me just to nod my head and just let a bunch of terrorists blow them all up?"

He propels me further down the sidewalk.

"The Brotherhood aren't terrorists," he says. "We're freedom fighters!"

"Freedom fighters? You make it sound as if going around murdering people is heroic or something."

He looks at me incredulously. The rain that's streaming down both our faces trickles down my back in cold rivulets.

"Erm, hello? That's what you tried to do, isn't it?" he answers angrily. "You weren't so concerned about anyone else when you threw a grenade into the middle of the circus ring!"

"That's not fair," I say. "There was no one in there. Well, only one person, and he deserved to die!"

Like so many times before, I see Silvio's face, looking up at me, his eyes widening in shock as I threw the grenade that killed him.

Felix looks around anxiously again. "What do you think you were doing when you dropped that bomb? Fighting for freedom, that's what. You inspired us – you did exactly what we all would have done, given the chance. What was the alternative? That you let them keep on treating you like some kind of performing animal? That you let them kill you?" His eyes burn with passion. "Asking nicely for things to be different, waiting for some Pure with a conscience to miraculously gain power and make things a bit better for us, that's not enough. If we want real change, we need to tear things up, blow this world apart. I'd have thought you, of all people, would see that!"

His words are vicious slaps; they make my head reel. Maybe he's right. I *did* blow up the arena and I *did* kill Silvio. And I've never regretted it, not once. So what does that make me? A terrorist, or a freedom fighter? If the cause is justified, if it's important enough, shouldn't you fight with everything you have, even if it means people might get hurt along the way?

And there's the sticking point: *people might get hurt.*

People dying isn't an unfortunate consequence for groups like the Brotherhood; it's their aim. It's their sole purpose.

"Look, no one's going to lose their life," he says, reasonably. "Well, none of the Dregs anyway." He sighs, heavily. "If I tell you what we're doing, will you shut up about it?"

"I'm not sure. Maybe."

"The Brotherhood are storming the Cirque. We're going to seize control of the whole place as soon as it opens. Surely that must please you? We'll get the Dregs out first; liberate every single one of them. It's all been properly planned."

I shake my head. "You'll never do it. The security in there's going to be unbelievable, especially on opening night."

"We will. We know exactly what's going on in there. There's more than one insider providing us with information. And I tell you something else: that's just the start of it. There's a revolution coming. The tables are turning."

My heart is tight in my chest. Of course I'd like to see the Cirque destroyed once and for all, of course I want the Dregs released, but this feels far too dangerous, far too risky.

"Listen," Felix says. "We know the Cirque layout. We know how to get in. We've got guns. We've got bombs. It can't fail. All this crap they keep telling us about how Laura Minton is going to gain power, about how things are going to come to a peaceful end, it's all bullshit. And she knows it too: she ain't as holier than thou as she makes out, I'll tell you that for nothing. We have to seize power, not go to the Pures cap in hand and beg for it!"

There's a silence. I get what he's saying, I can't even begin to argue with it, but it still feels wrong.

"Does Kadir know what you're planning?" I ask.

He laughs, a cold, hard laugh.

"Kadir's a bully and a thug, surely you've worked that out by now, despite my mum's romantic take on it." He looks into my eyes, unblinking and intense. "If he finds out this has leaked, we're all dead, so you'd better keep your mouth shut, you understand?"

After a moment, I nod, reluctantly.

"The only people we're interested in targeting are Pures. You hate the Pures as I much as I do, don't you? You must do after everything they've done to you."

"Not all Pures are evil, you know," I say.

"Yes, they are! Every last one of them. Look at what they stand for. Fight hate with hate, fire with fire. It's the only way."

"That's not true. Jack was a Pure, Ben was a Pure. They aren't evil. They're the bravest people I ever met."

"Once a Pure, always a Pure," he sneers. I picture his face when I asked him to let Jack in, how he refused to shake his hand, how his lip curls with disgust every time he looks at him. "There's plenty of people I know who'd like to tell your Benedict Baines exactly what they think of him, laying his hands on one of our Dreg girls. He should keep to his own kind!"

"That's beyond offensive!" I fume, outraged. "One of *our* Dreg girls? I'm no one's possession! That's the problem, don't you see? We're all people! There are plenty of Pures who don't like the way things are either. We have to try and fix this mess together; it won't work otherwise. Planning attacks like that makes you just as bad as the people you hate!"

"They're going to be at the Cirque, aren't they? They'll all be enjoying the shows. Call that innocent? The Pures killed my dad and they've taken my brother. I don't even know if he's still alive." His voice cracks. "You know what? I hope we kill every last one of them: men, women, children, all of them! For every Pure that dies that's one less of them polluting the planet."

He turns around, his back to me. He's so angry. I know that

anger. I've felt it all my life, even more since they killed Amina. It's love, that's what causes it. Love and fear. He's heartbroken and grieving. Just a lost and frightened boy who wants his brother to be safe.

What would I do, in Felix's shoes? What if it was Greta in there? Or Ben? What lengths would I go to, to try and get them out?

Any lengths, that's what. I'd put my own life on the line in an instant. I'd destroy anyone who stood in my way to protect the people I love. It's awful, thinking of that place reopening, wondering if Emmanuel, Ezekiel, all my friends are in there, getting ready to perform. Knowing that if not, they're probably already dead.

I reach out a tentative hand, rest it gently on his shoulder. He shakes it off angrily and whirls around to face me.

"Get your hands off me!" but then he slumps forward, lurching towards me.

I catch him in my arms. "I just want my brother back," he says, his voice smaller: plaintive, like a child's. "I just want him safe." He clings on to me and his whole body judders with the force of his great wracking sobs.

Eventually, he stills in my arms. Pulling away from me, he wipes his face with his sleeves, leaving dirty smudges in the tear marks. When he looks at me again, all the sadness, all the vulnerability has gone.

"The best thing you can do is stay out of things," he says, the tough guy mask firmly back in place. "Keep your head down, forget what you heard. There's a plan. It's a good one. It's an important one. It has absolutely nothing to do with you. The only people who are going to get hurt in that circus are Pures, that's all you need to know. You of all people should approve of it, and I'll tell you something else: we'll do anything to succeed, anything, and that includes getting rid of anyone who might try and stand in our way!"

He regards me coldly. "Time to make your mind up, Circus Girl. Whose side are you on? Ours, or theirs? There's only one answer, isn't there?" and then he turns and sprints away.

Silvio steadies himself, looking down incredulously at his chest where I've just shoved him. I glare at him, maintaining my position between him and the machine.

I haven't let myself look at him directly for long before. Now I can't stop staring at him. His face doesn't appear to be made of flesh at all any more. It's plastic, I think, or plaster, a smooth alabaster finish somehow stretched over his skull. That's why it's so white.

"I beg your pardon?" When he speaks, only his mouth moves; the rest of him remains static.

"I said: no one's pushing that button."

He moves his hand around me, feeling for the button. I shift on my feet and block him.

He raises up his cane, waggling it in my face.

"You sure you want to persist with this little stand-off, Baines?"

"You're not allowed to hurt me," I say. "I heard what my mother said."

"Wrong. I'm not allowed to leave visible scarring. She hasn't forbidden punishment at all. In fact, she's actively encouraged it. There are several settings on this little cane of mine. I can make my mark on you mentally instead of physically, if I so wish."

I take a step backwards.

"Are you frightened?" he says, quietly. "You should be."

He slams the door of the booth shut, taking a step towards me. "You can't get out of here unless you know the combination."

I look across the arena at the performers, all frozen in place, staring up at us nervously.

All except Sean.

"That boy needs help!" I tell him, urgently.

Silvio reaches his arm forward. I move back, but I'm wedged into the corner now and it's only about two foot by two foot in here.

I dodge to the left and he darts towards me again, holding his cane in front of him like he's jousting. We dance around the booth before he finally makes contact.

It's not a burn I feel, or even an electric shock; it's a jab. The prick of a needle.

Suddenly, pain in my head, like it's being crushed by a vice. I try to move, but I'm rooted to the spot. It's as if I've turned into a statue. I can't move my head, can't move my mouth, can't even blink my eyes. The only part of me that's still animated is my heart: pounding, pounding, pounding.

I think I might die. I want to die.

Silvio grabs hold of me and manoeuvres me to face down over the stage. Whatever's about to happen, he's going to make me watch. I try to look away, but even my eyeballs are frozen into position.

"I hate you, Benedict Baines," he whispers into my ear. "I've never hated anyone like I hate you and Hoshiko."

He wrenches up my head and lifts up my limp arm, swinging my hand round towards the button. I will every inch of my strength to resist, but it's no use.

He slams my hand down on the button.

I wish I could close my eyes.

Four ropes tumble out of the trapdoor, swinging just above the clowns' heads. The Pierrot clown steps forward and ties each of their hands to a rope, looping it around. There's no need for the teardrops painted on his face now, because he's actually crying, the make-up on his face streaked and ghastly, as he weeps on the stage.

He's only young. Younger than me by quite a few years, I reckon. He should be in school now, getting an education, preparing for life. He should have the world in his hands.

What have they done to him in here? What have they done that makes him step forward and tie his friends up like that? Was it worse than this?

They've hurt him, that's for sure. Threatened those he loves, maybe worse. That's what they did to us: took Priya away, mutilating her to teach me a lesson. Strung Amina up in the arena because they knew she meant more to Hoshiko than anything. They take your love, take your loyalty, and use it against you. They turn it into a weakness.

Violins begin to play, the bows saw backwards and forwards, screeching and screaming discordantly.

The ropes jerk up and down in time with the ear-splitting music, flinging the boy and girl up and down like rag dolls. Quicker and quicker, higher and higher, splaying their bodies out way up high and then throwing them down to the ground as they drop again and again and again.

They don't look like people any more at all.

Behind me, pressed up far too close, Silvio gives a slow hand clap.

When the jerking eventually stops, the boy and girl drop down to the floor. They lie there, still.

Silvio leans over me to call down to them.

"OK. A bit tame, maybe, but it's a start. Tonight's show will be different, of course." He turns to me. "Tonight, the front row will all be given the opportunity to pick from a lucky dip. There'll be firecrackers in there, air rifles, that kind of thing. We've even added some bona fide rotten tomatoes, just to ham up the slapstick element. The audience can pretty much throw whatever they like at them while they jerk on the rope."

He sighs, regretfully. "There is one problem, of course. It might not be the most cost-efficient idea I've ever had; we're going to get through an awful lot of Dregs in this act! Like you said, it already looks as if one of our clown friends down there has tooted his last horn, and this is only the first scene – there's so much more to come! Oh well, it's all in the name of entertainment, I suppose, and it's not as if there's a shortage of resources in this city. They keep on breeding like flies down there in the slums!"

I try to speak but my mouth won't open; my jaw is locked shut.

"Now, Baines," he admonishes me. "You have disappointed me. I can't trust you as much as I thought. This role obviously holds far too much responsibility for you. It looks like we'll have to find something else to do with you. Hmm, what would be appropriate? Oh, don't worry." He pats my head. "I'll think of something. I *do* love a challenge!"

He's destroyed me.

I've only been here a day and he's won already.

I've found my bearings again and I tread my cold and sodden way back to the little hut where Rosie, Jack and Greta are all waiting outside. Greta hurls herself into my arms.

"We were so worried. You were gone ages. Where were you?"

"Thank goodness!" Rosie cries, her lovely face crinkled with relief.

What good would it do to tell her about Felix? It's not as if she's going to be able to change his mind – he's absolutely committed to his cause – and it would just make her worry even more.

"I got lost," I tell them. "I walked Nila and Nihal home and I couldn't find my way back. This place is a maze."

"We were about to send out a search party," Rosie says. "All three of us were in a terrible panic. We thought you'd been kidnapped again. I was just about to go to Kadir. Speaking of Kadir, it's lucky you're back in time; he wants to see you and Greta."

My heart leaps. Maybe he has news on Ben. "Did he say why?"

"No. He just said he only wanted you two and that there's someone he wants you to meet. Oh yes, and please bring Bojo."

My stomach loops the loop. Someone he wants us to meet. Rosie said Kadir could get things done. Maybe he's rescued Ben from wherever he's been and brought him here.

"Let's go!" I say. "Come on, quick!" And I dash out of the hut, Greta and Bojo trailing along behind me so slowly that it's excruciating. I tug on Greta's hand, yanking her along behind me.

"Hoshi!" she yelps. "You're going to pull my arm off!"

"Well, move faster, then! Please!"

As we pass Rosie's neat little shack, we both look in to see if Felix is in there. He is. Greta waves at him, but he just glowers at us through the tiny window.

At Kadir's, we're ushered straight in, right past his men, to his office/throne room, where he's sitting majestically on his chair. He stands up when he sees us, casting his arms out warmly.

"Welcome, my friends!" He beams. "I'm ready to cash in the favour you owe me sooner than I thought."

Raising his hand, he clicks his fingers in that over-the-top authoritative way that's already becoming familiar and one of his men immediately appears.

"Please bring a seat in for the young ladies," Kadir says. The guy returns with two chairs and Kadir signals to us to sit down. "We'll need two more," he tells the man. "And a table. For our meeting."

"Meeting with who?" I ask. I can't breathe properly. It must be Ben.

He smiles, enigmatically. "All will become clear shortly."

He turns his attention to Bojo. "I'm so glad you brought along my new friend!" he croons, and reaches into one of the pockets of his long robes. He whips his hand out, brandishing a banana.

Greta gives a theatrical gasp.

"You got him one!"

He laughs and holds the fruit out enticingly to Bojo, who leaps immediately on to his lap and snatches hold of it. Peeling it with his tiny hands, he looks just like a little wizened old man, the banana puffing out his cute monkey chops as they chomp up and down.

The door opens and another one of Kadir's guys enters: Sven, the man from last night. He ushers in a group of people; four men, all dressed in black, surrounding a figure entirely concealed by a large dark cloak. I stare at it. It can't be Ben; he'd have said something by now.

One of the men steps forward. "We need to body search you, for weapons," he says brusquely, and they pull us up and begin roughly patting us down. I try and wriggle away from the invasive hands.

"What are you doing? Get off!"

Next to me, Greta is attempting to squirm out of the grasp of the man searching her, too, but they just ignore us, continuing with their mechanical search. Thankfully, it only takes a minute to ascertain that we aren't concealing anything under the thin rags we're wearing.

The man searching Kadir takes longer. He pauses as he pats down his robes, and his eyes widen in alarm. Kadir throws his head back and roars with laughter at the man's shocked expression.

"Is that a banana in my pocket, or am I just pleased to see you!" The man doesn't laugh. He reaches into the folds of the gown and pulls out another banana. Kadir laughs even more.

Despite myself, I smile, and the figure, who's been silent so far, throws back her hood and joins in with Kadir, a hearty, throaty laugh. Bojo jumps out of Kadir's arms and snatches the banana from the man, running with it to the corner of the room and watching us all furtively. The woman laughs even more loudly.

Long auburn hair, tanned face, a determined thrust to the jaw.

Laura Minton. What's she doing here?

She steps towards us, smiling delightedly, and seizes both my hands, clasping them warmly in hers.

"Hoshiko," she smiles, and then turns to Greta. "Greta! I'm so very pleased to meet you both!"

She turns towards Kadir and he sweeps down low into a dramatic bow.

"Hoshiko, Greta, I'd like you to meet our next Prime Minister!" he declares.

BEN

Silvio's watch beeps suddenly. When he glances down at it, his eyes widen and his jaw slackens, stretching the taut plastic of his white face even more.

"Your mother is here, again. She wants to see us immediately."

He starts firmly slapping my face on both sides.

"Come on, Benedict, shake it off. I only gave you a mild dose, just enough to scare you. It should be wearing off by now."

Despite what he said earlier about her encouraging punishment, he doesn't want my mother seeing me like this. Is he right to be nervous? What will she say? Will she care? She might do. She's a control freak, and I'm her possession, not his.

I feel a tingle in my fingers. I wriggle my toes. Swallow.

As quickly as it seized hold of me, the drug has worn off.

I try to stay frozen, just to keep Silvio panicking, but when he prises my eyes open with his fingers and leans forward, staring at my pupils, I feel his hot, rancid breath on my face and I can't do it. Pushing him away, I take a step backwards.

He gasps with relief.

"Good boy! You're back with us. I knew I'd issued just the right amount!" He smirks. "Any more and it might have been a different story, of course. I could kill you, you know, any time I liked, with just a few prods of this cane. Not just yet though, we'll play our little game a bit longer. I expect that's why your mother's here; she's probably after an update. I've promised her I will quickly make you see sense. What do you think?" He takes his cane out and twirls it between his hands. "Have you had enough of your little holiday at the circus yet?"

The doors fling open unceremoniously, and there she is, my mother, and she's got company. Two familiar faces flank either side of her.

"How delightful!" Silvio croons. "A family reunion!"

Kadir's men bring in a table and chairs and the four of us sit down. After a moment, one of the men returns with tea and biscuits. Real, proper biscuits. On a plate. I can't help myself, I snatch one and cram it into my mouth. It's not even stale.

I catch Laura looking at me.

"Sorry," I mumble.

She smiles.

"Nonsense. You knock yourself out, girl."

Next to me, Greta, munching away happily, is actually sighing with pleasure.

I take another one, prising out one of the chocolate chips which nestle in it with my teeth. It melts on my tongue. Then I stuff the whole biscuit in my mouth and crunch it up.

Once the second one's finished, I feel a little more in control.

I look at Laura and Kadir, warily. They both smile. They're both so friendly. They're the good guys, aren't they? So why do I feel so vulnerable? Why do I feel like they're hawks, circling above Greta and me, delicious little field mice they're about to pounce on and devour?

"Greta?" Kadir smiles down at her, paternally. "Wasn't there something you asked for?"

She gasps, clasping her hands together.

"Chocolate cake?"

"That was it. Chocolate cake. Now, let me think … did I manage to find some chocolate cake?"

Whenever Kadir speaks, I can't help staring at his jewelled tooth. It doesn't sparkle when it's away from the candlelight; it just looks like it's rotten, or has a big lump of food stuck to it. It's only when you look closely that you see it's not something decaying, but a pretentious, oversized gemstone.

He claps his hands and Sven appears. In his hand, a plate, and on the plate, a huge chocolate cake, thick with fudgy icing. There are candles in it. Seven of them.

Greta gasps again. She looks like she could burst with excitement.

"Ah, that's right, I did!" Never in all my life have I heard a more condescending tone of voice than Kadir's right now. "Here it is! And what's this I see? It has candles on it! Seven candles! Now, who around here is seven?"

"Me!" Greta says, then looks suddenly downcast. "But it's not my birthday." Her little lips pout. "We don't know when my birthday is. I forgot the date."

"Well then, today's as good a day as any! Have you ever had a birthday cake, Greta?"

She shakes her head, gazing at the cake with shining eyes.

They're all grinning at her. Kadir, Laura, even the usually sinister men in the corner.

I look at her face again. She's spellbound. Completely transfixed by the cake.

Tears sting my eyes and I feel my lip tremble. I've never seen her this happy, so I don't know why I suddenly want to cry.

Kadir reaches forward and lights the candles.

"What do I do now?"

"What do you do? You blow them out, of course! Remember to make a wish first! You'll need a different one now; I made this one come true already!"

Greta opens her mouth wide, takes a deep breath and then closes it, puffing out her cheeks.

"Stop!" Laura Minton says, suddenly. "Haven't you forgotten something, Kadir?" She rolls her eyes at Greta. "I don't know, these men, useless, the lot of them! We have to sing 'Happy Birthday', of course! Come on everyone, join in! *Happy birthday to you, Happy birthday—*"

She breaks off. "Don't make me sing it on my own!" she berates us, and then begins singing again. This time, Kadir joins her and, under his scrutinizing glare, even the men in the corner mumble the words half-heartedly.

I catch Greta's eye, then smile at her and mime along, bobbing my head to the rhythm.

When we finish, Greta screws her eyes shut tight and blows out all the candles at once. Laura claps her hands. "First time! That means your wish will definitely come true!"

"Will it really?" Greta asks.

"Oh, for sure! And now we get to eat the cake! I expect you'd like the first piece?"

Greta nods excitedly. Then she hesitates and smiles at me, coyly. "Hoshi can have it."

"Oh, what a delightful child! So well mannered! Tell you what, Hoshiko can cut you both a piece, how about that?"

The whole room looks at me expectantly, even Bojo.

There's a knife on the edge of the plate. I've never cut a birthday cake before – I've never even seen one. I lift the knife and plunge it down into the thick icing, slicing off a great slab of moist, gooey cake. All things considered, I think I do a fairly good job.

I hand it carefully to Greta, who gazes down at it with love.

"Aren't you having a piece?" she asks me.

"I will in a second. You enjoy yours. I just want to talk to these guys a minute."

She looks at me with questioning eyes and, when I nod my approval, she sinks her teeth into the cake, smiling at me with a big chocolatey grin as she eats, her lips and cheeks already covered with brown smudges.

Laura and Kadir watch her fondly for a moment and then look at each other in some kind of silent exchange, and then at me.

"OK," I say, my eyes flitting between them. "Who's going to tell me what this is all about?"

BEN

I suppose I ought to feel something, seeing Father and Francis after so long, but I don't. I feel nothing at all.

Silvio claps his hands at the performers on the stage. "Leave!" he orders, and they move out, carrying Sean's inert body awkwardly between them. I still haven't seen him move.

"We require a progress report," demands my mother. She glares at me, coldly. "According to your father, I've been too harsh on you."

My father's eyes are full of tears and he's shaking. He looks smaller than before. He looks like a weak old man.

"What have they done to you?" he says.

I lock eyes with him. I don't blink.

"Not much. Put me in a prison cell patrolled by wolves, forced me to electrocute innocent people, drugged me when I refused to, just the usual. Nothing as bad as the boy they've just dragged offstage. I think he might be dead, in case you were interested." I smack my forehead with my open palm. "Silly me. He's just a Dreg. Why would you be concerned about him?"

My father turns to my mother. "I told you. I told you Sabatini would take it too far." He glares at Silvio.

My eyes turn to Francis. He hasn't changed. He's still wearing the same smirk he had when I saw him last, the exact same smirk that was on his face when I confronted him about Priya.

He's the reason they found out I'd been talking to her. Because of him, they hauled her out of the house and murdered her. Because of him, they turned her into a circus exhibit.

Uncontrollable rage seizes hold of me. I grab him by the scruff of his neck and push him backwards. The shock on his face pleases me. I pull back my fist.

Before I can make contact, the guards intercept. It takes two of them to pull me away.

I think even my mother is shocked; her face has turned a little paler than usual and her nostrils have flared angrily.

"Benedict! Has your time with the Dregs turned you into an animal?" she gasps.

My father steps forward. He puts his hand on my arm. I look down at it, resting there.

"Come home, son," he says. "Let's start again. Please, just come home."

"Come home?" I spit the words out. "I don't have a home with you, a home with *her*."

I turn to my mother. "I don't care what you do to me, don't you see that? You can be as nice or as nasty as you like – it doesn't make any difference! I'll never be your little boy again, never! I'll never be a part of you, a part of what you are. You don't care about me! You don't even know me! You just want a cardboard cut-out, someone who'll stand there next to you to boost your stupid election campaign. Someone who'll help you get back that wholesome family image you spent so long cultivating. Well, you know what? I hope you lose. I pray to God you lose! Tell you what, why don't I send Laura Minton my DNA? Find out exactly what it is you're so keen to hide!"

Her eyes seethe with hatred. When she looks at me now, it's the same way she looks at Silvio, the same way she looks at any Dreg. I repulse her. I revolt her.

"I told you. I told you it was necessary," she says to my father. "Do you see now? What he is, what he has become?"

My father's eyes are still fixed on me, like he can't tear them away.

"There must be another way!" He's pleading, not with her though, with me. "What can we do? What can we do to make you come home?"

What does he want from me?

I know what the others want. They're easy to read.

My mother wants to bend me, curb me to her will – that's all she's ever wanted – and Francis, standing there, that smile lingering on the edges of his mouth, I know exactly what he wants.

That's the funny thing about me and Francis: we've always been so different to each other. We've never got on, never been close. I hate him for what he did to Priya, hate him for everything he is. I hate him as much as I hate my mother, as much as I hate Silvio: I hate him more than anyone … and yet … I know him better than I know anyone too. Better than I know Hoshi, even.

Hoshi fascinates me, captivates me, intrigues me, but can I always read her emotions? Can I predict how she's going to react in any given situation? No. Hoshi's way too complex, way too complicated. I don't think I could ever really say I *know* her, even if I was to spend a thousand years trying. Not like I know this little weasel, smirking at me. I've always known exactly what's going on in his head, always been able to figure out what motivates him, what pleases him.

He catches my eye and his smile curves wider. He's happy.

I'm doing exactly what he wants. He wants me to be the rebel. He doesn't want me back in the fold. He likes being the golden child.

I turn back to my father. He's the only one I can't read. He's always been softer than the others, more pliable. Maybe that's why he and my mother work together. She's told him what to do, how to behave, what to think, and he's been happy to oblige.

Now, though, his expression is all his own; it doesn't reflect either of theirs. He's not looking at me in frustration and rage like my mother, or glee, like Francis. He looks bereft, broken.

What can we do? he says. Does he really want to know? Does he care enough to listen? I tried once before, to talk to him. He told me to stop being romantic. He told me not to cause any scandals for my mother. He told me to be a good boy and behave myself.

Positioning my body away from the others, I move closer to him. The tears welling in his eyes spill over. He's crying. I've never seen him cry before.

For the first time, I feel something other than coldness and anger. I don't know what it is. It isn't love.

"I'm never coming home," I say to him, quietly. "But you could listen to my reasons why, that would be a start. You could hear what I have to say. You never know, I might even tell you something that makes you change your mind about things."

He just stares at me, the tears spilling down his face. Then he nods, sadly.

"Oh, for God's sake, Roger, don't let him manipulate you like that!" my mother tells him, crossly.

She turns to Silvio, hovering uncertainly in the corner.

"Ringmaster," she says. "Have him. No strings attached; call it a gift. We're done with him."

Silvio's face lights up like a Christmas tree.

"You mean I can do whatever I like with him?" He licks his lips. "You mean I can use him in the shows?"

My mother glares at me. I glare back. My heart is pounding with fear, but I'll never let her see.

"What I mean is what I say. Do what you want. Parade him in the shows, hang him from the rafters right now, whatever you like. He's nothing to us. Our son is dead. I never want to hear him spoken of again."

She turns and walks away, turning back at the door. My father and Francis remain where they are, looking from her to me; even Francis looks uncertain.

"Well, let's get out of this godforsaken place, shall we?" she calls to them. It's a command, posed as a question.

Francis turns and scurries after her.

My eyes meet my father's once more.

"Roger!" she barks, impatiently. He reaches out a hand, rests it on my hair for a moment. "Goodbye, Benedict," he whispers to me. "I wish it didn't have to be this way." And then he turns away, scampering obediently over to my mother and Francis, waiting by the exit, and the three of them leave. I watch them go, but none of them, not even my father, look round.

Laura Minton smiles at me.

"Tell me, Hoshiko, how much do you know about the current political situation?"

"I know you're taking on Vivian Baines," I answer. "I know they say things will be different under you, that you're going to change things if you win, change things for the better."

"That's right. I am and I will. It's not going to be easy; this country has been segregated for a long, long time. We've been patient, but the time is now."

"So, what have Greta and I got to do with it?"

She laughs. "Smart girl, this one. Gets straight to the point, doesn't she? Well, Hoshiko, we're hoping you'll agree to help us. Kadir tells me you saw the showdown last night, on TV?"

I nod. "Vivian Baines was faking it. Ben would never go back to her, never."

"Oh yes, she was faking it, I have no doubt about that. But why would she bother? Why would she go to so much trouble to attempt to convince the world that Ben's back in the fold?"

"Because she's a control freak. Because she's a bitch."

She laughs, dryly. "Well, I won't disagree with you there. But it's also because she knows how important you and Ben are together. You're notorious, you two – many people see you as inspirational, as heroes. You blew up the circus, and then escaped from it." She smiles at me. "*You* ran off with the Dreg Control Minister's son, the very woman who wants to be the next Prime Minister. You can't get more radical than that.

You're a very important figure; I don't think you realize the influence you could wield."

"So what do you want me and Greta to do?"

"I want to interview you, use it for the finale of my campaign. I want you to give insiders' perspectives of the Cirque. It's about to reopen, did you know?"

I nod again.

"Baines has made it a central part of her agenda," she continues. "She's gone from publicly condemning it to promoting it. She's put a lot of her money into its revamp. The opening night marks the official climax of her election campaign. Do you know why?"

I shake my head. "No, not really. Ben said she always used to go on about how it was an extravagant waste of money."

"Well. She's changed her story now. She's desperate, that's why: making it bigger and better than before is the only way she can come up with of drawing a line under what happened with you and Benedict. It's her way of demonstrating to the world that you didn't achieve anything, that the Pure and Dreg divide is as entrenched as it ever was. She's wrong, of course. It won't work, not if we don't let it."

She leans forward, her voice earnest. "I'll be honest with you, Hoshiko, this election is too close to call at the moment. I have my staunch supporters; Baines has hers. It's the ones who are sitting on the fence we need to win over. The ones who know, deep down, that change is necessary and right but are afraid of it nevertheless.

"The circus has become a key symbol in this election. Vivian Baines wants to use the publicity surrounding opening

262

night to her advantage. She's going to make it her victory parade, a visible symbol of Pure dominance over Dregs. We need to take that away from her. If we can knock her off the hot spot; if we can storm the networks instead with footage of you girls talking about your experiences, spelling out just how horrific circus life is, I think we can bring the waverers onside."

She places her hands over mine again, leaning in even more closely. "This needs to be hard-hitting. Real, emotional, powerful stuff. You're famous, Hoshiko. You're famous and you're beautiful and you beat them! You made it out of there. *You* can steal her thunder. *You* can steal the show. People will follow where you lead. If you stand beside me, we can win over all of those people who might stick with Baines just because they're afraid of change, just because they're afraid of the brave new world we can bring!"

She's good, this woman, better than Baines, even: I can see why she's managed to get so far. Her words are rousing. They make me feel hopeful for the future. There's still something about this whole situation that doesn't feel right, though. Kadir's chair is pushed right up to hers. The two of them so close together, as thick as thieves: the Pure politician and the slumlord.

"What *is* the alternative?" I ask her. "What exactly are you going to do if you win, and what's *he* got to do with it?"

"Kadir and I are allies," she answers immediately. "Isn't that right, Kadir?"

Kadir nods, silently, his eyes never leaving my face.

"If things go our way, the country is going to be in turmoil for a while," Laura Minton says. "We need change, God knows we do, but we also need order to prevail. We can't just let things descend into chaos, can't let anarchy take hold. The Dregs have been oppressed for so long, they will need careful managing if they're granted their freedom. Changing the infrastructure, building the housing we need, the schools we need, is going to take years, decades even. Kadir understands that, but not everyone does. I will need him on hand to govern things when I take control, to keep the slums calm, to stop people getting hysterical."

She says it with gentle authority. She speaks like she's a benevolent angel, and she is, compared to Vivian Baines, but I don't like the way she says *when I take control*. I don't like anyone having too much power. It scares me.

"So Kadir's going to work for you, is that what you're saying?"

Kadir frowns at me.

"I don't work for anyone. We'll be a team, working together for the good of the country." He turns to her. "I'm going to be an important part of the cabinet, right? I'm going to be given a title?"

She nods. "Oh yes. You're vital to me," she purrs. She turns to me again. "Kadir and I are on the same side. We're on your side and we just need this one thing from you. What do you say?"

I look at Greta. She's nodding at me and grinning as she licks her fingers.

"Look," I say. "I'm already the most wanted criminal in the country. If I speak on film, the people who hate me now are going to hate me even more, and Greta too. I'd love to help, but I can't put us in any more danger than we already are, I just can't."

There's a heavy silence and then Kadir speaks, quietly.

"May I remind you," he says, "that we had a deal. I've guaranteed you safe asylum in my slums. I've protected you from kidnappers, set myself in direct opposition to the police for you. I've given you food, I've given you lodgings. I thought we were friends."

My slums. Both of these people are hungry for power, and power-hungry people are always a threat.

There's a long silence.

"Think about it," he says. "Where would you be now, without my support?"

"So, you're blackmailing me now?" I say to him. "If I don't do it, you'll take away your protection. You'll turn us in, that's what you're saying, isn't it?"

"No. No, I'm not saying that, of course I'm not. I'm just pointing out that I thought we were friends. Friends look after each other; friends help each other. I've helped you, now it's your turn to help me."

I look back at Greta. She's quietly helped herself to another piece of cake and is feeding little bits to Bojo. I don't think she's even listening.

I look at Laura Minton. Why am I so wary of her? I must be mad.

She wants Dreg equality, she says. She wants to build houses. She wants to build schools. She wants to do all of the things I've never even really let myself dream of.

The alternative to Laura Minton is Vivian Baines. Vivian

Baines, who I can't believe, even now, is related to Ben. Cruel, vile Vivian Baines who sees us as vermin, who wants to finish us all off for good.

"Do you know what?" I say. "We'll do it. We'll do it because we hate Vivian Baines and we hate the government and we hate the Cirque and because it's about time people know what it's really like in there."

"You're doing the right thing," Laura says. She turns to Kadir. "I'll make the necessary arrangements." Throwing the hood over her head, she stands up and, flanked by her guards, she sweeps out of the room.

BEN

Apparently, Silvio has important places to be, so he doesn't get to exercise any of his horrid little fantasies on me, for now at least.

"I'll put my thinking cap on." He smiles at me. "Think of something really special for you."

For the rest of the day, the guards throw me into the dormitory cells. There's no one else in there: everybody's rehearsing for the show.

All I can think about is Sean, lying there motionless on the floor. I don't even know whether he's still alive.

I tread the corridors so many times that I'm surprised my feet don't wear a path out on the floor, and I keep trying the door, even though I already know it's locked from the outside.

Lifting my arm up, I push my hand through the flap the meat for the wolves came through, feeling for a bolt on the other side, but there's nothing. The rough metal scratches at my wrist and, when I pull it back through, it's grazed and bloody. I look at the blood suspiciously. It's very dark – it doesn't look fresh. I don't think it's all mine; it must come from that meat they pushed through.

What kind of meat is it? I remember what I saw that night, in the Cirque butchery, I remember what Hoshi said about the Recycling Room – that Silvio told her they don't like to waste anything – and I shudder.

There are two buckets in the corner. I choose the cleaner-looking one of the pair and slosh the murky liquid over my arms, scrubbing and scrubbing at them until the dark smears are gone.

I feel weak with hunger.

If no one comes soon, I think I may actually go crazy.

Eventually, the door opens.

It's the performers. They all look solemn. I scan their faces, hurriedly, looking for Sean's.

It's not there.

Leah and the other clowns are at the back of the group. I push through the others to get to them.

"Where's Sean?" I say. "He's not—?"

Leah shakes her head. "He's OK."

I lean against the wall. "Thank goodness."

There are smears on her face where the make-up hasn't been removed properly and her eyes are pitted and dark.

"Thank goodness? You really think so? It been like that every day for weeks. First the motorbike, then the electric shocks. He's not dead, but I expect he wishes he was. What's there to look forward to, for Sean, for any of us? It'll be worse when we open. Way worse."

"Where is he?"

"He'll be here soon. They're treating him. It's lucky Silvio wants him kept alive, I guess."

"I'm sorry. I wanted to stop him. I didn't know what to do."

"It's not your fault," she answers. "You were brave today." She smiles, forlornly. "Brave and stupid."

The rest of the boys from the clown show nod their agreement.

"You tried," says the boy who was dressed as Pierrot. "Didn't do us any good, but you still tried. We know that."

He thrusts out his hand.

"I'm Ravi." He gestures to the others. "Sorry we weren't exactly welcoming before."

"It's fine," I answer. "I'd hate me if I was you."

Emmanuel comes forward. He hands me a crust of dry bread, and several of the others pass me small items of food too: an oatcake, a slither of cheese, even an apple.

"We figured they hadn't fed you." He smiles. "We smuggled out what we could."

I look down at the food. They've been in this circus for weeks, for years, some of them. They've never been fed properly in their whole lives. They watched me, just this morning, eating a cooked breakfast with Silvio while they were given pigs' swill, and yet they've brought me food. Me, Benedict Baines.

"Thank you," I say. "It was really good of you to think of me, but I'm not hungry."

"Nonsense. We have had our fill. We'll be offended if you refuse it." I search Emmanuel's face. "I mean it. They fed us well tonight. They want us strong for the shows. You'd better eat it quickly though: if the wolves smell it, they'll go crazy."

My blood runs cold. I'd actually forgotten about the wolves. Unbelievable, I know, but I'd been too busy thinking about what happened in the rehearsal and all the stuff with my family and worrying about Hoshi, Greta and Jack to spare them any thought.

Not again. Not another night like last night, trembling alone in the corner.

The second the alarm sounds, everyone quickly scurries away to their tiny cells. I run to mine, shut the door, shoot the bolt across.

I start to think about the nature of wolves.

I've watched TV programmes on them and read a lot about them online. I got a book once too, out of the school library, full of glossy pictures and interesting facts. Something about them has always fascinated me. I think it's their contradictory nature: the way they seem so wild and unrestrained but actually depend for their survival on an accepted social hierarchy.

Wolves are pack animals. They rarely fight amongst each other, not to the death, anyway. They share food. They don't attack humans, not unless they're desperate or provoked, or unless the human is alone and vulnerable: young or visibly weak.

They don't attack humans unless they're desperate or provoked.

These wolves aren't desperate. They're fed well every morning, far better than we are, if last night is anything to go by.

An idea comes to me, a very risky, very stupid idea.

I stand up, walk to the door, pull the bolt back.

I slam the bolt back across. What am I thinking of? I lean my head against the bars, staring out into the corridor.

I remember reading some stuff on an American website about how to avoid a wolf attack. *Stand your ground. Don't run away. Don't scream.* That's what it said.

What would happen if I stood my ground? Would they attack me? Would they kill me? Would they leave me alone? I'm not visibly weak, even after all this time on the run. Not yet.

I hate the thought of spending another night hunched up in a corner, listening to them prowling outside. I've always been claustrophobic but the last year or so it's got worse. When Amina and Jack hid me in a prop box at the circus, my heart hammered in my chest so hard that I thought it would burst.

They were big, though, those wolves, all of them were big, especially that alpha, with its shaggy black coat and staring yellow eyes.

Who am I kidding?

I'm not the kind of boy who stands up to wolves. What would be the point, anyway? I'd just get myself killed for no reason. I tried to stand up to Silvio before, and look where that got me.

I check the bolts are tightly pulled across and slink back to my corner.

After a few minutes, the door to the cells opens.

There's a pounding above and the wolves all rush down the stairs to hurl themselves at the iron gate. Even though I'm waiting for it, it still makes me jump, still makes the hairs on my arms stand on end.

The gate lifts up and they tumble through and stream down the corridor just like they did yesterday.

I don't look. I crouch down, cover my head with my arms, put my hands over my ears.

It doesn't work though.

I can still hear them, yapping and snarling, still hear Maggie's cries as they start up again. Still smell them. Still feel them as they rush past, sniffing for blood.

Once Laura's gone, Kadir steps towards me, placing a hand on my shoulder.

"You've made the right choice," he says. "She's an amazing woman, Laura Minton. She's going to do amazing things."

"I hope you're right." I look at him. "You'll still do what you said, won't you? You'll still see if you can find out about Ben?"

He smacks his palm into his forehead. "Silly old me! I almost forgot about that! I *have* found out where he is!"

I clutch hold of the table to steady myself. How could he forget something like that?

"Is he OK?"

Kadir winces and tilts his hand back and forth in front of him. "Hmm, yes and no, I suppose. He's having quite a difficult time of it from what I understand."

"What do you mean, a difficult time? Where is he?"

"There's no easy way of saying this ... he's in the circus."

My heard jerks up.

"He's what? What do you mean?"

"His mother had him put in there to teach him a lesson, show him how bad life as a Dreg can get. She's desperate for him to show public repentance, apparently. She needs the PR. Like Laura said, her campaign's in trouble and the Cirque's at the heart of it."

This can't be real. This must be a joke. I have the strangest desire to laugh. Of all the news I'd been steeling myself to hear, this wasn't it.

"What are they making him do?" I cry. "They're not making him perform, are they?"

He's silent for a second, and then he answers. "I believe they intend to, on opening night. I believe Vivian Baines has told Silvio Sabatini they can."

My heart stops beating.

"Silvio Sabatini? Silvio Sabatini's dead. I killed him."

He shakes his head.

"I'm afraid not. He survived, apparently, against the odds. He's making his first public appearance on opening night."

I feel like I'm under water; everything around me is whooshing away from me.

All this time, I thought he was dead.

We were running from the police, running from Ben's mother, but I still felt safer than before, just from knowing that *he* couldn't hurt *us* any more.

I spent years in that circus, living under Silvio's all-seeing eye. Years, keeping my head down, desperately hoping the next one on his hit list wouldn't be me, wouldn't be any of us.

Silvio or the Cirque: what was the bigger evil? It's interchangeable: Silvio Sabatini was the Cirque and the Cirque was Silvio Sabatini. Both had the same swagger, the same strange charisma – something within them that made you draw your breath, that fascinated you, despite yourself. Both were just veils of glitter and sparkle and lights thinly draped over a dark, cavernous black hole of inexhaustible evil and cruelty.

There's no one on this planet who loved to hurt people as much as Silvio Sabatini did. And now this man's standing in front of me and he's telling me he's alive.

He's alive and he's in the Cirque and he's got Ben.

"You have to get Ben out of there!" My voice is high and hysterical. "Silvio will kill him! You have to save him!" I grab hold of Kadir and shake him.

Greta rushes over. She's been playing some kind of tag game around the room with Bojo.

"What's going on?" she demands.

"Ben's in the Cirque," I wail, "and Silvio's in there, too. He's alive!" Her jaw drops open and she bursts straight into tears, clutching at me.

"Please," I beg Kadir. "Please get Ben out! Before the show starts, before tonight!"

He casts his hands up helplessly. "How can I? The place is a fortress!"

"You must be able to. You said it yourself: you know things, you know people. There must be something you can do!"

"You're right. There are things I can do. Plans to deal with the circus are already in place. The best thing you can do is concentrate on making the film."

I stare at him, incredulously. "You've just told me that Ben's in the circus. You've just told me that the devil is still alive and he's in there with him and you want me to make a *film*? You know what? Go to hell. Until you get Ben out of that circus, I'm not saying a word to any camera and that, *friend*, is a promise."

Grabbing hold of Greta, I run from the room.

Once we're outside, I keep running through the tiny streets, pulling her along next to me.

"Hoshi?" she says, tugging at me. "Hoshi, stop!"

But I can't stop. Chemicals rush through my body, a surge

of rage and fear. The adrenaline sweeps me along. Where to, I don't know.

"Stop, Hoshi!" Greta screams. "I'm frightened!"

This halts me in my tracks. I crouch down low and I grab hold of her and I squeeze her tight.

"I'm frightened too," I tell her. "I'm more frightened than I've ever been in my life."

BEN

I don't know how much time passes. Half an hour, maybe, three hours, eight: it's impossible to tell.

Then, something that didn't happen yesterday. A beeping sound from the far end of the corridor. Cautiously, I peep out. The food hatch at the far end opens. The wolves rush towards it, crushing each other and leaping up with frenzied yelps. No food appears though.

Instead, the furthest gate slams down suddenly, trapping the wolves in the space at the end.

They turn, as one, and hurl themselves at the gate. The sound is unbearable as they bark frantically. They're so strong that I think the gate will fall as they pound against it, but it holds fast.

At the other end, behind the opposite gate, a figure emerges from the darkness.

It edges down the stairs, sweeping the area with a gun, then calls up behind it.

"All clear."

Another figure appears. The light above it flicks on. Silvio stands there, a ghastly white spectre at the top of the stairs. He claps his hand and a guard behind him moves forward, dragging a third person with him.

It's Sean. His face is bruised, but he's standing upright and he's conscious.

Silvio starts talking, but I can't hear him over the frenzied wolves.

He turns around, steps back to grab something, then steps

forward again. He's holding a megaphone, one of those really old-fashioned ones – a circus prop, I guess. He puts it up to his mouth and his voice, tinny and echoing, just about carries over the wolves' howls.

"Can you all hear me? I do hope so. I'd hate you to miss out on the details. This boy here, I have been advised, will not be fit to perform tomorrow night. He is evidently not made of as strong a mettle as is required to succeed in the Cirque. He is weak. He is, quite frankly, pathetic! He's only been electrocuted a few times, only been injured on a handful of occasions, and yet his body is, apparently, unfit for purpose and he will not be able to adequately fulfil his duties. My dear ladies and gentlemen, I'm sure you will agree, this simply will not do! We cannot have folk like this weakening our little circus family! If I cannot rely on this boy on opening night, of all times, what use is he to me? Luckily for me, this is not a problem I need to lose sleep over. Fate has given me a contingency plan; a convenient replacement for this useless piece of junk."

He kicks at Sean, whose head slumps forward.

"Baines! Baines! Where are you?"

He lowers the megaphone and leans forward, scanning the cells. I pull my head back.

"Very well, you wish to remain hidden. I can't say I blame you. Being the focus of my attention rarely does anybody in here much good! Well, Baines, wherever you are, the good news is that you will take this boy's place tomorrow night. You're very fortunate, he has several starring roles on the cards. The fact that you are untrained and unskilled will only serve to make things more interesting!"

He grabs hold of Sean with one hand, thrusting him forward towards the edge of the steps.

"This boy has failed us! He has let us all down! We no longer have use of him. I hope the wolves are hungry!"

There's a scream, and the sound of crying and begging rises above the wolves' yelps.

Silvio lifts the megaphone away so that we can all see the leering grin on his plastic face, before raising it back.

"Ah, come on now! Where's your sense of charity? Surely you would not begrudge your lupine guards a treat?"

He pushes Sean forward and he tumbles down the stairs, landing in the space between the first gate and the stairwell.

At the other end of the corridor, the wolves hurl themselves against the gate even more ferociously. The last time I saw animals this desperate it was the lions, back in the old Cirque.

They were being tormented by human bait, too.

At the top of the stairs, Silvio raises the megaphone once more. His loud, booming ringmaster voice rises above the prisoners' screams and tears, above the wolves' yelps and howls, rises above everything.

"Ladies and gentlemen, it's feeding time!"

Dragging Greta along, I run back to the shack and, muddled and hysterical, we tell Jack and Rosie what we've just heard. Both their eyes widen in shock as we talk.

"I knew I should haven't let Ben give himself up like that!" says Jack, angrily. "I should have known his mother would want retribution!"

His words make me feel even worse.

"It's all our fault!" I cry. "He gave himself up for us! Oh my God!" I clutch Jack, desperately. "Kadir said they're using him tomorrow, in the shows! We have to do something!"

His face mirrors my own panicked thoughts. "What can we do? We don't have any bargaining tools. We don't have any power."

"Laura Minton must have power! She wants me to do a video about the circus, to support her campaign. I'm not doing it unless they get Ben out!"

Rosie's eyes widen further.

"Laura Minton was here, in the slums?" she asks. "You spoke to her?"

"Yeah, I spoke to her. I told her I'd do it, but I'm not going to now. Not until Ben's out of that place! That's what I said to Kadir."

Rosie looks even more worried than before. "Laura Minton and Kadir aren't the sort of people you deliver ultimatums to, Hoshi. Laura Minton might be the leader of the country soon, and Kadir's … well, Kadir's Kadir. You can't just tell them what to do!"

"I'm not afraid of them!" I answer, ferociously. "They'll

have to find a way to break Ben out of there if they want me to do anything!"

She winces. "When I said Kadir was a good man, I meant it, sort of. He's good to his friends. He's good to the people who respect his position, the people he commands. But he's tough too, Hoshi – really tough on people who cross him." She steps away from Greta and turns towards me, lowering her voice. "You must have heard those sounds last night. He was torturing those men, Hoshiko, for daring to cross him. They'll be long dead by now. You need to be careful."

"What's he going to do? Give us up? I don't give a damn if he gives us up! Let's turn ourselves in right now! They might let Ben go if we do!"

"Why would they let him go?" Jack runs his fingers through his hair. "I told Ben I'd look after you two. What do you think Ben would want you to do, Hoshi? He'd want you to stay safe. That's what he wants more than anything. You know that!"

"Well, that's just rubbish. That's just you two – you and Ben with your sexist macho crap!"

His head jerks back like I've hit him. I don't care though. "I'm sorry, Jack, but it's true! Greta and I are both tougher than Ben and you. We've seen things you couldn't even imagine in your worst nightmares! We'd be far better off in there than Ben is! Ben's soft. He's soft and gentle and all the things I'm not. They'll destroy him in there!"

"Hoshi?" Greta pulls at my arm. "It's OK. They won't hurt Ben, I promise!" She smiles up at me. "When I blew out the candles, I wished for him to be safe. I wished that we'd all be together again. Laura said it would come true!"

Her little face is so eager to make everything all right. She thinks she's solved all our problems. God, I love her so much. I reach down and sweep her into my arms.

"I think it's going to take a bit more than blowing out a few candles to save him, Greta," I sob. My eyes seek out Jack's over her shoulder.

"Silvio's alive. Did you know that?"

The colour drains from his face. I've told him a lot about Silvio.

"No way. How did he survive that blast?"

"Because he's not human, that's why, like I told you all along!"

There's a shocked silence.

There were always rumours flying around at the Cirque about Silvio. Where did he come from? How did he have such power in the Cirque when, at the end of the day, he was just a Dreg, like the rest of us?

People said his mother was a Pure; a rich girl who fell in love with a Dreg. They said she died and his grandparents had her lover – the father of Silvio, her child – killed.

The family were very important, far too high up to ever publicly acknowledge who he was, but they didn't totally turn their backs on him. The whole time he was in the Cirque, somebody, somewhere was pulling the strings, giving him control of the place; letting him do whatever he liked to the rest of us.

Maybe they're the reason he survived. Maybe they've lovingly nursed him back to health. Maybe not. Maybe I was just right all along and he's the devil.

The devil's supposed to be immortal, isn't he?

Suddenly, the cardboard door of the shack is ripped away and five of Kadir's men burst in. Not Sven, but some of the others. One of them grabs hold of Greta, wrenching her from me and pulling her roughly out of the door.

She struggles with him but it's no use: he's a great big man and she's a tiny girl.

"Get off her!" I scream. "Get away from her!" but another of the men has grabbed me, twisting my arms behind my back. Two of the others are restraining Jack and another one has a rough hold of Rosie.

"Stop!" My voice is hoarse. "Let her go! Stop!"

Jack's struggling, Rosie's struggling, I'm struggling. We all are, but it's no use.

I flail around in the rough arms which hold me, all the while my eyes on the window, watching helplessly as the big man throws the little girl with white hair over his shoulder and carries her off into the darkness. Watching helplessly as he takes my Greta away from me.

BEN

Sean is still slumped on the floor, leaning against the entrance gate. As it slowly rises, he tips forward into the main corridor.

At the other end of the short corridor, the wolves are smashing against the insubstantial gate which is all that's separating them from Sean. It hasn't started to lift yet.

Sean's alone out there. Alone and bleeding.

Wolves rarely attack unless a person is visibly alone and vulnerable.

Before I can change my mind again, I pull back the bolt and step out of my cell.

I stand in front of Sean in the middle of the corridor, bracing myself. Facing the wolves.

"What are you doing?" someone hisses, and then a chorus of frantic voices calls to me. "Get in! The gate's going to open at any minute!"

I look to the left. Leah's clinging on to the bars of her cell.

"You can't stop them!" she cries. "They'll kill you!"

"Well, something's got to," I answer. I'd probably sound quite tough if my voice wasn't shaking so much. "And I'd rather it was them than Silvio Sabatini! Anyway, wolves rarely attack people." I glance back at Sean, lying on the floor listlessly. "Not unless they're vulnerable."

Leah's eyes cut from me to Emmanuel, in the cell opposite her. She raises her hands up in a questioning gesture. Even over the wolves, I can hear my heart thudding in my chest. After a moment, Emmanuel nods, curtly.

Simultaneously, they stride out from their cells. The three of us stand shoulder to shoulder, blocking the wolves' path to Sean.

Leah's eyes meet mine. "Strength in numbers, right?"

She's right. They're less likely to attack if there are more of us standing here, fronting them.

And so we wait. Wait for the gate to raise. Wait for the wolves.

I feel a little stronger than before, now there are three of us.

"Don't panic." I raise my voice so they can hear me over the desperate wolves. "Don't show fear. Stand your ground."

There's the sound of another lock being pulled across. It's Ravi, his face set with grim determination. Then another lock pulls back and another person joins us. Then another, and another.

I feel a little hand in mine; Ezekiel has worked his way between me and Emmanuel.

Emmanuel looks down at him. "No," he says. "All kids back in the cells. Anyone over thirteen can stay."

Ezekiel frowns and folds his arms together, crossly.

"No," Emmanuel repeats.

"What if we go to the back, near Sean?" Ezekiel says. "They won't be able to get us but they'll see that there's more of us then."

He's bright, this boy, bright and brave.

Emmanuel looks down at him, sternly. After a few seconds, he nods. "OK. Kids to the back."

"This is madness! You're all mad!" A woman starts crying from inside one of the cells, a loud, hysterical wail. I recognize the sound from last night.

"Maggie, stay in the cell if you like, but for God's sake stop making that bloody noise!" Leah hisses. "Didn't you hear what he said? Don't show fear!"

There's a few loud, heaving intakes of breath from Maggie and then blissful silence. Finally, out of her cell, she appears: Maggie, the last one of us. A frail, emaciated-looking woman. She's probably not much older than twenty, but she looks it. Her face is full of lines, taut and skeletal, her thin neck is scrawny and her skin hangs from her arms in drooping folds. She's shaking and she gives a loud gasp now and then, but she's out of her cell. She stands near the back, but she faces forward.

I close my eyes for a second. Vivid pictures flash in my mind: snapping jaws, lunging paws, teeth sinking into flesh.

I push the thought away. This will work. This has to work.

When the second gate begins to rise, not one Dreg remains in their cell. The wolves lunge towards us. A streaming, rolling mass of fur.

"Stand your ground," I repeat. "Don't show fear."

They stop short. They stare at us. Their hackles rise and they strain forward.

We face each other, one pack to another.

HOSHIKO

Once Greta's disappeared, the men drag me, kicking and screaming, along the winding paths of the slums to Kadir's.

There he is, sitting on his throne in the flickering candlelight. Bojo's already settled comfortably on his lap, munching away contentedly on another banana. Fickle bloody monkey.

"What have you done?" I scream. "Where is she?"

He smiles, patronizingly. "Calm down, there's really no need for all these theatrics. She's safe. For now."

"What do you mean, for now? Where have you taken her? *Why* have you taken her?"

"Stop. Breathe. How about you gather yourself together for a moment and listen to what I have to say?" he asks, in the same irritating tone. "Do you think you can do that?"

I glare at him. "Where is she?"

"When you are prepared to listen with composure, then I will talk to you."

I concentrate on breathing, in and out.

"Now, are you feeling a bit calmer?"

I nod, frantically.

"Please—" He gestures towards the chairs, still in the middle of the room from our meeting. I step forward and perch impatiently on the end of one of the chairs.

"Do you know how old I was when I seized control of these slums?" he says, quietly. "Seventeen. How did a seventeen-year-old kid come from nothing to rule over the whole place? I saw an opportunity, that's how. An opportunity to fill a vacuum, and that's what I did.

"My parents were weak: weak and downtrodden – born victims. They just accepted whatever life threw at them, like pretty much everyone you see out there. I was the youngest of six brothers, still might be, who knows? Maybe some of them are dead by now, maybe they've spawned a few more. They never had time for me, any of them. My brothers used me as a punchbag, day after day after day. What did my parents do? I hear you ask. What protection did my doting mother and father offer me? None, that's what. They didn't even notice, or didn't even care – I'm not sure which. I was a nuisance to them, that's all, just another mouth to feed.

"As soon as I could, I hit the road. Left the shitty little slum I came from and made my way here, to the biggest, shittiest slum of them all. They used to say the streets of London were paved with gold, did you know that?"

I stare at him, willing him to stop talking, willing him to get to the bit where he tells me where Greta is.

"There was no gold here when I arrived, though, just mountains and mountains of rubbish, gangs fighting on them like dogs.

"There was a *need*, you understand, a *need* for leadership. A *need* for guidance. A *need* for regulation.

"What made me any different, you might wonder, from everyone else? I'll tell you, shall I? Determination, that's all. Determination and strength. Not physical strength, mental strength. I'm strong..." He taps his temple with one hand. "Strong in here. I see what needs to be done and I do it. I don't beat around the bush, don't arse about first, I get things done. I came, I saw and I conquered."

I'm going to burst in a minute but I know if I interrupt him, he'll drag this out even more.

"Now, as you know, I have been very generous to you and your friends. I have provided you with a home, with nourishment, guaranteed you protection in the slums and put my own neck on the line to ensure you get it. I have actively defended you from harm. I asked only one thing of you, Hoshiko, one little thing, and you have refused to do it. Does that seem fair to you?"

"I didn't refuse! I said I'd do it as soon as you got Ben out!"

His brow furrows. "You were not in the position to attempt negotiations or make demands. You were indebted to us, and besides, you should have been as keen as I am to help Ms Minton out."

I can't be quiet any more.

"Where's Greta?"

"Do you know what, Hoshiko, something about you reminds me of myself. You've got balls, more balls than most men I've met in my life." He pauses. It's the longest pause of my life. "Greta is being held, somewhere not far from here. As soon as you deliver what I have asked, she will be released without further harm."

"Without further harm? What do you mean? What have you done to her?"

"I am not a cruel man, despite what people will tell you. I never use violence for the sake of it and I do not seek trouble out. Hoshiko, this doesn't have to be difficult. You make the film. You get Greta back. I promise you, she will be free the moment you produce something suitably impactful and, unlike you, *I* don't go back on my promises."

"I told you: get Ben out of the circus and I'll do anything you ask!"

"There you go again. You told me. *You* told *me*. You still don't seem to understand! *I* control things around here. *Me*, not you. *I* tell *you* what to do. With all due respect, your boyfriend really is not my problem, and there's a lot more at stake here than him. He'll be fine anyway; I'm sure his mother is behind the scenes somewhere, protecting him from afar."

Maybe he's right. Ben's mother won't let Silvio actually harm him in there, will she? But if I make that video, how am I ever going to get him out? I'll have no leverage at all then and, despite what Rosie seems to think, this man is never going to help me just out of the goodness of his heart. Everything he's done so far has been a calculated gamble – so I'm in his debt and he can get something in return.

Even after all the things he's seen, even after all the things I've told him, Ben's still never really been able to comprehend what it is to live in an institution like the Cirque. Nobody could. Not unless they've lived it, day in, day out. Not unless they've felt the continual anguish of looking around at their friends and family every night and wondering which of them is going to be the next one to die a horrific death. Not unless they've feared that death but found themselves craving it too – knowing it's the only hope they ever have of getting out of there – the only means of sweet relief there is. Not unless they've been dressed up, paraded out there and forced to smile and shine for an audience who'd love to see them fall.

Even if they don't physically hurt Ben, he won't cope in there. His heart is too big for that place; all he has inside him is compassion. It will break him, being in there.

I have to get him out.

But Greta's my baby sister. She's always been my baby sister.

"You shouldn't have to think this hard about it, Hoshiko. I'm running out of patience."

"What if I refuse to make the film until you return Greta to me?"

Kadir's voice is soft but his mouth has a cruel curve to it and his eyes are as sharp as needles as he carefully and slowly enunciates every word. "Then you are more foolish than I thought."

Last night, this man had two men tortured and killed for defying his orders, and today he's kidnapped my little Greta. What will he do to her if I don't follow his exact commands?

"Just tell me what you want me to do and when," I say. "Whatever it is, I'll do it."

He nods. "That's more like it. Now, you just keep being sensible and nobody needs to get hurt. It's late now; nothing else is going to happen tonight. Let's both get a good night's sleep and I'll be in touch in the morning. Make sure you're up bright and early – Laura Minton is keen to get this done."

A good night's sleep. Does he actually think that's possible?

"Can't Greta come back with me now?" I ask. "Please. I've learnt my lesson. I promise, I'll do what you and Laura want anyway."

He laughs. "Nice try. Don't look so worried; Greta's my insurance policy, that's all. You keep being sensible like this and I won't have to hurt her at all."

I've never had murderous thoughts before, not even for Silvio, but I'm having them now: graphic, violent ones. I can't stay in the same room with this man any more.

"I'll be waiting," I say as I turn and leave. And I repeat what I said before. "I'll do anything you want as long as you don't hurt Greta."

Once I'm outside, I lean against a wall, taking deep breaths.

The two people I love more than anybody else in the world are in danger and hurting and alone, and it's all my fault. It's all because of me. I'm going to lose them. I'm going to lose Ben and Greta. It's like Amina all over again.

And then I stop trying to hold it all in and I drop down on the path and I clutch my stomach and I cry and I cry and I cry.

BEN

The wolves' yellow eyes are narrowed and the hair on all of their necks has risen up. Their lips are curled back, revealing sharp, fanged teeth, and there's a collective sound emanating from them – a low, rumbling growl.

They draw back on their haunches. Ready to spring, ready to attack.

I remember something else from the website.

"Wave your arms in the air," I instruct the others. "Jump up and down. Make yourself look as big as possible. Take up as much space and make as much noise as you can."

I raise my hands up, clapping them together up high, like I'm about to break into song. I start making strange, guttural animal sounds, deep, like a gorilla. I feel like an idiot, but I keep doing it.

The wolves' staring eyes swivel towards me as one. I'm not imagining it; they definitely appear a little less aggressive and poised to leap now. They look a little uncertain, a little puzzled, if it's possible for wolves to look puzzled.

Emmanuel mimics my war dance. He manages to look intimidating, rather than just insane, as he makes the same deep noises and smacks his hands together in the air. After a few seconds, the others all join us.

We roar and wail and cry and jump up and down. We pound our fists, pound our feet. I stop feeling ridiculous. I feel powerful.

And that's how it goes for a few minutes. Our pack, facing the wolves.

We are a unit. We are strong.

Suddenly, as if their minds are connected, as if they are in agreement somehow, the wolves simultaneously drop their aggressive stance and disperse out of their attack formation, sniffing around nonchalantly where they are. A few of them sit back on their haunches and slowly wash themselves, and some of them wander back in the other direction.

It's as if they're trying to stay cool, to save face; as if they don't want to admit what just happened. The noise we're making slowly dies away as everyone stops shouting and punching and clapping.

We lower our arms down. We look around at each other.

The biggest wolf of all breaks out of his position and edges forward. He slumps towards Emmanuel, Leah and me in the front line. I hold my breath as he sniffs at us disinterestedly and then wanders off to the other end of the corridor, staring up at the hatch and waiting for his food to arrive.

Emmanuel's face stretches into a wide grin. He gives me a high five, and then we all whoop and laugh and hug each other and congratulate ourselves.

I look behind me. Sean is sitting up and Leah and Ravi are crouched down next to him, hugging him.

He catches my eye over their shoulders and nods at me.

I nod back, with a small smile.

We've done it. We've taken on the wolves and we've won.

Together, we're invincible. Together, we can do anything.

HOSHIKO

By the time I make it back to the shack and fill Rosie and Jack in on what's happened, it's already halfway through the night.

We don't talk about it much – what is there to say? – and, once Jack's walked Rosie home, we spread the blankets out on the dirty mud floor and lie there in the darkness waiting for morning.

I can't think about Greta. I shut my mind off from thoughts of her, push them away every time they rear their heads back up again.

I let myself think about Ben instead. Not about where he is now, but about how lovely and sweet and good he is, and how glad I am that I had all those months with him.

Everyone says you shouldn't make judgements of people based on first impressions, but I don't think that's right at all, not in my experience. I think you can tell exactly what a person's like in just a short space of time. Not because of the colour of their skin or because of the clothes they wear, but by the light in their eyes, by the way that they smile, by the way they hold themselves.

I think it's been true of everyone I've ever met.

As soon as I saw Vivian Baines, I knew she was evil. It was all there in the icy coldness of her stare, the haughty arch of her eyebrows, the arrogant thrust of her chest. And Silvio always had his slick, sadistic little smile and that glint of crazed excitement in his eyes that told you straight away that he was mad, power hungry and deadly.

It works the other way too, I'm sure it does. I loved Amina from the first day I arrived in the circus. You only had to look at her to know what a calm and wise soul she was – you'd have to be blind not to see it – and even if you were, you'd know it just by spending five minutes in her presence, just by listening to her talk.

I've loved Greta too, with all my heart, since the moment Silvio threw her down at my feet and ordered me to train her up. Her beauty and grace start on the surface and go all the way through, right to the very core.

Emmanuel, Ezekiel, Jack: it's been the same with all of them and it's how it is now, with Rosie. I've only known her a couple of days but, for some reason, I completely and utterly trust her. Even her son, Felix – he's angry, he's got issues, but underneath all that hurt and anger, he's got a good soul. A good heart. It's all there when you speak to him.

People think I was naive and silly, I suppose, to fall for Ben so quickly back then, when it all started. I'd only met him a short while, they'd say; I didn't know him at all.

They're wrong, though, if they think that. I did know him. I knew him as soon as I looked into his eyes, all the way back there in the arena. I knew a part of him was vulnerable and hurting, like me. I knew we belonged together. I tried to pretend I didn't, but the feeling was too strong. It overwhelmed me. I don't know why we're connected, but I know that we are.

Ben's good and kind and soft and vulnerable and lovely and now he's there in that awful, awful place. He'll try and stay strong and brave for me but he'll be scared and he'll be afraid, and he'll be lonely. And Greta will be scared too, wherever she is.

I wish I was with them now. I wish I could hold them both close and make them feel better.

BEN

We seem to have formed a mutual pact with the wolves to give each other a wide berth. Every now and then, one of them moves a little closer, sniffs at one of us and then wanders off. We keep the youngest kids in the middle of the group, just in case one of the wolves attacks or tries to grab someone, but it doesn't seem to be an issue.

Propped up against the wall is Sean, still weak, but alive. I make my way over to him, offering him the food that Emmanuel and the others gave me.

He takes some bread, devouring it, before he looks up at me again.

"Thank you," he says. "I didn't deserve that after the way I treated you."

I lower myself down next to him.

"I'd have hated me too, especially after what Sabatini said. It's not true, you know. I never asked to be in charge of anyone."

He smiles weakly. "Good thing your mum's relaxed your terms and conditions, then. You're one of us properly now, so I hear, whether you like it or not."

He's right: I am. All the division between us has gone now. I'm here, in this place, with these people, and tomorrow I'm going to be paraded with them in front of an audience. To do what? I don't know. I don't feel frightened, though, not tonight. Let the fear wait until tomorrow. Tonight is for unity. Tonight is for togetherness.

I wish Hoshi was here. What would she say? I smile to myself and hug my arms together. She'd be proud of me.

I hope I get to tell her, one day, that we took on the wolves and won.

It's a special night, in an odd way. I'll never forget it. The atmosphere is laden, a heady mixture of adrenaline and euphoria, of sadness and resilience and love. We probably should sleep; I don't think anyone's had much at all for months, but I think we all feel too wired; besides, no one wants to let their guard down just yet.

For most of the night, we sit together in the widest part of the corridor and talk, sometimes as a whole group – one person telling a story or explaining something to the rest of us – sometimes in small groups of people. We take our turns to be on the outside, on guard in case the wolves suddenly turn, but it never happens.

In the centre, encircled by us at all times, the youngest children curl up on the nest of thin blankets we've piled together in a heap. There are eight of them, snuggled up together like puppies, and they drop off almost immediately. Some of the women cover them tenderly with the rest of the blankets and we all smile at them, sleeping so peacefully in their little cluster. Looking at them gives me the same feeling I get every time I look at Greta, and the one that Ezekiel has already started to give me. It's a feeling of protection so strong; a feeling of tenderness, but also of fear. A feeling of outrage.

Hoshi was as young as them when she was ripped from her family to perform in the Cirque. Her childhood was stolen from her, just like theirs has been. All she's ever known, all her life, is hardship and pain, and it's all they'll ever know, these sleeping innocents.

How dare they put them in here? Here, in this circus, at the mercy of wolves and lions and far scarier, far more evil beasts: beasts like Silvio Sabatini, beasts like my mother. How dare they?

I'm part of this pack now and these sleeping children in our midst are our cubs. I know one thing for sure: we'll defend them with our lives if we have to.

I'm riding around and around on a carousel, my stomach lurching, my head reeling, faces flashing before my eyes.

Ben, holding a gun to his temple. Greta, screaming as they drag her away. Amina, dead, swinging up high in the arena. My mother sobbing as they drag me away from her. Kadir, his gold tooth glinting in the candlelight. Vivian Baines, her arm wrapped around Ben, her face smug and victorious. Silvio, laughing malevolently, reaching for me, reaching for Ben.

Round and round and round I go. Ben, Greta, Amina, Kadir, Vivian Baines, Silvio, Ben, Greta, Amina.

Round and round and round and round.

Whirling, whirling, whirling. Image after image. A montage of fear and terror.

All night I slip in and out of the same vivid, feverish dreams, reality and nightmare blurring, so that I don't know what's real and what isn't.

When there's a tap at the door, I jump upright, gasping, and throw it open to reveal Kadir, standing there in the murky dawn light.

"You ready?" he asks.

I nod. "Let's go."

And closing the little door, I slip away, leaving Jack sleeping behind me on the dusty floor.

BEN

I discover a lot as the night passes: how Silvio is worse than ever, how my mother has been coming here a lot, how she's using the circus as a platform for her leadership battle.

I spend a lot of time chatting to Emmanuel and some of the other performers about Hoshi. Hearing them talk about her makes her seem closer somehow.

Ezekiel works his way inch by inch from the designated children's area in the middle until he's right next to me. He seems as keen to talk about Hoshi as I am: I think she must have been the first person in here to show him any kindness. It was a mutual bond, I know; Hoshi's talked about this little boy a lot, and I can see why she's so attached to him. You can't help but smile when you look at him, with his deep brown eyes and his mischievous grin

"What will you be doing in here once the shows start?" I ask him. "Is it the tightrope? Hoshi said you were a natural."

He frowns and the smile drops from his face for once. "No, not that, not exactly." He bites his lip and doesn't say anything for a moment and then the grin's back on his face. "Hoshi will be impressed, won't she, when she finds out we stood up to the wolves?"

He's trying to change the subject. Whatever he's doing, it's bad enough that he can't bear to talk about it.

At the back, someone raises their voice suddenly, speaking loudly above the rest of us.

"Sorry, everyone. Erm, can I just say something for a minute?"

300

It's Sean. He's on his feet, leaning against the wall for support. He looks awkward and embarrassed at all the eyes turned on him. I don't think he's the kind of person who likes being the centre of attention.

"I wanted to say thank you," he says, his voice shaking. "What you all did back there, it was amazing. You saved my life, all of you, and you risked your own to do it."

"Like I said yesterday, that's the circus way," Emmanuel answers, in his rich, wise tones. "In the face of adversity, we look after each other, as best we can."

"That's why I have to tell you all something," Sean says. "Something I'm supposed to keep secret."

He looks over his shoulder and glances around.

"There aren't cameras in here, are there?" he says. "Or bugs. They can't hear me?"

"No," Leah answers. "They think the wolves are security enough."

"OK." He looks around at us all. "There's no one in here who wants to be here, right? There's no one who wouldn't rather be out there, even if it is back in the slums?"

"Of course not!" someone calls out, impatiently. "Stop asking stupid questions and get on with whatever it is you have to say!"

"OK," he says again, and he lowers his voice, speaking in a breathless whisper so that I have to lean forward to catch his words.

"You've all heard of the Brotherhood, right?"

The Brotherhood. They're the group who tried to kidnap me and Francis that time, in the football stadium. They wanted

301

to kill us; that's what Mother and Father and the police said after they hanged them all. I thought they'd been wiped out, thought that was the end of them. Obviously not.

Everyone else is nodding, even the youngest of the kids who are still awake. "Well." He takes a deep breath. "They're planning an attack on the Cirque, on opening night!"

People are looking around at each other, shocked at this sudden news.

"How do you know?" someone calls out.

He lowers his voice even more, so I have to really strain my ears to make out what he's saying.

"My brother's in the group," he says with quiet pride. "He got a work assignment, in here, when they were still building. He's been coming in here for weeks; shifting all the building rubble and carrying it away. We've managed to talk to each other a few times. I've been giving him information, as much as I can, about the layout and what it's like, and he's been reporting back to them." He looks towards Emmanuel for approval. "That was the right thing to do, wasn't it? I mean, they aren't going to attack the Dregs; it's only the Pures they want. They've got it all worked out."

"So why is it supposed to be a secret?" Ravi asks. "If it's so risk free, why aren't we supposed to know?"

"Because they don't want word getting out. They've got huge plans. They've got guns and they're going to storm the place and set us all free!"

Maggie, the perpetually petrified woman, shrieks out, "We'll all be killed! They'll blow us all up!" A few voices join in, agreeing with her, but Emmanuel stands up and raises his hand and they fall silent.

"Maggie, you may well be right. If they come in here with weapons, it may mean some or all of us get hurt, or worse, but the fact is, we'll all get killed at some point or other anyway in this place. If it comes to a choice between taking a chance with an outside group who want to break us out, or sitting back and taking what they throw at us in here, I'd support the group anytime."

It's as if his words are enough for everyone; even Maggie stops protesting.

"Does anyone disagree?" he asks. "If so, state your concerns now. Everyone is entitled to an opinion, everyone. This is a democracy." He looks frankly at Sean. "If we decide as a group to report what we've just heard, then that's what will be done."

Nobody speaks.

My heart is racing.

Emmanuel is looking at me, his eyes shrewd.

"Ben?" he says softly.

I look down at the ground, avoiding eye contact with anyone. I get why they think it's a good idea to support anybody who wants to bring this place down. I really do, but I'm not sure I can just go along with it.

My mother and father always said the Brotherhood were cruel, ruthless killers; everyone did. The police, the press, everyone said they were evil.

I'll never forget the fear I felt inside when they grabbed me; the absolute certainty that I was going to die. My parents celebrated when they were captured and hanged, their bodies swinging up there in front of the PowerHouse.

I think about what Sean just said. *It's only the Pures they want.*

Does that make it OK? Maybe it does. No one who's here on opening night will be innocent, after all. They'll all have come here to watch Dregs suffer and die. They deserve everything they get and more, don't they?

That was you a few months ago, the voice in my head says. *You wanted to watch the shows too, until Priya and Hoshi showed you the truth. Isn't it better to try and re-educate people? To try and make them see that what they're doing is wrong? How does more violence solve anything?*

It's not right to attack people. It's not right to kill. It doesn't make a difference what side you're on.

"My mother might not win the election," I say, without looking up. "Laura Minton might. Things might change anyway, without people getting attacked."

"People will get attacked, Ben." Emmanuel's voice rings with conviction and certainty. "People have been getting attacked in the circus ever since it first began. People were attacked today – you, Sean, all of us in our rehearsals. And people will die tomorrow night, whether the Brotherhood infiltrate the place or not, Silvio's already promised that." He gestures towards the little children, curled up in the middle, sleeping obliviously under their blankets. "We don't have time to wait for the election. And I think you must see why what happens to us in this place makes it very hard for us to believe that the Pure public will suddenly find their consciences when they do go to the ballot box. Even if Laura Minton does win, even if she does fulfil her promise and shuts us down, it could be weeks before it happens, even longer maybe. And if she doesn't, well…" His tone becomes almost apologetic. "Things aren't going to get any easier in here with your mother running the country."

I look back at him, at his noble face, ripped apart by lions. I look around at all of the people gathered about me, all of them already bearing scars and bruises as souvenirs of their time here. I look down at Ezekiel. Whatever he's doing in here tomorrow night, he can't even face talking about it. I see Sean and Leah when they were being electrocuted, their bodies jerking spasmodically.

What's the alternative to fighting back? Accepting it, I suppose, meekly turning the other cheek?

No. If we do that, we might as well just all lie down right here and die.

"It's OK," I say. "It's necessary."

"That's it, then," Emmanuel says. "We're in. Agreed?"

"Agreed." There's a unanimous chorus. He turns to Sean.

"What's the plan, then?"

"I don't know," Sean says, apologetically. "Felix got moved out last week, when the building work finished, and I haven't heard anything since. All I know is what he said to me the last time I saw him."

"And that was?"

"Be prepared on opening night; get ready for war and get ready to run," he says.

There's a hum of excitement around the group.

Ezekiel nudges me with his arm, grinning up at me excitedly.

"We're going to get out of here!" he says "I can go back to my mum and dad, you can go and find Hoshi!"

I smile back down at him. I like what he's saying. It's definitely not going to be that simple, but there's hope now, where there was none just a few hours ago. We've taken on the wolves and we've won. We've proved ourselves a match against one set of predatory beasts with blood on their minds; maybe we can prove ourselves against another.

I follow silently after Kadir as he leads me through the forlorn pathways of the slums.

I have to think practically now. I have to make the video as quickly as I can and get Greta to safety.

Once she's safe, I need to find Felix and speak to him alone. I need to find out when the Brotherhood are planning on storming the Cirque. They hate Pures, Felix has told me that. What will they do if they get hold of Ben?

They won't listen to him when he tells them he's not like the rest. They won't see how kind and good he is. They'll just see Benedict Baines, Vivian's son. They'll want to finish off what they started before – when they targeted him and his family a few years ago. It'll be the biggest coup of their lives if they can capture him, if they can kill him.

I shiver.

I won't be able to carry on without him. Not after everything we've been through.

At the edge of the slums, there's a car waiting for us, outside the fences.

I look at it doubtfully.

Maybe this is the wrong thing to do, after all.

"Greta's still back there somewhere, isn't she? I want to get her back, not go further away from her."

Kadir grips my arm, propelling me firmly towards the car. "If you want her back, you know what you have to do."

BEN

As morning approaches, we make our way back into our cells, bolting the doors behind us. Sean takes the one furthest from the guards' entrance and, once the doors open and the wolves rush out, he stays tucked in the corner while we all come out for headcount.

None of the guards ask where he is. They must just assume the wolves have finished off every last bit of him. The thought of how different things might have been makes my stomach churn.

Silvio isn't at breakfast, which is a blessed relief, but apart from that, it's the same procedure as yesterday: the others feeding from troughs like cattle, while I sit at my own little table of delicious food.

This time, though, all the glances I get are sympathetic. There's no prickling hostility any more, no more angry waves of resentment.

I wait for an opportunity to throw some food their way, but the guards keep their watchful eyes fixed on me and I can't risk anyone else getting hurt because I've tried to do something stupid. I don't even get the chance to hide any away to give Sean later on.

The guards blow their whistles and begin shepherding us all out.

I stand there, blinking in the light, watching everyone else as they scurry off in various directions.

"Ahh, Benedict!" Silvio glides up to me in his golf buggy. Behind him, crouched in the luggage compartment, Ezekiel peers up at me, his face sombre for once. "Has this little guy told you about his act yet? He hasn't? Oh, that's even better! I shall enjoy studying your face closely for your initial reactions. You don't really need to rehearse for what I have in mind for you tonight and, as you're my special guest, I thought I'd give you the morning off, just to spectate. All you need to do is sit back, relax and enjoy yourself. It'll be just like old times! Of course, you may wish to get involved; it's a highly interactive show, and I speak from personal experience when I say how much fun it is! Isn't that right, Ezekiel?" He turns and grins inanely at Ezekiel, whose head is bowed.

"Well, what are you waiting for? Jump aboard!"

I try to catch Ezekiel's eye, but he won't look up. I'm not sure what to do.

"Come on, Baines!" Silvio orders. "The Spider's Web awaits!"

The Spider's Web? Morbid fear grips hold of me as I step on the board at the back of golf buggy and we trundle off across the Cirque.

HOSHIKO

Laura Minton sits behind the wheel of the car, dressed up smartly in a woollen day dress and a suit jacket. She smiles at me warmly when I climb in, clasping my hands in hers. She wipes hers clean on her dress straight afterwards, though. I don't blame her; I can't remember the last time I had a wash. I run my fingers through my hair. It's all matted. My clothes are dirty. I'm dirty.

"Hoshiko, it's so good to see you again. I just know you're going to do a marvellous job with this. You don't need to look so worried! We're on the same side."

She doesn't even mention Greta. I scowl at her. "Let's just get this over and done with, shall we? Where are you taking me?"

"A studio. It isn't far, just a few miles away. We've cleared everyone out today, so we'll have the place to ourselves."

Kadir and his men are climbing into the seats behind us.

Laura talks to me as the car drives away.

"This really will make a big difference you know, Hoshiko, if we get it right, but we've only got one shot. You said you saw the broadcast the other day?"

I nod.

"Baines has plummeted in the polls since then. And yet a year ago, even the idea of a public debate like that would have seemed unthinkable. Do you know who changed things?"

She raises a questioning eyebrow at me and I shake my head.

"I'll tell you who changed things. I'll tell you who the real hero is. It's Ben, your Ben. He made the speech that changed everything."

Her words make me feel so proud. I wish Ben was here now so I could tell him that. I don't think I ever told him how brave I thought he was. Why was I so cold and moody with him so often? Why didn't I spend more time telling him how I really felt? Why did I waste so many days?

"Do you know, Ben was cut off within minutes when he spoke out. Doesn't matter, though; the damage had already been done. In fact, the censorship just gave his words more power, made them even more notorious. He woke the rest of the country up from their slumber. It's not as if none of us had ever thought those things before, it's not as if none of us hadn't wanted to say them, it's that until Ben, it just wasn't something anyone ever considered actually doing."

"People should have spoken out," I say. "Going along with what someone like Vivian Baines says makes you all as bad as she is."

Laura Minton sighs.

"You're right. I'm not trying to excuse things, I'm just trying to explain the way things were. The culture of the political classes in this country, for years and years and years, has been to *comply*. Keep your real views to yourself, play the game, keep your head down."

Ahead of us, the PowerHouse looms over the city. Underneath the images of Greta, Jack and me, the pure gold statue beams its smile down from the top of the heap of Dregs it clambers on.

Laura nods towards it.

"That place was gripped by fear. Fear that if you said too much, if you questioned anything, if you dared to speak out, they'd turn on you. You'd lose everything: your home, your family, your Pure status. You'd be thrown into the slums and left to rot."

She says she's not making excuses but it doesn't sound like it to me. Ben gave up his status, he didn't even think twice about it. And Jack didn't wait until he thought it was safe enough to speak out. He sacrificed everything to save us.

I don't bother saying that though. What would be the point? I just sit back and listen to this woman trying to justify why it took so long for her to try and do the right thing.

"Turns out, loads of us were sympathizers, maybe even most of us, but nobody was brave enough to say it out loud, not until your Ben."

She looks over to the PowerHouse again. "More and more people in that place are coming out pro-Dreg every day. More and more people are speaking out against Baines and all that she stands for. The tide has turned and your Ben was the one to turn it. Even if we lose the election next week, the fact that I'm even running on an openly pro-Dreg platform, the fact that it's too close to call, that's a victory in itself."

When she looks at me, her eyes shine with glee.

"That test I asked Baines to take? Her resistance proves that she's complicit in the lie! We've put her in an impossible position. If she takes the test, who only knows what genetic murk might be floating around in her supposedly superior blood? She can't risk it, but the more she refuses to take it, the more she calls it illegal, the more uncertain of who she, or any of us, actually are she looks. She's damned if she does, and damned if she doesn't.

"The empire she's built up is crumbling. Things will never be what they were. She'll never be able to take us back to that time when everyone kept their head down and kept quiet. The emperor's got no clothes on and, for the first time ever, none of us are pretending otherwise."

If Ben was free, if Ben was with me, maybe her words would make me hopeful, but right now, they just make me feel more frightened than before. If Vivian Baines is desperate and angry, she'll be looking for someone to take it out on. Who better than the poor circus folk? Who better than her own son: the one who was the first to speak out against her, the one who lit the spark that ignited this whole inferno?

If his actions have damaged her, won't she want to damage him, too? Punish him? Make him suffer?

And if I stand up now and speak out against her, won't I make it even worse?

Next to me, Laura Minton is still talking.

"We need to make sure you're seen by as many people as we can in one go. What we want to do is shoot the perfect interview with you and then flood the PureWeb and TV channels with it in one big assault. I've got a sponsor who owns a technology company and he's promised me he can do something amazing with it. What you say needs to be sharp, dramatic and impactful. This could be it, Hoshiko, this could be that final nail in the coffin!"

I suppose what she's saying sounds good, but I don't care. All I want is to get Greta and Ben free: the rest of the country can look after itself.

I guess that's not really true. I care about everyone in the circus. I care about Emmanuel and Ezekiel and all the others.

I picture all their faces; their dear, dear faces. I picture all the other faces, the ones who never made it, dozens and dozens of faces. I picture Amina. I feel her in my heart. Amina would never have these selfish thoughts I'm having. I know what exactly she'd say. I know exactly what she'd do.

We must fight injustice, Hoshiko, that's what she'd say. *For ourselves and for others. We must fight with all we have.*

She gave up her life to save me.

I need to make it count. I need to stop being self-centred. I need to fight. For her. For all my lost friends. For all those poor people, trapped in there right now, bracing themselves for opening night.

I owe them this.

I pivot around in my seat. "I'll do it anyway, I promise," I tell Kadir. "Please, if you just bring Greta back. She can speak with me. She wanted to do it all along."

"Ah yes, Greta!" says Laura, her eyes flicking up to glance at Kadir in the mirror. "I thought we were using her too?"

She doesn't know what Kadir's done. If I tell her, will she stop the car right now? Will she insist they release Greta immediately? If she does, will they do what she says?

Kadir fires me a warning glance. "She's not coming. It's complicated. Hoshiko's the big pull though, right? That's what you said. And we've got the monkey, too. He'll look good on the camera."

She nods. "They'll do. I'd rather have Greta on camera too, though, even if she doesn't speak."

"See, we *need* her," I say to Kadir.

314

He looks at me again, a hard and angry look that makes me feel even more afraid for Greta. "It's just going to be Hoshiko, I'm afraid," he says to Laura. "And Bojo here. They should do the trick, shouldn't they?"

Laura smiles. "They'll do."

As the car drives through the streets, she scrutinizes me with little sideways glances, and that look of slight disgust crosses her face again. "We'll need to get you a bit more camera ready. You can have a proper wash at the studio. Plus, I have a surprise for you. I think you'll like it."

She laughs. "Don't look so worried! This is going to be fun, Hoshiko! You're going to be a star again! Screw Vivian Baines, with her cheap trickery and her brand-new torture extravaganza! You're going to steal the show before her very eyes. I tell you what, Hoshiko: you, me, Kadir, between us we have more power than that woman will ever know. We're going to blast her out of the game. We're going to tear her and her circus down."

Crossing the courtyard, it strikes me again how much bigger this place is than the old, travelling Cirque. It's huge, like a city within a city; no wonder Silvio uses a golf buggy to get around. We whizz along, past the huge Arcadia hill, past dozens of other buildings, all different shapes, all different colours, past the fairground rides, the massive Ferris wheel and the dodgems and waltzers, past a hundred stalls and tents and sideshows to the last building of all, right at the far end of the Cirque, nestled next to the huge fences.

It's a black-and-khaki-green shed, unassuming and dingy-looking. It looks like it's been built from old shipping containers, and the paint is flaking away here and there. It doesn't fit in at all with the pristine showiness of everything else, but there's something cool about it – like it doesn't have to try as hard as the other buildings, like it can't be bothered. The writing on the sign above the door is in a street graffiti style, and it takes me a second or two to work out what it says: *The Gaming Zone*.

Silvio takes his cane and swings himself out of the buggy. "Come on!" he barks at Ezekiel and me, and we both get slowly out and follow him through the door.

Inside, it's unlit, except for old-fashioned arcade machines which fill the large room, their screens flashing hypnotically. Silvio digs at us with his cane, shepherding us across to another door. Ezekiel still won't make eye contact with me. His gaze is fixed steadfastly to the floor, and his beaming smile remains noticeably absent from his face.

When we're through the second door, Silvio prods Ezekiel

forward to a narrow staircase, immediately to our left.

"Go and get ready. Full costume and then into position!" he commands.

Ezekiel scoots up the staircase, disappearing at the top. I can hear his footsteps moving around above our heads.

I look around the room, trying to work out what kind of place it is.

Twelve large black chairs are all lined up in a row. Padded leather, headrests – gamers' chairs. In front of each one is some kind of control panel: a joystick and various other buttons and levers. They face a pit, opening up in the ground in front of them. It's full of huge segregated blades, like rows of vast jagged teeth, jutting upwards.

Above, about eight metres off the ground, a rope canopy stretches all the way across the room. It reminds me of football goal netting, but the criss-crossed squares are bigger: each one about two metres wide.

Perching ominously at the far end are twelve spiders. Not real ones: huge model ones, each about the size of a motorbike. They all have black, furry bodies with eight spindly legs sprouting out and yellow, lifeless eyes.

Silvio lowers himself on to one of the large chairs, his legs dangling childishly, and leans forward to the control panel in front of him. He presses a button and the panel lights up. There's a whirring sound and the spider directly opposite him slowly revolves forward on to the roped web. Its eyes flash bright yellow. He moves another lever and one of its hinged legs rises up and waves at me, the silver pincer on the end opening and closing.

"Please," he says to me. "Choose your arachnid!" His white skin is almost luminous in this light and his pale blue eyes gleam. I don't think I've ever seen him look so gleeful.

I stand there, rooted to the spot.

"Where's Ezekiel?"

"Do you know, I was thinking the very same thing? He really should be ready by now!"

There's a sound, from above our heads. "Ah. Here he is, right on cue!"

About four metres above the web, a panel in the ceiling has opened up. A tiny figure springs down, landing nimbly on the web and crouching there, holding on to the ropes with his hands and feet. Transparent wings, six delicately moving legs, one fat cushioned body, one petrified little face. He's in costume, but it's definitely Ezekiel.

The fly, trapped in the web and surrounded by spiders.

The car slows to a halt outside a large, newish-looking building, and Laura gets out. I pull my door handle, but it's locked, and I have to wait for her to come round and let me out. Kadir and his men are marching on ahead of us.

The place has the echoed hush of an empty building. Laura flicks the lights on and leads me through the corridors. She stops outside a room with a large star on the door. When she rests her hand on the handle she turns to me with a smile.

"See that star? It means VIP. This is where the most important guests prepare. You're no exception."

I look away and roll my eyes. Am I supposed to be impressed?

She opens the door and ushers me into the dressing room.

The light in here is subdued and cosy and the soft red carpet feels luxurious beneath my feet. There's an elaborate mirror taking up one wall with a padded chair in front of it, and a dressing table crammed with beauty products.

It reminds me of the Cirque, of my own dressing area. It's a lot nicer, of course: it's meant for the Pure elite, not just a circus Dreg like me, but it has the same smell to it – the smell of make-up and hairspray. My body gives a little shiver of excitement, betraying me, betraying Greta.

Laura opens up an internal door, revealing a toilet and a huge walk-in shower.

"There are towels here," she smiles, "and shower cream and body lotion. Take your time. We've got the whole day."

She might have the whole day but I need to do this as

quickly as I can. I need to save Greta. I glower at her angrily but her fixed smile meets mine.

What would she say if she knew Kadir had kidnapped Greta? I think about telling her but I really can't afford to anger Kadir right now.

"One more thing," Laura says. "We've only got one chance to get this right. We need to knock Vivian Baines off her pedestal. We need to make such an impact, cause such a stir, that everyone will be talking about you, not her. The appeal you hold for most people is that they recognize you, and that you're beautiful and glamorous. You're a circus star, or you were, not so long ago. We want you to make an impact, and we think you'd do that more if you looked the part. Don't look so worried!" she laughs. "I've got a gift for you." She opens the door of a large cupboard and gestures to the wall.

There's a costume hanging up. It's my black cat outfit from before. My trademark, the costume that earned me my nickname, the costume I always perform at my best in. I step towards it. The tiny sparkles in the ebony fabric catch the light and wink brightly at me.

"How did you get this?" I ask, as I caress the cool material.

She grins. "It's complicated. We knew someone, who knew someone, who knew someone. Are you OK to wear it?"

I nod. "I guess so. If you think it'll help."

I get a funny feeling when I look at it. I feel like I'm about to go out into the arena, like I'm about to perform.

I guess I am, in a way.

"I'll leave you to it," Laura says. "Take as long as you need."

When she's gone, I stare about me.

The toilet is clean and white with soft toilet tissue, as much as I like, next to it.

I've never had a shower to myself. I step into the large cubicle and turn the dial until water gushes out of two big nozzles on the walls. I spring back; it's cold. Not for long though; it warms up quickly. Running warm water. I step under it. The steam mists around me and the water jets down over my head. I put my head back and let it stream over me. It's lovely. My whole body tingles.

There's a shower gel dispenser. I squirt some on to my hands and soap myself with the frothy lather.

The water runs off my body, brown and murky.

I feel like I could stay under here for ever.

This is no good, I berate myself. Every second that I'm standing under here, pampering myself, is another second that Greta's being held somewhere. I turn the shower off, drying my hair roughly with a soft, fluffy towel.

I sit down at the little dressing table and stare at myself. I can't remember the last time I saw my face in a mirror. The months on the run have made me look gaunt. At least in the Cirque, we were given semi-regular meals. My cheekbones jut out now, where they didn't before. I don't look healthy and my eyes betray the panic I'm feeling inside. Panic for Greta, panic for Ben.

Still, if I'm going to do this, I might as well do it right.

I wonder where my make-up artist, Minnie, is. I wonder what she's doing, right now. Picking up the make-up brush, I begin to turn myself back into a showstopper.

BEN

"Come on!" Sabatini demands, impatiently. "Sit down and get playing! It'll be no fun on my own!"

"Are you mad?" I ask, which has to be the most stupid question anyone's asked, ever.

"I knew it!" He sighs, theatrically. "I really do think I know you better than I know anyone! I knew you'd refuse! And I thought to myself: *That's fine, let him refuse, let him just sit back and soak it all up. Tonight, he'll be a real part of the show. Let him enjoy this final day as a bystander.*" He smiles at me. "You're a teenage boy, after all – that's exactly our target market."

I look towards the door. It's locked. I look back at Silvio. For once, he's not holding his cane. One hand is on the joystick, the other lingering over a gun attached to a holster. "OK." He grins. "Let the fun commence!

"Call it paranoia, but I don't like sitting with my back to such a violent and savage criminal as yourself, Baines. I've learnt the hard way to keep you where I can see you at all times."

He points to the middle of the pit of jagged metal in front of him. "Get into the centre, will you?"

"No." I glare at him.

He sighs again. "Your heroic protests really are getting dull. You have no power here, Benedict, surely you've realized that by now, no bargaining chip whatsoever. If you don't do what I ask, I'll shoot you. I'll shoot him first, and then I'll shoot you."

He rises up from his chair, takes the gun and waves it nonchalantly up at Ezekiel, crouched nervously in the middle of the web.

"You won't shoot Ezekiel, not before the show."

I take a step towards him.

"Oh, Benedict. I know you so well, and yet you don't know me at all! Of course I will! There are loads of kids who could take the place of Fly-Boy up there. True, they may not be as adept as him quite yet, but the Pures won't mind if the flies don't stand a fighting chance! Most of them like as high a death rate as possible, especially lads your age. And as for you, there's nothing I'd like more than to give you a matching wound on your other leg! Perhaps I could stick you up there instead of him; after all, your mother has bequeathed you to me. No! I'll stick to Plan A for you – it's just too good not to!"

He aims the gun up towards Ezekiel.

"I'm running out of patience…"

What can I do? He's right. He holds all the cards, and a loaded gun.

I edge my way through the maze of serrated blades. They're packed in so densely that there's only just enough room to squeeze between them and they look even sharper and more deadly close up. Maybe, if Ezekiel falls, I'll be able to catch him before he hits any of them.

"I've had this attraction in mind for the longest time," Silvio calls over to me. "For ages now, I've been trying to think of ways we could make the Cirque more interactive, ways the Pures could really feel a part of things. My original vision for it was as an act for Hoshiko and Greta. When Hoshiko's caught, I'm hoping I can persuade your mother to let me have her for a while before she's executed. It really would be such a pull if we could get her in here, such a crowd-pleaser!"

323

I try to resist the power of his words; try to keep the barriers I've built against him in place, but I just can't do it. Not when he's so casually talking about using Hoshi like that. Not when he's talking about her death. I squeeze my hands together. I'd like to ring them around his white little neck. I'd like to snap him in half.

He sits back down and starts moving the spider. It propels its way forward, scuttling at an alarming pace on its eight mechanized legs towards Ezekiel.

All I can see of the little boy from below are his hands and feet, scrambling away as the spider advances.

Silvio leaps up from his chair and starts another spider up, cutting Ezekiel off from the path he was running down. Ezekiel turns around, darting back the other way.

Silvio moves to a third chair, intercepting Ezekiel with another spider, then jumps up and runs to work a fourth one, calling across to me. "Just imagine how frantic and fast-paced it'll be with twelve on the go at once! A battle of wits, a battle of egos! Who will be the first to catch him? Who will be the first to knock him down? And he's good, isn't he? A natural up there, just like I always said he'd be. Who knew your girlfriend would be so easily replaceable! Don't know why I didn't have her killed off years ago! Oh my!" He dashes across to another chair and moves the spider across the web, then sprints to a sixth one. "I just cannot wait for tonight!"

I study myself critically in the mirror. I don't look like me. The make-up on my face seems garish after so long without wearing any. I smear the red lipstick away.

When I step into the studio, though, Laura gasps and gives a little round of applause.

"Oh, Hoshiko! You look simply stunning!"

There's a woman standing with her who I haven't seen before. She's wearing a short, tight-fitting dress and her foundation is slapped on so thickly that her face looks orange. She's smiling at me with teeth of brilliant white.

Kadir and his men are all here too, staring at me. I don't like the looks on their faces, not at all. They're the same looks the men watching the shows used to wear when Silvio made me put on some skimpy outfit or other and twirl on the rope over their heads.

I cross my arms together, glaring at them.

"I'm not saying anything while they're in the room."

Kadir shrugs his shoulders.

"Fine," he says. "Really not bothered as long as you get it done."

He and his men turn and leave, casting smirking looks over their shoulders as they go.

"Hoshiko" – Laura smiles brightly – "may I introduce you to Alison Devine?"

The woman steps forward, her smile growing even wider.

"I don't suppose either of us need any introduction," she simpers. "We're equally recognizable, I'd say."

I stare at her. I've never seen her before in my life. There's an awkward silence for a moment or two.

"I'm sorry," I say. "I don't…"

"Hoshi, Alison is the presenter of the national breakfast show. One of the biggest stars in the country." Laura smiles apologetically at the woman. "Hoshiko went straight from being incarcerated in the circus to a life on the run – it's natural that she wouldn't be as aware of famous faces as the rest of us, even household celebrities such as yourself. The Pures we're trying to win over certainly know who you are, though, and that's what counts. I can't tell you how delighted I am that you've agreed to do this."

"I thought *you'd* be asking me questions," I say to Laura. "I thought that was the whole point."

Laura grimaces. "It's not quite that simple, I'm afraid. If I'm seen publically consorting with a wanted criminal, there could be all sorts of recriminations. I'd be blatantly flouting the law again and I don't think I'd get away with it this time. I'd have to go into hiding, and, what would be even worse, Vivian Baines could use it stop me running for office. We can't afford to provide her with the opportunity."

"But if you're going to use it as part of your election campaign, surely it will be obvious to everyone that you're behind it all?"

Laura nods and grins. "It will. Baines will know it, the country will know it, everyone will know it. No one will be able to prove it though, and that's the important thing." She laughs. "It will drive Baines crazy!"

"What about you?" I say to Alison Devine. "Aren't you scared you'll get into trouble?"

She sighs, dramatically. "This thing is bigger than even me. We all have to make sacrifices for the cause. I'll go into hiding immediately after the interview, lay low until after the election. Laura will win, I'm sure of it. You'll be granted a pardon and we'll both affirm our places as national heroes." She flounces her hair. "It's a gamble, but it's one worth taking."

She indicates towards two chairs which have been placed in the centre of the room, then shepherds me over to them and pushes me gently down into one. "The camera's all set up. We can do the zooming in and close-ups after the filming, so all we need to do is sit down here and have a chat about the Cirque.

"Remember, our objective is to win the audience over to our cause. Graphic, explicit details are good – the gorier the better – but you need to charm them too; they need to identify with you. People love a good romance, so might exploit that angle. And emotional displays always go down well." She coughs, as if she's embarrassed. "If you feel the urge to shed a few tears, don't hold back."

I can feel my heart pounding.

Greta's trapped somewhere, frightened out of her mind or worse, while I've been putting on a leotard and plastering make-up on my face. And Ben. Ben's in the circus. With Silvio. Silvio must hate Ben and Greta and me more than anyone. We blew up his arena. We nearly killed him. What's he going to do to Ben? And what about the Brotherhood? They're attacking the Cirque. When? And how? They don't want to harm any Dregs, Felix said, but Ben's not a Dreg, he's a Pure, or he was until a few months ago. The Brotherhood hate all Pures. They want to kill as many Pures as they can.

I have to speak to Felix. I have to find out what they're planning. I have to find out when.

But first I need to make this video. I need to get Greta released and then work out how to save Ben, and I need to do it as quickly as I can.

"Ooh, I nearly forgot! Hold on a minute…" Laura leaves the room and comes back with Bojo. "He might not be able to say a lot, but he's a good visual prop!" She laughs. When I look at Alison's grinning face, I can't help feeling like I'm some performing animal too, being put on display to serve the purposes of others. I haven't felt that way for a long time now. I haven't felt that way since I was in the Cirque.

Alison takes a lipstick from her bag and reapplies it quickly. Then she casts a final critical eye over me. Her brow furrows and she pulls her whole make-up bag out.

"Ready?" she asks me, after a couple of minutes of prodding at my face with her brushes and products.

"Ready," I answer.

"Right." She leans forward and presses a button on the camera.

She turns to me and then turns to the camera, her smile even wider than before. "Good morning, England! For months now, you've all wanted to know one thing. You've all been asking me the same question: who will I be voting for next week? Where do my allegiances lie? I've kept quiet, until now. Now, the time has come for me to tell you the answer. There is one candidate in this historic election who stands for justice. There is one candidate who stands for change, who stands for equality. There is one candidate who stands for what is right. Let it be known, I am standing firmly on the side of Laura Minton. I'm brave enough to back her, are you?

"Not sure? Let me try to persuade you. Today, I have a worldwide exclusive for you. No, your eyes do not deceive you! She's here, before your very eyes! The Cat! Hoshiko, the former circus star! Some say she's a criminal, I say she's a hero, and she's right here next to me, ready to tell the world her story!"

She turns to me, her brow etched with concern, her expression oozing sympathy.

"Hoshiko, can you tell me first about Benedict Baines? When did you meet? Was it love at first sight?"

I feel my chest fluttering in panic and my fingers tingling with anger. What's this got to do with it? What's this got to do with anyone except me and Ben?

"I'm not going to talk about Ben." I say, abruptly. "That wasn't what I agreed to. I'm not going to talk about anything except the Cirque."

Her smile freezes. "OK," she says tentatively. "Tell me, what do you think it was that made Benedict feel he wanted to storm the Cirque like that? Was it the sense of injustice he felt when he saw how the Dreg performers were treated? Or was it more personal; was it just a case of Pure boy meets Dreg girl, Pure boy falls for Dreg girl, Pure boy rescues Dreg girl?"

This is useless. She wants me to tell them all a love story, and this is about so much more than that.

I move away from her and push my chair forward so that I block her out of the camera shot. I stare into the lens.

"Let me tell you about life in the circus," I say.

And then I take a deep breath and I begin to talk.

BEN

After ten long minutes, a buzzer sounds and the spider Silvio's currently chasing Ezekiel with comes to an abrupt stop.

"Damn! Better luck next time!" he cries. "Get down and get changed!" Ezekiel crawls quickly to the centre of the web and pulls himself back up into the space above.

Silvio peers at me. "Would you believe it, Baines, I'd forgotten you were down there? I was so caught up with the desire to catch the boy! I came pretty close a few times too, did you see? It's so irritating! So irritating and so addictive! That's what we're aiming for; people getting so close to knocking him down that they just have to keep on going. *Just one more go*, they'll tell themselves, *just one more try*. Before you know it, they're a few hundred pounds down! Oh yes, this is going to be an absolute gold mine, I can just feel it!"

He nestles down in the big black chair he's sitting in and rests his hands over his stomach.

It feels wrong, keeping quiet after what I've just witnessed. I step up to him and stare into his strange, colourless face.

"Hoshi was right. You *are* the devil and this place *is* hell."

"You're too kind! And Hoshi may well have been right. Isn't the devil immortal?" He lowers his voice into a stage whisper. "You see, I rather believe I am too, Benedict! After all, I've already risen from the ashes once! I think I'll be here ruling over my dominion for ever!"

I shouldn't have said anything. The only reason he showed me what he's doing to poor Ezekiel was to get a reaction out of me. The best way to resist him is to keep silent.

He chuckles. "Funny, I've gone the other way somewhat with the persona I'm adopting for tonight. Perhaps I should have gone for Lucifer instead of... No, I've done that one before. Still, the juxtaposition between your suggestion and mine are most interesting!"

I stare off into the distance, trying to zone out completely, but it's impossible.

"Right, I have last-minute arrangements to be getting on with; your mother's wish for me to include you in the shows has rather changed my plans. Do you know what Arcadia means, Benedict?" He leans forward and scans my face. "You don't, do you? I am surprised! I'd have thought a boy with your education would know about all that classical stuff. Still, you never did have much going on between the ears, did you? Your actions over the last year have more than proved that!

"Arcadia means paradise. Arcadia means perfection. And it's a good name, for that is what our opening ceremony will be. Perfection on a plate! Especially now that you will be there, with your Purity shining down from the stage for all to see! We're holding our opening ceremony in there, you know, and then the circus acts begin for real. Not long until Ezekiel will be up there again, scrabbling around for his life!"

He pulls himself up from the deep chair.

"Just a few hours now before those doors open and the Pures come spilling in! I'm off to meet with your dear old mum again now: she can't stay away from this place."

And then he turns and taps his way out of the arena, leaving me there in the centre of the great maze of metal: just another fly caught in his web.

HOSHIKO

"I was five years old when they ripped me apart from my family. When three huge men with angry faces burst into our home and grabbed me one day. My little brother was screaming. I was screaming. My mother was sobbing as they pulled me away from her, shoved me in the back of a van and drove me away.

"A life sentence for showing a bit of agility, for being able to do a few backflips.

"I haven't seen my family since. Perhaps they're all dead. It's not unlikely – there's not much food in the slums, there's no real medical help if you get ill, and it's cold, so cold in the winter.

"When I got to the circus, I was thrown into a dormitory with the other people you call Dregs. Forced to train, forced to perform.

"How do you do that? Make a child perform even if she doesn't want to? How do you get her to comply, to do what you want? Well, you beat her, you whip her, you Taser her and, sometimes, that's enough. It doesn't take too much to scare a five-year-old child who misses her mummy.

"Sometimes, though, it takes a little more than that. Sometimes you have to really harm her, or harm others, just to make sure she knows exactly what's at stake.

"I've seen people murdered, and not just during the shows, not just in the name of entertainment. I've seen people shot dead right in front of me, because they happened to be in the wrong place at the wrong time. It's not unusual in the Cirque.

"The only reason I survived for so long was because of the other people you call Dregs. They took care of me, became my new family. They understood, because they'd been through the same thing. They all looked after me, but one person in particular took care of me. She loved me when I most needed love. She gave me her food, she gave me her time, she gave me her wisdom. Her name was Amina.

"Her name was Amina and they murdered her. They hanged her by her neck in the arena we performed in, just to teach me a lesson. Afterwards, they sold her body parts in an online auction, I believe. I don't know how much she fetched.

"But I don't suppose you want to hear about that. Those kinds of details aren't really what fascinates you about the Cirque. You want to know about the performances.

"How does it feel to be a circus star?

"Well, sorry to burst your bubble, but it's not much fun in the circus, for the performers at least.

"It doesn't really make much difference if you're an acrobat, or on the trapeze, or in with the lions. Whatever your role is, it's all the same in the end. There's always a crowd of those people who call themselves Pures, a crowd of those people who are apparently superior, apparently better, watching you suffer. Calling out, crying out, for your death. Desperately waiting for you to fail: to slip, or get mauled, or get shaken to death, or ripped to shreds, or set on fire."

I turn to Amanda. The syrupy smile has gone from her face.

"You asked me about Benedict Baines. Benedict Baines came to the circus, saw what went on there and hated it. Benedict Baines had the courage to question, the courage to judge for himself."

I turn back to the camera.

"You all know who his mother is; you all know the beliefs he was brought up with. He fought against them. He saw them for what they were and he rejected them. He used his head and his heart and he made up his own mind. If he can do it, you can too.

"The day is coming when you get the chance to stand up and change things. You have a vote. Use it. Use it to do what's right. Don't listen to the propaganda, the lies, the false facts you've been fed all your life.

"The people you call Dregs don't have a voice; it was taken away from us long ago. Taken away because we were the wrong colour or the wrong creed or because our parents' parents happened to come from a different place to you.

"You have a voice though. You have a chance to make things right.

"The Cirque only exists because it has an audience. It's time to take them on. Stand up to those around you. Question them, challenge them, show them that there is another way. There is another truth."

I pause. I stare hard into the camera.

"We are all flesh and blood. We all feel. We are all human. Be stronger, be better, be like Benedict Baines. Have the courage to stand up and fight for justice. Put that cross on that piece of paper. Make a difference. Vote for what is right. Vote for change."

Amanda leans forward and presses a button on the camera. When she looks at me, her eyes are brimming with tears.

"Wow," she says. "You wonderful, brave girl. No wonder they wanted you to speak."

She places a hand over mine and squeezes it tight. "Well done. You've just helped us change the world."

Hoshi told me once that meeting me made her change her mind about good and evil. She said that before me she thought that all Pures were evil but that, after me, she'd never look at things in that black-and-white way again.

We were holed up in one of the safe houses the resistance arranged for us: hiding in plain sight, Jack called it. We spent time in a few houses like that one: apparently ordinary-looking houses on apparently ordinary streets which provided safe havens and refuge for people in danger from the authorities.

We didn't even have to worry about suspicious neighbours twitching net curtains because the houses in the rest of the street were all owned by undercover resistance agents and their families – people like Jack used to be – apparently law-abiding citizens who trimmed their lawns and kept their flower beds neat, went to work and kept their heads down while doing everything they possibly could to help the Dregs and provide for anyone in trouble.

The houses were our favourite places of all: warm and cosy, with well-stocked cupboards and clean, warm beds.

I remember when we first got to that place, how Hoshi and Greta kept opening the fridge as if they thought the milk, yoghurts, fresh fruit and vegetables would just vanish if they didn't keep checking on them. There was a bathroom upstairs, and Greta used to turn the hot tap on and off again and again, like it was magic, which I guess to her it was. Hoshi would run her big warm baths overflowing with bubbles and she'd spend hours just splashing around in there.

The TV didn't work but there was a big cupboard full of board games and a pack of playing cards. Jack was trying to teach us how to play this old game called Trumps. Greta and he were both obsessed with it for a while, so Hoshi and I used to take the opportunity to go to one of the bedrooms for a "rest".

For the first time ever we had privacy: space and time to get to know each other properly. We didn't just talk, of course. There were other, special moments in that house that I'll remember for the rest of my life. I smile thinking about it. If I had to choose my most favourite place in the world, that house would definitely be it.

Anyway, Hoshi and I were talking one day about the fact that my mother was running for office against Laura Minton and she said that she thought that good was stronger than evil and good would win in the end. I remember being really surprised – Hoshi always seems such a realist, and all the stuff she's been through can make her seem a bit spiky at times. When I asked her about it, though, she said that being with me had made her more hopeful.

"People wouldn't be capable of feeling like this if we weren't all meant to look after each other," she said.

"But what about people like Silvio?" I said. "And what about my mother?"

"Silvio was an abomination, but maybe he wasn't born that way. Maybe it was the terrible injustices he suffered when he was young that made him like that. And no offence, Ben, but there aren't many people in this world as warped as your mother."

She snuggled up even closer in my arms.

"What I mean is that I think now that there's good in most people, whether they're Pure or Dreg, or there would be if they weren't so brainwashed and deluded. How could someone as sweet and perfect as Greta even exist if the world's evil? And think of everything Jack's given up for us – three strangers he'd never even met. So many people have helped us, even though it put them at risk. Amina and Priya and all my family in the Cirque, and all those people now, bringing us food, helping us hide, helping us survive. For every bad act we've seen, there have been loads of good acts. Loads of times when people have put themselves on the line for us – when they've done all they can to protect us."

She looked up at me, and I looked back. We just stared at each other for the longest time before she said, "There's so much goodness in people, Ben. It's stronger than evil, it has to be. One day good will win through, I'm sure of it."

I agreed with her at the time. It made sense then. It made sense last night too, when we stood up to the wolves.

It doesn't make sense now though.

If Hoshi and I were still together, maybe I could still believe it. Without her, I can't see anything good any more. Not when I've just watched that little boy scrambling around up there, fighting for his life.

The circus will open tonight. People will pay good money to come and join in with whatever horrors have been planned, the gorier the better. Silvio and my mother have won this game. Evil holds the trump card and it beats Good hands down, again, just like it does every time.

I'm in such deep thought that it startles me when Ezekiel

appears, back in his normal ragged clothes. He looks up at me, the cheeky grin back on his face. What on earth is there for him to smile about?

"It's OK, Ben," he says, gently. "Don't be sad. I'm sure your mother won't let you be in the shows really."

I hear myself making a strange noise, a cross between a splutter and a sob.

"I was sad because of you," I tell him. "Not me. Are you OK?" What a stupid question.

He nods and slips his hand into mine. "It wasn't so bad. I'm much quicker than all those spiders; I'm going to be fine."

I stare down at him. He's just been through all that and his first thought is to comfort me. He's trying to make *me* feel better about his ordeal.

No wonder Hoshi said he was special. He is.

"Do you know what I think?" he says.

I shake my head.

"Tell me. What do you think?"

"I think it will all be OK. I think all this will stop soon. That's what happens in all the stories, isn't it? The good guy always wins."

I feel my eyes welling up. I rest a tentative arm around him and he instantly throws his around me and hugs me tight.

"Ezekiel," I say, looking down on his glossy curls. "I think you must be right. With people like you in the world, it can't be all bad. With people like you in the world, there's always room for hope."

I wipe the tears in my eyes away before he can see them, and together the two of us make our way back across the courtyard.

Avoiding Laura and Amanda's attempts to hug me, I scoop Bojo up, pivot away from them and head straight back into the entrance hall.

"I've done what you wanted," I say to Kadir. "You can let Greta go now."

"Don't worry, my child. I've already given the orders. She'll probably be home before you. Now, that wasn't so bad, was it?"

I don't say anything. I clench my fists, my nails digging into the palms of my hands.

"Don't you want to get changed?" he asks. "That costume is rather different from the usual slum attire."

"There's no time. I just want to see Greta."

"Have it your own way," he says. "Next time perhaps you'll do what I ask in the first place. I don't like playing games like this; it's much easier if everyone just does what I want from the start."

I stare at him, swallowing hard so that the words inside me don't come out. I can't risk antagonizing him while they still have Greta. If they've done anything to hurt her, I don't know what I'll do.

BEN

It's still quiet when we make our way outside. For a moment, I think about running away, seeing how far I could get, but I know there's no point. Besides, I don't know if I could do it now, turn tail and just leave Ezekiel and Sean and Leah and Emmanuel and all the others. I know I can't do anything to save or protect them, but it would feel cowardly now, to leave them behind.

All those nights, Hoshi would wake up with a jolt, sit bolt upright, fling the blankets off with a scream. The circus was haunting her, she said, memories of what had gone on in there and fears for what was happening right now to the people she'd left behind. She was guilty, she said, guilty of putting herself first, of leaving them all to their plight. I didn't really understand what she meant then. I mean, I felt sorry for her, but I couldn't see why she could ever imagine any of it was her fault.

As soon as we heard what they were building over here, I'd catch her and Greta staring across, watching its progress with morbid fascination.

"They're my family," she'd say. "They're a part of me and I abandoned them."

I didn't get that at all. I'd never had that feeling before; never felt that sense of duty, that sense of unity, of being bound together. I never felt it with my family: even when I was a little boy, there was always an empty space deep down inside. I only felt it once I was with Hoshi and Greta and Jack. Only understood then that family isn't about blood at all. Family is about loyalty. Family is about love.

Now, in this terrible place, I understand what she meant. I've only known the people in here a couple of days but their faces will haunt my dreams for ever. I feel bound to them already. Opening time approaches thick and fast and for every urge inside telling me to turn heel and run, there's a contrary one, a strange, strong one: a need to see this through together.

I look around at the different arenas and attractions, at the rides and the stalls. It doesn't look like a place of horror. It looks like somewhere wonderful things happen. It looks like a place of childhood dreams, of childhood magic.

Everything is new. Everything gleams with fresh paint. Lots of things shine, lots of things sparkle. Even the rubbish bins are bright and attractive, each one in the shape of a different circus animal.

There haven't been any deaths since I arrived, not yet. There's been electrocution and beatings and horror already, but no deaths.

One thing's certain, though: it won't be long until someone dies. This place has been built for torture, built for death. Which one of us will be the first?

I feel a tug on my arm.

"Are you OK, Ben?" Ezekiel says, worry furrowing his little brow. Then he points at the sky. "Ooh, what's that?"

I look up. The light above is fading already. High above the smudged pink sunset, tiny black dots hover, hundreds of them, spreading out as far as the eye can see. They aren't birds, I don't think – there are too many of them and they're too round, too uniformly spaced out.

I shake my head, bewildered.

"I don't know. I've never seen anything like it before."

"Do you think it's aliens?"

"No," I laugh. "Well, maybe. I don't know what else it could be."

Across the courtyard, Silvio appears with my mother. Her arms are crossed, her lips are pursed, her eyes glide over me like I'm invisible and then back up at the sky.

Simultaneously, a beam of light appears out of each one of the black dots, wide and strong, projecting down across the city.

"They're projection drones, I think," I say to Ezekiel. "But I don't know what they're doing."

One of the beams reaches down into the courtyard, its pool of light forming a wide circle between us and Silvio and my mother.

I gaze across London. Everywhere, light beams, pouring down from the sky.

The first time I ever saw Hoshi it was in a beam of light like this. A holographic image they projected upwards the day the Cirque first arrived in the city. I saw her dance across the sky. A wave of longing seizes me. I close my eyes. I can still see her now, still feel that tingling when I looked into her angry eyes.

Ezekiel's intake of breath, a gasp of wonder, makes me open my eyes.

There she is. My Hoshi. Not in my imagination any more, not in my memory, but there, right in front of me, the same images as before. Across the city, a hundred other Hoshis mirror her: free and fluid and fantastic.

It's beautiful. It's like a poem. It's like a miracle.

And then, above me, to the left of me, behind me, everywhere: her voice.

We are all flesh and blood. We all feel. We are all human.

My eyes don't move from her. They drink her in as she jumps, tumbles and tumbles and tumbles through the sky and lands, perfectly, right in front of Silvio and my mother, whose mouths both hang open in shock at this lovely, lovely vision; braver, better, brighter than they could ever hope to be.

I don't know who did this, and I don't know how, but, my God, it's phenomenal.

Ezekiel reaches out an incredulous hand towards her, pulling it back when it grasps at nothing. I know how he feels.

I wish she was real. I wish I could touch her.

Her words ring out like bells pealing across London, loud, proud and true.

There is another truth. Vote for what is right. Vote for change.

The car drops me at the edge of the slums and I push my way through the fence. Sprinting as fast as I can, I head down the labyrinth of winding paths.

Coming towards me, out of nowhere, is Greta.

She sees me at the same time and we run towards each other while poor Bojo scrambles out of the way with an indignant chatter.

I pull back, crouching down low so that we're level, and scan her for any signs of injury.

"What did they do to you?"

"I'm OK," she says. "They were nice to me. Well, they just ignored me most of the time, but they did let me have some of my cake."

"You sure? You sure no one touched you?"

"No, honestly. They were really busy." She looks at me with a strange excitement in her eyes. "They locked me in a room, but I listened at the door. There was a keyhole, and when I looked through it, I could see them. Felix was there for a while, with a load of other guys. I heard them talking."

She glances over her shoulder, cups her hand to my ear and whispers into it. "It was the Brotherhood, Hoshi, Felix has already joined them. They're storming the Cirque. Tonight! Kadir knows about it! He was giving them guns, loads of them!"

My heart freezes. "They're going into the Cirque tonight? Oh my God. Greta, this is bad. This is really bad."

She looks puzzled. "Why? I thought you'd be pleased. You can't *want* it to open!"

"Because the Brotherhood are ruthless!" I say. "If they raid the circus, Ben's going to be in even more danger than he is already!"

"Why? They're going to free the performers! They're going to get everyone out. That's all they kept saying – that they were going to turn the tables, show the Pures what it was really like to be in there. They don't want to hurt any Dregs."

"Ben isn't a Dreg though, is he? He's a Pure. The Brotherhood hate all Pures. He's Vivian Baines's son! He's leverage!"

"But Ben's one of us now."

"Not to them. They'll just look at him and see his mother. If they get their hands on him, they'll hurt him just to spite her." I shiver. "He'll be a prime target!"

She gasps. "What shall we do?"

"I don't know. We have to get him out." I pause for a second. "Surely, they'll fail; I don't even understand how they think it's possible to storm a place like that. There's so much security. How the hell do they think they're going to get in there?"

"They've got a government van and security passes," she says. "Laura Minton has given them to them. They're all official."

"Laura Minton knows about this?"

"They've promised to keep her name out of it, but she's in on the whole thing."

I feel so shocked. Laura Minton is the face of respectability. And yet … she's allied with a slumlord. She's facilitating terrorism. She's playing a dangerous game.

Laura. Kadir. The Brotherhood. Are they really that different from each other? They're all prepared to use subterfuge and violence to get what they want. They all think the end justifies the means.

Are they right?

Maybe they are. Maybe what Felix said is true: how is it different from what we did when we escaped? I'd have used that gun if I'd had to, I know I would. If I hadn't blown up the arena I'd have been captured. Greta and I would be dead.

I take Greta's hand and we walk to the little stretch of patchy wasteland right on the edges of the slums. I look around. It's quieter here; I don't think anyone can hear us.

"Right," I say to Greta. "Tell me exactly what you heard them say, every last detail."

"They've got passes and a van ... they've got weapons ... and they're storming some building called Arcadia. They know the timings: they said that all the Dregs and all the Pures are going to be in there at the same time for the opening ceremony. Felix has been doing undercover work for them – it's how he's earned his place in the group. He's been going in with a work permit, meeting his brother and reporting back to the Brotherhood."

Poor Rosie. Felix has spoken to his brother and he didn't even tell her. And now he's a fully-fledged member of the Brotherhood. He's going to break the law, commit violent crimes maybe. If he gets caught, they'll hang him. Why would he risk everything like that?

Because he wants to save his brother. Because his life isn't worth living anyway.

Suddenly, the sky ahead fills with tiny black dots, way up high. Out of each one, a beam of light, and then an image.

Greta's jaw drops open.

"Hoshi! It's you!"

She's right. It is me. I'm everywhere.

The biggest drone of all is hovering directly over the PowerHouse. There, for all to see, the country's most wanted criminal is somersaulting on the head of the gold statue of the government headquarters, calling out for change.

On the other side of London, I'm there too, dancing in the circus.

I wonder if Ben can see me. I wonder what he thinks.

Greta gazes up with a huge grin of amazement on her face. "Isn't it brilliant!"

People are already coming out on to the streets. Crowds gathering here and all over the city, pointing up at the sky.

I look at the images again and my heart plummets like a stone. Vivian Baines will see them. If they do what they're intended to – if they steal her thunder and weaken her campaign – she'll be really angry. She'll be desperate to get her revenge.

What if her hatred for me is bigger than her love for Ben? No, love's the wrong word. Someone like her, someone with stone for a heart, isn't capable of loving anyone. How *does* she feel by now, about her wayward son? She gave up her chance of catching me to make sure he didn't kill himself. Why? What for, if it wasn't love? She'll be after an apology from him, I guess. She'll be after remorse. What if he's already made it clear to her that he won't change?

I know Ben. Not the Ben she thinks she knows; not the confused and uncertain boy who struggled for a while to work out right from wrong. I know the real Ben. Ben as he is now.

Brave, strong, loyal. If she's spoken to him he'll have told her exactly where to go.

Silvio killed Amina to get at me. Kadir kidnapped Greta so I'd do what he wanted.

Vivian Baines can't hurt me while I'm on the run.

She can hurt him though. What if she decides the best way to punish me is to finish him off once and for all?

"Greta, is there anything else you can remember? Anything at all." I'm gripping her arm too tightly, but I can't help it.

Greta's brow furrows. "That's it, I think. Oh yeah, pickup time's at dusk. Meet at the agreed rendezvous, whatever that means."

I look to the west. The sun is already low in the sky.

I start running.

"Where are you going?" asks Greta, dashing along next to me.

"I'm going to find Felix. I'm going to follow him." I look down at her. "I'm going with them. I'm going into the Cirque."

BEN

Once Hoshi finally vanishes, everyone stays still for a moment. Fixed in position. Numbed. Awestruck.

Eventually, I feel Ezekiel squeeze my hand and he grins up at me.

"That was like real magic wasn't it?"

I nod.

"It was real magic. Only Hoshi can make magic like that."

I walk towards my mother and Silvio, my smile wide, my heart swelling.

"What do you reckon? Amazing, wasn't it?"

My mother's face is so pale it's nearly as white as Silvio's.

"I should have told them to shoot you all when I had the chance!" she spits at me. "The biggest mistake I ever made was allowing you to survive and letting her run off again! Correction, second biggest mistake. The first was giving birth to you in the first place!"

I keep on smiling. "I can see why you're angry. Talk about stealing the show! You may as well give up now; you'll never compete with that!"

For just a second, I have the upper hand. For just a second, she's panicking, but then a new expression settles on her face. Her eyes meet mine and she's victorious again: self-assured, smug, in control.

"Ah, Benedict. You never did know when to keep your mouth shut. You're right, in a way. She's upped the ante, your girlfriend – only something truly dramatic can compete with that. Fortunately, this evening's performance provides the very opportunity."

She turns from me to Silvio.

"I've changed my mind. What you suggested before, we'll do it. I was wrong to listen to my husband; wrong to hold on to maternal feelings which should have long been dead and buried."

She turns back to me, musingly. "I don't know why I resisted: the advantages are threefold. Firstly, any limelight surrounding your girlfriend's little acrobatic display will be mercifully short-lived. Secondly, it will finally end your Bonnie and Clyde scenario once and for all. Thirdly, I get to dispose of an embarrassing problem."

She reaches out a hand and pats me on the head.

"Sometimes the apple really does fall far from the tree. Ringmaster, you may go ahead with your plans. Goodbye, Benedict, goodnight and God bless."

As she walks away, Silvio claps his hands with delight.

"Oh my! I never even really dared hope that your mother would say yes to my little request! You know, Baines, tonight was always going to be fantastic, but with you in the starring role it's going to be just spellbinding!"

HOSHIKO

I wait round the corner from Rosie and Felix's while Greta creeps up to peek inside; she's smaller than I am and less likely to be seen.

"He's in there," she says when she comes back. "As soon as he comes out, we can follow him."

She thinks I'm taking her with me. "Greta," I say, softly. "You have to stay here."

"No!" she cries. "No way! I'm not letting you go without me! We work as a team, we always have!"

I look at her, my beautiful Greta. Last time she was held captive, she stole a gun and came and rescued me; this time she's managed to uncover top secret plans to raid the Cirque.

Silvio, Kadir, the Brotherhood, they're all the same. They all underestimate her because she's tiny and because she's a girl. What fools they are!

I tilt her chin up and look into her eyes.

"Greta, I need you out here. I need someone who knows what's going on, to tell Jack and Rosie if things don't go to plan."

"We should tell Jack now! He could come with us!"

"He'll try and stop us. He's been absolutely worried sick about you; I've never seen him so upset. He won't let us do it."

"That's because it's a stupid idea! It's dangerous, Hoshi, and it won't work! How can *we* take on the Brotherhood? Take on the circus? It's silly to think we could!" She crumples into me and starts to cry. "I don't want you to leave me again!"

I hold her tight.

"I know," I whisper into her hair. "And I don't want to go, but I've got to do it, Greta. I've got to try and get Ben out of there. I need you to be strong. I need you to cover for me with Jack and Rosie. Tell them I'm with Nila and Nihal."

"What if you don't come back?" She gulps the words out through convulsive sobs.

"If you haven't heard from me by tomorrow, you can tell Jack the truth," I say. "But you will. I'll come back, I promise and this time, I'll have Ben with me."

There's a movement from outside the shack. It's Felix, hood pulled over his head, slinking off down the road.

"I've got to go." I hug her one more time.

"I love you, Hoshi."

"I love you too," I whisper back, and then I follow after Felix, leaving her there, crying in the shadows.

BEN

Once my mother has gone, Silvio looks me up and down, like he's assessing my worth.

"Hmm. We should be OK; you're about the same size as the boy the wolves finished off last night. There might need to be some minor adjustments though – I want everything tonight to be absolutely perfect! Come with me!"

He ushers me away from Ezekiel, right through the courtyard and into Arcadia. I keep my eyes focused ahead of me. I will not be impressed with anything this place has to offer.

He takes me backstage, opening a door to reveal a giant wardrobe, crammed full of costumes hanging up on racks. Rifling through, he pulls one from the back of the rail.

"Now, this was originally intended for wolf boy, but you're far more suited to the role. I think the outfit will fit, and the life you used to lead, the life you turned your back on, should have prepared you perfectly!"

He holds the costume up in front of me.

I look at it. I don't know what I expected, but it wasn't this. I start laughing and, once I start, I can't stop.

"You want me to dress in that?"

"Benedict!" He looks really offended. "This is the costume of a god! Tonight, you will become Pan, ruler of all Arcadia! Things could not have worked out better!"

I don't believe it: he's being serious.

"Well," he barks. "Put it on!"

"Now?"

"Yes! I need to check it fits." He lifts his cane up and waves it in my face. "And do it quickly!"

I take the costume off the rack, pull my rags over my head and wriggle my way into it. All the while he's watching me with that creepy grin on his face.

The costume is incredibly uncomfortable. The trousers are tight and itchy and it's hard to stand up properly in the hooved shoes, but Silvio seems more than satisfied.

"Oh my!" he gushes. "Your Pure blood shines through no matter how much you seek to deny it, Benedict! You look far more handsome and godly in it than the Dreg boy would have done! Far more regal! Oh, that reminds me." He goes to a big plastic box at the side of the room and rifles around inside. "How could I forget?" he cries, and places a crown on my head.

"And there we have it," he beams. "The illusion is complete!" He wheels over a full-length mirror and then twirls his hands forward and bends low in an extravagant bow. "Welcome to Arcadia, your Greatness!"

I look into the mirror. Just when I thought nothing about this place could surprise me any more, he's turned me into this. I'm dressed as a goat. A goat wearing a golden, jewel-encrusted crown.

Felix heads quickly away down the winding alleys of the slums. I follow close behind, always ready to duck back if he looks around, but he never does. When he reaches the fences, he slips through a gap and out into No Man's Land.

I creep softly after him. He walks for another minute or two before turning off into a big car park.

It's empty, except for a van, right in the far corner. Even from this distance, I can see the government crest on it. I shiver; it reminds me of Ben's mother.

Felix crosses the car park and heads over to it.

I stay on the outskirts. If I step out into the open, they'll see me straight away.

I hear voices and spring back into a doorway. Two more men walk past, both dressed in dark clothes, both with shifty looks on their faces, both carrying large bags. Brotherhood: you can spot a mile off that they're up to no good. They cross the road and head towards the van.

I run as quickly as I can around the perimeter of the car park, skirting around it, so that I end up coming in from the opposite side and duck down behind the straggly, ugly bushes separating the car park from the street. I can hear the low murmur of voices and see the back doors of the van, tantalizingly close.

After a few minutes, a man comes round and opens up the door. He lifts up the bags, looking around quickly before loading stuff from them into the back of the van. Guns, just like Greta said.

My heart beats faster.

"Carlos," someone says. "Get round here a minute." He chucks the last bag in and disappears to the front, leaving the back doors of the van open.

This is my only chance.

I creep out from the bushes and jump into the van, crouching down at the back as low as I can.

I can hear voices clearly now.

"OK. We've got all the paperwork, we just need to stay calm and confident and we should get in no problem. Everyone set for this? Felix? We don't want any first-time nerves giving the game away."

"I'm ready," Felix's voice answers.

"You sure you're committed?"

"One hundred per cent. I've been waiting years for this."

"Good. When we get there, I'm in charge. You wait for my command. Right?"

"Right."

"OK. One last thing. Everyone sure they got away all right? Nobody was asked any awkward questions? Nobody got suspicious? You know the first rule of the Brotherhood: trust no one. If anyone thinks they might have been exposed, now's the time to tell me."

No one says anything, including Felix.

"Let's go. Felix, shut the van up."

There's the sound of feet coming round the side of the van and then Felix's face peers in, squinting in the gloom.

I press myself backwards, but it's no use: he sees me straight away. He jolts his head back, his eyes alarmed and panicked.

"Felix?" the voice from the front calls. I can feel the weight of them all piling into the van, just the other side of the thin panel separating us. "All set?"

He stares at me for a moment and then turns away.

"All set," I hear him say as he slams the doors shut. He jumps into the passenger seat in front of me, and then the engine fires up and we drive off into the dusky night.

BEN

Silvio looks at his watch. "My goodness, it's nearly showtime! Only two hours to go until the finale. I can't be doing with babysitting you! I've got to find a last-minute standby for wolf boy in the clown show, and in the Wheel of Death. I have to say, I could do without losing a performer at this late stage. It was quite annoying really, him being eaten like that. Oh, who am I kidding! I'd make the same decision all over again: you know it and I know it! The impact it must have had on your lot's morale is worth all the headache it's causing."

He reaches up a hand, stroking my cheek softly, his deathly white face etched with false compassion. "What was it like? Seeing them devouring him?"

My skin crawls under his touch. I'd love to tell him where Sean is now. I'd love to describe exactly what happened, exactly what we did.

"Hmm." He rubs his chin. "Maybe I should just stick you in his place for everything, not just the opening ceremony? It's the obvious choice, and your mother did say I could do what I like. Yes, that's what I'll do, if you happen to survive. Oh, Benedict, you are in for a busy night. Anyway, I must stop all this chit-chat! Get back into your normal clothes, will you. We need to keep this costume pristine for the big reveal!"

He stares at me while I get changed and licks his lips. "Life on the run certainly hasn't done any harm to your physique, Baines, has it?"

He steps closer and I move away, hurriedly.

He lifts his arm and speaks into his watch.

"Come and take the Baines boy away, will you? Lock him up until further notice."

From nowhere, guards appear at his command and drag me away through a fire exit at the back of the room. At the door, I look back over my shoulder. He stands in the middle of the stage and beams at me, raising his hands high in the air. Then, seemingly by magic, he disappears. How did he do that? There's no wires above where he stood, or obvious trapdoor in the floor. Does he have special powers?

Maybe Hoshi was right; maybe Silvio really is the devil.

HOSHIKO

The men don't talk much on the journey; maybe they're all psyching themselves up for whatever it is they've got planned. I stay crouched down in the back of the van while it drives across the city, not moving an inch, even though my legs cramp up and my arms go all stiff. Eventually, we slow down. I think we must be in traffic, or some sort of queue, because we stop and start sporadically for ages.

After about ten minutes, I feel a rush of air as the window is wound down.

"Good evening, gents. All right if I take a look at your passes?" a voice outside says.

There's the sound of rustling papers before the voice continues. "We haven't got you down on the list. Only authorized personnel are permitted, tonight in particular."

"We were given the approval weeks ago, by the government security services," the driver in front of me replies, his tone assured and confident. "It's all there in the paperwork. Extra security. For opening night. There's a lot of VIPs here, they need full protection…"

There's the sound of footsteps walking away and then voices talking close to the van.

"We can't afford to hold up the queues any longer," I hear another voice say. "They're in a government truck, they must be legit."

"They look more like Dregs than Pures," the first voice says. "I don't like it. Something feels wrong."

"The paperwork looks OK?" asks the other voice.

"Yeah. It's just…"

"You know what these security firms are like; the government want them to look intimidating. They probably use them for all their Dreg raids and interrogation and stuff." The voice drops lower. "We can't afford to mess around giving government heavies a hard time."

"No, I guess not," the first man says, and then after another few seconds I hear him again at the window. "Sorry about the delay," he says. "Go on through." And the window closes as we slowly roll forward.

We drive for another minute or so more and then the van stops and there's the sound of the handbrake being pulled up and the engine being switched off.

Now what do I do?

Light pours in as the doors swing open and Felix's face appears, glaring at me angrily.

"Quick!" he hisses. "Get out, quick!"

I don't need telling twice. I scramble out and dart off between rows of cars.

I look up. I was just in time; the guys are all at the back door of the van now, peering around suspiciously. They aren't doing a very good job at looking inconspicuous, if you ask me. The way they're huddled together in their dark clothes carrying those big black bags, they might as well have a sign declaring "We're terrorists." Still, the government van and passes seem to be all the accessories they need to persuade people, because they've passed the hardest hurdle already.

They're in.

And so am I.

I look around. The long rows of cars line the length of the field we're in, and ahead, bigger and brighter than ever before, there it is.

The Cirque.

The spectacular Ferris wheel, all lit up, towers above everything else, and there's a helter-skelter, the excited squeals of Pure kids sliding down it already filling the night. There are other rides too: roller coasters and dodgems and waltzers, whizzing round and round, the people in the carriages screaming with delight.

Pures mill about everywhere and there's music and stalls and tents and sideshows and I can see a man in stilts walking along, and jugglers and clowns moving amongst the crowd.

A thousand lights flash and whirl and wink, and that circus smell of popcorn and smoke and sweet sugary doughnuts, freshly cooked, lingers in the air. The smell of oil and fire, of cold night air and heated bodies. The smell of excitement. The smell of life. The smell of death. It's the smell that hits me, the smell that gets me, the smell that fills my senses and makes me close my eyes with the strength of the memories that flood in.

I'm transported back there, once more. Back to the arena, back to the wire. Back to soaring through the air, arching, gliding, flying. So free; and yet not free at all.

I can feel it now. Feel myself leaping forward off the trapeze, catching hold of Amina's hands, springing lightly on to the wire. For so long, we were seamless up there, we moved as one, the perfect team. It was magic.

And then I see Amina falling again. I see her murdered body swinging on the same wire, and I shudder. That's what I have to hold on to: the cruelty and the violence and the horror. That's what's real. How can I, of all people, be seduced by the Circus?

I pull myself together. I don't have time for this. I need to find Ben. I become aware, all of a sudden, of voices getting louder, coming out of nowhere along the line of cars.

"I told you to bring it! What's the last thing I said to you? Sebastian, bring your jacket!" says a voice crossly, and a Pure woman and a young boy appear, weaving their way through the cars and stopping at the one next to me. The woman clicks her car keys and the lights of a nearby car flashes as it unlocks. She comes round to open the door and looks at me, suspiciously, crouched down by the next car. I get to my feet and walk off quickly.

It's only then that I notice the Brotherhood have gone.

I head quickly across the field.

What do I do? Anyone looking at me will know who I am straight away. Maybe I should start performing so that they think I'm one of the acts? I could easily do a few somersaults, a few backflips. No, everyone will have seen the drones. I must be more recognizable than ever.

I'll have to hide somewhere until things die down a bit and the Pures head inside, to the shows. I look around but there's nowhere to go: everywhere is all brightly lit up, everywhere is busy and bustling.

The only thing I can do is to creep to the outskirts and try and remain as hidden as possible.

I keep my head down low and dart through the open gates.

I'm back in the circus.

BEN

The guards take me outside and lead me across the main courtyard.

It's dark already and they've opened the huge gates. Crowds of people are streaming in, chatting, laughing, shrieking. The lights are on, the music is playing, the rides are whirling, twirling, whizzing, the food is sizzling and frying. The Cirque isn't a hushed ghost town any more, quietly snoozing while it waits for something to happen. It's alive and awake and buzzing.

The big queues in front of each ride make it hard to see what's actually happening on them. Strobes and lasers flash, things spin and soar in the air, but I can't tell if the screams are Dregs in pain or Pures in ecstasy, or both.

The guards are so busy staring at everything that it slows their pace right down. I get plenty of time to absorb what's going on, whether I like it or not.

Right in the middle of the courtyard, there's a big crowd of parents with young children, queueing to buy huge balloons, the biggest I've ever seen.

The balloon seller is a clown, on stilts, standing nearly as high as the balloons. As we get closer, I see that it's Ravi.

At the front of the queue, a dad is handing over some money while a mum helps her daughter choose a balloon. The girl is about eight, I reckon, all wrapped up in a white fur coat.

"I want that pink one!" she says, pointing at the biggest balloon of all, and Ravi stoops down to pass it to her.

"I've told you before, Verity, don't touch the Dregs!" her mother hisses, and reaches over to take it from Ravi herself, a look of disgust on her face. They move off with their balloon, the girl clutching firmly on to the curled ribbons of string. "Keep hold of it the whole time, Verity. If you don't, the balloon will float away and I'm not buying another one at that price!"

Their airs and graces and snobbery make me feel physically sick inside. How can they be so self-assured of their superiority in the world? So certain of their *purity*?

I try to pull away from the guards, but they tighten their grip on me. "Hey!" My voice sounds hard and brittle, like it could crack. "Are you proud of yourself? You really think it's OK, do you, bringing your precious daughter here? You really want her to grow up thinking that what they do here is acceptable? That it's entertaining? People will die here tonight, I should think. Human beings. Does that make you excited?"

The whole family stare at me in shock and the crowd of people waiting to buy balloons all turn and look at me. On every face, horror at my impertinent outcry.

The guards drag me away, kicking and struggling, while the crowd look on, outraged and affronted.

My behaviour has horrified them. *My* behaviour is socially unacceptable to *them*.

If it wasn't so tragic, it would be funny.

HOSHIKO

It's hard to find somewhere to hide. Everywhere is lit up and more and more and more people just keep spilling in.

My cat costume sparkles when the lights shine on it, so I try to stick to the darker places. Luckily, there's so much going on everywhere that nobody thinks to pay any attention to the Dreg girl lurking in the shadows.

I circulate slowly around the vast Pure pleasure ground, all the time my eyes scanning the crowds, searching for people I know, wanting, and not wanting, to see them. Most of all, I look for Ben.

I stick to the quietest, darkest places, and that's why I find myself around the back of one of the rides – *Dodge a Dreg*, it's called. It's a bumper car track, open at the sides so I can see exactly what's happening.

Coloured cars are driving around a rink, hooting their horns. There are two Pures in most cars, sometimes couples: the boy behind the wheel, the girl screaming next to him. More often, though, it's a parent and child, the child behind the wheel but the parent's hands reaching over and steering the car. Some of the cars have one rider, usually a teenage boy, and they're the ones who are driving their cars the fastest and ramming them the hardest into the other vehicles.

On the front and back of each car, bound tightly by thick straps, is a person: a Dreg, I assume, dressed in contrasting colours to the car.

Every time the cars ram into each other, the people attached to each one are crushed together. Only their lower bodies are fastened to the car, so their torsos move with every crash, reverberating back and forth. The faster, more skilled drivers –

the teenage boys – slam into the back of the slower cars, again and again and again, their jaws set with determination as they spin their steering wheels. The drivers in front are oblivious to the impending impact until it's too late, but the poor Dreg strapped to the back must be able to see it coming, see the car as it approaches, see the triumphant glee on the riders' faces.

I can't tell if there's anyone I know on the cars; every person has their face painted like a clown and is wearing a different coloured wig, so it's impossible to tell.

When the ride finishes, the Pures all climb out, chattering excitedly and laughing to each other. The Dregs stay fastened to their cars, their heads hanging low while more riders get ready.

This is even worse than it used to be.

I'd have said such a thing wasn't possible, if you'd asked me. I thought it was hell before, when the Pures just watched, but now, in this fairground, they're active participants. They are the instigators of the violence: the power has been put in their hands and they are loving it.

I've let myself forget just what it's like, being in this place. All those months with Ben have softened me. I learnt from him and Jack to look for the good in Pures, to give people a chance to redeem themselves. I let go of hate, for a while. Now it's back. Now it floods through my whole body.

I can't watch this again. It feels wrong, skulking behind here, looking on while these poor people suffer like this. I move away quickly.

I didn't come here to hide, and I certainly didn't come to spectate.

I came here to find Ben.

BEN

The guards move more quickly now, hurrying me away from the crowds so I can't cause any more fuss.

They manoeuvre me all the way across the courtyard and unlock the gate that leads to the Dreg holdings.

The first guard waits at the top of the stairs while the other one walks me down the stairs and pushes me into a cell, then takes a padlock from his pocket and locks up the door.

I hold on to the bars. "Do you really think this is right?" I ask him. "What happens here? You saw those kids. You see what happens in rehearsals. Do you sleep well at night?"

He looks around and up the stairs and then steps closer, responding quietly. His eyes are bloodshot and shadowed with dark circles.

"No. To answer your question. I don't think it's right, and no, I don't sleep well. I do this to pay the bills, that's all. It doesn't mean I like it."

He turns away from me.

When he reaches the door, he places something on the floor.

"When they come to let you out, this is where the keys are," he says, and then adds quietly, "Good luck tonight, I really hope you make it."

I hear the guards' footsteps overhead as they walk off.

I count to sixty. Everywhere is silent.

"Sean," I say. "Sean, it's only me, Ben. It's OK, you can come out now."

At first there's no movement at all, and then he emerges

slowly from one of the cells. You can tell by the way he's dragging himself along that his body hasn't healed yet.

"What are you doing in here?" he says quietly.

"Silvio wants me out of the way until the opening ceremony."

"Did you see any of the others?"

"I saw Ravi selling balloons. I didn't see anyone else, just Pures queueing for the rides and stuff." I point to the keys lying in the corridor. "Can you unlock my door?"

He picks them up and fumbles with the padlock, his poor, injured hands clumsy.

Finally, it clicks.

I push the doors open and step out. "Thanks."

"Thank *you*," he says, his voice cracking. "For last night, with the wolves."

We smile at each other, awkwardly, then I reach out a hand and he takes it, holding it limply in his broken and bloodied one.

Only a couple of days ago, he saw me as his enemy. Now we're brothers. Not brothers like me and Francis – linked by biology and nothing else – but brothers like me and Jack. Brothers whose experiences bind them tightly together.

Being in a place like this does that to you, I guess.

That must be why his real brother's group call themselves the Brotherhood, because they stand together, because they're trying to fight back together, because they feel stronger in their unity.

If they somehow manage to get into this place, bringing in their weapons and their anger, what will I do?

I'll stand with them, that's what, if they'll let me. I'd fight for all my brothers' freedom, whatever the cost. I know that now.

"So what happens next?" Sean says.

"They're coming back for me in an hour or so. I'm taking your place in the big opening ceremony."

He smiles ruefully. "Sorry my fake death has landed you in it."

"It's hardly your fault," I say. "Do you know what I'm supposed to be doing?"

He shakes his head. "They wouldn't tell any of us anything. Silvio just kept saying it would be better if we were unprepared, that the Pures would want to see genuine shock on our faces."

He looks around the cells. "Hold on," he says. "What are you still doing here, anyway? You can get out of here – those are the master keys, I reckon. They probably unlock all the doors."

"Where would I go? Everyone will recognize me."

He nods. "You're probably right, but if I were you, I'd rather take my chances out there than just sit in here and wait for them to come back and drag me along to the opening show."

Maybe he's right. Maybe I should just go out there and take my chances. No. I can't. The thought of staying down here, waiting obediently for them to come and take me, is awful, but going out there again, after what I've just seen? I don't think I can bear it.

"It's the same for you, though, isn't it?" I say. "You could go out there if you wanted to. Your brother's supposed to be breaking in tonight, isn't he?"

He nods, his face grave.

"That's all I've been thinking about; Felix and his crew are going to storm the finale. Felix knows I'm supposed to be in it. When he doesn't see me, he'll think I'm already dead."

"What are you waiting for then? You might be able to find him."

He shakes his head forlornly. "Look at me. I can hardly move. The guards'll seize me straight away. I'm supposed to have been wolf food. They'll kill me as soon as they realize."

"But they'll find out eventually anyway. You can't stay hidden down here for ever."

"I won't need to if the Brotherhood succeed."

It's futile, what his brother and his gang are planning. There are guards everywhere. They aren't even going to make it as far as the main entrance and, even if they do, they'll be mowed down before they've taken five steps. I don't say that though. I don't say anything.

"You don't look like a Dreg," Sean says. "Even now. If you can avoid Silvio and the guards, and if you keep your head down, you might be able to last out there, for a while at least. You could look for my brother. He looks exactly like me – you'd recognize him straight away. Tell him I said you're different from the others, that I said you're a good lad. Tell him I'm not dead."

"I tell you what," I say. "Let's go out together."

"No." He shakes his head. "I'll just draw attention to you."

"It doesn't matter really, I'll never get out past the guards anyway. You're right though: we might as well as give them the runaround a bit before they catch us, and if you brother *has* made it inside, you can tell him and his gang not to shoot me yourself."

He closes his eyes, squeezing them shut tightly. When he

opens them, there's a spark of life in them that wasn't there before.

"Come on then," he says. "Let's go and join the revolution."

I move away and run quickly across an open area to the next ride, duck down behind it and then move on to the next one.

Across the square there's a band playing, moving along in a big procession: a classical orchestra with soaring violins and strumming harps. Twelve tiny children, dressed as angels, tumble simultaneously at the front. I strain my eyes but I don't recognize any of them. They must be newly selected – God, they've trained them up quick, and they're good, all of them; flipping and turning as one. Behind them are two fire eaters, the flames they create flaring up into the air before they devour them. As they move closer, my heart jolts. I know them. Alex and Archie, they're called: friends of mine, friends of ours.

I can't watch. I turn my head. Look instead at what's in front of me.

Big mistake.

Up high, a flashing sign is lit up with the words *Fatal Blow*. Below it, Pures are lining up, taking it in turns to strike a rubber cushion with a giant hammer as hard as they can. Every time someone slams it down, a big iron ball whooshes up a vertical panel. The harder the hit, the higher the ball goes.

I raise my eyes. I know I shouldn't. I know what I'm going to see.

There's a person, right at the top, trapped in a bubble of glass. The Pures are trying to hit the cushion with enough force to make the iron ball shoot up high enough to hit him.

They've made him wear his leopard-skin thong, the same one he used to wear in the lion show.

It's Emmanuel.

A woman steps up. Swinging the hammer behind her, she whirls around and pelts the rubber cushion. The bar rises all the way up, whacking right into Emmanuel. The whole pole lights up in multicoloured strobes while an alarm loudly sounds. It must hurt like hell, but he stares ahead, unflinching, proud as ever, as they cheer and jeer below him.

I stare up at him, but he never looks down. I step forward, right into the main area in front of him, to get his attention. I don't know why. I don't know what the point is, but I want him to know I'm here.

The procession moves closer and closer while I stand there, right in the middle of the square, in full view. And then I see a horse, a golden palomino. I'd know that horse anywhere; it's still just as beautiful, just as thoroughbred, just as Pure.

A white figure stands on top of it, smiling and waving down at the crowd gathered around him, all gasping, all cheering.

It's a ghost, it must be. Same height, same gestures, same maniacal grin but devoid of colour. His clothes are white. His face is deathly white. Everything's white except his glowing eyes of blue.

The procession comes to a standstill. The golden halos of the children light up as they begin to sing. Angelic, choral voices, their crystal tones soaring through the night.

Behold! Behold!
He has risen! He has risen!
Hallelujah! Hallelujah!

Right in the middle of them, standing on his horse's back, his arms thrown out wide, his head thrust towards the heavens. Silvio Sabatini, back from the dead.

BEN

I unlock the door slowly and poke my head out, scanning the dark and silent field.

Over the fences seeps the glow of a thousand lights and the noise of the fairground.

Slowly, I creep across to the gate and try the keys in the lock. It clicks open.

I beckon to Sean, who's peering out nervously from the top of the stairs, and he runs across as quickly as he can. Once he gets to me, he bends over double to get his breath back. It takes a while for his breathing to steady, but when he pulls himself back up, that same light of hope is still there in his eyes. I try and smile at him. There's no point showing him that all I feel is the promise of doom.

We slip through the door and into the Cirque.

When we aren't instantly seized, I look about and allow myself a quick sigh of relief. Nobody has noticed us. There's nobody near where we are at all; everyone seems to be gathered across the square, lining the main thoroughfare and watching a procession moving through. It's a band, a full orchestra and a choir, singing in angelic voices. All the children are at the front, dressed in white, tumbling and turning and, in the middle, Silvio is standing on his horse. There's no sign of his cane now, no sign of any injury at all. His arms are thrown out, Christ-like, as he gazes up into the sky.

I look at Sean and roll my eyes.

"What an idiot."

He laughs.

"We'd better get out of here before they get any closer."

I glance around for somewhere to go.

To the far left, there's a carousel, noticeably quieter than all the other rides. It's an old, traditional one by the looks of it, with no sick adaptations. I think it must be meant for little kids and their parents, but it's empty. All the Pures who've come here tonight, even the ones who've brought their children, are after as much Dreg suffering as they can possibly get for their money – nobody wants good old-fashioned fairground fun any more.

"That carousel. On the count of three, make your way over there."

Sean looks over to where I'm pointing.

"OK. One, two, three. Run!"

It's the shock that roots me to the spot. I don't run away. I don't hide. I don't do anything except stand there, mouth wide open, gaping at him. His gaze scans over me. And then his head jolts back round. His eyes lock on to me and they stare.

I stare back.

Finally, far too late, I pull myself together.

Behind me, on the *Fatal Blow* attraction, another Pure is about to attempt to bang the rubber cushion hard enough for the iron ball to reach Emmanuel.

I snatch the hammer from his hands and run as fast as I can across the square, but when I turn back, it's too late.

Silvio's down off his horse.

He's slowly crossing the square towards me, and his eyes are hungry.

I'm too exposed.

An old-fashioned carousel looms up in my path, revolving slowly. I run around the back of it and jump on to it.

It's just a traditional ride, no horrid Dreg torture twists going on here, and that probably explains why it's so quiet. I don't think there's anyone on it. I move into the middle, crouching down behind a horse and carriage, which bobs serenely up and down. As the carousel rotates slowly round, I peer out. Silvio's still crossing the square, moving towards me. He's looking around, though. He doesn't know where I am. He's walking with a cane. Maybe I can get away. I keep my eyes fixed on him.

Just as I turn out of view, he sees me.

I edge my way slowly around to the other side, pressing my body against the middle point.

BEN

We crouch down on the carousel, hiding behind a horse and cart.

Across the square, Silvio is still standing on his horse, smiling and shouting something down to the people gathered around him.

Suddenly, his expression changes. He's gazing, transfixed, across the Cirque. He's seen something he doesn't like, something which has shocked him.

It must be Sean's brother and his crew.

I look across, following his gaze, but it's not a gang of men I see.

It's one girl. One girl, running across the square. One girl, jumping up here, on to the carousel.

Not just any girl. My girl. My Hoshi.

She's on the other side. I can't see her any more but she's metres away from me.

What's she doing here?

I stand up. I have to get to her, but Sean grabs my arm and pulls me back down. "Wait!" he hisses. "Pick your moment."

HOSHIKO

I creep my way along behind the horses.

Where's Silvio?

A hand clamps down on my back and someone spins me around.

I'm staring into the face of the ghost.

"Ah, Hoshiko! What a pleasant surprise!" It's a voice that makes my blood run cold and my legs crumple beneath me. A voice that makes the nausea rise up in my throat and makes me lose my breath with fear and shock and loathing. A voice that's haunted my dreams for as long as I can remember.

I try to raise the hammer up but it's too late. He wrenches my arm behind my back and the hammer falls, landing with a metallic clang behind me. The other hand hauls me by my hair off the carousel and throws me to the ground. By the time I look up, loads of people: the whole population of the Cirque, it seems, are gathered around us, staring at him, staring at me. All the people who were watching the parade must have seen him leap off his horse and limp across the square and they've all followed him, gathering more people along the way. He doesn't look quite so messiah-like now, standing over me with his fist raised.

"It's her!" someone shouts out. "The Cat!"

More people appear then, out of nowhere, and the crowd pushes forward towards us, frenzied.

"Hoshiko, where have you been?"

"Where's Benedict Baines?"

"What are you doing here?"

Silvio turns to them and then looks at back at me. His strange white face is ecstatic.

"Yes! Yes! The Cat is back!" he cries jubilantly. "Just in time for tonight's opening ceremony!"

BEN

It's the hardest thing I've ever done, but I crouch in the shadows and wait as Silvio jumps on the ride, his injuries suddenly forgotten.

I hear a sound and see a hammer fall to the floor of the ride. I watch silently as he throws Hoshi to the ground, then turns to address the gathering crowd.

I glance over at Sean. He points to the hammer.

I crawl over to it, keeping behind the pastel-coloured horses whenever I can.

I lift it up. It's heavy enough to knock someone out. Heavy enough to kill them, maybe.

I look down at Silvio below me and pick my moment, just like Sean said.

I crouch low, spring up and jump, swinging the hammer as I drop.

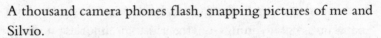

A thousand camera phones flash, snapping pictures of me and Silvio.

He keeps his vice-like grip on my arm and pulls it behind my back, standing behind me, facing the crowd.

The guards have gathered quickly and they manage to restrain the surge, but it's a struggle.

Suddenly, I feel his grip loosen and he slumps forward into me and then tumbles sideways on to the ground.

BEN

As Silvio falls, an astonished Hoshi turns and faces me. The guards are already moving towards us, raising their guns. There's no time to talk, no time for anything. She grabs my hand, and we turn together and run, as fast as we can, bullets whistling past our heads.

"There's nowhere to go!" I gasp as we run. "We're heading straight to the fences!"

Hoshi points to the huge Ferris wheel. *The Wheel of Misfortune*, Silvio called it. It must be popular; there are loads of people milling around in front of it, looking up at it and pointing.

"Head that way."

"Why?"

"More people. They can't shoot at us if we're amongst a load of Pures."

She's right, I guess, but the Pures won't protect us, especially not the ones who come here. They're as likely to kill us as Silvio. Still, I don't have any better ideas.

We run towards the crowd.

Suddenly, bright light from up ahead, images projecting down.

The drones are back.

Just as we're running towards the Big Wheel, the sky lights up and the crowd of people we're running towards all stop what they're doing to stare.

It's the holograms again. Hundreds and hundreds of me, all performing at different times on a loop. Some versions of me are jumping up high, others crouching down low and springing up; some of me are tumbling through the air, some of me are soaring. They're so damn realistic. They don't look like images at all.

Around each image, purple and gold fireworks soar. The sparks dance and shimmer against the night sky and the smell of gunpowder and smoke fills the air. The images have been choreographed so that they are perfectly in sync with the fireworks. When I somersault, they somersault. When I leap up, they leap up. When I fly high, they do too.

Loud, so loud that it drowns out all the other noises, my voice, on repeat, saying the same thing, again and again and again.

We are all flesh and blood. We all feel. We are all human.

Vote for what is right. Vote for change.

For a while, everyone's distracted. Even the guards have stopped, staring in confusion at the dozens of versions of me dancing around in front of them.

Ben could blend into the crowd if he slipped away without me now. He doesn't even look that different from all the other Pures. Dirty old tracksuit bottoms and scruffy tops must be fashionable, because they're pretty much what every single teenage boy around here seems to be wearing too.

I'm the one who usually stands out, especially in this costume. Not today though. Not right now. If I start performing, they won't be able to tell which one of the girls they're looking at is me.

"Go!" I tell Ben. I push him towards the wheel. "Lose yourself in the crowd."

"No! Not without you. Not again."

"I'll find you," I tell him: the same words he said to me the other day. "They'll be looking for us both. We can get away if we're not together." He stares at me, his beautiful eyes frightened and unsure.

"Trust me," I say. "Watch."

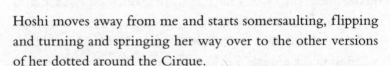
Hoshi moves away from me and starts somersaulting, flipping and turning and springing her way over to the other versions of her dotted around the Cirque.

The sound of her voice fills the air.

We are all flesh and blood. We all feel. We are all human.

Vote for what is right. Vote for change.

The lights, the rides, the wheel, all of it, fades into insignificance when Hoshi moves like that. Nothing can compete with the brightest light of them all.

Time stands still, just for a few seconds, as the whole of London stops in its tracks and holds its breath, spellbound.

Finally, the guards gather themselves together and move towards her. None of them are looking at me. Why would they when the most beautiful girl in all the world is performing on loop right in front of them?

If I can just distract them for a second, they won't know which one is her.

"Hey!" I call. "Over here!"

Their heads whirl around.

"He's there! Get him!"

I turn and run towards the crowd of people queuing for the wheel, pressing myself into the crowd.

I look over my shoulder.

They're coming.

I move through the crowd, pushing myself forward. The guards are blowing whistles now and everyone's facing towards the noise, trying to see what all the fuss is about. Even the attendants are distracted.

Hoshi was right though; they aren't firing any shots.

There's a carriage open, ready and waiting for riders, but nobody's getting on.

I jump on to it and it rises slowly upwards.

I'm riding the Wheel of Misfortune.

Out of the frying pan and into the fire.

For a while, everywhere is chaos.

Panicked people are running in every direction. The guards' whistles have confused them all and there's a herd of people heading away from the rides and towards the main exit.

Carving a path through them, I see the white figure of Silvio.

He's standing still amongst the pandemonium in the middle of the Cirque while people rush past him like rats fleeing a sinking ship, his eyes darting over all the somersaulting versions of me.

I can't freeze. I have to keep moving, have to keep performing.

I somersault and turn along in time with the firework display surrounding me.

From the corner of my eye, I watch him. His gaze lands on me, scrutinizes me for a second and moves on to the next Hoshi.

Then he heads towards the big wheel.

I look up at the enormous carriages on their slow, cyclical path.

One half of each one is dark, but the other half is lit up, its insides glowing brightly against the dark night sky.

Most of the pods are empty; the queue must have disbanded when the guards started blowing their whistles. Just above my head, though, rising slowly upwards, there's a boy in one of the carriages, his face pushed up to the glass, looking down at me.

It's Ben.

BEN

At first, I think I'm all alone in the carriage. I sink down on the seat lining the edge and let myself breathe for a moment or two.

The area in front of me is shrouded in dark curtains. Then, from behind it, muffled sounds.

Someone, or something, is in there.

The half of the carriage I'm sitting in is open-topped. In the middle, there's what looks like a steering wheel on a central column, with two buttons on it.

Sneak Peek, one says. The other: *Release the Beast*.

I don't know what they mean. I don't even want to think about it. All I know is that I won't be pressing any buttons.

As I move upwards, Silvio's voice fills the pod. Even after hitting him over the head with a hammer, I can't escape this man.

Welcome to the ride of your life! You've been brave enough to climb aboard the Wheel of Misfortune! Are you ready for the big reveal? When the carriage gets to the very top, your battlers will be revealed! One Dreg, one savage beast. What horrors will your Dreg face? Will it be a lion? Will it be a bear? Will it be tarantulas? Listen, what can you hear? Are there any clues? Will your Dreg make it to the bottom? There's the sound of his manic laugh and then a loud alarm.

"Ladies and gentlemen, it's sneak peek time! Want a quick reveal before we get to the top? Go on, you know you do! Why not take a look?"

The *Sneak Peek* button pulses with red light. Morbid curiosity moves my hand towards it. Someone I know must be in there. But with what?

No. I won't play their sick games.

"Five seconds left! Will you take your sneak peek?"

I move away from the button and cover my ears. I press myself up against the glass, as far as I can from the other side of the pod.

You can see the whole circus from here.

All the way across the other side, six black figures move stealthily along the walls towards the Arcadia arena. The Brotherhood. They've made it inside.

Far below me, a stream of Pures are heading towards the main gates. I scan the crowd, looking for Sean, but I can't see him anywhere. It's then I notice one solitary figure standing still amongst the thronging masses. Silvio. Around him, around them all, red and gold fireworks, and a dozen acrobating Hoshikos. And there, looking up and staring at me, the real Hoshi. I'd know her anywhere.

HOSHIKO

The mistake I make, for the second time, is staying still as I stop and stare up at Ben.

Ben's mouth is open wide. He shouting something at me, frantically, pointing over my shoulder. I turn around. Silvio is moving steadily towards me.

The Wheel of Misfortune is right in the far corner of the Cirque. There's nowhere else to go.

I run towards it, jump up on to the scaffold frame and start climbing, up up up towards Ben.

BEN

I watch helplessly as Hoshi scales the scaffold of the wheel towards me.

Why is she doing that? Once the wheel gets to the bottom, I'm caught. Silvio's already there waiting. There are guards moving towards us from all parts of the circus.

Hoshi's getting closer. I flinch as Silvio and the guards fire rounds of bullets up towards her, but she's so quick and light that they miss her every time.

The carriage keeps moving upwards, right to the top of the wheel.

Then Silvio's voice again. *"You chose not to take a sneak peek! Time to end the suspense. Are you ready?"*

The black screen in the middle of the pod lifts up.

HOSHIKO

A bullet ricochets off the glass near my ear. The guards have the wheel completely surrounded now and their aim is getting more accurate. I weave to the side and jump up to the next level.

I move up the left-hand side, past each carriage slowly making its upward ascent. As I pass each one, I can see straight into the half of the carriage that doesn't have a roof. Ben's must be near the top by now. If I can make it up that far without being hit, I can drop down next to him.

I know they're going to catch us both, but maybe I can get to him first. I'm not making the same mistake ever again. This time, we'll face whatever they've got in store for us together.

We should never have separated. It doesn't work when we're apart.

BEN

Behind the screen, there's a thick sheet of glass. Beyond that, the rest of the carriage is divided in half again, segmented by a gridded gate.

In one section, crouched up in a ball, right in the corner, Ezekiel.

In the other, prowling, snarling, angry at being kept in such a small space, a huge tiger.

HOSHIKO

Somehow, miraculously, I dodge the bullets and make it right to the top. This one has to be Ben's carriage. I scramble up the smooth glass sides, gripping on for dear life, and drop down, right inside.

I fling myself straight into his arms but he doesn't throw his arms back around me, not like I thought he would. He doesn't react at all.

I pull back and look at him.

He's rooted to the spot. His face is as white as Silvio's and his body is shaking. He's staring, transfixed, at something.

I spin around to see what he's looking at.

Ezekiel, face-to-face with an angry tiger.

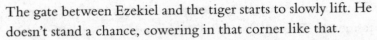

BEN

The gate between Ezekiel and the tiger starts to slowly lift. He doesn't stand a chance, cowering in that corner like that.

Last night, with the wolves, he was ready to fight. He wanted to stand next to me, right at the front.

"Stand up, Ezekiel!" I yell. "Stand up and fight! Come on! You can do this!"

On the other side of the glass, he scrambles to his feet. He looks at me, his face full of doubt and fear.

"That's it!" I yell. "Show him how tough you are!"

He faces the tiger. It crouches down low, staring at him.

He jumps in the air and lands with his legs wide. He waves his arms, makes fierce noises, just like we did last night. My God, he's so brave.

It's no good, though. The tiger throws its head back and roars. It's not like the wolves; it's huge and frustrated and ferocious and the only thing in its proximity is Ezekiel. It's not going to be intimidated by this six-year-old boy.

Ezekiel's panicked eyes flick over to me and back to the tiger.

It pulls back on its haunches.

I can't look any more.

What is it they say in these situations? Fight or flight? Why on earth does Ben think that Ezekiel is going to be able to fight a tiger? The only answer here is most definitely flight.

The ceiling of Ezekiel's half of the pod is supported by white metal bars criss-crossing over it.

"Jump, Ezekiel!" I yell. "Jump up to the bars!"

At the same time, I bang as hard as I can on the glass panel dividing us from the tiger. I push right up against it and pound it with my fists.

The tiger turns to face me while Ezekiel leaps up behind it and grabs on to the bars with his body, gripping on with his feet and hands. He's even more agile than he was before, when I first saw him at selection.

The tiger steps closer towards me so there's just millimetres dividing us. I stare aggressively into its eyes. I'm so close that I can see the strings of saliva when its mouth opens in another roar.

I snarl and roar back at it.

Next to me, Ben joins in.

We need to keep its attention focused on us.

The tiger launches itself towards us. I stop myself from flinching back as its body comes into contact with the glass, shaking it with his huge might. The screen doesn't come anywhere close to shattering though. There'd be Pures in here normally; they'll have made certain they're well protected.

Ezekiel has moved right over to the top corner and he hangs there, staring down at us. His little face looks so frightened.

How long does this ride go on for?

BEN

We aren't going to be able to keep the attention of this tiger for much longer, not when there's fresh meat in there, dangling just above it.

It's still trying to get to me and Hoshi at the moment, though. It raises itself up on to its hind legs, pushing its paws into the glass. Its claws look sharper than razors.

Silvio's voice fills the pod again.

Has your Dreg survived their battle? Have they made it around the Wheel of Misfortune? There's just one minute remaining! One minute left to enjoy the ride of your life!

Next to me, Hoshi yells and stamps even harder.

I join in.

The tiger hurls itself against the glass one more time and then turns away, searching the pod for Ezekiel.

It doesn't see him at first, but then it raises its head and looks up. It crouches back and springs.

Hoshi and I both scream out helplessly as it jumps.

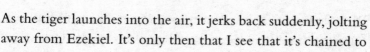

As the tiger launches into the air, it jerks back suddenly, jolting away from Ezekiel. It's only then that I see that it's chained to the floor.

The chain's long enough for it to prowl around the whole pod but, when it jumps up, it stops just short of Ezekiel.

The tiger tries again but is pulled back.

Ezekiel just needs to hold on, to stay pushed tight. If anyone can do it, he can.

"Hold on!" I cry.

He pushes himself upwards so that he's pressed against the glass roof as the tiger lunges at him, again and again.

He can't hold on much longer, though. His body starts to sag down in the middle.

The tiger's paws swipe again. This time, they don't miss.

BEN

Ezekiel flinches upwards as the great paws lunge at his body, leaving behind five sharp red gashes on his exposed stomach.

"Don't let go!" I shout. "You can do this!"

He looks down at me. His eyes full of pain and fear.

The tiger lunges again.

The tiger misses Ezekiel the next jump, and the one after that.

Ben and I keep shouting to try and get its attention again, but it just ignores us; it would much rather have the meat it can smell.

After an eternity, Silvio's voice fills the pod again.

Five, four, three, two, one!

The chain holding the tiger pulls it backwards, reeling it in like a giant fish, and the gate between it and Ezekiel drops back down with a clang.

Ezekiel hangs up there for a few seconds more and then drops down to the floor. He crawls over to the glass towards us. He puts his hands up and I crouch down and touch them with mine.

He's crying. "You did it!" I cheer through the glass. "You did it!"

Ben bobs down and puts his hands over mine.

And then the carriage stops moving and the doors swoosh open and the guards grab hold of all three of us.

BEN

While we've been in the pod, they've somehow managed to lure the fleeing masses back into the Cirque, and there's a big crowd watching as the guards pull me from Hoshi and drag us off in different directions.

I never even got to speak to her and now I don't even have time to say goodbye.

Still, Ezekiel's in one piece, and Sean's out here somewhere, looking for his brother and the Brotherhood, and they've made it inside – I'm sure it was them I saw earlier. And Hoshi's images and what she said – they're bound to affect my mother's election campaign.

The tide *is* changing. There *will* be a brighter day.

We've taken on the Cirque before, taken it on and won. We can do it again, all of us together this time. We *will* do it again. We're strong now.

Whatever they put me through, I'll never let them win. Even if it means I have to die, I'll damn well go down fighting.

There's no point begging or screaming, so I don't bother saying anything.

I just let them pull me right across the fairground to the back of a big building that looks like a hill. They drag me through the corridors and throw me into a room.

I'm alone for a moment. Then there's the sound of lots of footsteps, and in walks the new strange white Silvio with Vivian Baines, surrounded by her entourage of guards and security.

She closes her eyes when she sees me, like she can't bear to look at me. Her hand flutters to her chest and she breathes in and out dramatically, as if she's fighting back nausea.

I know how she feels.

When she opens her eyes, they shine with hatred.

"Finally, I have you! The little tramp who bewitched my son!" she hisses. And then she slaps me. Crack! Right across the face.

My head reels back. My fingers itch, desperate to hit her back. I move forward and the guards immediately close in around her.

"He's not your son," I say. "Not any more. He hates you."

Her nose wrinkles up in disgust, like it always did when she looked at me.

"Perhaps he'll change his mind when we finally get rid of his distractions. That's assuming he makes it out of here alive."

Fear grips me, squeezing the air from my lungs. What does she mean?

She turns to Silvio. "It's not often you surpass my

expectations, Ringmaster, but on this occasion, you have certainly managed to do so. I've had police forces across the country hunting for this bitch for months, and now here she is, back in the Cirque. It's all gone full circle – it's almost poetic. I suppose I should thank you; you've made things much easier for me."

Silvio preens himself proudly, basking in her praise. I'm pleased to see a large egg-shaped lump on the top of his head where Ben cracked him with the hammer. If only he'd done it a bit harder and finished him off completely.

I won't let their words and their threats scare me. I won't let them win.

"What have you done with Ezekiel?" I demand. "He's injured, he needs treatment."

Silvio rolls his eyes. "So much melodrama! That was just a scratch! Nothing that will stop him being in the line-up for my opening ceremony!"

I stare at him, my curiosity prickling, despite myself. This is the first time I've had the chance to look at him properly.

So many times, this man has haunted me in my dreams, and now here he is, in real life, looking more like a phantom than a real person. His eyes have the same evil glint as before. His voice drips with the same cruel silkiness, but the rest of him is altered beyond anything I could have ever imagined.

"What's happened to you?" I ask him. "Why are you dressed up as a freaky ghost? It's not Halloween yet, is it?"

His eyes narrow.

"I assure you, Hosh-i-ko, I am very much alive. Someone like you could never have the power to destroy someone like me. Do you know what kept me going all these months? What fed me? What brought me back from the brink? The thought of seeing you again. The thought of exacting my revenge."

"Well, I hate to say it, but you look a teeny-weeny bit silly." I turn to Vivian Baines, but not before I hear his little gasp of outrage and shock. "I've just had a thought." I smile at her and flutter my eyelashes. "I should really start calling you Mother now that I'm on such *intimate* terms with your son. What do you say, Mummy dear?"

There's an audible snort of amusement from one of the guards. She whirls round.

"Who laughed?" Her voice is cold and steely. There's no answer. "I said: who laughed?"

Silence again.

"I'm waiting," she says.

The seconds tick by.

Finally, one of the guards speaks.

"It was me, ma'am. I was just clearing my throat."

"Get out," she says to him. "Get out now and don't come back. You can collect your final wages on Monday."

He turns and leaves. Nobody says anything else.

She turns back to Silvio.

"Have this girl executed," she says. "Immediately."

I look at him, all white and ghostly and grinning, and my blood runs cold again.

"Madam," he says, silkily. "If you would permit me to make a suggestion?"

She peers at him. "Very well. What is it?"

"The opening ceremony is due to begin in just a couple of

minutes. As you know, your son has already been assigned a role. Perhaps if this girl's termination was to occur live, in front of an audience, it would have a greater impact on him. He'd witness her death for himself, perhaps be *involved* with it in some way, and the public would see her finally being punished for her actions. It would be a victory for both of us. Your son, the audience, the whole world will realize once and for all that the Cirque, the government, the Pures, will never be vanquished!"

She muses for a second.

"Do you know, Ringmaster, I think you may have a point. It would do him good to see it with his own eyes, plus, it would be wonderful entertainment too. My family have a box to ourselves, you say?"

Silvio nods vigorously.

"Very well. Stick her in a costume and get her out there. Let's watch our little Greek god try and rescue her, shall we? Let's watch his face when he realizes he can't."

I don't think I've ever seen Silvio look so jubilant. "Oh, you won't regret this, madam! I have the perfect role in mind for her! Forget about her little acrobatic display from earlier: this will be all anyone's talking about!" He looks at his watch. "Oh my! There's no time to spare! If you will excuse me, madam, I will make the necessary arrangements."

"Yes, yes, run along, little man. Just give me one guarantee – whatever happens out there, whatever you've got planned, the girl doesn't make it off that stage alive."

He smiles. "Rest assured, madam, the only person who could possibly desire her death more than you, is me. I give you my word, she'll die tonight."

BEN

After what seems like for ever, the doors are thrown open and a guard enters.

"Time to get ready," he says. "The show's about to start."

He manoeuvres me down the corridor and pushes me into the dressing room.

Every single performer is in there: Emmanuel, Leah, all of them, and they're all in costume. The men and boys are all wearing rough hessian tunics and brown sandals. They look like they're about to perform as shepherds in a school nativity play; they're even carrying crooks and wearing long fabric headdresses.

All the girls and women except Leah are wearing loose white dresses. They all have a band of white flowers on their head and their hair is flowing in waves. Leah's dressed in white too, but her gown is tight-fitting, and shimmers and glows with soft light. Her hair has been pulled back off her head into a tight bun and there are illuminated wings fluttering, somehow, on her back.

The door opens again, and Ezekiel's thrown in like a bag of rubbish.

I run to pick him up. He's stopped bleeding. The cut looks nasty but shallow.

He throws his arms around me.

"You saved me!" he says. "You and Hoshi saved me!"

I look over his head at all the others.

"He saved himself," I say. "He was brave and brilliant. Is everyone else OK?"

409

"We're all here," Emmanuel says. "Every last one of us. We've all been out there – I think pretty much all of us have got injuries, but nothing to stop them using any of us in the opening show."

Minnie, the make-up artist, steps forward with my costume.

"You might as well wear it," she says. "They'll make you go out there whatever happens."

I know she's right and I don't want to put her at risk, so I pull the stupid thing on over my clothes.

The eyes of the whole room are staring at me.

"Why are they dressing you as a goat?" asks Ezekiel, incredulously.

"I have absolutely no idea!" I answer.

He's grinning from ear to ear and the light's already back in his eyes again.

"I look really stupid, don't I?" I say.

After a second, he nods shyly and starts to laugh.

I look down at my funny little goat legs and join in with him, and then so do the others.

For a few seconds, we're all laughing together until there's a buzz as the door lock is released and Silvio appears.

He's still wearing his white robe, and his feet are bare.

He points at Leah.

"You!" he commands. "Get your costume off!" She stands up. "Now!" he says, sharply. "Time's running out!"

She takes off the dress while we all look away, trying to allow her some dignity. After a moment, she steps forward, back in her normal clothes, and holds the gown out to Silvio.

He seizes it from her and hands it to a guard, waiting behind him. "You know what to do," he says.

He turns back to Leah.

"A last-minute change of plan – someone else needs this costume. You will be delighted to know you've had a reprieve, for tonight at least! You can join your comrades as a supporting cast member in what will surely be the deadliest show of all time! I've got far bigger fish to fry than you tonight!"

My heart begins to pound. It's for Hoshi; it must be.

He looks at me and smirks, as if he's enormously pleased about something. "Come," he beckons. "Come hither." I don't know what part it is he's playing, but he's certainly getting into it. Even his language has changed. I swear he actually thinks he's Jesus or something.

"Who do you mean?" I ask. "Me?"

His arms sweep across the room inclusively.

"Why, I mean all of you, of course!" He throws his arms out wide. "It's showtime!"

Alone in the room, I wait, my heart beating hard against the walls of my chest.

They're putting us both onstage; that's what Silvio said. I don't want Ben to have to watch me die.

The door handle turns and a man comes in, a Pure, about fifty years old, I reckon. I know straight away who it is, even though I've never seen him before. It's Ben's father. He's got the same blond hair, the same eyes.

"Thank you," he whispers to a guard behind him. "I'll only be five minutes."

He shuts the door.

"I haven't got long," he says, hurriedly. "They don't know I'm here. I just want to ask… Do you love him? Do you love my son?"

"Yes," I say. "More than anything."

He clutches at the wall.

"He's good," I tell him. "And brave, and kind. You should be proud of him. You should love him too. Not for who you want him to be, but for who he is."

He looks at me. His eyes are watery and he's shaking.

"I *am* proud," he says. "And I *do* love him. I wish I'd got to tell him that. I tried to stop her. I tried, but she won't listen!"

"Well, make her listen then!" I say.

His face crumples. "She's never listened to me. She doesn't listen to anyone! She does what she wants, she always has!"

Ben's never said that much about his dad; just that he wasn't around that much when he was a kid. I always had the impression, from what he did say, that he was a bit of a yes-man, that he just let Ben's mother make all the decisions and went along with them. Judging from what he's saying now, I was spot on.

Funny, I thought I'd hate him if I ever met him, but when I look at this broken man opposite me, snivelling and wringing his hands, I don't feel hate at all. He's far too weak and pathetic to hate.

Maybe it's not all his fault. He's lived with a bully for years. Maybe she made him like that. There's got to be some backbone somewhere in there. He's Ben's father, after all, and God knows Ben didn't inherit anything from his mother's half of the gene pool.

He says he loves Ben. If the last year has taught me anything, it's that love can be strong. Love can be much, much stronger than hate.

Very cautiously, I put my hand on his. He doesn't flinch or shake it away; he stares down at it, and then he looks at me, and his face is full of regret and heartbreak.

"Stand up to her," I urge him. "Stand up for what's right. Stand up for Ben. It's not too late," I say. "It's never too late."

He makes a funny sound, like he's choking.

"I have to speak to her!" he cries, and then he pulls his hand away and runs off through the door.

Seconds later, it opens again and a guard comes in carrying a costume. A white sequined dress, full of light and sparkle, with wings on the back.

"Put this on," she commands.

I scramble into the dress while she waits, impatiently. She clicks her fingers and, from behind her, Minnie appears.

After so long, it's so good to see her. I want to hug her. She looks at me, her face full of emotion, and I can tell she feels the same.

"Hurry up!" snaps the guard. "The show's due to start!"

Minnie scrubs my face quickly with a flannel, then pulls a brush through my hair and twists it into a bun behind my head. She puts some mascara on me, and dabs shimmering silver on my cheeks and lips.

"Quick!" snarls the guard, and she pulls me out along the corridor and through a little wooden door, pushing me up a tiny narrow staircase. At the top, she forces me roughly down into a chair. Wrenching my hands back, she clips iron cuffs on to them, doing the same with my feet. Before she leaves, she pulls a tight iron brace down over my body, clicking it down into latches at the bottom of the chair.

I hear her feet echoing as they dash back down the stairs, and the sound as she locks the door at the bottom.

I look around. I'm in a tiny, circular room.

There's light creeping in from under the cracks in the door and the sound of people, lots of people, not far away.

I must be above the stage in the theatre.

There's music and cheering, and the noise of the crowd gets even louder. They're chanting something. "The Cat! The Cat! The Cat!"

The show's begun.

Prodding me with his cane, Silvio ushers me to the left wing of the stage and dashes hurriedly off.

The band are playing: beautiful, elegant music soars through the forest.

The lights are so dazzling that I can't see the audience, but I can hear them all right. They're very loud, very excited.

The music stops, and a hushed silence gradually settles over the whole place.

Above, the ceiling looks just like the sky. There's a cloud hovering up there with sunlit gilt edges. As I look at it, a group of children materializes right in the middle of it, cherub-like in white gowns, wings and halos, as if they're descending from heaven. Their voices fill the arena.

Behold! Behold!

He has risen! He has risen!

Hallelujah! Hallelujah!

Slowly, slowly, Silvio emerges from the cloud, stopping right in the centre of them, about eight metres above the woodland stage.

"Ladies and gentlemen, welcome to the Cirque!" he cries. The crowd are roaring and clapping.

"Yes!" He sweeps his arms wide. "Yes, it really is me, your very own world-famous ringmaster! I have risen again! Lo! I am resurrected and the darkness has vanished! I am Pure now: the Purest of Pure!"

There's some booing. Sabatini doesn't seem the least bit fazed by it though. He holds his hands together beatifically and smiles serenely, waiting calmly for silence. Finally, he speaks again.

"Ladies and gentlemen, I am not the only familiar face you will see tonight! For your delight and delectation, we have staged a romantic reunion!"

"I would like, if I may, to tell you a story. Are you all nestled comfortably down in our woodland glade? Then I'll begin...

"Let yourself be transported back to simpler times, the times of the ancient Greeks. Ladies and gentlemen, welcome to Arcadia, a rustic paradise where nymphs and dryads frolicked at ease among the trees."

The sound of pan flutes and wind chimes fills the air and, one by one, every other performer is pushed from the opposite wing, out on to the stage. They stand there uncertainly, looking at each other. That's what their costumes are supposed to be, then: nymphs and dryads, whatever they are.

"Holding dominion over this rural Eden, ruling with grace and gravitas, was Pan. Pan: grandson of Zeus. Pan: half man, half goat. Pan: god of the shepherds, god of fertility, god of all that is wild!"

The guard shoves me on to the stage, towards a circle, embedded in the grass. As soon as I'm standing on it, it starts to protrude from the ground, rising upwards so that I'm elevated above the main stage too, not as high as Silvio and the angels, just about two metres or so. I stare around me. What do I do now?

The audience are all whooping and chanting. My eyes have adjusted now. They're all standing up, clamouring to see. Above them, level with Silvio, there's a wooden platform, suspended between the branches of two trees, with wooden eaves like a tree house. I guess it must be the VIP box because looking down from it, eyes on the stage, eyes on me, are my mother, father and brother. My mother looks stony-faced. My father looks stricken. My brother looks delighted.

"For many years, Pan ruled his kingdom in peace and prosperity!" Silvio chimes. "But a change was coming to Arcadia…"

The lights darken and, above our heads, storm clouds gather in the sky.

"Where's the Cat?" someone shouts out from the back, and then the crowd join in, clapping and chanting and drumming their feet on the floor as they chant.

"The Cat! The Cat! The Cat!"

Silvio waits patiently for silence, smiling tranquilly.

"All in good time, my dears, all in good time. Now, as I was saying, a change was coming to Arcadia. One morning, as Pan wandered in his forest, he gazed into a lake, and there he beheld the most beautiful maiden he had ever seen! Just one look at her reflection was enough for him to fall desperately in love!"

The lights dim and there's a dramatic fanfare. A spotlight appears on the rocky cliff above the waterfall and its walls slowly part to reveal a cave.

Inside, looking down at me, bound in chains, is Hoshi.

HOSHIKO

I was expecting to be looking out on to a circus tent but, instead, a forest glade stretches out below me, sunlit and tree-lined. It's packed with people though, clamouring to witness the show, pushing and shoving to get the best view. It's still the Cirque then, whatever they've done.

There's a platform opposite me, strung up between two trees. It must be the royal box, because there, just as she said she'd be, is Vivian Baines, looking up at me with a victorious smile on her face. Ben's weaselly-looking brother is next to her and my heart sinks when I see his father, sitting on the end.

What was the point in him coming to see me? I look away.

He was my last hope.

Below me, there's a stage, lined with blossoming trees. And there, standing in the centre, looking up at me, is Ben, my lovely, lovely Ben, dressed as a goat.

Any other time it might be funny, but not now. Now the fear I feel is reflected in his eyes.

Silvio dangles from the ceiling, pretending to be an angel, I think. I can't help but give a little snort to myself at the irony of it all. He's narrating some sort of story.

"Pan simply could not live without the love of the beautiful creature who had so entranced him. In vain, he searched, but he could find no trace of her. As his hunt continued, he began to go mad with longing. His kingdom was neglected, and decay and rot crept into Arcadia."

The music changes from the soothing sounds of flutes to harsh and jarring piano and bass.

Below, the green leaves of the trees turn yellow, then orange, then brown, and the blossom begins to fall like snow. The flowers wilt and the lush green grass turns brown and dry.

"Finally, after many months, high above a cascading waterfall, Pan glimpsed the maiden he had longed for with all his heart."

The area all around me lights up and the audience burst into applause.

"When Pan saw that the beautiful nymph was a prisoner, he was determined to reach his heart's desire and rescue her, despite the many fearful obstacles placed in his path…"

Silvio clicks his fingers and a trapdoor slowly opens on the floor of the grassy stage.

Rising up from the depths, a huge cage. Inside, snarling, snapping and growling, a pack of angry wolves.

BEN

Glass walls descend across the front of the stage, ensuring the safety of the Pure audience as the cage full of wolves rises up, resting between the gushing waterfall which separates Hoshi and me.

The wolves' frantic cries drown out the water, the music, Silvio's voice, everything.

Emmanuel and the others huddle together in the far corner of the forest stage.

Silvio reaches into the folds of his gown and pulls something out. He clips it on below his chin: a microphone.

"Pan was desperate to free his love from the chains which bound her so cruelly. But little did he know that he had been enchanted! The beautiful nymph who had stolen his senses from him was nothing but an illusion, a wicked spell cast to entice him! She was really an evil gorgon monster, jealous of Pan, intent on destroying all Arcadia. Even if he managed to survive the deadly traps she had laid, he would die anyway! For her name was … Medusa! Just one look into her eyes would turn him to stone!"

HOSHIKO

The audience gasp and boo as my costume changes from white to green, and the twinkling lights of my wings flash bright red.

"Have you heard of Medusa, ladies and gentlemen?"

I have no idea what he's going on about, but the audience seem to: they're all shouting out, hysterically, the same thing.

"Snakes! Snakes! Snakes!"

"Yes, that's right! You do know your Greek mythology! Medusa, the evil gorgon monster, had hair made of venomous snakes!"

There's a click above me, and a hatch in the roof slides open.

I try to jerk away but it's no use, I can't move.

I close my eyes as whatever it is that's dangling above me descends. As it settles on my head, all I feel is warmth and a kind of vibrating tremor all around me.

I won't be a part of this performance. If I don't see it, it's not here. If I don't hear what Silvio's saying, he can't hurt me. If I don't react, I'll disappoint the audience.

The theatre vanishes, everything vanishes. I take myself to another place. I'm in the safe house, in the bedroom, with Ben. There's nobody there but us.

There's a collective gasp from the audience as something slowly appears above Hoshi's head.

I see her try to shift, try to jerk her head back, but she can't move. There's nothing she can do as the writhing, seething mass above her is lowered down to settle right there on her head.

She's wearing a helmet of snakes.

There are screens either side of Hoshi now, amplifying what's going on. The snakes are held there by their tails and they're all trying desperately to free themselves, whipping their black and red bodies outward and flicking out angry forked tongues.

My heart is beating so fast that I feel like I'm going to explode.

Hoshi doesn't look afraid though. She isn't screaming or hysterical. Her eyes are shut. Her face is tranquil.

"Ladies and gentlemen. The snakes were death adders! The deadliest snakes in the world! Just one bite meant certain death!"

One bite?

I have to get her down from there.

"Hoshi! I'm coming!" I shout just as the cage door opens and the wolves tumble out on to the stage between us.

Ben's voice penetrates my thoughts, shaking me out of the place I've gone to in my head.

"Hoshi! I'm coming!" he's yelling, again and again.

I open my eyes. He's still standing on the grassy podium and he's shouting at me. The audience are very loud, though, and I can't see him clearly enough because something keeps obstructing my view. Something flicking and moving in front of my eyes.

I gasp as I look into a sharp, beady eye, millimetres from my head. I shift my eyes to the left, then to the right.

There are snakes on my head.

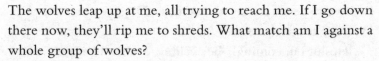

BEN

The wolves leap up at me, all trying to reach me. If I go down there now, they'll rip me to shreds. What match am I against a whole group of wolves?

I'm not.

I need my pack.

I look to the wings. The rest of the Dregs are all still there. The wolves haven't even noticed them yet; their attention is all focused on getting to me.

Emmanuel looks up at Hoshi, then at me. There's fire in his eyes. I look at the others. There's fire in all their eyes. Every single one of them is bracing themselves; every single one of them is straining forward.

They all look towards me. I lift up my hands and signal to them. One, two, three. On the third count, they surge on to the stage. They move as one, marching towards the centre. I jump down so that I stand among them and, together, we face the wolves again.

This time isn't like before, though. It's not a case of both packs mutually respecting spaces. We need to get past them, get through them. We need to get to the waterfall.

I take a determined step forward. Everyone else does the same. Step by step, we move towards them. They face us, ready to pounce. The biggest wolf snarls, right at me. I stare back at it. I don't blink. I snarl back. Emmanuel starts the chanting and clapping this time, and everyone joins in. We chant, we clap, we howl, we stamp our feet, we stare down the wolves.

For a few moments, they seem uncertain what to do. Then

they begin to edge backwards, hanging behind the alpha of the pack. Their hackles are no longer up; their stance is no longer poised.

As one, we slowly move closer.

I'm still eye to eye with the biggest wolf. Its lip curls back even further. I take a deep breath and move forward. With a gentle whimper it crouches down low, its head to the ground. The rest of the wolves do the same. Every single one of them, submissive and still as we cross right through them towards Hoshi.

HOSHIKO

I try to zone out again, but I can't. One of the snakes is exploring my face; I can feel it slowly moving across. I keep my mouth shut and try desperately to fight the hysteria welling up inside me.

Below, people are on the stage while the wolves crouch down meekly, allowing them to move towards me.

Maybe none of this is real. Maybe I'm dead already.

The audience are quiet now, watching with a collective tension.

No longer in his angelic position, Silvio is off the stage. He's up on the platform, talking to Vivian Baines. You'd think she'd be happy, seeing me like this, but her face is red with rage and she's talking to him animatedly. It looks like she's spitting. His face looks even paler than it did before and his head is hanging low.

There's another sound above me and the ceiling opens up again. A basket appears, more snakes pouring out of it. One of them is huge; it's got to be over twelve feet long. It must be a boa constrictor. It moves like liquid, flowing towards me.

BEN

The snakes twist around the tiny circular space towards Hoshi, their tongues flicking in and out.

She's rocking backwards, trying to manoeuvre out of their way, but even if she could, there's nowhere she can go; there are more snakes behind her and with each shuffle she just gets closer to them. Each time she moves, the snakes raise their heads at the sound and move nearer to her.

"Hoshi!" I call up. "Hoshi, listen. Stay very still. Don't move. Don't make a sound! They can sense the vibrations!"

HOSHIKO

I know Ben's right, but I can't do what he's saying. I can't stay still. Not when they're writhing about on my head with their tongues flicking in and out. Not when I can feel them, cool and slow, slinking up my legs. Not when the huge boa constrictor is beginning to coil itself slowly around my body. Not when it's squeezing me like this, tighter and tighter...

BEN

There's no time left. I have to free her, now. There's a huge snake coiling around her body and the smaller ones are massed all about her.

I grab hold of the rocks around the waterfall and try to scramble up, but it's no use. They're cardboard scenery, that's all, collapsing and crumpling beneath my weight as I fall back to the ground.

What now? There are vines tumbling down over the rocks, but they're fake too and won't take my weight. I look around the stage. There's nothing I can climb on. How am I going to get to her? I run to the back of the waterfall. There's a door there but it's locked shut. Sean's got the set of keys we had, and anyway, there are two armed guards standing in front of it.

I run back to the front.

Hoshi's covered in snakes now. Not just her head any more, her whole body.

I look desperately at the others.

Emmanuel steps forward, assuming command with just two words. "Human tower."

He bends forward and about ten of the other performers do the same, forming a circle, so their backs make a flat platform in the centre. More performers climb up on to their backs, standing on them and bending down to form another layer.

They move into formation quickly, the heavier ones on the bottom and the lighter ones on top. The tower of people tapers inward, getting narrower and narrower so that the top layer, made up of just two people, almost reaches Hoshi.

Nearly, but not quite. It just needs one more person.

Every single Dreg forms part of the tower, even Maggie. The only ones left are the tiny children, all of them either crying or staring around open-mouthed.

I move forward. I have no idea how I'm going to do this. I feel someone tugging at me. It's Ezekiel.

"It's my turn now," he says.

"No, that's the top of the tower. Whoever gets up there has to free Hoshi. They have to go in with the snakes. It's too dangerous. It has to be me."

"The tower will collapse. You aren't light enough," he says. He flashes me an apologetic little smile. "You won't even get halfway. You've never been trained and you're not an acrobat. It has to be me."

There's a groan, an involuntary one from Ravi, who's part of the group holding up the whole tower from the bottom, their faces red and strained.

He's right. The tower won't take my weight, but I can't allow him to put himself in such danger.

"There isn't time!" Ezekiel says, hurriedly. And without another word, he starts to scramble up the bodies.

Should I stop him? I should. I look up at Hoshi. She's glaring down at me, shaking her head agitatedly from side to side. She shouldn't be moving. I know why she is though; I know what she's trying to tell me.

But she'll die if she's not rescued soon.

And so I just stand back and watch. Watch with the rest of the packed auditorium, while a six-year-old boy scrambles up a human tower into the snake pit.

HOSHIKO

I've never felt so angry with anyone as I do with Ben right now. He *knows* I want him to stop Ezekiel; that's why he's looking away. He's letting a six-year-old boy risk himself to save me.

It's wrong. It's selfish. It's awful.

I'll never forgive him if something happens to Ezekiel, never.

Ezekiel springs up the pyramid of performers in no time and, within seconds, he's up here with me, grappling with my shackles.

There are snakes everywhere now. Their heads all swivel round at once at the sudden movement and commotion he makes.

There's a hiss, and then another one. The boa constrictor wrapped around my body unravels itself.

They move towards him.

BEN

I can't watch. I shouldn't have let him climb up there. I should have stopped him.

Right at the bottom of the rising tower of people, Emmanuel's eyes are closed tight and he's whispering something to himself. I think it's a prayer.

I look back up. The snakes are all moving from Hoshi to Ezekiel. He's already undone the cuffs and is now working frantically to free her from the brace.

And then he does it. Hoshi is free. She stands up and throws the crown of snakes off her head. She moves forward, but it's too late.

With a cry, Ezekiel falls to the floor, his body jerking, He's been bitten.

I crouch down and scoop him up in my arms, shaking the snakes from him. His eyelids are drooping and his breath is rasping.

"Help him! Someone help him!" Ben's shouting, all the Dregs are shouting. The audience are still silent: mesmerized, I suppose, enjoying the show.

I look down, look all around. What can I do?

Then, a cry from the royal box.

"Benedict, I've got the antidote!"

Ben's father is hanging over the wooden balcony. He throws something on to the stage: a glass vial, spinning as it flies through the air.

BEN

Instinctively, I catch the bottle as it drops.

I look back up at my father.

"It's an antidote!" he shouts. "I told them you couldn't be in the show. They gave me this to shut me up, in case something happened. It's effective, but she needs to administer it quickly!"

Behind him, Mother's mouth is gaping open. Francis's face is a mirror image of hers. Sabatini's up there with them, looking on in shock. He doesn't know what to do.

I turn around and throw the antidote up to Hoshi. Still holding Ezekiel, she catches it deftly with one hand.

I turn back to face my father.

He's astonished me.

"Thank you!" I call up to him.

There are tears in his eyes.

"I'm sorry," he cries, while the rest of the audience look on. "I'm sorry for everything."

Ezekiel is drenched with sweat now. He jerks and then turns rigid in my arms.

I don't stop to question. I pull the cap off the bottle and pour the whole lot into his mouth.

His body relaxes a little and his breathing calms. His eyes open weakly.

As if they can sense his weakness, the snakes crawl back up my legs towards him.

I've used up all the antidote. How long until one of us gets bitten again?

I lift him up in my arms and stand on the edge of the platform, but beneath us, the tower of performers has already collapsed.

BEN

Hoshi stands on the edge of the waterfall, cradling Ezekiel.

"Join arms," I tell the others. "Make a landing mat!"

And that's what we all do, join both hands with other people and stand there, arms stretched out, in a long line.

"We'll catch him!" I call up.

Hoshi stares down at us.

The snakes are curling up her leg towards Ezekiel.

She lets go and he drops, right down into the middle of us.

We've got him.

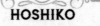

HOSHIKO

Some of the audience start cheering.

I look down at them. How do they feel? What are they thinking?

Suddenly, a gunshot.

The front doors fly open.

Dark figures, glinting metal, moving forward.

The Brotherhood. They're here.

They've come to get us out. They've come to rescue us.

In my head, Felix's words, from before:

Time to make your mind up, Circus Girl. Whose side are you on? Ours, or theirs?

All at once, I know what to do.

BEN

We're all bracing ourselves to catch her, but Hoshi doesn't jump down into our waiting arms. Instead, she unravels a snake, coiled about her torso. Raising her arm, she hurls it, right over the stage and into the audience. Immediately, there's the sound of screaming and a mass of bodies desperately clamours for the door.

Hoshi tosses snake after snake down into the crowd.

Then she crouches down and springs from the tower. As she soars, she seizes hold of one of the vine tendrils hanging around her cave. Arcing right across the stage, she drops down on the other side of the glass doors; the audience side.

She pulls at them, wrenching them open.

The wolves turn at the sound.

There's nothing between them and the Pures now; the screaming, hysterical Pures.

Their terror couldn't be more evident.

You shouldn't show fear to wolves. They'll see it as weakness. They'll attack.

Hoshi darts neatly out of the way as the wolves spring off the stage, snarling, into the crowded woodland glade below them.

I look up at the trees. My mother, brother, father and Silvio Sabatini are all staring down at the pandemonium.

"Ben," my father shouts. I can just hear his words over the screams. "I'm sorry!"

The Brotherhood have already swarmed up on to the stage and Hoshi is down too, next to me. She grabs my arm.

"Run!" she yells. "Out the back!"

"Stop!" one of the armed figures shouts, waving his gun dangerously towards all the performers. "Where's my brother? Where's Sean?"

"He's dead!" Silvio shouts from above. "Just like the rest of you will be soon!"

"If Sean's dead, you're all dead." The gunman turns to face the audience. He sweeps his gun left to right across the crowd.

Next to me, Hoshi is screaming. "Felix. Stop! Stop!"

"Sean's alive!" I shout. "Your brother's alive!"

But he doesn't hear me.

Below, one figure is moving towards the front, fighting against the desperate masses trying to get out. He's holding his hands up high in the air.

"Felix! Felix! Stop! I'm right here."

I hear Hoshi screaming frantically next to me.

"Felix! Your brother! He's down there!"

Felix stares at her, then down into the crowd. His eyes widen as he sees his brother below him, and the hand with the gun in drops down to his side.

Sean looks up at his brother. He's smiling at him, a smile of reassurance, a smile of love. "I'm here!" he calls again, before the smile on his face freezes, replaced by shock.

Right at the other side of the room, there are more gunshots: a Cirque guard, firing up on to the stage. The Brotherhood wrestle him to the ground, but not before he hits his target.

Next to me, Felix slumps down to the ground, a pool of red blood forming around him.

Sean vaults up on to the stage.

"No!" he shouts. "No!"

But it's too late.

For a minute, the world stops turning and I watch him cradle his dying brother in his arms.

Poor, broken Felix.

He was so hurt by the world, so damaged by it. He wanted to destroy all the Pures, and now they've destroyed him: the Cirque; Silvio; Vivian Baines; the messed-up society we live in. They're what's killed this angry, vulnerable boy who's known nothing but violence and heartbreak.

If I ever get out of here, what on earth am I going to say to Rosie?

"Quick!" one of the Brotherhood shouts. "Get the performers out now, while it's chaos down there! That little kid needs medical treatment!"

Emmanuel is cradling Ezekiel in his arms like a baby.

"Let's go!" I shout. "Let's get him out of here!"

BEN

"This way!" I call out. "There's a fire exit in the costume room!"

I run in, pushing the lever on the door. It springs open and we cascade out into the night.

I look back at the theatre. There aren't many people left in there; they've all run out of the front doors, chased by the wolves. I look in the royal box for my family, but they aren't there either, and neither is Silvio.

There are sirens sounding and guards running towards us, but some of the Brotherhood are with us and they have guns too. They group around us, shielding us, weapons pointing outward.

Someone blows a whistle, piercingly loud. It's a policeman.

"Let them go!" he shouts. "The wolves are attacking out there! We have to save the Pures! Let the Dregs go!"

The guards and police turn away from us and run back towards the main courtyard. All you can hear is the sound of screaming.

"Run!" someone shouts. "Run!"

We move forward.

There are two guards still, on the gate.

"Open it now!" one of the Brotherhood shouts. The guards hesitate. "I said: open it!" he roars, aiming the gun right at them. They do what he says.

I look at Hoshi. Ashen-faced, she fires me a poisonous glare. She's angry with me for letting Ezekiel climb up to rescue her.

"I'm sorry," I say. "I didn't know what else to do."

"He'd better be OK," she says.

"He will be," Emmanuel's deep voice answers from behind us. He's running too, carrying Ezekiel effortlessly in his arms. "He's sleeping. He's peaceful."

Hoshi scowls at me. Then she grabs my hand and we join the stream of Dregs running out of the Cirque.

EPILOGUE

HOSHIKO

It's been six months now since the day the circus fell. Six months since poor Felix died. Six months since Vivian Baines was vanquished. Six months since the election result that changed history.

England's a different place now: a brighter place. The air is full of promise and hope.

What was the turning point? What was it that made the Pure voters turn out in their thousands and vote for equality for all?

Ben says it was my speech and the holograms of me they spread through the city, but I think the trigger point was him, way back when he spoke out before we escaped from the Cirque. If the son of Vivian Baines herself dared to stand and be counted, couldn't other people?

Folklore says it was the day we blew up the circus, the day I threw the grenade that so very nearly vanquished Silvio Sabatini.

Maybe it wasn't any of that. Maybe it was the way that Vivian Baines so visibly floundered when Laura Minton threw down the gauntlet and challenged her to have her genetic heritage assessed.

What I think is that it was all of those things combined and it was more than them too, things bigger and greater than any of us – reason and goodness and justice. Regardless of our actions, hatred and bigotry would never have reigned supreme for ever. There's light at the end of every dark day, I truly believe that.

And so far, Laura Minton has proved as good as her word. As soon as she got that landslide result, she rushed through emergency legislation. Discrimination based on race or ethnicity is a criminal, prosecutable offence now and, officially speaking, there's no such things as Pures and Dregs any more. Of course, it will take a lot more than a change to the legal system to make things right. There's still deeply entrenched hatred and resentment from both sides of the divide, but it's a start: a really good start.

I still don't like Kadir, but I do have to reluctantly admit, he's doing a pretty good job so far of keeping things calm amongst the masses. The government are going to tear the slums down, they say, as soon as enough new houses are built, and already, life for the people living in them has changed dramatically. They earn wages now, they have access to health care and, from next September, every child under the age of sixteen, including my Greta, will go to school.

I look around at the solid brick walls of our home. The first real home I've ever had. Laura Minton arranged homes for all of us Cirque veterans as soon as they shut it down. She said it was the least the country could do for us.

It's not big, but it's cosy and warm here and, when we lock the door at night, I feel almost safe.

In frames on the walls there are photos: Greta and Bojo; Ben and me; photos of Jack; photos of Ezekiel and Emmanuel. In every one, we're laughing and happy and hopeful.

They don't tell the whole truth, those photos. They don't show how fragile we all are, how damaged we've been by the life we've led, the experiences we've had.

Some clever person with a lab coat and a degree has arranged a rehabilitation programme for everyone who suffered at the hands of Silvio Sabatini and the Cirque. Group therapy; individual therapy; post-traumatic stress counselling; cognitive behavioural therapy – you name it, we've had it. It helps a bit, I suppose, but no amount of talking will ever fix what's broken, not really.

There's one more photo I have, but I keep it hidden away under my mattress, and I only take it out when nobody's there.

It's a photo of me, from way back in the days of the old Cirque. I'm in my black cat outfit. The light catches on the spangled costume so it looks like I'm made of sparkle and shine. I'm standing on the wire, toes pointed, back arched, head held high, while the crowd below me cheer.

I haven't even told Ben and Greta I've got it and I certainly wouldn't tell my counsellor: she'd have a field day.

Why do I keep it? she'd ask. What am I clinging on to? How does it make me feel?

Those are questions I don't want to address, with her or anyone else, and so I push the yearning and the longing back down and I concentrate on the here and now: on Ben and Greta and our little home.

The official search starts next week to reunite the circus children with their families. Of course, lots of people are already back home. Ezekiel is safe with his parents; Sean and Rosie live together, just down the road to us; and Emmanuel has found his brother and sister.

Nobody's asked about Greta and me though. I don't know why. If they're out there somewhere – our mums and dads; our brothers and sisters – they must know what's happened. We're more famous now than we ever were. We don't talk about it much, but I think we both know, deep in our hearts, that something isn't right. Surely, if there was any way they could have come forward for us, they would have.

The television's on: the news channel. The headlines flash up. They're talking about Vivian Baines again. They've set a date for the start of her trial. She's being prosecuted for crimes against humanity. They say she'll go to prison.

They're looking for Silvio too, but there's been no sign of him since the day the Brotherhood stormed the Cirque. The police think he must be dead, but they've never found his body. There are rumours now and again that he's reappeared, sightings of him living rough around London, but they never come to anything.

Even if he is alive somewhere, he's got no power now. He's replaced me in being the country's most wanted criminal. Instead of Ben, Greta, Jack and me, it's his face that scowls down from the Wanted posters beamed up on the walls of the PowerHouse.

Once they catch him, he'll be tried and sentenced. He'll finally be made to pay the price for everything he's done, just like Vivian Baines.

They're covering the protests on the news report now – the ones that happen every time Vivian Baines has to make a public appearance. The people who are demonstrating against her, the ones who are calling out for her to pay for her crimes, shout the loudest, but they aren't the only ones who turn up. There's a strong minority faction who won't be silenced. They want her reinstated. They want things to go back to how they were before. They see this as a blip.

I click the television off. I don't want to hear this. Not today.

I stir the pot on the hob, and the smell of meat and spices fills the room. I love cooking: chucking a little bit of this and a little bit of that into a pot and creating something aromatic and hearty and delicious. Greta and I shop for ingredients together, both of us revelling in the sheer indulgence of being able to pick something up from a shelf, pay for it and take it home to keep.

I look at the clock. Ten to six.

They'll all be arriving any minute now. I'd better get changed.

I put my dress on and run a brush through my hair. Then I close the curtains and cast one more critical eye at the big table which fills the room.

Right on cue, there's a tap on the door and the guests all come pouring through it one after the other.

"Quickly," I tell them. "We need to get into place."

Once everyone's seated, I look around the table.

We aren't exactly a joyful bunch, but we're getting there.

To my left, Rosie and Sean. They'll both grieve for ever for Felix, their lost boy, but they're smiling today and they're here, with us, and that's all anyone could expect of them.

Next to Rosie, Jack, his arm around Alice, his fiancée. She came back as soon as it was safe and the pair of them are busy planning their wedding. She's just like you'd think Jack's partner would be: warm and wonderful.

On the other side of the table, Ezekiel and Emmanuel. Emmanuel's chuckling at something Jack has said and his booming laugh fills the room.

Looking out of the window, waiting excitedly with Greta, Nila and Nihal. They're family already, these two lovely children. Ben sees them every day now and Greta already loves them like a brother and sister.

There are two spaces left at the table.

A knock at the door signals the final guest, and we all look around at each other nervously. I don't know if I've done the right thing, inviting him. I don't know how Ben will react.

I open the door up and we smile at each other, politely and awkwardly. He gives me a bunch of flowers and I thank him and show him to the table, where Jack makes awkward small talk with him.

Ben's father.

I sent an invitation to Ben's brother, Francis, too, but I knew he'd refuse. He says he still hates Ben and he hates me and he hates Dregs. I'm glad he didn't come.

"He's here!" Greta calls, excitedly. "Turn off the lights and get ready, everyone!"

BEN

It's been a long day. I've been volunteering on one of the work groups, breaking the Cirque down and levelling the land where it stood.

It's therapeutic work. I think it's doing more to heal me than any of the counselling courses, but it's hard, physical work and it makes my legs ache so much that it feels like I'm dragging myself through the streets back home.

I just want to get back to Hoshi, but as I turn into the road and look towards our house, my heart sinks with disappointment. The lights are off; nobody's in.

I put my key in the door, fumble for the light—

"Surprise!"

"Happy eighteenth birthday!" Greta shouts out excitedly, and they break into song.

I stare around, lost for words.

Nila and Nihal, Sean, Rosie, Ezekiel, Emmanuel, Jack, Alice, Greta.

There's someone else here too. A pale, nervous figure, standing still and silent amidst the singing and the laughter, his eyes full of apprehension and worry.

After a moment, I step forward. He steps away from his place at the table, meeting me halfway, and for the first time in oh so many years, I hug my father.

Over his shoulder I catch Hoshi's eye. She's by the sink, putting some flowers into a vase. She's wearing a new blue dress and she's more beautiful than I've ever seen her. She looks as unsure as my father.

"Is it OK?" she mouths.

"Did you arrange this?" I mouth back, and she nods, smiling shyly.

She's organized this. Hoshi's gathered together all the people we love. Hoshi's cooked the meal that smells so good it's making my mouth water. Hoshi's made that cake that sits in the middle of the table, and Hoshi's done what I'd never have been brave enough to do and invited my father, who I haven't seen since that day in the circus when he threw the antidote up for Ezekiel. Hoshi, who has every reason to hate him, has asked him for me, because she knows I want to try and forgive him but I might need a nudge in the right direction. She's done it all for me. My Hoshi.

I cross the room and hug her hard while everyone breaks into another round of applause.

Holding her tightly, I thank God she exists.

"Thank you, Hoshi," I whisper in her ear. "Thank you for everything."

SILVIO

They've all forgotten about me. They think they've defeated me. They think I'm running scared.

They're wrong.

Even my family have forsaken me now, after I got too close. I knocked on the door of their elegant home in my darkest hour only to be turned away: still just a shameful secret to be denied.

I don't care. I don't need them anyway. I don't need anyone.

Lurking in the shadows, I bide my time, waiting for the right moment. I cannot be erased from history like this. I will rise again, just like I did before.

Before long, it will all collapse, this brave new world.

Once the Pures see the truth – once they realize what equal rights for all really means – they won't be quite so keen on the idea.

They'll soon get fed up with sharing their schools and hospitals and parks and restaurants with Dregs, with seeing their hard-earned taxes frittered away on the shiny new welfare system.

Vivian Baines's supporters have not gone away: they're just waiting, like me, for the rest to realize their mistakes. They'll all be begging to have her back soon, all be begging to have the balance restored.

And when she's entrenched in her rightful position of power, as she will be, she'll want to bring the circus back. She'll put me in charge again. She'll put both Ben and Hoshiko in it. She'll let me do what I like with them.

Like an animal, like a Dreg, I forage in bins for scraps of

food and find another newspaper with another picture of them: the happy couple, the people's heroes. I caress them with my fingers, smudging and blurring their faces before scrunching them up into a ball. Then I do what I always do: light the paper and watch them crumble to ashes.

My time will come again, I know it will.

ACKNOWLEDGEMENTS

I have loved writing this book, mostly because of the support and guidance of my brilliant editor, Lauren Fortune. From the moment I started working on it, Lauren has been on hand with advice and suggestions and has made the whole journey feel possible and, for the large part, stress free. I'm so proud of *Show Stealer*, and it wouldn't be here at all – and certainly wouldn't be anything like the shape it's in now – without Lauren.

I am also blessed to have Alice Sutherland-Hawes as my agent. Her professionalism, warmth and humour have been invaluable to me and I am so excited to be continuing my writing career with her support and vision. This has been a hugely successful year for the Madeleine Milburn agency, and I am proud to be represented by Maddy, Alice, Hayley and the whole team.

Massive thanks to everybody at Scholastic, especially Olivia Horrox, who I will miss like mad. Thanks so much, Olivia, to you and to Róisín O'Shea for doing such a phenomenal job marketing *Show Stopper*, and to the foreign rights team for all of their hard work. Thanks also to Jessica White and Peter Matthews for helping to iron out all the creases.

When I first saw the cover of *Show Stealer*, it lived up to its name and took my breath away. Andrew Biscomb and Paola Escobar, thank you so for being so hugely talented.

This book has been a collaborative effort in more ways than one. Last year, while experiencing a bout of writer's block, I put out a plea on Facebook for ideas of unsavoury circus rides and fairground attractions. Turns out, I have a lot of friends and family with minds nearly as twisted as mine! Thanks to all of you who made such brilliant suggestions, and special thanks and co-author credits – for ideas which I took and ran with – to: Elliot Sadler, Rachel Sadler and Faye Bravant for the deadly Ferris wheel; Nassrin Schott for the Globe of Death; Caroline Gordon-Johnson for the idea of Silvio seemingly disappearing from the theatre by magic; and David Glasspool for the Dreg bumper cars. Huge thanks to Kerrie Lewis Graham for first planting the idea of using genetic heritage testing in my head. The story wouldn't have been the same without any of you!

Since I wrote *Show Stopper*, I have been privileged to get to know many people in the UKYA world through Twitter and Instagram and at various bookish events. Thank you to all of you, the UKYA community is just the best. Thanks especially to Zoe Collins, for being such a great advocate – it's been wonderful seeing your career progress and develop so formidably over this year. Thanks also to Nicola @ PrythianBworm for always being especially lovely about *Show Stopper*. Thank you to Josh Martin, for helping me to get to grips with Scrivener, which made this novel soooooo much easier to write, and to Alice Broadway and Lisa Thompson for giving me help and advice whenever I've asked for it.

The title of *Show Stealer* is thanks to Jay Kenobi and Kirsty Stanley, who suggested it to me at YALC 2017. Who knew that Star Wars cosplay could be so helpful?

I was writing this book when the Grenfell Tower tragedy occurred and Molly Ker Hawn organized the Authors for Grenfell auction. Talented children's poet Paul Minton (not heard of him? You should have, his book *Miss Winter's Demise* is brilliant and hilarious) bid for the chance to name a character in the book. Laura Minton, I hope you like your dad's gift.

As ever, the biggest thanks of all go to my wonderful husband, Mark. Not only do you support me practically and emotionally but you have offered me the most insightful advice throughout for both of my books. I could never have done any of this without you, especially now that you seem to have somehow landed yourself the enviable role of being my unpaid and unofficial accountant and PA.

Thanks always to my wonderful family. My sisters, Katie and Gemma, for always being there for me. My gorgeous boys, Will and Adam and, last but not least, my mum and dad, who this book is dedicated to. Mum, thank you for always dropping everything to give each draft – and there have been many – a read-through and for being able to sniff out a typo like a police dog on a drug raid. And huge thanks and lots of love to both of you for being generally awesome and for proudly waving the flag (and wearing the T-shirt) for *Show Stopper* wherever you go.

Hayley Barker has a BA (hons) degree from Birmingham University and has taught secondary school English for eighteen years. She is a huge YA fiction fan and says being published is the most exciting thing that has ever happened to her. Hayley was inspired to write *Show Stopper* and *Show Stealer* by her fears about the growing wave of crime and animosity against minority groups in England. She lives in Essex with her husband and two young sons.

Twitter: @HayleyABarker
Instagram: @HayleyBarks
Website: hayleybarker.co.uk

Praise for *Show Stopper*

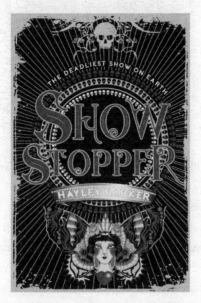

"It hangs life and death, love and despair perilously in
the balance. A brutal but brilliant young adult read"
The Sun

"Dazzling and dark. Heart-breaking and uplifting"
Escapades of a Bookworm

"This book is I.C.O.N.I.C…
Extremely emotional and action-packed"
Voracious Bookling

"A thrilling, dark romance"
The Book Activist